WESTIN
A DARK COWBOY ROMANCE

RAYA MORRIS EDWARDS

Westin

By Raya Morris Edwards

FIRST EDITION

Developmental and line editing: Lexie at Morally Gray Author Services
Proof and copy editing: Alexa at The Fiction Fix

Cover design: Maldo Designs
Cover photography: Michelle Lancaster @lanefotograf

This book is for anyone who wants a hot cowboy to put his hat on your head and his collar around your neck.

Important Author Note

This book contains scenes where the main characters are together while she is legally married to someone else. There is an ongoing debate between the MCs if what they're doing is cheating and whether or not the FMC's abusive marriage is legitimately open.

There is no cheating between the two main characters, Westin and Diane.

While this book can be read as a standalone, if you are going to read the entire Sovereign Mountain Series, it falls after *Sovereign*. To get the fullest picture of both Sovereign and Westin's stories, they should be read in order. Additionally, this book contains a few brief scenes that are also in *Sovereign*, but differ in *Westin* due to the change in POV.

A Note on Dialect

In an effort to remain true to my characters, this book contains many instances of dialect inspired by my own experience living in rural America. Some words, phrases, and sentence structure may be unfamiliar to you, but they are intentional and correct.

Due to this book being written in immersive first person POV, some of this bleeds into the narrative, not just the dialogue. There are many different ways to speak a language and instances of unusual sentence or word choices are intentional for the purposes of authenticity.

Warnings & Tags

Please bear in mind that this is a dark BDSM romance and it contains instances where BDSM may not be practiced properly throughout for the purposes of plot and character development.

As always, DO NOT look to fiction for true and accurate depictions of these practices.

This book includes topics and on page depictions of DV, grief, death, unaliving, heavy use of weap*ns, emotional tr*uma, as well as frequent and explicit s*xual content.

So you are aware, on page depictions of DV are in Chapter 13 and 29.

Before beginning, I encourage you to read the detailed list of content tags at rayamorrisedwards.com/westin.

CHAPTER ONE

DIANE

My bare feet rest on the dusty porch steps. My brother, David, stands by the barn, face shaded by his hat. The trailer backs up slowly, beeping and flashing lights as the horses in the paddock watch with blank eyes.

The trailer comes to a halt. Jensen Childress kicks the truck door open and jumps to the ground with a puff of dust—he's a handsome man with a cut jaw and a dirty hat on his head. Two of his cowboys appear at his heels, and I take that as my cue to check dinner.

I scramble to my feet. I'm wearing a cotton sundress that buttons up to my neck and leaves my legs bare from the knees down. It's only the beginning of the summer, but it's shaping up to be a hot one. I wish I could wear shorts, but all the men stare at my ass when I do. Except for Jensen; he's always respectful.

"You watching the beef?" David snaps. "It's almost time to eat."

I want to flip him off. Maybe I'd have done so when Nana was still alive, but not since David slammed me into the hallway wall so hard he knocked the faded family portrait on the ground and cracked it down the middle.

That's the last picture we have of our parents, taken when I was a baby and he was five years old.

Who knew that little boy would grow up to be such a dick?

I nod and slip back through the screen door. The big ranch house is quiet as I move down the hallway, stirring up dust, reminding me I need to clean myself up before we have company. I step out the back door to where the beef is cooking. It's a huge piece, and I have to push hard to get the spit to rotate. Fat sizzles as it hits the open bed of coals.

I wipe my forehead. I'm grimy, and my hair is greasy from cooking all morning and afternoon.

In the distance, a truck revs up the driveway. I recognize it as one of the two remaining Garrison brothers, and a chill runs down my spine. They're both so fucking mean, especially Avery. He's the oldest, and he's got eyes like a snake watching a bird.

I consider it a mercy that the middle brother, Clint, passed recently. He used to watch me with a hungry, unsettling gaze.

The truck door with GR emblazoned in red opens, and the youngest brother, Thomas, who's a few years older than me, jumps out. I slip back, unwilling to be noticed. He has always had a thing for me, and sometimes, it feels aggressive. I find him immature and unsettling, but I tolerate his presence because I have to. His family is important around here, and we need their business.

The beef is done; it just needs to be taken off and wrapped in foil to keep hot.

I creep back into the house and find David talking with Jensen on the front stoop. He glances up, narrowing his eyes. Jensen gives me a polite smile, taking off his cowboy hat.

"Can you carry the beef in?" I ask.

A crease appears between David's brows. I know he wants to chew me out for interrupting, but he also knows I can't carry it by myself. He sighs, pushing past me into the hall. I follow, keeping my distance.

He's annoyed, so I stay quiet, holding the door open as he brings the beef inside and lays it on the kitchen counter. Then, he wipes his hands and gives me a hard stare.

"You'd be more useful if you'd been a boy."

He slings those words casually, like they don't hurt. My eyes sting, but I keep it to myself. It's not the first time he has expressed that sentiment.

"Make the potato salad. That much you can do." He jerks his head and grabs his hat, pushing past me. The screen door slams.

The clock over the stove chimes five. I need to get upstairs and wash, but David's right. I still have to make the potato salad. Wrathfully, I switch off the gas stove and dump the boiling water down the drain, filling it up with cold water to set.

I rip off my apron and stomp upstairs to my room at the far end of the hall. No one can hear my rage, so it's alright to let it out.

The floor is worn by my feet. This has always been my room, every pivotal moment of my life centered in these four walls. It holds my childhood, the treasured memories like my Nana braiding my hair in bed while we watched the stars come out through the window. It was my escape when Nana fell asleep and never woke up.

I turn on the shower in the bathroom and circle around to the big window overlooking the yard.

The mountains spill out in the distance like sentinels holding up the sky. Down below, Thomas and Avery Garrison stand by the barn with David. They're in a circle smoking cigarettes, all just shooting the shit, talking about nothing. Tonight, after dinner, they'll get drunk and burn trash in the back field. It's the same thing every time.

Tomorrow, hungover and in a bad mood, David will slam everything in the kitchen trying to make a cup of coffee.

Quietly, I lift my middle finger and flip him off in secret. Then, I pull the curtain. My dirty dress goes in the basket, and I step into the shower. I've had endless chores to do since this morning, and I'm sticky with sweat and dust.

I hurry through, jumping from the shower with my soaked hair hanging down my back. It feels like something exciting is going to happen. Tomorrow, I turn twenty-one. No one has mentioned my birthday, but that doesn't surprise me. We haven't celebrated anything since Nana left.

Since she died.

But I keep telling myself she just left. She slipped away into the next room, where it's a little too dark to see her face anymore.

I grab a hand towel and dry my hair. Then, I pull on a sundress. It's stretchy yellow material, and it clings to my upper body, the knee-length skirt flared. It's long enough that I can bend down without hearing one of the men whistle at me.

I scowl, feeling faintly murderous, and head downstairs.

In the kitchen, I grab a bowl and start making potato salad, chopping the red potatoes into messy chunks, dicing up onions until my eyes stream.

Somewhere in the distance, Red the border collie starts yapping. I dump everything into the bowl along with a splash of pickle juice and mix it up. There—it can sit for a minute.

Wiping my hands, I creep softly to the door and press my forehead against the screen. Six more trucks line the drive.

Two trucks for the Garrisons—Thomas and Avery.

Then, there's Jensen and two more of his men. They came in different trucks, so that leaves just one, and I can't tell who that belongs to. There's a faint symbol on the side, but it's half-covered in dried mud.

The sun is sinking below the horizon as I slip back to the kitchen. Working quickly, I finish everything and lay the dishes on the main table, save for the meat. That, I carefully slice and lay on a platter, waiting for it to be taken out. Standing back, I wipe my hands.

It looks good, everything the way David wants it.

I hate David. Maybe not enough to hurt him, but enough to make his life hell. Nana told me it wasn't worth it to hate anyone. She said if they were bad enough, I'd leave them at the gates of heaven, so there was no point in it.

"Don't use up your energy on those who wrong you, baby," she'd whisper, running her fingers through my hair. "Vengeance belongs to the Lord."

Then, she'd hum a slow, mournful tune until I fell asleep, one I have no name for, though it still haunts me.

I disagreed and spent my nights plotting against David. He got snakes in his room, burs under his horse's saddle blanket, and salt in his coffee until he was big enough that when he pushed me, it hurt.

Now, I just have to take it.

I slip upstairs again and comb out my dry hair, letting it fall in waves down my back. My fingers trace over my face, touching the bridge of my nose. I'm pretty, I know, but I don't know how to use it to my advantage.

Maybe tonight, that changes.

Tomorrow, I'm twenty-one, old enough to legally drink whiskey. It's time to be a woman; at least, that's what I assume.

No one taught me how. Nana died before she could.

I put my boots on. They're new, and the bottoms are hard and loud on the stairs as I move. Red starts yapping again, and I freeze at the bottom of the steps.

There's something going on outside.

Heart thumping, I burst onto the porch. The men are fighting over by the barn, Avery Garrison lunging at someone while David holds him by the shirt collar. The Garrisons are big men, but my brother is bigger. He's got him reined in. Dust rises. Inside the barn, the horses kick at their stalls, spooked by the disturbance.

It doesn't surprise me that the men have been here less than thirty minutes and they're already fighting, especially not since Clint Garrison died a few months back.

Everyone north of South Platte has been walking on eggshells since that happened. The Garrisons are a prominent family around these parts. The middle brother's death sent shockwaves through the community.

I drag my eyes back to the men.

A storm is brewing.

Jensen stands in front of the other Garrisons, keeping them back. His pistol is out, held at his thigh and pointed down. Jensen doesn't fuck around; he's got perfect trigger discipline. When he wants to shoot, he'll point and—*bang*. There'll be nothing left but a hat fluttering in the wind.

He won't shoot, but he still has it out, just to let them know he could.

My eyes shift. The object of Avery's ire is another man, one I've never seen before. I blink, focusing on him. He's tall, about six-four, with dark chestnut hair. My stomach swoops in a way that feels...good.

I like the way he looks, maybe more than I should.

He's a large man, broad shoulders and big hands. His jaw is covered in a short beard, and it's tensed hard. He has good features, a strong, straight nose, low brows.

I can't tell how old he is, but I know he's too old for me, probably thirty-two or three. There's no gray in his hair, but he has light laughter lines around his eyes.

Those could just be from the elements. I can tell he's a wrangler, that he works a ranch. There's something about the confidence it takes to live in that world that runs like the blood in their veins.

His black hat is off, hanging by his thigh. I tilt my head, trying to see the symbol on the crown.

Avery yells something. Jensen shoots into the earth, and everyone calms the fuck down. There's something about a gunshot that induces either panic or sudden good behavior.

"Shut the fuck up," Jensen barks. "Back off."

He pushes up against Avery, their faces inches apart. I can see they're arguing, jaws tense. Jensen gestures with the gun still pointed down to the earth. Then, Avery throws his hands up and steps back, shaking his head.

He takes his hat off and wipes his face.

David releases a short sigh. "I have to be able to do business, Avery," he says, loud enough that I can hear. "I got grain to sell."

"Fuck it," he says. "You do what the fuck you want, David. It's your farm."

Three more trucks pull up the drive, and I recognize them as some of the men who work on the Garrison and Carter ranches. They're all the same: big, loud, and handsy when they get drunk. After I finish dinner, I'm going to make myself scarce.

I'm not foolish enough to stick around after dark.

The truck doors open, and more men than can legally be inside tumble out. Some, I've seen around, some I haven't. I step back through the screen door and watch from the safety of the house as they gather by the barn.

They do this every year after David gets a feel for how much feed he can sell. The surrounding ranches meet, talk it over, and place bids. This year, there are more men than usual. The spring has been unusually hot, and they anticipate a hard winter.

Clearly, some of the new wranglers know the man in the black cowboy hat. They start talking, and I see the situation diffusing slowly until they finally break apart and head towards the porch.

Heart pounding, I duck into the kitchen and pull a jug of iced tea from the fridge. Their boots clatter down the hall. I gather glasses from the cupboard and carry them to the table. The men enter the room, talking and laughing so loudly, it makes my ears ring.

I keep my eyes down, but it does fuck all. It's seconds before I feel someone brush against my hip. I know it's probably one of two people, and they're both named Garrison.

"Why so shy?"

I glance up, meeting Avery's gray stare. A little part of me hoped that, despite how much I hate Thomas, he was the one standing beside me. Avery makes my blood run cold, the kind of man who definitely bullied everyone growing up. He spends so much time torturing anyone who isn't big enough to hit him.

Part of me thinks he won't put his hands on me.

The other part thinks if he got the opportunity, he would.

"Hi, Avery," I say, pretending my mouth isn't dust dry.

He bumps me with his leg, like he's trying to flirt. I glance up again. He's handsome with those steel gray eyes and shock of blond hair, but the expression on his face is always meaner than a snake.

"You make all this?" he asks, leaning in until the side of his body touches mine.

I try to bite my tongue, but I can't.

"No, Avery. It just appeared this morning," I say tartly.

He laughs, but he's not amused. "Better watch that mouth."

I made a mistake sassing him, so I go quiet. He's up against my body now, but no one notices in the crowded room. They're all standing around with their arms crossed, feet apart, talking among themselves. I try to shift away, but there's a chair blocking me.

He sees I'm trapped, and he likes it. It glitters in his steel eyes.

"Where are you gonna go?" he says under his breath.

"Maybe if you quit dry humping her while she's trying to serve dinner, she wouldn't be trying to run off."

We both spin as the room goes quiet. The words came from the chestnut-haired cowboy with the black hat. Up close, our eyes meet, and I feel something I've never felt before: a little zing, like I brushed up against a blanket on the line, loaded with static electricity.

My fingers clench around the plate I'm holding. Avery straightens and takes a step back, his stare glacial.

"Fuck off," he says. "Sovereign Mountain trash."

My heart skips a beat as the pieces fall into place. Clint Garrison died while making a business deal at Sovereign Mountain Ranch. He was run over by a herd of cattle, spooked by something in the hills. David said he got trapped in the mountain pass and his horse threw him, leaving him dead in the dust.

Sovereign Mountain is the black sheep of cattle ranches here in Montana; Clint's death didn't improve their reputation, but they're also the biggest, wealthiest operation in Montana. David sells them grain, as he does everyone, but he never goes out of his way to do business with them.

My eyes flick up and rest on the black hat, and I realize what the insignia on the band is. SMR—Sovereign Mountain Ranch.

I swallow hard.

"Go on," says the man, stepping between us. "Get."

Avery's livid, but the room is watching us. David clears his throat and pulls out his chair at the head of the table. Taking advantage of the distraction, I duck away and circle the table to make sure everyone has what they need. Then, I disappear into the kitchen with my heart pounding.

I'm not eating with them tonight. I'll eat whatever is left later—a small price to pay for getting out of that suffocating dining room. In the kitchen, I pour a shot of whiskey into the bottom of an old jam jar and go sit out on the back porch.

I'll probably need another glass by the time the night's over.

The men eat, and I hear them in the kitchen as they start drinking. I wish David would let me hide in my room, but he says I have to stick around because I'm the woman of the house. It would be rude to disappear.

He pretends he doesn't know I've spent the last few years dodging hands.

It's not like he'd say anything anyway. The worst perpetrators are the Garrisons and, other than Sovereign Mountain, they're the biggest operation out here. David does a lot of business with Garrison Ranch; he'd gladly trade letting me get felt up in the barn for pick of their cattle before auction.

I hear the front door slam, one after the other, as they leave. Quietly, I move back into the house and enter the dining room. The table is a wreck. I go get the cart and start piling dirty dishes on it.

Slam. Crash.

A little part of me wants someone to hear my displeasure.

There's nothing left of the meal. My eyes burn as I push the cart back into the kitchen. There's bread and butter; I can eat that. After I rinse the dishes and load them to be washed, I pull out a stool and reach for the bread box.

"There's a plate in the microwave."

I turn. The cowboy in the black hat stands in the doorway, half shadowed.

"What?"

He takes a step. "I put a plate for you in the microwave."

I stare. "Why?"

"Because you didn't come to the table," he says, crossing the room and leaning on the counter.

Why is my heart pattering so hard against my ribs? He takes off his hat and runs his hand through his short hair, slicking it back. His eyes are hazel, a mix of green, gray, and brown. They're bright and piercing under lowered brows. I take a second to look him over. He's handsome, and for some reason, I'm not afraid of him.

I don't know why.

He's big, with broad shoulders. He's rough—I see the calluses on his hands—but he doesn't feel like he would hurt me. He rests on his elbows and fills the space over the counter, fixing those brilliant eyes on me.

"Why didn't you come to the table?" he asks.

I swallow hard. "I don't like some of them."

"The men?"

I nod.

He cocks his head, eyes narrowing. "Why? Did they do something to you?"

For some reason, it's embarrassing to admit that they harass me. I drop my eyes, picking at the table.

"Sometimes they try," I say finally.

"Which ones?"

I snap my gaze back up. The way he said it sounds...dangerous.

"Why does it matter?" I whisper.

Maybe he hears the defeat in my voice, because he doesn't answer. I glance down and notice he's got a thick scar on the knuckle of his thumb. Perhaps from a branding job gone wrong.

His fingers are long and lean with the short white scars on the backs of his hands and forearms, the ones I see on men who work with barbed wire a lot. Gloves and long sleeves will only do so much.

"What's your name, darling?" he asks, his voice low.

"Well, it's not darling, that's for sure," I say.

I cringe, expecting him to get pissed off the way Avery did. Then the corner of his mouth jerks in a smile. He looks at me, head down, eyes up, amusement glittering in them. He has a toothpick in the corner of his mouth I didn't notice before, but I see it now, and I can't look away.

He flicks it to the other side with his tongue.

"You've got a little sass to you," he says.

I lean in, elbows on the countertop. I don't know where the courage to get closer came from, but the desire is there.

"Do you like it?" I whisper.

"Maybe I do."

"I'm Diane," I say. "Diane Carter."

He straightens and holds out his hand. "Westin Quinn."

Tentatively, I shake it. His hand is so much bigger than mine, and it engulfs me in a firm grip, wrapping me in warmth for a second before he withdraws. He leans back down so he's eye level with me, his elbows planted on the table.

"How old are you, Diane?" he asks.

The way he says my name sends a thrill through me. Di-*ane*. I like the little drawl he adds to the last syllable. My toes curl in my boots.

"Does it matter?"

His jaw works. "Yeah, it does."

I sigh, brushing my hair back. "Twenty. I'll be twenty-one at midnight."

His brows rise. "You're just a little thing. You can't even drink yet."

"I am not. How old are you?"

"Thirty-seven next month."

My jaw drops, and it takes me a minute to pull myself together. For some reason, the fact that he's older than me makes my toes curl even harder. My legs tingle, and the feeling creeps up my thighs and centers in my core.

Right where I feel like maybe it shouldn't.

He's so handsome, but it's the way he's looking at me that makes me feel something brand new, like I'm interesting, not just a potential place for him to get off. I stare, watching as he absently picks an apple from the fruit bowl. He rolls it in one hand, tossing and catching it.

"That scare you?"

I shake my head. "There's nothing to be scared about. We're just talking, sir."

His pupils blow, but I'm not sure why. He straightens and puts his hat firmly back on his head. "You're a little young, aren't you, darling?"

Indignantly, I put my hands on my hips. "For what?"

He crosses the room, pausing in the hallway. "If you don't know what for, you're definitely too young."

For some reason, I'm crushed that he's leaving. "Where are you going?"

He tosses me the apple, and I catch it.

"Call me after your birthday," he says. "It was nice to meet you, Miss Carter."

"That's tomorrow," I whisper. "My birthday is tomorrow."

He dips his head. "See you tomorrow then, darling."

I don't tell him not to call me darling this time. He walks out, and the doors slams behind him. I stand there, knuckles white. It doesn't occur to me until later, when I'm in bed staring at the ceiling, that I can't call him. He didn't leave his number.

I turn my head, staring at my bedside table.

My eyes fix on the round, red apple. I didn't put it back in the kitchen—instead, I carried it up to my room. Now, it sits on my table, reminding me of him.

I only know three things about the cowboy in the black hat, and I run them over and over in my mind until I fall asleep.

He comes from Sovereign Mountain.

His name is Westin Quinn.

And he's thirty-seven years old next month.

Everything else is a mystery.

CHAPTER TWO

WESTIN

BEFORE

I'm seven years old when my father puts a gun in my hands and lifts it.

In the distance, the tin cans waver in my eyeline. He steps back, resting his hand on his hip, and I glance over my shoulder, keeping the gun steady.

He's watching me without offering any corrections this time. Inside, I glow with pride. My father isn't a bad man. I'd go so far as to say he's an honest man who loves his family, but his jaw is always set at a grim angle.

He looks out at the world like a bullet from the barrel of a shotgun. If it threatens him, he'll shoot back.

And my father doesn't miss. For me, at seven, that means the pinnacle of achievement is to be a man who shoots and never misses.

I turn back around and huff out a breath. It's hot, high summer.

My finger squeezes.

Bang.

Bang.

Bang.

All three tin cans flip off the fence railing. My father squints and takes his hat off to wipe his face with a bandana. Sweat etches down his neck, wetting his collar.

"Good. That's good," he says.

I drop the magazine out and hand it over. He watches me intently as I put the gun back in the holster at my belt. It's too big, and it hits my knee as we start down the hill. We don't talk much, me and my father, but that's alright. I don't expect a lot of words from him.

My mother stands in the doorway of the ranch house. She's much younger than my father, but neither of them will tell me how old they are.

My father has lines around his eyes and silvery hair while my mother is beautiful with long auburn hair and always smells like cinnamon. She doesn't have a single wrinkle on her skin.

She hugs me, taking the gun off my belt. I hear her say something to my father, their voices low. I'm thirsty, though, so I don't stick around.

I hang my hat and put my boots away. In the kitchen sits a tray with two glasses of lemonade. My father doesn't drink anything but lemonade and water. I grab one and empty it.

My mother will be inside in a moment, and she'll want me to clean up, so I duck into the bathroom off the kitchen. One step ahead.

Their footsteps sound as I scrub lye soap up to my elbows, the way my mother showed me. She likes everything clean and neat. Their voices rumble, unintelligible. I finish up and turn the water off so I can hear what they're saying.

"I don't know," my father says. "He kinda fucking scares me."

I freeze, my stomach twisting.

"He's a good boy," my mother says, her voice soft. "He's just...older for his age."

"He shoots like a grown man. I've never seen anything like it," my father says. "It's unsettling. But I'd be a fool not to make sure he uses a skill like that."

Unsettling—it feels like I've been punched in the stomach.

"He's a little young to be shooting with you," my mother says tentatively.

"Don't start on that," my father says. "He acts like a grown up and he's fucking seven. He can handle his shit."

My mother gives a sigh of defeat. "Of course."

I stay in the bathroom for a while after. Finally, the dinner bell rings, and I eat in silence. All the ranch hands are lined up, and I sit with them instead of next to my father. I always do—he says that's where children should sit. He eats at the far end of the room, my saint of a mother at his side.

He has a big presence: confident, belligerent, and aggressive to the world, but lenient towards anyone who obeys him.

The next day, my father takes me out to the field behind the barn. It's hot, the air filled with the whine of cicadas. In the distance, lined up in the plowed field, sits a row of tin cans.

They're a lot further out than they were yesterday.

My father flips his wrist and looks at his silver watch with its worn leather band. It belonged to his grandfather. It's eight in the morning. I haven't had breakfast yet.

"I've been giving it some thought," he says. "Let's see what you can do."

He gives me his gun. I check the chamber, spin it, and click it into place.

"You want me to shoot them all, sir?" I ask.

He nods. "You got fifteen seconds."

My brows shoot up to my hairline. "I don't know if I can."

He taps his watch. "Ready....and go."

The tin cans waver in my eyeline. My breath goes still...and then I let it out in a soft puff. The cans come into focus. My finger squeezes, and I account for the kick.

I account for everything without noticing.

The breeze.

The distance.

The sun in my eyes.

My heart knows where each bullet needs to land. The cans flip off the railing, one after the other, leaving nothing but a whisp of dust.

The cicadas are silent.

"Good," my father says. "Let's go again."

We go again and again until my mother rings the bell for breakfast and we head inside to wash up. This time, my father tells me to sit with him at the big table. For the first time, I see the clear connection between pleasing him and his affection.

I don't have to work to please my mother. She loves me so hard.

My father slows down as I enter my teens. In high school, I meet my closest friend, Gerard Sovereign. I don't notice it for a while, but he's just as hardheaded and willful as my father, just less cold.

I want to resent my father, but instead, I become everything he wanted me to be without realizing it. When I'm old enough to strike out on my own, he gives me and Sovereign a piece of land. I have a steady aim and a willingness to do anything to succeed while Sovereign has the drive and the business sense to run an empire.

We build Sovereign Mountain Ranch.

Sovereign takes the helm, and I stick to what I do best—spinning a chamber and making sure no one stops him.

Ranch work is rewarding, but lonely. I find my comfort in the usual places—bars, the beds of women I won't see again—until my loneliness is numbed enough that I can go out and face another day. Until a year into working together, Sovereign makes a comment about it.

"What's the point of it?" he says one day while we're out in the field.

"Of what?" I ask.

"The women, the bars," he says. "You're just coming back to an empty bed anyway."

That hurts, but it snaps me out of it. In that way, he and my father are one and the same.

As he gets older, my father sells the rest of the farm to us and moves to South Platte with my mother. I bought the house for them so my mother would have somewhere to live when he was gone. For her, not for him.

My father and I sit at the table together, one day in my early twenties. He's gray, his eyes weak now, but he's still as stubborn as a mule. I'm a grown man, taller than him. Steam rises from my coffee, spiraling in the morning sun. My mother goes outside to gather strawberries from her boxes on the back porch and leaves us alone.

"When are you giving me a grandson?" my father says abruptly.

I freeze but recover quickly. "I'm not with anyone."

"So get a woman," he says, his voice flat, like it's that easy. "I got your mother, and I've kept her this long."

I rise under the pretext of warming my already-hot coffee. Through the window, my mother stands in the backyard. She looks so young compared to him, so free and hopeful. My mother is a caged bird, the door soon to be opened.

I find I'm happy for her.

"You're old enough," my father says.

"I'm working on it," I murmur.

That was a lie. My father died without grandchildren. The older I got, the less I idolized him. He taught me to be a man, to shoot and fight and push my will onto others, but he forgot to teach me to be more than that.

Oddly enough, it's Sovereign who shows me I'm worth more. He's the first man who doesn't ask me to prove myself. He's got a no bullshit approach to the world. In his mind, we're brothers, and that's that. My skills have nothing to do with it, and it's my choice to use them for the good of the ranch.

We take care of the land, and the land takes care of us. The world turns, and suddenly, I'm thirty-six years old. I did my best not to become my father, but in the end, I found myself with nothing at all to show for it.

No wife. No family.

All I have is my resolve to do better. It's kept me single and buried in my work for decades, right up until I made the foolish choice to go to Carter Farms to barter for some extra grain.

NOW

My eyes fall on her first while she's setting the table. Avery Garrison, public enemy number one in my eyes, is harassing her. I scare him off, and she leaves before I can get a good look at her face.

I catch sight of her through the window. She's sitting on the steps, facing away. My mind goes right back to being a boy and watching my mother cook for hours, only to eat leftovers after everyone was done.

I put food on a plate and shut it in the microwave.

Then, I eat with the men in the dining room. She comes in after everyone has cleaned their plates and walked out with the table in disarray.

I stay in the hall, transfixed.

She's in a yellow sundress with a tight bodice and loose skirt, the straps barely clinging to her shoulders. When she turns, a thrill like electricity goes down my spine.

Goddamn, she's pretty.

Her mouth is full but pursed, like she's pissed. Her big, dark eyes have a droop to them, and her lashes are heavy. Her face is oval, her chin pointed, her lightly freckled cheeks rounded. There's a fresh, girl-next-door look to her, but it's dulled by annoyance.

She slams cupboards, clearly angry about the mess.

I can't help but smile. I like her fire.

She pulls out a stool and reaches for the breadbox. I step out of the hall.

"There's a plate in the microwave," I say.

She jumps, whipping around as her lips part.

"What?"

"I put a plate for you in the microwave."

She stares at me like I'm speaking another language. "Why?"

No one has ever cared if she ate or not, that much is obvious. We start talking, but I barely remember anything because I can't stop looking at her mouth, the way it moves when she talks. Her white teeth flash, her pink tongue flicking out to wet her lips.

God, she's gorgeous.

My heart does a somersault. I think love feels a bit like this—but then again, what the fuck do I know about that?

It all comes crashing down when I ask her how old she is, and she says, "Twenty. I'll be twenty-one at midnight."

Fuck that; she can't even have a drink at a bar. Right away, my mind goes to my mother standing in the back garden. My stomach is uneasy as we speak. I have an urge to stay, but a tingle of shame holds it back.

I go home, my hands white-knuckled on the steering wheel of my truck.

That night, it's hot, and I can't sleep. Even with the fan on and the window open, I'm tossing and turning. When I finally fall into oblivion, I dream about her face.

Head back, golden hair like a waterfall.

She straddles my hips. I'm not inside her, but her pussy is bare against my cock, rubbing back and forth up the sensitive underside, all wet and hot.

"Fuck me," she begs.

I've always been restrained, but this time, I'm not. I need this woman. In my dream, I reach between us and guide my cock into her pussy. Pleasure rises, I gasp, and my eyes fly open.

I'm in bed, propped against the headboard, and I pull the sheets aside.

Goddamn it.

I'm late for chores because I have to shower and strip the bed, but it gives me time to get my head on straight. When I get to the barn, I'm pulled together.

Sovereign and I head out to check fences. The early morning is clear with the promise of heat later on. All I can think about is her face when she told me today is her birthday.

I said I'd go back.

But all I can think about is my mother in that fucking garden, so close to the door of her cage.

So I don't go.

We move through the day, and I find myself alone once again, sitting with my back against the headboard, staring out at the moon rising through the trees.

CHAPTER THREE

DIANE

I turn twenty-one without a word of acknowledgement. The men eat breakfast and leave. David tells me not to forget to muck out the chicken coop before he heads out.

After I clean up breakfast, I go to the barn and feed my horses, Gracey and Sunshine. They're both bay mares I broke myself. As long as I take care of them, David doesn't care that they're useless.

I head back inside and grab a basket from the laundry room. We have six dozen chickens in the backyard, and they're in peak laying season. We're getting upwards of four dozen eggs a day, so tonight, I'll make breakfast for dinner.

I gather the eggs, still warm from the nesting boxes, and bring them into the laundry room to wash. While I'm drying them, I hear David come through the front. He's walking fast, like he's looking for someone.

I freeze as his boots get closer. What is he doing back so soon?

"Did I see you talking to Thomas Garrison last night?" he says.

I turn, wiping my hands. "No, I didn't."

He frowns, taking off his hat, his face streaked in dust and sweat.

"Next time, make sure to talk to him," he says. "He likes you."

"I don't like him," I say.

"I don't give a fuck," David says, turning and heading back down the hall.

I follow him and set the bowl of eggs on the kitchen counter. David wipes his face on the dish towel, leaving dusty smears before he pours a glass of water and drains it.

"Why do you care?" I ask.

He glances at me. "Because it's good to be on the Garrison's good side. You can't stay here for free forever."

I stare at him, eyes narrowed. "I think I pay my way."

He turns, leaning on the counter. "Making food isn't the same as running this farm."

"Okay," I say before I can bite back my words. "Make your own food. You can't boil water."

He lifts a hand, the one holding his hat, and points. "You watch your mouth."

"I didn't say anything wrong," I whisper.

His eyes flash. "You shut your goddamn mouth, Diane, or I'll shut it for you."

I'm going too far. Reluctantly, I do as he says and shut my mouth. He slams his hand on the counter to back up his words and strides from the kitchen. I wince as his boots echo until the screen door slams. I hear him calling one of the hired hands.

Wrathfully, I go back to my chores. One of my tasks is self-imposed, so I have to do it as quickly as possible so I don't get accused of wasting time. Quietly, I tuck some shears and flowers from the side garden in a basket and disappear from the house.

A deer trail runs along the fence line to the west. I take it, hidden by the tall grass, until the ground flattens. Down below, a hundred yards off the path, is a little valley, the deepest point encircled by a wooden fence with a gate tied with twine.

I push it open and enter the Carter family cemetery. At the far end sit two metal plaques, one beside the other—my parents, who never really had a chance to live before an accident took them. I'm not sure how I should feel about their death. They're my parents, but I never knew them.

To assuage my confusion, I keep their graves clean, the grass cut, and lay flower wreaths on them every week.

Beside them is my Nana's grave, the only one in my immediate family with a headstone. It cost David and I a small fortune, money he complained loudly about having to spend. The only reason he did was because I cried in front of the funeral director, and he didn't want to look bad.

I sink down, taking out the shears. The grass isn't long, but I like it to be even all over. As I cut it back, I find myself chattering about everything.

Except the cowboy from Sovereign Mountain.

Those feelings are a little shameful.

I complain about David for a while and let Nana know I still hate the Garrisons. Then, we talk about the new calves and the ducklings we had this spring. Ants crawl over my bare feet and my neck sweats from the sun. I weave the flowers into three wreaths and lay them down, making sure everything looks perfect before getting up and brushing off my clothes.

I have to get home to my chores before anyone notices I'm gone.

By the time I'm done cleaning out the chicken coop and barn, it's time to start dinner. I haul a load of green onions from the garden and start cutting them into a bowl on the porch. In the distance, I see David and Jensen on their horses in the side pasture.

Jensen runs a construction company, but he's more of a cowboy than anything. He's got no woman, no place to be other than wherever pleases him. Some days, he's putting flooring in a house, and other days, he's rounding up cattle at one of the ranches. No one really knows much about him, but he makes good money.

He's also handsome, but not my type—not like the cowboy in the black hat.

Westin Quinn.

Not in a way that tugs at my mind at night and makes my face flush.

I wish I could say I forgot all about Westin, but I didn't. I lay in bed all night with a strange warmth simmering deep inside, remembering how he looked me up and down. When I got up, there was a restless ache between my legs.

My cheeks are hot just thinking about him. I need to stop, so I haul the chopped onions inside and make dinner. I don't try to eat with the men; I just go sit in Gracey's stall in the barn. The sun sets through the window, casting a golden light down over my bare legs and feet.

I can't get Westin Quinn off my mind.

I'm not totally sheltered. I know about sex in the abstract. I've skimmed salacious romances and seen a little porn by accident. When I was thirteen, Nana sat me down and gave me The Talk. She was straightforward but not particularly helpful in regards to what I feel now.

What I feel isn't just mechanics; it's a flood of all the little things I noticed about him yesterday. How square and strong his hands looked. How his eyes glittered beneath the brim of his hat. How good he smelled when he leaned close.

I shiver.

He looks like he knows all about dirty, shameful things that no one talks about in front of me.

The sun sets. My birthday is over, and no one came, least of all Westin Quinn. I peel myself off the stall floor. The barn is quiet; the only sound is frogs trilling in the pond at the bottom of the hill.

Wearily, I put the horses to bed and pull the barn door shut. Then, I go inside and clean up the dinner mess the men left. When I put the last dish away, I'm too tired to prepare my own meal, so I make bread with butter and carry it up to my room. The house is quiet, and I know David's already asleep. The men have an early day tomorrow, although I don't know where they're headed.

Nana used to make cake for my birthday, vanilla with a dusting of powdered sugar and a single candle on top. I tear off a piece of bread and let it sit on my tongue, pretending it tastes like cake.

My throat is tight, but I get it down.

After I finish eating, I lay down, keeping perfectly still. Outside, the horses nicker, the frogs sing. My twenty-first year starts today; I hope it's better than my twentieth.

Maybe something exciting will happen.

It could be false hope, but I feel like it will.

Nana told me hope is as unpredictable as a meadowlark in the grass, hidden from view until someone steps too close. And then it bursts up into the sky, rising, trilling, black against the gold sunset.

There are no meadowlarks in the fields by the house. David hays them, and it scares the birds away.

CHAPTER FOUR

WESTIN

I should stop myself, but I don't think I can.

My body is restless. I have a hunger that I know only one thing can satisfy, and it's that sweet face, dusted with freckles, framed by golden waves. I didn't think I had a type, but I know I do now.

And it's Diane Carter.

Every part of her.

It's like someone lit a fire in my chest, and it just keeps growing, stoked by every second I turn our brief conversation over in my mind. I swear, I remember everything. The way her lips moved when she spoke. Her soft voice, edged with a little vocal fry.

I've felt desire before, but not like this.

This is a fucking fever. I'd do desperate things to satiate myself.

The night of her birthday—the day I promised to visit her but didn't—I pace the gatehouse floors.

Back and forth.

I take a shot of whiskey, then another.

The moon is full, so I go outside in the hopes of walking until I'm tired enough to sleep. It's almost eight, so everyone is settling down. As I move through the employee housing, I see Jensen sitting on the porch of one of the vacant houses. Sometimes, when he's helping with a job in the morning, he'll stay overnight.

He takes a drag of his cigarette. "What're you doing out so late, gunslinger?"

I wince. He doesn't mean it badly, but the name unsettles me.

"Walking," I say.

He stretches out his legs, blowing smoke at the sky. "Want to go shoot shit?" he drawls.

He's not from here. He showed up from Kentucky when he was in his early twenties, tight lipped about his past but willing to work. Sovereign was one of the first to give him a job. Even after over a decade out here, he still drawls like he's in deep Appalachia.

I consider his proposal.

"Yeah, alright," I say.

We go down to the shooting range, a strip of rocky land with a hill that comes up to catch strays. Jensen takes his empty beer bottle and puts it on the rail, taking his time getting back to me. He fits his hat on and hangs his cigarette in his lip.

I know what he wants.

"How much?" I ask.

"Five bucks," he says. "Spin and close your eyes."

Jensen has a lot of dumb ideas, but I usually go along with them, so I'm not any better. I cock my pistol and spin once until my foot is exactly where it started. Then, I point, take a beat, and shoot blind. Glass splinters.

I open my eyes.

"Goddamn it," says Jensen.

"Give me five dollars, motherfucker," I say, holding out my hand.

"Best I can do is a cigarette."

"That works too."

We fuck around for a while, shooting loose cans. Then, it gets too late, and I don't want to keep anyone up, so we head back up the hill. I'm agitated, and nothing can get my mind off how much I need to see her again. It's eating me up inside, burning me, making me desperate to get my mouth on her in the hopes she can quench my thirst.

It's her birthday, and I said I'd go see her, but I didn't.

What's holding me back? My guilt over how young and unsuspecting she is?

Jensen and I sit on the porch, and we have another beer.

"I'm not sure what's going on with you, gunslinger, but you seem agitated," Jensen says.

I consider lying, but instead, I tell him what happened in the kitchen. He listens, quiet until I get to the end.

"Well why the fuck didn't you go?" he says.

I shrug. "Twenty-one is pretty young."

He nods. "But she's a grown woman, and if it isn't you, it'll be somebody else. Judging by the ages of some of us out here, he'll be a good bit older than she is."

He has a point. Maybe that's all I need. Just one excuse, and all my flimsy resistance comes tumbling down. I stare up at the moon, a pale silver disk overhead. She's down the hill and a ways down the road, laying in her bed. Maybe she's thinking about me.

Maybe her hand slips under the blankets.

I clear my throat. "I'll go see her in the morning."

Jensen shrugs. "Ain't no harm in it."

Those words turn over in my head as Jensen leaves and I go upstairs. If I'm being honest, I take a shower and jerk off to the memory of her in my dream. My body doesn't want to rest, even after I finish, so I just lay against the headboard and count every second until I get to see her again.

CHAPTER FIVE

DIANE

The next morning, I roll out of bed and pull on some faded cut-offs. They're too short to wear without getting bothered, but all the men are gone in the city until dinner. I can dress how I want.

My bare feet carry me over the floorboards. It's a good day to get some cleaning done; the kitchen is cool and empty. I grab a muffin from the freezer, heat it up in the microwave, and have it with a cup of coffee.

Maybe I'll take Sunshine out and ride the fence line. It's going to be hot today, but right now, the sun is still buffered by the mountains. We could ride the northern border and be back before noon.

To hell with the chores. I can get them done by the time David gets back tonight.

I walk out onto the front porch, and my heart stops, jumping so far up my throat, I feel my ears roar. There's a man sitting on the chair by the front door.

And he's wearing a black cowboy hat.

"Good morning, Miss Carter," he says.

"Mr. Quinn."

He's got his knees spread, his hat pulled low. All at once, I feel naked, and I wish I'd put on longer shorts. I glance down at my body, and it looks different today, somehow more feminine, even though my curves are small.

He's not looking, his eyes are lowered.

"Why are you on my front porch?" I ask, moving around to stand in front of him. The railing pushes against my lower back.

This time, he looks up and takes his hat off. His hair is the nicest shade of deep brown, and it's brushed back, somewhere between short and a little bit long. It's just long enough that I could play with the waves on top, but not enough to touch his neck.

His gaze cuts right through me and makes me feel naked.

"You get left here all alone, darling?" he said, his voice low.

My mouth goes dry, and I realize I don't know this man at all.

"No," I say quickly.

"I saw David and the others leave on my way up the road."

"Well, he's coming back. Really soon."

He shakes his head. "No, he's heading down to Lancaster to the auction there. They won't be back until around about seven."

I dig my toes into the worn floorboards. "What's that to you?" I ask.

He rises and towers over me. I shrink back, cowed by his height. My eyes run down his blue shirt, the sleeves rolled up to reveal his forearms. I stare at those barbed wire scars, distracted.

"I thought I'd come by to say happy birthday," he says, his voice husky.

Like he's feeling something.

"Thanks. It was yesterday," I say.

"I'm taking you out, Diane." His voice is quiet, firm.

Dead silence falls between us. Does he mean on a date?

The breeze rustles the trees and blows my hair back over my shoulder, the wind tugging it. Deep down in the pit of my stomach, heat tingles and makes me want to press my thighs together.

"I...I don't know if that's a good idea," I say.

He clears his throat, and his intense stare rests on me for a long moment. "Are you going to ask me inside?" he says finally.

For a second, I think about refusing him. Then, I remember there's a pistol underneath the kitchen sink, so I nod and lead the way inside. He sets his hat on the kitchen counter, standing between me and the hall. It should scare me, but it doesn't, just like it didn't the first time.

"You want an iced tea?" I ask. "I can spike it."

The corner of his mouth turns up, and he leans on the counter. "Sure, that'd be nice."

I make two, filling the glasses with ice, lemonade, tea, and a shot of whiskey. It's early in the morning for a drink, but standing next to him, I need a stiff shot in my system. He takes a sip, and I can't keep from staring at how big his hands are on the glass.

"So, what do you say?" he says, setting it aside.

"About taking me out?" I ask. "Like on a date?"

"Yeah," he says, locking gazes. "Like a date."

I want to recklessly say yes, but then I remember David and what he said about Thomas Garrison yesterday. I have my doubts he'll give a cowboy from Sovereign Mountain his stamp of approval over a Garrison.

Maybe I should lie and say I'm taken.

One look into those hazel eyes, and I know he can read me like a book, so I opt for the truth.

"My brother wouldn't like that," I say with a sigh.

"Why's that?"

I bite my lip. "Well, he's trying to set me up with Thomas Garrison, on account of them being so important. I don't think he'd approve of you."

He smiles, like he knows something I don't. "Don't worry about your brother, darling. I'll take care of that."

"You don't have to live with him," I say.

He cocks his head. "What does he do?"

"Nothing," I lie. "He's just mean, bossy."

"Does he hurt you?" Westin asks.

There's something dark and dangerous creeping over him, making my hair stand on end.

I push back the memory of the handful of times David lost his temper with me. He shoved me on the porch steps once, and I split my lip on the railing. He slapped me around a bit, but only once did he take me by the neck and slam me into the wall in the hallway so hard, my head snapped back and left a hot, tender spot on the back of my skull.

I saw the regret in his eyes a second after, as soon as he saw the blood seep from where I'd bitten my tongue.

He let me go and left the house in a rage, like I'd done something wrong not him. When he came home, he told me I shouldn't bait him the way I do. After that, all he'd done was verbally berate and threaten me. Maybe he was right; it's hard to say.

I wasn't sure if I should blame him for it. The only other men I know are the Garrisons, and they're meaner than David.

It hits me all at once that this is my future if I bend to David's plans for my life. I'll be married to a Garrison. I'll keep my eyes on the ground, my head down, and eat leftovers alone in the kitchen. I'm well on my way to that already.

I take a sip of my drink to steady my nerves. I don't want to live my life scared.

I want to run free.

I want to love so hard and messy that I feel like I'm in ecstasy every night. I want to drink whiskey and ride horses, fall for a man who makes me feel the way Westin does. Someday, when I'm ready, I'll have babies and let them do that very same thing when it's their time.

I know one thing for certain: I don't want Thomas Garrison to be the man who knocks me up.

"Fine," I say. "If you can handle David, you may take me out."

His face breaks into a smile, flashing white teeth. My stomach swoops—he's so damn handsome, it makes my head spin.

"Just promise you won't do anything to me?" I say.

"What?"

"Promise you're not going to kidnap me and tie me up or something."

His eyes glint, and he circles the counter until he stands right over me. My heart thumps so hard, my ears roar, and I take a step back and bump into the sink. He takes a step forward until I can smell the scent of aftershave or soap. It's nice, clean and sharp.

"I can't promise you both of those things," he says.

My mouth is dust dry. "You want to kidnap me?"

He shakes his head. "No, darling, I won't kidnap you."

Heat rushes through me.

"You want to...tie me up?" I whisper.

He leans in, and his hands brush my elbows, gathering my wrists. My heart is thrumming so fast, I can hear it in my ears. He pins them gently against my lower back and bends down until I feel his breath on my neck.

"Don't lie and say you don't like that idea a little bit," he says.

I can't think of a single thing to say to that.

He lets me go, and his hands brace on the sink, on either side of my body. His eyes drop, lingering over my cleavage. Over the rise of my breasts, down to the sliver of naked skin on my belly. Over the curve of my hips in my shorts, down my bare legs.

"You're a pretty woman," he says quietly.

My hand comes up, pressing against his chest to keep him off me, for decorum's sake only. It's warm, and I feel his heart thump under my fingers.

It's beating as fast as mine.

CHAPTER SIX

WESTIN

She goes upstairs. I wait in her kitchen, tapping my hat against my leg. The clock over the stove etches out the seconds. It's still early with plenty of time for lunch, so I'm not in a hurry. We both have all day.

I hear her boots on the floor upstairs after a while before she comes slowly down the steps, like she's feeling shy.

I don't say a word, because there's nothing in my head.

She's stunning.

Her dusky blonde hair is tied in a braid down her back, flyaway bits around her face. The hair near her scalp is darker, the sun having bleached the rest blonde. It's long enough for me to get my fingers tangled up in those curls.

Her short sundress clings to her upper body and flares out below her waist. It hits the middle of her thigh, leaving those long legs bare down to her cowboy boots. Her thighs are lightly freckled, and I follow them with my eyes, up until they disappear under her skirt.

I'd like to explore that later, with my tongue.

"Is this okay?" she asks, voice hushed.

I put my hat on. "More than okay."

Her face breaks into a smile. She's got a full mouth, and she pouts it a lot, like she disapproves of something. Now, it's pulled back in a little smile as her eyes glitter.

I'd do a lot to see her smile like that again.

"Where are we going?" she asks.

I jerk my head. "Anywhere."

"So you won't tell me?"

I shake my head. "But I promise I'll have you back by two. How's that sound?"

She nods. "This is probably reckless, isn't it?"

I fill the space between us, and she jumps when I take her hand. "Don't worry about that."

She follows me as I lead her down the hall. My truck is parked just off the porch, and I open the side door, but she's too short to climb into the passenger side. She gives me a look, and I lift her up. For a second, her soft body presses against mine.

My dick twitches.

Then I put her into the seat, slam the door, and get into the driver's side. She smooths her skirt primly. Trying not to stare at her legs, I put the truck in gear and drag my eyes to the road as we head down the drive to the state route below.

We're a mile down the road when she puts her hand on her head and sighs.

"Forgot my hat," she says. "My hair bleaches in the sun."

"You can wear mine," I say.

She bites her lip and glances at me again. I can tell that tickles her, because she has to turn to cover her smile.

We head down a side road leading to a one-lane town about ten miles from Carter Farms. It's got a post office, a gas station, and a grocery store, plus a creek that leads to a swimming hole a little ways down. That's as good as it's going to get for a date out here.

"What's your middle name, Westin Quinn?" she asks, shifting to face me.

"Why?"

"I'm curious about the man taking me out."

"River," I say. "Westin River Quinn."

"Who do you work for?" Her jaw works, like she's interrogating me.

"Gerard Sovereign. And I don't work for him—I work *with* him."

Her brows rise. "I know who that is, but I've never met him."

I glance down, distracted by her bare thigh. The window is cracked, and the air blows her skirt up a few inches. Her thigh is so smooth and tanned. I'd like to run my palm up and down it, maybe grip right above her knee.

Fuck me, I'd do anything to feel both those soft thighs wrapped around my head.

"Do you like it?"

I tear my eyes away. "Working with Sovereign? Yeah, I do. I have partial shares in the farm, I live on it, and I work when and how I choose. What's not to like?"

She mulls this over. "How'd you meet?"

"We were friends as kids."

Her eyes get distant. "That sounds nice. I've...never had any real friends. We live so far out of the way, and Nana did most of our schooling."

That strikes me as sad. I know David Carter well enough to know that he's not the type to think about anyone else. If I had to guess, she has been cooped up on the farm doing chores and cooking for most of her life. I know I've never seen her in town before.

Lost in thought, I pull off the road on the other side of the town. There's a gravel stretch and a dirt path that runs down to the creek. Across the road is a little convenience store with a single gas pump.

I get out of the truck, circle it, and lean in her open window. She chews her lip, suddenly shy.

"You want to come inside?" I ask. "Or should I pick something out for you?"

She smiles. "I trust your judgment," she says.

"Alright," I say. "I'll take my keys so you can't make a run for it."

She smiles. "I'm not making a run for it, Mr. Quinn."

I take my hat off and fit it on her head. "Be right back."

The store is empty except for a man smoking on the porch and the clerk. I move through the aisle to the deli at the back and pick up two sandwiches. There's a liquor shelf and a row of cigarettes below it, so I grab two bottles of green tea and a whiskey before I head to the front.

I'm almost to the register when the kiosk by the door stops me short. Medicine, bandages...and condoms. Pausing, I look down at the minimal options.

Do I need a condom today?

What are my intentions with her?

If I had my way, I'd pull that truck off in a private space and lift her into my lap. I'd let her unfasten my belt and take my cock out. I'd dig my hands into her soft hips and work her down onto my length.

She'd gasp, and her big, brown eyes would widen. Her lashes would flutter, her nails drag down my neck.

"Can I help you?"

I jerk my head up to find the clerk is staring at me expectantly.

"No," I say, setting my things down.

"Did you need anything else?"

I glance back at the condoms and take my wallet out. "No, this is it."

When I step onto the porch, Diane is standing outside the truck. My hat is big, and it sits too low, close to her eyes. Her flyaway curls flutter in the hot wind. She's got her arms crossed over her chest.

"Where are we going now?" she asks.

I jerk my head towards the dirt path. "Down there."

She circles the truck, staring down the hill. "What's down there?"

"Just a place to sit," I say.

A place to be alone.

She doesn't wait for me. Short skirt swaying, she moves down the dirt path. I follow a few steps behind until we bottom out at the dusty bank of the creek. The trees move slowly overhead, and the air is hot already. It's private, which makes it a hot spot for couples trying to skinny dip or fuck on the bank.

But she doesn't know that.

She starts taking off her boots. I sink down and set the bag aside. Her legs are long, even though she's not that tall. They keep grabbing my attention, pulling my mind under her skirt. I rest my elbow on my cocked knee, squinting up at her as she tugs her socks off.

"You want to go wading?" she asks.

I shake my head. "No, I've got the best seat in the house right here."

She blushes again, and it's the prettiest thing I've ever seen. Without thinking, I beckon her, and to my surprise, she comes, standing between my boots with her hands tucked behind her back.

"Have you ever been kissed, Miss Carter?" I ask.

Her blush deepens as her eyes dart down. She's embarrassed, but she's got no reason to be. Finally, not meeting my gaze, she shakes her head.

I have two reactions at the same time: surprise and satisfaction.

"Come here," I say, reaching for her waist.

She gasps when I lift her and set her on my lap. Her skirt rides up and bares her thighs. I lean in, my hand sliding to her lower back. The air between us is thick, like static electricity.

Her lips part, and my eyes fall.

"I hope you weren't saving that first kiss for anyone, Miss Carter," I say quietly. "Because I think it's mine."

Her throat bobs.

I lean in and kiss her softly. At first, she tenses, and I rub her back in slow circles absently because I'm occupied. Her lips are so fucking soft, and the feeling of them on mine goes right to my dick. I'm rock hard under my zipper.

All I know is, I can't be too much, too soon.

But, God, I want to be. I want this woman with every fiber of my being.

Instead, I go slow and let her catch up. She's clumsy at first, but as the kiss goes on, she figures it out. Slowly, I increase the pressure until her lips part. Then, I kiss her long and deep, giving her a taste of my tongue.

Her thighs stiffen, and she fucking moans into my mouth. My entire body burns. We break apart, and she's so pretty, all flushed and panting in my lap.

"Can I have that again?" she breathes.

She could ask me for the moon, and I'd drag it down for her. I grip her by the nape of her neck as my other hand moves up between her breasts, cradling her face, holding her head steady so I can lean in and really kiss her this time.

Her hips buck.

I die a little inside, knowing she's feeling things between her thighs that I can't see, taste, or touch. My head spins, and my heart thumps so hard, I feel it in my mouth.

She tastes like sweet lightning.

Like she's going to fuck me up, good and hard, and I'll just keep drinking because she's so good. I swear that, as her lips part and she offers me the tip of her soft tongue, the ground shakes.

Something good is coming.

And so is something cataclysmic.

Mindlessly, recklessly, I flip her onto her back on the bank. She gasps as my mouth runs down the side of her neck. My teeth graze her collarbone. My hand slides down, down, down to the hem of her dress.

I pause. I'm so horny for her, I didn't put all the pieces together until now. If she hasn't been kissed, she definitely hasn't been fucked.

I pull back and her dark eyes are dreamy with desire. Her full mouth pants as her breasts heave under her thin dress.

She's my judgment day, my test of what kind of man I am.

She probably thinks I'm a good one, but she doesn't know about the tin cans, the bodies in the ground, or the list of names carved into my bed. Names I've been scratching off, one by one, as I take care of them.

I should let her go—tell her I'm no good for someone as sweet as her—but I don't. Instead, I slip my hand up under her skirt.

She gasps, and I catch it in my mouth. This time, the kiss goes on and on as I move my hand back and forth over the seam of her panties right below her navel.

She moans, her hips riding up. I break contact.

"Is it too much too soon?" I ask.

She shakes her head. "Don't stop," she begs.

Her thighs shudder and my heart thumps. We're on the shore, her on her back with her thigh cocked. Our bodies mold together, and I swear I can feel the blood pump in her veins.

I shift my hand, slipping my fingertip under the seam.

"What are you going to do?" she whispers.

I move over her, keeping my weight up so I don't crush her frame. My mouth runs over her throat and goes lower, kissing the faint swell of her cleavage. I should stop right now, but I can't—I don't want to.

I want to push her skirt up and eat her out, right here on the riverbank. It's summer, and I haven't gotten laid in forever. I've been like a bull on the other side of the cow pen since we met, all tied up in knots and hornier than I've ever been in my life.

Something changed in that kitchen, a shift strong enough that it made me set aside my guilt about how young and vulnerable she is. For the first time, I've met a woman who looks at me, really looks at me, like I'm a man who could love her right.

Like I'm more than just a gunslinger.

My hand dips down, and I feel a little patch of trimmed hair. Then, there's soft, naked pussy and, God—my fingertips slip over her wetness.

Fuck me.

Her thighs tremble, and a gasp slips from between her lips as her nails pierce my chest. My hands tighten on her panties, and I *need* to go down, to taste all that sweet arousal on her cunt. But she bats my arm away, and I drag my gaze up to wide eyes.

"What are you...going to do?" she whispers.

Her voice is raspy, but it's not scared. Head spinning, I bend down and kiss her open lips harshly. I know she feels the drumbeat in my body, the one I hear in the distance, getting closer with every second I'm not buried in her sweet pussy.

This is inevitable. I have to have her, even if it means taking her virginity on the bank of the creek.

I pull back. There's no fucking point in lying.

"I need you, Diane," I say hoarsely.

Her throat bobs. "Like...how?"

I brush her hair back, my thumb dragging down her cheek. "I need to touch you, kiss you...be inside you. God, girl, I feel like I'm fucking dying."

Heat waves rise from the dusty riverbank where our bodies lay together. Her lashes flutter, and I know my words are a million filthy images in her mind. I see it in her flush, feel it when her hips rub on me, just a little bit.

"I...um...I haven't...."

I nod. "I can guess."

My eyes rove over her face. Her big, dark eyes have a little droop to them that I find so sexy, especially when they're hazy with desire. Her full mouth parts, showing me a flash of white teeth, one tooth slightly overlapping the other. The pink tip of her tongue flicks out and wets her lips.

I'm so hard it hurts. My hand tightens on her body.

My girl. This could be my girl.

All soft, warm, sun-kissed skin, dotted with summertime freckles. Blonde curls so fine, they feel like silk in my calloused hands.

I should stop. She's twenty-one years old.

She doesn't know what she's getting into, consorting with someone like me. Up at Sovereign Mountain, we do things with little regard for anyone's law but our own.

This girl doesn't know who I am.

Or what I've done.

If I was a better man, I would take her home with her virginity intact, but I've never been particularly good—just good at pretending I am so the world doesn't guess what I do in the dark.

But I can't pretend with her—something about those brown eyes makes me honest.

I know what I'm going to do, even if I shouldn't, and so does she. The inevitability is intoxicating. When our eyes meet, it thrums like wire through a fence. We're going to fuck.

"Do you want to do that...here?" she whispers.

"Would you rather it be in bed?"

She nods. "Yeah, I think I would."

Reluctantly, I extract my hand from her panties and help her to her feet. She's flushed as she puts her boots back on, and I take the opportunity to lick my fingers.

My head spins.

She's sweet with a little hint of tartness, and *fuck*, I need more. I want it saturating my senses. Before I fuck her, I'm going to eat her out. Thoroughly.

She's getting a lot of firsts today.

We're both quiet as I take her hand and lead her to the truck. She hands my hat back to me, and I set it on the dashboard. The engine rumbles as I pull back onto the road, and she clears her throat.

"Are you going to tell anyone?" she whispers.

I glance over. Her arms are wrapped around her body. I slide my hand down her thigh and grip it, holding her tight.

"No," I say firmly.

"I don't take the pill."

"I'll pull out," I say.

"Maybe you could use a condom?" she says, glancing sideways. I can tell she's not used to conversations like this—she's glowing pink.

I shake my head. "No, I'll pull out."

She starts biting her thumbnail. I rub my palm over her bare thigh in slow circles. After a while, she takes that hand and twines her fingers through it, and as we drive, some of the tenseness ebbs from her body.

We pull up the drive, and I park behind the trees, even though no one is home. She lets me lift her out of the truck, and I stay a few steps behind her, watching her short skirt twitch as she walks.

And I toy with the idea of not pulling out.

CHAPTER SEVEN

DIANE

My heart is jumping out of my chest.

His hand is big and rough around mine as I lock the front door and lead him down the hallway. I swear, I've soaked through my panties.

I didn't have a sip of whiskey at the creek, but I feel so fucking drunk—drunk off his kisses, off his mouth on my neck.

His hand on my pussy was the most intoxicating thing I've ever felt, and down between my thighs thumps a raw, hungry heartbeat.

It's wild, so strong that it feels like a primal urge I don't quite understand.

And I need to satisfy it.

His hand lingers on my lower back, guiding me as if I don't know my own stairs. It feels good; I want him to take control. I don't want to have to do anything but lie back and let him show me what he can do.

I let him into my bedroom and push down the hook and eye lock. Slowly, I turn to find he's looking at me like he's starving.

Bright, watchful hunger.

My stomach swoops. This room has been my only safe space since Nana left. Nobody comes up here but me, and now he's standing by my metal framed bed, larger than life. It's making my heart jump up my throat.

He's a lot of unknowns, but I like the edge that gives him. I like his bright, hazel eyes, his short beard, and his chestnut hair. I like that he's all hard muscle and scars and tanned skin. I like that he smells good, like fresh laundry on the line.

There's also another side to him I can't ignore.

It's the dark side I haven't tasted yet, the flicker of something rough in his gaze. *Hunger*. Maybe he can't control it. It's the way his voice drops deep in his chest and the gravel that comes out when he wants me.

It makes my toes curl in my boots.

My mouth is dry; it's sinking in that I'm at a pivotal point in my life. I'll always look back and remember today was the day, that he was the first man to fuck me.

It's not who I expected at all. I never expected to hope he'd be the last, either.

His belt clinks. He's taking off his gun and hanging the holster on the bedpost. Our eyes lock, and he guides me to sit, my heart picking up when he kneels at my feet.

His throat bobs, the space between his collarbones flushed. A trickle of sweat catches in the dark hair on his chest.

He tugs my boots and socks off and sets them aside. Then, without any hesitation, he puts his hands up under my dress and slips my panties down, peeling the wet fabric right off.

It happens so fast. His hands move quickly. Then, he's got my pink and white panties in his calloused palm.

His fist closes, crushing them as he brings them to his face, and my jaw drops. Heat rushes through my veins and pulses in my bare pussy. I shaved the other day; I have no idea why, but now I'm glad I did, because I'm so sensitive. My hips shift, and I feel soft skin and wet arousal.

I'm ready.

At least, as ready as I'll ever be.

"Please," I whisper.

He cocks his head. “Please?”

“I need you.”

He rises, and suddenly, I’m looking straight at him, hard in his pants. I swallow, staring at the rise under the zipper. There's a raw drumbeat spinning out of control between my thighs, and I tilt my head back as he lifts me by the waist to lay me out on my bed.

He shifts between my thighs. His boots clatter to the ground, and the rough fabric of his pants pushes up as he cocks his knee. His muscled thigh presses against my bare sex. I gasp, resisting the urge to rub myself on his leg.

“It’s gonna hurt, darling,” he says.

I nod, swallowing. The air between us feels heated, almost feverish. My hands slip up between us and plant flat on his chest, feeling the muscle rippling beneath his shirt.

I don’t know what I’m doing, but I know what I want. Dizzy, I find the buttons and start undoing them.

One after the other, until they fall open.

My eyes drop.

He’s well-muscled, the kind that comes from hard, physical labor, so perfectly imperfect with ridges and scars. My eyes move lower, following the dark trail from his navel down to his belt. My fingertips hover over the hair on his chest, and then I run them through it, mesmerized by him.

He turns to toss his shirt, and my eyes widen. Across his upper back, he’s got a single word etched into his muscled shoulders, almost like...like someone branded him.

Gunslinger.

My stomach twists.

He’s not like the boys my age.

He’s a man, and not a very domesticated one. Maybe, if I’m being truthful with myself, he’s too old and too dangerous to be in my bed.

But God, I need him.

His lids flicker, and his hand runs up my hip, moving along my side to tug my zipper down. For a second, I want to hesitate. No one has ever seen my breasts before.

I clear my throat, and his hands pause, his bright eyes inches from mine.

"Why do you have that word on your back?" I ask tentatively.

His eyes flick down, like he's hiding something.

"I had a job, and I fucked it up," he says. "That's what I got for getting caught. Could have been a lot worse."

He tugs at my dress, and it slips down my body. His eyes are distracted, lingering on my bra. I made it—I make most of my clothes—and I feel a little pride that he likes what he sees. I'm a good seamstress.

Or maybe he's just looking at my breasts. That's more likely.

"Is the word...a scar or a brand?" I whisper.

"It's a brand," he says.

I don't have time to process his words before his hands are on my back, flicking my bra open. He peels it off, and my breasts fall out, exposed.

His eyes drop. My nipples tighten.

I don't have to ask if he likes them. From his expression, it's obvious the rest of the world has fallen away. He moves in, pulling me closer and sliding one hand around my back to hold me up. With his other, he bends me until my spine arches and my breasts push into his face.

"Jesus Christ," he groans.

"What?" I whisper.

Instead of answering, he kisses the underside of my left breast. My body lights up. His mouth is pure heaven. My head falls back, and the ceiling of my room spins. His hot, strong tongue runs over the tip of my nipple, and a tiny gasp slips from my lips.

It circles the sensitive peak as he moans, and I pulse deep inside.

His free hand tugs my dress until it slips off. Then, he lowers me onto my back, thighs spread, no panties.

"Wait," I gasp.

He's not listening. Those piercing eyes are locked between my legs. I squirm, uncomfortable with being inspected so closely.

"Be a good girl," he says, flicking his eyes up to mine. "Stay right there, darling."

"You're staring at me," I manage.

"You've got the prettiest cunt I've ever seen. Of course I'm staring."

Something about that word, one I've never had the courage to say, falling from his lips makes me weak.

My brain hums, and I worry my lower lip, stalling and unsure how to respond. I don't get a lot of compliments, especially not dirty ones, but thankfully, I don't have to answer him, because he leans down and kisses my stomach so gently, I shiver.

His tongue darts out and circles my navel. The sensation shoots down to my clit, making my thighs tremble. Then, he moves down past my dress bunched around my waist and starts kissing along the inside of my thigh.

His mouth is dangerously close to my sex, and a tremor runs down my leg at the idea.

"What are you doing?" I whisper.

He looks up. "We've got hours, darling. And I've got nowhere to be but between your legs."

"What?"

He doesn't answer. My heart patters out of control, and for a second, I consider begging him to stop so I can gather my thoughts.

But what's the point of thinking when just feeling is so much better?

He takes my wrists, wraps them up in one hand, and holds them to my lower belly. I'm pinned down and exposed. My pulse hammers, and I wait with bated breath.

I feel it—his tongue, hot and hungry—curl over my sex and drag up to my clit.

Oh God, I'm going to die.

He licks over me again and zeros in on my clit, lapping gently with the tip of his tongue. I want to bury my hands in his hair and keep him right there forever.

I squirm, twisting my wrists. His grip tightens, steady and firm, and my brain buzzes. There's something so deliciously dirty about being in bed, in the middle of the afternoon, with a man's head between my legs.

This is everything I never knew I wanted.

My toes curl on the quilt as my lower back arches and I push my pussy up against his mouth. Just a little, to let him know I like what he's doing.

He growls softly, like an animal, but doesn't lift his head. His tongue keeps working over my clit, keeping a slow, steady pace. I'm the only one who has ever touched that place. It feels good when I do it, but not the way it does under his tongue.

Something sparks deep inside me, and I can't help myself. My eyes flutter, the ceiling spins, and a moan works its way from my mouth. It sounds strange, like it came from someone else, not me.

He releases me and grips my hips, driving into me harder with his tongue. Hazily, I realize my hands are in his hair now, holding his head right where I want it.

When did I get so bold?

The spark gets hotter until, suddenly, it catches fire. Then, my pleasure is a train leaving the station. I can't stop it, not even if I wanted to. I'm dimly aware of my legs going stiff, of my hips lifting off the bed, needy for more.

His rough hand moves to rest on my belly, keeping me down.

His tongue never stops, never relents.

My head spins. Sweat breaks out across my skin, the sheets sticking to me. I'm on the edge of a cliff about to plummet off. It might ruin me, but there's no stopping it now as it hits me like a thunderclap.

"Westin," I cry out.

He groans and buries his face deeper between my thighs, giving me his tongue to ride. It's warm and a little rough as I grind my clit on it, eyes rolled back, savoring the swells of ecstasy rolling through my body.

It isn't the same kind of pleasure I give myself. It's glorious and dirty, and so much better because it's forbidden.

We shouldn't be here together; he shouldn't have done this.

But here we are, and he did it.

CHAPTER EIGHT

WESTIN

She's going to fuck me up.

And I'm going to let her.

Her body shakes, and I drag my tongue over her perfect pussy as her orgasm dies away. She's soaked with sweet, tangy arousal, and I want it all, so I lick it off her pussy and inner thighs until it's gone.

Her eyes are glassy, her cheeks flushed. Her teardrop-shaped breasts heave, catching my eye. God, they're beautiful. Her nipples are upturned and a soft blush pink. Her bra was tight, making them look small under her dress, but when I unhooked it, out spilled the prettiest, softest breasts I'd ever seen.

Everything about her is perfect.

My cock is rock hard, aching to slip inside her. But more than that, I'm aching to be her first. When she'd admitted she was a virgin, the dark undercurrent I like to keep hidden sparked.

She's beautiful and so fucking sweet.

And maybe it's selfish, but I have to be that man.

The first...and last.

The thought makes my head spin. I've known her for two days, and I'm already ready to lay it all on the line. I'm not sure what will happen tomorrow, but I know for certain there's no world where I fuck this woman and leave.

No, if I fuck her, she might as well be branded with my name.

And I'm *going* to fuck her.

She moans as I reach between us, and her head falls back. She's draped over the pillow, her head hanging back, her beautiful throat marked pink where I'd kissed her by the river.

Her thighs tremble as I slide up and brace my knee, unzipping my pants, pushing them down low enough to unleash my cock. It slaps against her thigh, rock hard.

Her pussy leaks, dripping on the sheet.

Fuck. Me.

My cock jerks, leaving a bit of wetness on her skin. Her breasts heave and her pink nipples tighten. Mindlessly, I bend to put one in my mouth and suck.

"Oh." The air rushes from her lungs.

I push my hand between us again and run my fingertips over her pussy, letting her slick arousal coat them. Gently, I press my middle finger deeper until it slips inside her cunt.

Her nails come out, digging into my upper arms.

"Ouch," she whispers.

I push my finger in another inch, intoxicated by her soft, wet pussy and the way it grips me. She's tight, probably too tight to be doing this today. Having her first kiss and losing her virginity is a lot all at once.

That isn't going to stop me, though. She's here, naked and willing. I'm not a good enough man to walk away.

"Does it hurt?" I asked.

She shakes her head once. "It did at first. Not much anymore."

I flip my hand, searching for that sweet spot. Her lips slowly part, and when I find it, the breath leaves her lungs in a rush.

"Oh," she gasps.

I circle her G-spot, rubbing gently to make her thighs tremble again. "I want to touch every place on your body that makes you feel good, darling."

Her lids flutter, eyes rolling back.

She's so soaked, it's dripping down the curve of her ass. Slowly, I explore her pussy with that finger before I pull it free and lick it clean, getting to my knees.

Her eyes drop like a stone, and her brows reach her hairline.

"I'm going to fuck you now, darling," I tell her.

She nods, wordless as I bend down and kiss her mouth. When I pull back, she follows me with her lips, like she doesn't want to stop.

"Say yes," I order softly.

"Yes," she breathes.

I sink down until our bodies are tangled. Outside, birds trill, and hot wind moves through the window screen, brushing our naked skin.

Her hands touch my upper arms, nails digging in. Her big brown eyes widen as she feels my cock at her entrance, the head of my cock finding the slick heat of her pussy. She bites her lip and winces.

I push until she whimpers.

"That's a good girl," I praise.

I slip my hand under her neck, holding her head in my hand. My hips don't relent as her inner muscles spasm and her breasts heave, nipples hard, brushing up against my bare chest.

I'm halfway in when I hit resistance. I hesitate, but not once does it occur to me to stop. Her spine tenses; maybe it's better to just get it done. I thrust hard, sinking to the hilt inside.

"Oh," she breathes, tears springing to her eyes. One slips down her temple and mingles with her hair.

"Does it hurt, darling?" I murmur, kissing away that tear.

"Yes," she gasps. "It hurts, but don't stop."

I can't help the moan that moves up my chest. Bracing myself on my knee, I pull out halfway and lift so I can look down to where we're joined. She's soaked, the entrance of her sex swollen with a trace of pink, a hint of blood. It sinks in that I did this to her, but I'm not sure if I'm triumphant or ashamed.

Most likely the former.

I spend a lot of my time trying to be a conscience for Sovereign, but I don't have much of one myself—at least not when it comes to staking my claim on Diane.

My brain is empty as my hips move of their own accord, thrusting hard. She gasps, eyes rolling back. I'm bare inside her, skin against skin. I made a choice when I walked out of that convenience store that I wouldn't wear a condom. It feels like a crime to put something between us.

We're way past that anyway. If she gets pregnant, it doesn't matter. Either way, she's my woman. Fuck that I've known her for a grand total of two days.

I shift closer, letting her body meld with mine. We're both hot and dotted with sweat, mingling together and staining the sheets. She's bleeding more than I expected, but she doesn't seem to notice. Maybe she likes the pain—she's writhing like she does.

Her hips move with mine as I fall into a steady rhythm, and she's rising to meet my thrusts like she loves it.

The bed hits the wall, clattering. The hot breeze makes the window screen shake. The room is permeated with the scent of metal and summertime honeysuckle.

I'll remember it as long as I live. It smells like the day Diane Carter became mine.

CHAPTER NINE

DIANE

He hurts me, fills every part of me to the brim, but he feels like being alive. If he breaks me in the process, I'm happy to be broken.

I've been rusting away at Carter Farms, hoping for my life to start, and here he is, all muscle and sweat and a maybe-it-could-be-something-more. I'm delirious, but I swear, I can see him coming back to me at night.

He kind of looks like he could make me his bride.

And I like the thought of that, though it sounds ridiculous, considering we barely know each other. He's different. I've never held much stock in romanticism, but I wouldn't mind hearing him whisper sweet things to me or bring me flowers from the field in July.

Maybe even promise to be more than just a kiss and a fuck in the afternoon.

His body stiffens abruptly, pulling me from my silly thoughts. His eyes change; he goes from fucking slowly to rutting hard, chasing something that makes his breath come in harsh pants.

His gun, hanging from the bedpost, clatters.

I whimper.

Then, in one, fluid movement, he jerks his hips back and swears under his breath. I look down, and his cock is out of me and in his hand, wet with my arousal. He comes on my inner thigh, and it's warm as it hits my skin. His jaw goes tight as his hips jerk one last time before he's done.

I'm faintly disappointed he didn't do that inside me.

But also relieved.

He sits back on his heels. His pants are still on, a leather belt hanging open at the hip. His chest heaves, glittering with sweat. He tucks his cock back into his boxer-briefs and runs a hand over his face.

"Let me clean you up, darling," he says, his voice a low rumble. "You got any washrags?"

"In the bathroom," I whisper.

He stands and flashes the brand on his broad, muscled shoulders. The scar tissue is thick, like someone took a hot poker and raked it over his skin, digging in to make sure he was branded for life.

My stomach twists. People are cruel, I know that, but sometimes, it shocks me just how much.

He comes back to the bed and cleans the cum off my thigh before he wipes his hands and tosses the rag in the laundry basket. I sidle over to make room for him.

He stretches out, looking absurdly big on my twin bed. I let my gaze run over his hard stomach. It's so sexy, and I feel my battered pussy tighten.

I look up at him, head spinning. He bends and kisses my forehead, something gentle and dark in his eyes, but I don't know enough to understand it. It reminds me again that I'm out of my depth.

Too much, too soon.

Maybe he was right to ask me that on the riverbank.

What he did to me in this bed while all the men were in the city was too much, too soon. I should have refused instead of welcoming him like rain after a drought.

The only problem is, I don't regret it. I'd do it again in a heartbeat.

I part my dry lips. "You hungry?"

He shakes his head. "No. You?"

"A little."

He picks up the apple I placed on the bedside table the other night, the one he tossed to me before disappearing. He has no knife, so he bites a piece from it. I watch as he takes the chunk from his mouth and puts it between my lips.

Breathless, I open.

It's the sweetest apple I've ever had.

We lay on the tangled sheets as he feeds me, bite by bite, until it's gone. Taking it from his mouth and putting it into mine. It's so intimate; I never dreamed it was possible to feel this close to anyone.

When it's gone, I slide down so my head is on his thigh. It's thick and hard with muscle. I'm fully naked, and I don't mind that he's looking, studying my body like he wants to memorize every inch of it.

"What do you want most in the whole world?" I ask, staring up at the ceiling.

He rumbles in his chest, leaning his head back against the wall. "What you just gave me."

I glance at him, thinking he's joking, but his face is sober. I can't find the words to respond, so I pick at my nails. There's a smudge of blood on the side of my finger.

"What do you want, darling?" he asks.

"Everything," I sigh.

He's silent for a long time, and I wonder if he thinks I'm silly. Finally, he lays his hand on my chest, right between my breasts, like he's feeling my heart thump.

"That's a good thing to want," he says. "You'll get at least part of it at some point."

I laugh, even though he's not joking. He gathers my right breast in his grip, squeezing it. His rough thumb moves back and forth over my nipple, and the feeling trickles down my belly to my clit, making it tingle.

Downstairs, the grandfather clock chimes. It's late afternoon. I sit up slowly, trying not to wince at the twinge between my legs. He catches me by the elbow and kisses my mouth hard. When we break apart, he gives me a look that pierces right to my soul.

"You're so beautiful," he says.

His voice is hoarse and low. I believe every word he says.

I don't know how to respond, so I curl up against the headboard and pull the sheets over my body. He stands and gets dressed, the gun holster back on his waist.

His expression is sober as he picks up his hat, and my hands are a knot in my lap. I glance up, and I don't know why, but I want to cry.

"You better go before the men come back," I whisper.

He kneels beside the bed. I shift to the edge and let my legs hang down between his boots. He's so big, his head is level with mine.

He runs his hand down my calf to my ankle. His head dips, and he kisses the arch of my foot.

My stomach flutters.

"You're pretty sweet, Diane," he says. "I'd like to see you again."

I swallow. "Um...do you think we're moving too fast?" I whisper.

He shakes his head once, not hesitating. "I've never been surer about wanting to get to know somebody. If you want me to fuck off, Diane, you'll have to shoot me."

I laugh weakly. He smiles, and I touch his face, enjoying the prickle of his beard.

"I kinda like you," I whisper.

His lids flicker as his throat bobs. "I more than kinda like you."

I bite my lip. "Too much, too soon, Mr. Quinn," I say, trying to make it into a joke. I mean it a little bit, though.

"I don't care," he says, voice hoarse. "What kind of flowers do you like, darling?"

My brows rise. Is he trying to get romantic with me?

"My favorite? The yellow lilies that grow in the spring," I say. "They're pretty, but they don't last long, so it's a waste to pick them."

He tilts his head, the corner of his mouth crooked. Then, his hand slides around the back of my neck, and he pulls me down to his mouth. I swear, I'm getting used to the taste of Westin Quinn. It's feeling familiar.

He makes me burn between my thighs when his tongue brushes mine. We break apart before he kisses my palms and gets to his feet.

"Goodbye, Diane Carter," he says. "I'll be back soon."

He leaves me sitting on the bed, stained sheets surrounding me. The front door slams, and I go to the window, holding the curtain over my body. He's leaving, heading down the driveway.

I know it's risky for him to be here, but it'll break my heart if he never comes back.

CHAPTER TEN

WESTIN

I've gotten a taste of that little blonde Carter girl, and now, I'm hungry.

God, no. I'm starving.

It's agony pretending nothing has changed. Sovereign Mountain turns with the rest of the world. I get up and head to the barn to saddle up Rocky and rotate the southernmost pasture to the east. Sovereign is already in the driveway, astride his bay gelding, Shadow. Jensen Childress sits beside him on a dappled gray mare.

"What are you doing up on Sovereign Mountain?" I ask, leading Rocky out.

"Came to help for the day," he says.

He gives me a look. Sovereign stares out over the eastern field, his eyes narrowed. He's a quiet man, but I've known him long enough to let him ruminate in his own world. He'll be back when he chooses.

I swing onto Rocky and stretch out in my stirrups to get adjusted. "What's the face for, Childress?"

"How's it going with the Carter girl?" he asks.

Wishing he hadn't brought it up here and now, I shrug. "Nothing to report."

"Nothing at all?" His brow arches.

"Nothing. Shut up, motherfucker," I say, shaking my head. "Next time, I'll make sure to read you the gossip column over breakfast before we're out trying to get work done."

Jensen laughs. "So I take it she's got you down bad," he says with relish.

He digs his heels into his mare, and they start moving. Sovereign swings Shadow around, and I'm right on their heels, heading out of the yard and down the valley to the southern field.

"Are you talking about David Carter's sister?" Sovereign asks.

"Yeah," Jensen says.

Sovereign glances at me. "Is she the one you used to go out with?"

"No," I say firmly. "She's a good bit younger than me, about the same age as your girl."

Sovereign's jaw twitches, and I know he's not hearing a word I'm saying. Luckily for me, Jensen didn't overhear. Sovereign has had it bad for Clint Garrison's widow, Keira, ever since he met her a few months back. He's waiting for her legal problems with her late husband's ranch to get sorted out. At least, that's what he says.

The truth is, when Sovereign met Keira, he fell hard. He has a habit of doing that in his relationships—falling hard and loving blindly. The next day, we invited Clint up to the ranch and ran him over with a herd of cattle. In my opinion, it would have been easier to fuck her and take her away, but Sovereign has a deep disgust for infidelity. He'd rather kill a Garrison and risk the legal consequences than commit adultery.

So, we killed Clint and spun it as an accident.

With Sovereign and I being responsible for Clint's death, he's not in an ideal situation to pursue his widow. Everyone in South Platte is still stirred up; I don't envy him having to clean up that mess to get the woman he wants.

At least my situation is a little more cut and dry.

Sovereign shrugs. "I've got no stones to throw. You fuck whoever you want."

"I'm not fucking her," I say quickly.

Jensen pulls up right beside us. “I heard her brother’s got plans to hitch her up to a Garrison.”

Sovereign gives him a sharp look, shifting his weight to swing Shadow around. I can tell the conversation is over, and thank fuck for that.

My blood bubbles at the idea of Thomas Garrison putting his hands on Diane. There’s no way I’ll let her marry him.

Over my dead body.

My mind wanders as we ride out and start moving the cattle. It’s a small portion of the herd, maybe a hundred and fifty head. They’re tired from the heat, and they move easily. The dust is a bitch, though. I have to stop and pull my bandana over my face to keep from gagging on it.

We get the last one secure, and Sovereign heads back to the barn—he has business in town with the bank. Jensen rides with me as I check the eastern fence. We’re both quiet until we get back to the barn and wash up in the gatehouse.

“Where you headed?” I ask.

“Carter’s Farm,” he says. “Care to join?”

I shake my head. “I’ve got no business there today.”

Jensen leans on the kitchen counter, drying his hands on a towel as he studies me.

“You like that girl,” he says.

I shrug. “So what if I do?”

I’m avoiding his eyes, but he’s shrewd. He always has been. Somehow, Jensen Childress knows everything about everyone’s business. The corner of his mouth jerks up, and he shakes his head, grabbing his hat.

“You already fucked her,” he says. “Goddamn.”

I keep my head down. “You judging me for that?”

He shrugs. “She’s a pretty little thing and I meant what I said before. But if her brother wants her with Thomas Garrison...well, you’ll get her into trouble.”

“She’s not in trouble.”

“Not yet, she’s not.”

Guilt creeps in, along with protectiveness. Jensen sees my scowl and relents.

"Listen, I'm going down to West Lancaster with David. You head down and see your girl, and I'll text you when we're leaving to come back."

"Really?"

"Go on," he says. "Let me get down there first."

Jensen might push a few buttons now and then, but he's a solid friend. I clap him on the shoulder before he leaves, his truck disappearing down the drive. It feels like it takes forever to get that all clear text from him. The cell service is poor at Sovereign Mountain, so I wait in my truck at the end of the driveway, in a clean shirt and everything.

Finally, it comes, and I'm on the road in a heartbeat.

My head spins when I think about pulling up her driveway and seeing her on the porch in one of those little sundresses, her boots dusty, her blonde waves falling down her back.

My heart pounds as I turn off the road a little way before the drive. I pull off but head up to the far western side of the field. On my way out last time, I looked up and swore I saw some of those yellow lilies.

Sure enough, they're on the fence line where the air is cool in the shade. I take a handful and head back down the fence, turning left to go up the drive.

Carter Farms is quiet, all the ranch hands are out in the fields for the day. The front door hangs open, and a barn cat lays on the porch, sunning itself.

I consider just walking in, picking her up, carrying her to her bedroom. Putting her through that mattress until we're both satisfied.

The screen door bursts open, and she steps out, all bright and beautiful—blonde curls and tanned skin. Our eyes lock as the breeze hits her skirt, tugging it around her thighs.

"Westin," she whispers. "You can't keep coming around here."

I take my hat off. "Seems I can."

Her cheeks flush, harsh edges softening. She digs the toe of her boot into the porch.

"Why are you here?" she whispers.

"Came to see my girl."

Her blush deepens. "I'm not your girl."

I climb the steps and put my hat on her head. "Yeah, you are."

Her breasts heave under her flowered sundress, short enough that it leaves those gorgeous legs bare.

"How'd you know I was alone?"

"Got a tip-off."

Her eyes drop to my hand. "Are those...lilies?" She bites her lip, her cheeks blushing pink. I snap one of the blossoms off and tuck it behind her ear.

We're both quiet, and I swear I hear our hearts beat in tandem.

"Are you trying to romance me?" she whispers.

"I'm just trying to make you feel special," I say. "To make up for fucking you like a whore in a little while."

Her jaw drops. I take her by the throat and pull her close, her pulse thrumming under my fingers. She's so much shorter than me, she needs the stability of my hand as I lean her back and kiss her mouth.

I melt. God, she tastes sweet like iced tea. There's a hint of lemon when her lips part, on the tip of her tongue.

My body roars to life, and I'm rock hard under my pants. I came here to talk, not to fuck her like an animal, but the intelligent part of my brain is shutting down. Her hand comes up and grabs me by the collar, yanking me even closer. A moan works its way up her throat, and the flowers hit the porch floorboards with a thump.

We break apart, panting, her brown eyes blazing.

"What are you doing to me, Westin Quinn?" she breathes.

"I could ask you the same, Diane Carter." I kiss her mouth again. "Do you need me, darling? Did it get you wet, thinking about being fucked?"

"Yes," she pants, pupils blown. "Please, take me upstairs."

I shake my head. "No. Get in my truck."

I take her hand and lead her down the driveway to where I parked. She tries to scramble into the truck, but I have to lift her. Her long legs flash as she settles herself in the passenger side and I slide in the driver's side.

She's still wearing my hat, my flower tucked behind her ear.

God, there's nothing prettier than the sight of her in my passenger seat, except maybe if I can get her back to the gatehouse and into my bed. That would be the prettiest thing I've ever seen.

I spread my knees, adjusting my seat back. Her eyes drop, and she bites her lip.

"Get in my lap," I say quietly.

Her skin blushes, and it lingers right between her breasts. On her hands and knees, she crawls across the seat and straddles my lap, pressing her soft body against mine, her hands flat on my chest.

"When I fucked you and you bled...did you like that?" I ask.

She gasps softly. I take her chin and force her to look me in the eyes.

"There's nothing to be ashamed of," I say.

She clears her throat. "Yes, I did."

My cock is so goddamn hard, fighting for release. Keeping my hands steady, I unfasten the delicate, heart-shaped buttons on the bodice of her dress one by one until the fabric falls away to reveal her breasts.

She's braless, and for a second, I'm speechless, totally entranced.

Her nipples tighten as I ease one shoulder of the dress down and fully bare her left breast. She moans when I cup its softness in my hand. Her eyes drop, watching my hard, calloused hand hold her soft breast.

My thumb drags over the pink of her nipple before I pinch it—*hard.*

She whimpers, pupils blowing.

"You liked that," I say.

My finger and thumb tighten, and she lets out a moan. I take her throat and compress the sides, gently but firmly so she feels it all the way to that perfect pussy between her thighs.

I know she feels it because her spine arches. Her hips rise, and she unashamedly tries to grind her cunt against the ridge of my cock.

I've always kept my sexual preferences under wraps. I know other men, like Sovereign, who share my interests and are more open about it, but I prefer to keep the streak of sadism I've always had locked away until the bedroom door is firmly shut.

It's a complicated thing to introduce women to. There has to be a foundation of trust first.

I don't know Diane well enough for rougher things, but I can test her here and there to see what her body enjoys. So far, she loves the little flashes of pain, and I saw how she responded when I pinned her to the bed.

"Again," she whispers.

I can't hold back my smile. She tenses as I lean in and take her nipple in my mouth. My teeth rake over it, just hard enough to sting. She moans and her hand goes between our bodies, boldly searching for my zipper.

I should say no, but I'm not a good enough man to do that. Everyone, even the ones closest to me, think I'm better than I am. Sovereign teeters so close to the edge of darkness, it's up to me to hold him back.

But who holds me back?

Who tells me when I've stepped over the line?

My hand fists, gripping her hair so my hat tumbles off and lands on the dashboard behind her. I fist her hair and drag her head back so she has to look me in the eyes.

"You want this," I say, my voice low.

She nods, swallowing hard.

There's no going back, not now that I've already had her. And now I've got this foolish idea I could be more to her than just sex.

One-handed, I hold her still by her blonde waves. With the other, I push between our bodies and unbuckle my belt, pulling it free. She gasps as I release her so I can put her hands behind her back and loop the leather around her slender wrists, and she gasps again when I pull it tight and secure her to the wheel.

I draw my zipper down and unleash my cock, shoving down the front of my pants. Fingers rough, I tug her panties aside and stroke over her soaked sex. Her breasts heave as she stares, in awe, when I lick my fingers to get her taste all over my tongue.

She whimpers. "Please, be gentle."

"You can take it, darling," I say. "I won't hurt you."

Her eyes widen as my cock pushes against her pussy. The head slips in, and I grit my teeth. Her full mouth parts, and her eyes roll back as I ease her down onto my length. Slowly; there's hardly any room.

"Please," she begs.

"Please...what?" I pant.

"Not all the way."

My hands grip her hips, working myself deeper. Her lashes glitter, her eyes glassy. Taking pity on her, I find her clit and stroke that swollen nub beneath my thumb, making her twitch and squirm.

"So fucking good," I breathe. "That's my girl."

This time, she doesn't tell me she's not my girl.

We both know better.

"I know you can take it all the way for me, darling," I say.

She groans, and her hips work, back and forth, as my cock slips deep inside her soft body. It's like tumbling into paradise. The heavy, roaring desire I've felt since I saw her slender legs, her short fucking skirt, and her big eyes is quiet for a second, placated by her cunt.

Then she flutters around me, and it roars back to life.

Fingers tight on her hips, I lift her an inch and slam her down. She cries out, but I don't relent. Distantly, I catch the sweet scent of her pussy as I rut my hips up against hers.

Our breath is loud. She's so wet, I can hear it as I thrust. It's stained on my work pants.

Hips moving, I bend until my mouth grazes her right nipple. She moans and pulls against the belt, keeping her to the wheel. Binding her with her arms back, her breasts exposed, just the way I like her.

I curl my tongue around her nipple, drawing a circle over the tight, pink flesh. Her moans are soft and breathy. I'm groaning in my chest.

How can I want someone so much, even when I'm buried in them?

She moans and her belly quivers, the muscles of her cunt working. I let her nipple go and lick up the soft curve of her other breast, nipping and biting it until I get to her other nipple. There, I do the same thing, sucking, grazing with my teeth.

"Westin," she pants.

I lift my head, hips still fucking up into her. "Do you want to come, darling?"

"Yes," she breathes.

"Beg and be nice about it," I order.

She falters, and I can't keep back a smile.

"I know you can be sweet," I say. "You're not all sass. I know there's a good girl in there who can be sweet and beg for it."

She gives me an impudent glare. I fuck hard, bouncing her on my cock. Her hair falls around her shaking breasts, her nipples still wet from my mouth, pink from my teeth.

I push her skirt up, baring her ass, and bring my hand down on it hard enough that she yelps.

"You're setting yourself up to get your pretty ass spanked, darling," I tell her.

"Please," she bursts out, face flushed. "Please, let me come. I'll do anything."

I grip her neck. "I bet you will."

Her eyes are glassy with desire. I push my hand between her legs and find her clit, rubbing it in earnest this time. Her thighs tighten, her pupils blown. My hips keep going, making sure my cock touches her G-spot as I fuck her soaked pussy. I see it coming in the deepening flush on her cheeks, the breathless whimpers spilling from her lips.

Her spine locks.

Her head falls back.

"Oh, God," she cries out.

I watch her, savoring every second. The pleasure hits, and her mouth shakes. It falls open, and I see a flash of pink tongue and white teeth. Her body spasms. Her breath hitches and holds.

"Let it out, darling," I soothe. "Keep on breathing."

She gasps, writhing. Her chest heaves.

"That's right, you just breathe through it. Keep those pretty hips going; ride every inch. Get it all out."

She's obedient in the throes of pleasure. Her body obeys my voice and hands as she does as she's told, down to the letter, hands still tied with my worn leather belt to the steering wheel of my truck.

The only thought I have in my head is a dangerous one.

Mine.

Mine.

Mine.

Sweet, little Diane Carter is mine, come hell or high water.

CHAPTER ELEVEN

DIANE

I only know one side of men, the rough side that makes me want to draw up and hide. The mean side that keeps me hating them.

In Westin River Quinn, I've discovered a new world.

My body tumbles down from its high. His lids are heavy, and his glittering hazel eyes are drunk on sex. He takes me by the hips and ruts his cock into me like he can't stop himself. My head spins, and I'm rising high in a new kind of euphoria, feeling things I've never felt.

When I first met him, he seemed so mild.

There's no mildness in him now.

My desire is soft and desperate. His is hard and driving. God, it drives on and on as he chases his climax. I see it in the way his jaw tightens.

And yet, his hands don't hurt me.

With one, he holds my hip and tugs me down onto him. With the other, he holds me by the throat. My head falls back and to the side. The mountains are a blue crack over the horizon. The sun blazes hot. The windows of his truck are down, and everything smells like hayfields.

He pulls me in, hand firm on my throat. His mouth meets mine, and I taste him, like leather and desire on my tongue. Inside, I ripple with pain as he gets closer to the end. It was like this the first time, right before he pulled from me and spilled onto my inner thigh. I know what's coming now.

He grits his jaw, our lips touching.

"Fuck," he groans.

He reaches behind me, and the belt around my wrist releases. In a second, I'm off his lap and on my back across the seats. He's on one knee over me, one boot braced against the door behind him. I see a flash of hazel, a glitter of sweat. Then, he comes on me, all over my naked breasts, swearing as he does. It hits my neck and chin.

My brain buzzes.

I want him to do that again and again.

My head lolls to the side. His hand is there, braced on the seat before my eyes. Those long fingers know how to touch me. Maybe they hurt me a little too, but I don't dwell on that. The pleasure is so much stronger.

He pushes himself upright and takes a bandana from his pocket. I lie still while he wipes my breasts, up to my throat. He rubs two fingers over the last bit and puts it to my lips.

"Open," he says.

I hesitate, but the part of me that needs him like air, like water, urges me to obey. So I do. His rough fingertips slip past my lips. I taste salt and Westin on my tongue.

Our eyes meet and my lips close over his fingers. My stomach has a pit in it that says one thing—I'm falling hard and fast.

"Good girl," he says, gently drawing his fingers from my mouth.

He sits back and I hear his belt buckle clink. The roof of his truck swims in my vision. His zipper hisses, and then he lifts me up, and I'm in his lap again.

"You alright, darling?" His voice is soft.

I nod, breathless.

His fingers move over the buttons of my dress, covering my breasts. Then, he leans in and kisses my neck. A low, guttural sound comes from his chest.

"You smell like mine," he says.

That goes right through my veins like fire. I'm breathless, but I smile, unable to hold it back. His eyes light up, fixed on my mouth.

"God, you're pretty," he says, distracted.

I think I might be scared, even if it is flattering, the way he's staring at me. I'm starting to think this is more serious than I thought. Maybe that part of me that wondered what it'd be like to belong to him is a louder voice than I anticipated.

"I guess...maybe I should go," he says.

It's clear that's the last thing he wants. I trail my fingers up his chest and rest two of them on his pulse point.

He keeps still, just letting me touch him.

"Do you want to come see my horses instead?" I ask. "The men will be gone for a while yet."

"Sure, darling," he says, smiling. "Let's go see your horses."

He gets out of the truck and tucks the front of his shirt in, circling to open my door. My heart patters when his hands touch my waist to lift me down. I don't think I'll ever get tired of feeling him pick me up.

We head to the barn. It's cool inside, the industrial fan whirring. Gracey and Sunshine are in their stalls due to the heat. It's not normally this hot this early in the year, and they need time to acclimate.

I lean on the door. Gracey pushes her head over the top and nuzzles my hair.

"What's this one's name?" Westin asks.

For a second, I just stare up at him. No one asks me about me or my animals. No one really cares. I've never had a man look at me the way he's looking now—like he gives a damn what I say.

It makes me want to squirm. Instead, I shrug like this is casual.

"Gracey," I say. "And that over there is Sunshine."

His mouth curves.

"What? You don't like their names?" I raise a brow.

He leans his elbows on the door. "I think it's sweet."

"Well, I was a lot younger when I named them," I say. "The names are from a book. But they fit them, I think."

"They sure do."

Sunshine throws her head hard, neighing. She's jealous. I step over and rub her gently with my fingernails. She has a white blaze down the center of her nose, and she loves when I scratch it.

"Do you have a horse?" I ask.

"Yeah, I have a gelding named Rocky," he says.

"Like that's any better."

He smirks. "I call him that because his gaits are all shit. Really jumpy and too slow, even when he gallops."

I turn around and tuck my hands behind my back, leaning against the wall by Sunshine's door. Westin moves until he's right before me, not caging me in but still reminding me what he's capable of.

That he likes to call me a whore, tie me to his steering wheel, and fuck me hard.

My toes curl. I look up through my lashes, but without warning, his face changes. It's stern now, like he's thinking about something that doesn't please him. He narrows his gaze, fixing it through the door to the driveway.

"You okay, sir?" I ask.

He nods, reaching in his pocket. He takes out a cigarette and puts it unlit in his mouth. "Let's go inside," he says. "We've got a bit more time, and it's hot."

His voice is stern too. Nonplussed, I follow him from the barn to the porch. He stands in the doorway and lights his cigarette and smokes. One foot on the porch, one in the doorway. I take my boots off and pad barefoot down the hall and into the kitchen to get some water.

After a minute, I head back to him. He's got a little bit left to smoke so I join him on the porch, handing him a glass.

"I didn't take you for a smoker," I say.

"I'm not really," he says.

"Can I try?"

He shakes his head. "You're too pretty for shit like cigarettes. It's bad for you."

I scowl. "You're doing it."

He glances at me. "Diane, I said no," he says, not unkindly.

I roll my eyes. He arches a brow.

"You better watch yourself," he says, his voice dropping.

He doesn't scare me the way men's threats usually do. This is a different kind of fear. It makes my heart pound, but it's laced with something sweet.

"Or what?" I whisper. "You won't touch me."

"No." He shakes his head. "But I'll tie you up with my belt and fuck the sass out of you."

Once again, I'm speechless. He flicks the cigarette butt into a potted plant.

"What's this about Thomas Garrison?" he asks. "I heard Jensen Childress say something about you getting set up with him."

There's an edge to his voice, but it's not directed at me. I shrug, rolling my eyes.

"They have a lot of money," I say. "David likes the idea of getting in good with them, like being family. He's always kind of pushed me to talk to Thomas, but I don't."

A trickle of sweat moves down his neck.

"Yeah? What's Thomas think about that?"

I sigh, sitting on the porch rail. My bare feet swing. "He always had a thing for me, even when we were teenagers. He used to be nicer, but the older he gets and the more time he spends with his brothers, the meaner he gets about it."

"Does he fuck with you?"

Westin takes out another cigarette. I watch him flick his lighter, a muscle in his forearm moving. Then, he inhales and exhales slowly.

His face is hard. Cold.

"Um, no," I say. "Sometimes Avery does, like he did the night we met. I kind of wish it was Avery that died, not Clint. Maybe you can invite him up to Sovereign Mountain too."

Westin's brows shoot up, and there's a second of silence. Then, he lets his head fall back as he laughs that rich, deep sound.

I frown. It wasn't that funny.

"I wouldn't worry too much about Avery or Thomas, darling," he says. "I have a feeling they'll sort themselves out."

"What does that mean?" I press.

He shakes his head. "Don't you worry about it."

I flip my hair, jumping off the railing. "I'm getting whiskey. You can't tell me no because it's my whiskey."

He laughs, following me into the kitchen. I take down a shot glass and a bottle and step out the back. This porch is cooler with wooden lattices on either end to block the sun.

I sit on the bottom steps, my bare feet in the dust. He sits behind me on the top step. I'm between his knees, back to him, his boots on either side of my body.

I find I like sitting like this.

"What are you doing here? Just talking?" I ask, pouring a half shot.

He tugs at my hair. "Just looking at you."

I glance over my shoulder. My stomach swoops.

"Why's that?" I whisper.

He cups my chin, fingers trailing on my throat. "Because I'd like to keep seeing you."

My heart hammers as I throw back a shot. It burns in my veins, giving me courage.

"You mean you want me to be your girl?" I ask.

"I mean, you *are* my girl," he says, thumb stoking the underside of my chin.

My head spins. He smells good, like sweat and the sex we just had in the truck. I take another half shot because what I want to ask requires bravery.

"Do you actually *like* me?" I whisper.

He rumbles, and I feel it through his hand. "Yes, I do."

The way he says it makes me go wild—firm, deep voice steady. No fucking around and pretending he doesn't care. It's straightforward, and that turns me on.

I shift, looking up at him from between his knees.

"I like you," I say. "Sometimes you make me roll my eyes, but I still like you."

The corner of his mouth turns up. His fingers caress my neck, slow and soft.

"Good girl," he says.

Electricity crackles. I'm right back where I was before he fucked me, hot and bothered and empty between my thighs. I want to be at the center of his world, the way I was tied to his steering wheel, his eyes and hands and body praising me, making me feel good.

Like there's nowhere he'd rather be than with me.

Maybe I just want to be tied up too. That felt better than I ever expected.

"I guess I should go," he says. "Before you get drunk."

The back of my head buzzes from the whiskey. My eyes fall to his zipper, at the level of my eyes. My tongue wets my lips. Into my head flashes an image of me with my face in his lap while he holds my head.

I know he'd feel good in my mouth; he feels so good between my legs.

"What're you thinking?" he asks.

"Can I do what you did for me?" I ask.

A crease appears between his eyes. "What?"

My hand goes to his zipper. His brows rise and he shakes his head. Disappointment fills my chest.

"You're a little tipsy," he says.

I roll my eyes. He reaches down and gives my thigh a light spank; not enough to hurt, but enough to make me want to straddle him. Then, he gets up and makes me go inside and have a glass of water.

"You're very responsible," I say, handing him the empty cup.

"No, just taking care of what's mine," he says.

I'm a mess inside after that. I'm so flustered, I don't know what to do with myself. So, I make food. He watches while I put together cold chicken sandwiches and take a jar of pickled eggs from the fridge. We eat standing at the kitchen counter, not saying anything.

Before he goes, after I'm sobered up, he kisses me. It's not a brief kiss or a swipe of his tongue. No, he sets me on the counter and kisses me like it's an experience.

Hands stroking my body. Mouth warming mine. He groans when I finally part my lips. He bites the tip of my tongue. I do the same to him.

He tugs down the front of my dress and leaves a little purple mark on my breast.

Like a secret only we know.

When he leaves, I feel like a new woman. For a few glorious hours, I'm soft and safe. Then, the men come back, and I put my head down and go about my chores.

CHAPTER TWELVE

WESTIN

I'm supposed to be the responsible one. The problem solver.

I don't feel responsible anymore. I'm all tied up in knots, so hot at night that I can't get any rest. It's good that Sovereign is distracted with his own woman problems, because I'm having a hard time keeping mine private. I prefer it that way. I've never been the type to talk about my love life, and I won't say a word about it if I'm not forced into it.

Nobody but Jensen will ask what's going on. Sovereign and I have been close friends for over two decades. We've never once talked about sex together.

It's just how it is. We both like it that way.

Jensen already knows, but he's nosy in comparison. I let him in a little because he helps me find ways to see Diane. But I do warn him; I'm not in the habit of putting my private business out there for everyone to speculate.

Having him in my corner is proving to be helpful. Jensen knows everybody's business. He does a lot of jobs for the surrounding ranches, including Carter Farms. It lets him keep tabs on David while I traipse over the field in hopes of seeing her.

He gets me time to see my girl. I pick up the organic cigarettes he likes when I go to the city.

Fair enough trade in both our books.

In June, there's a two week stretch where I don't get time to visit. We have a lot of repairs at the ranch, and Sovereign is distracted, so I have to pick up the slack. I think he's planning on going after his girl soon.

I'm not sure if that's a good idea or not.

I feel sorry for her, the same way I do Diane. Neither of them know what they're getting into, mixing up with Sovereign Mountain men. But Keira Garrison isn't my business.

I stick to who is—Diane.

It's the end of June when my personal drought ends. Jensen goes into the city and calls me to let me know he ran into David Carter. They're heading back to South Platte to talk to grain distributors and come up with some storage options for Carter Farms.

All I hear is that I have the go-ahead to see my girl.

I clean up and take the truck out to her place, making sure to park it in the woods and cut down through the western field. Everything is still, the air too hot for birds to sing. It's late in the summer for lilies, but I look anyway, and I'm rewarded with a single yellow blossom.

I pick it, holding it gently by the stem so it doesn't wilt in the heat of my hand.

The front door is open. Dust rises in puffs under my boots. Chickens scramble, clucking loudly, as I climb the steps. In the front hall, I see Diane. She's on her hands and knees, scrubbing the worn floorboards

I don't think I've seen her prettier. Her hair is tied up in a bandana, her skirt tucked up around her waist. I pause in the door, my mind going back to my childhood.

This is an all-too familiar scene. My father did this, showing up at the end of the day, always with a little gift in tow for my mother.

Maybe to apologize for being the man who fell in love with her.

She looks up before I can follow my thoughts to darker paths. Her face flushes as she scrambles to her feet, wiping her forehead.

"What are you doing here?" she asks.

"Came to see my girl," I say.

It's the same thing every time, and she eats it right up. Her smile flashes white teeth, and she comes down the hall and turns her face up so I can kiss her. I'm lost in her taste, how it makes my head go empty and my blood pumps hard.

We break apart. I tuck the flower behind her ear.

"You should let the lilies grow," she whispers, but she isn't displeased. "Do you want some lemonade?"

I'd like to eat her out more than I'd like lemonade, but I nod. She gives me a frosted glass and disappears upstairs. The house is perfectly still, scrubbed until the pale wood floorboards shine.

It's a nice home, big enough for a family.

I think about that for too long.

The stairs creak, and she comes down, barefoot with her hair wet down her back. Her boots are in her hand. She's in the prettiest cotton sundress, made of brown and gold stripes. It takes me a moment to realize it's handmade, probably from curtains.

I frown, wondering if David gives her enough money to buy the things she needs. She's too proud to take it from me, but next time I go to town, I'll bring her real fabric.

"How long is David gone for?" I ask, as if I don't know.

She sets her boots down and leans on the counter, giving me a nice view of her cleavage. Since we met, I noticed she's taken a lot more interest in her appearance. She was barefaced before, but now she wears a little makeup on her eyes and mouth.

She's softer too. Her voice isn't snappy when she talks to me, the way it was when we met.

"Probably after dark," she says.

"Anybody else home?"

She shakes her head. "All the wranglers are in the field or in town with David."

"Come here," I tell her.

I stand, pushing the stool in. She obeys, and her hands slip behind her back, the way they do when she's unsure. Before she can speak, I pick her up and lay her out on the countertop.

"Westin," she breathes. "Not here. This is where I make the food."

I don't really care. Her skirt slips up and, God, she's got no panties underneath. My mind goes blank. She's beautiful, soft skin, and bare pussy. I wonder if she keeps it that way just for me. The idea makes my head spin.

Just for me.

Her lashes flutter, eyes on the ceiling. "Westin," she says again.

I run my hand up, tugging one strap of her dress down to reveal her breast. No bra either.

"Say my name just like that, darling," I say, kissing the inside of her thigh.

She breathes it again, like a prayer.

"Close your eyes," I order.

She obeys, lashes against her cheeks. Her breasts rise and fall. A quiver moves down her stomach and her pussy clenches. When my tongue runs over the soft heat of her sex, her lips part and let out a moan.

"Oh God," she gasps.

"Just me," I say. "Just me and you, darling."

That's all I want. Just us in the kitchen, talking, eating the food she makes. Just her, spread out on our table while I pleasure her pussy until I can't take it anymore and I carry her upstairs. To our bed.

I want to live here with her.

Maybe David can visit Sovereign Mountain and have an accident like Clint Garrison did. The thought is pleasant. I mull it over as I drag my tongue across the soft, wet entrance of her pussy, dipping my tongue in a little more every time I circle it. She tastes like summer, like sweet lemonade.

I could eat her out for hours. Her silky thighs brush my jaw, her scent filling my mouth and nose. Her sighs and moans echo in the kitchen. This was worth every second of the wait. When she comes, my fingers inside her, a soft gush of arousal drips from my knuckles. I pull them free and lick them clean.

God, I could drink her neat, like whiskey.

I kiss up her body, lifting her to sit upright. Her eyes are glazed, her breasts heave.

"I want to do that for you," she whispers.

I consider her. Of course I like blowjobs, and I'd do a lot to get one from her, but I also like rough sex. I like degradation and choking and spanking. I don't want to slip up and give that to her before she's ready.

"Please," she begs.

My ego purrs. I kiss her again, letting her taste herself.

"Good girl," I say. "Let's get you down on your knees."

Her eyes widen as I lift her, and she sinks down. A fire sparks in the back of my brain, emptying my head.

"Tuck your hands behind your back," I tell her.

She does as she's told. Eyes big, lips parted. In one motion, I strip my belt off.

"You liked being tied up in my truck?" I ask.

She nods.

"Use your words, darling, I need to hear you."

"Yes," she says.

My cock throbs. Every nerve and muscle in my body is alight.

"I'm going to put this around your neck," I say. "I won't pull it tight. You tell me to stop if you don't like it."

Her eyes somehow get wider, and a slow, dusky rose blush creeps up her neck and stains her cleavage.

"Yes," she whispers. "I understand."

Gently, I loop it around her neck and pull it until it's around her throat, but not tight. Her breasts rise and fall quickly. I unzip my pants, pushing them down low enough to unleash my cock. It's hot, hard, and wet at the tip, ready for her mouth.

"Oh my God," she breathes.

It'd be a lie to say I haven't fantasized about exactly this, but reality is so much sweeter. I draw her closer, guiding her head with the belt without cutting off her air.

"Open your mouth for me, darling," I say.

Her lips part.

"All the way," I say, slipping the head of my cock between her lips. She widens her jaw, and her eyes lock with mine. I almost blow my load right there. My hips jerk, pushing my cock halfway into her mouth.

Her lids flutter as she moans, closing her lips around me.

"Pretty little slut," I say, brushing her hair back with my free hand.

She moans again, the vibrations teasing my cock. She's soft, she's wet, but most of all she's Diane, and somehow, I'm the lucky man who gets to have all her firsts.

And lasts.

I take a second to compose myself, cradling her chin in one hand and holding the belt in the other. Then, working slowly to get her acclimated, I fuck her mouth.

Gently, slowly, giving her all the time she needs.

She blinks away the tears that form. I can tell she's unsure what to do, so I take control and use her mouth so she doesn't have to do any of the work. It's still the best fucking blowjob I've ever had.

She tries to say something. I pull out, saliva clinging to my cock in a thin strand.

"You can go a little harder," she whispers. "I'm okay."

I lift my brows. She cocks her head.

"Harder, please," she says. "Sir."

How the hell she knows all my weak spots, I don't know. My cock jerks and pleasure sparks.

"Harder on your mouth or neck?" I ask.

She nods.

"Fuck," I say under my breath.

Who am I to deny her anything? I tell her to tap my leg if she wants out. Then, I push back inside and wrap the belt once around my hand and jerk it close. Her nails pierce through my work pants. She moans, her eyes rolling shut.

I fuck her mouth, and she loves it.

Pleasure moves through me in a rush. I consider pulling out to give her a choice, but I decide against it. This is the only time I've gotten to come inside her, and I'm taking it.

My cock goes rock hard. I push to the back of her throat and she gags, but she doesn't tap out. Hand in her hair, I hold her down on my cock and let go, pumping everything I have down her throat.

Clarity hits me like a wall of bricks, and I release the tension on the belt. She gasps around my cock. Her eyes lock with mine as I empty the last of my cum into her mouth.

She's the most beautiful thing I've ever seen.

I pull from her mouth and slip the belt from her throat. She snaps her lips closed, like she doesn't know what to do next.

"Did you swallow?"

She shakes her head.

"Show me," I order.

Hesitantly, she puts her tongue out. My cum sits on it, pooled in the dip in the middle. I'm still rock hard, and my cock throbs at the sight.

"Jesus fucking Christ, you're a dirty slut," I breathe. "Swallow it."

Her tongue darts in and her throat bobs. My head buzzes with satisfaction as I pull her to her feet and kiss her mouth, her neck, the dip between her breasts.

"You're so pretty," I murmur.

It feels like I've said some version of that a hundred times since we've met. She's just so fucking pretty, and I can't stop marveling when I see her big, brown eyes look up at me.

I might be done for, wrapped up around her little finger.

"Thank you," she says, unsure.

She needs reassurance. I set her on the counter and find a washrag. Her hands knot together in her lap. I wipe her face and hands, then spread her thighs and clean her there. By the time I'm done, the fire is back in her eyes.

"You alright, darling?" I ask.

She nods. "I liked that. A lot."

I think I might have met my match. She's new to this, but she's a natural when it comes to the fundamentals.

She jumps down and smooths her skirt. "You hungry?"

I'm not, but I am if she's cooking. "I could eat."

She starts moving around the kitchen, her cheeks still flushed. I sink down at the table, unable to keep my eyes off her. I'm just playing house in my head, pretending this is our home and nobody else exists.

It's heaven.

She makes a plate with cheese, fried green tomatoes, and ham. I don't want to leave, so I talk about anything I can think of. The haying season, coming up soon. The cattle we're planning to auction this fall. I get her to tell me a little about her grandmother, but not much. Her soft, brown eyes go from happy to sad, so I turn it back to things she likes.

She likes being outside, but she doesn't get to go out very much. We go upstairs, and she shyly shows me a box she has of pressed flowers, dried and preserved between two bits of clear plastic. Each one is labeled with their scientific name.

I ask her where she learned all this. She says she quit school when her grandmother died because David said she had to. But it's clear she's smart. The handful of books in a crate under her bed are worn through.

I listen to every word she says. I get the feeling I'm the first man who has.

"You like the yellow lilies best," I say. "What are those called?"

She's sitting against the headboard, feet bare. "Glacier Lily."

"Why don't you like me picking them?"

Her eyes go distant. "Nobody likes being locked up. I feel like...maybe I shrivel up being at home, just working in the house. I'd like to be able to go out, do what I want."

"Why can't you?" I ask.

I know, but I'd like to hear the particulars. She sighs, picking the wilted lily from her hair and turning it over in her fingers.

"David's not very happy with me most of the time," she says quietly. "I don't know why. I think he's just...all messed up inside. He was really young when our parents passed. He had to do a lot."

I'm quiet. She wipes her nose.

"I still hate him sometimes," she says. "Just because you got dealt a bad hand doesn't mean you have to be mean. There was a time when I did everything for him. Then, he just pushed me away."

If I had to guess, he started hating her when he realized she was a financial burden. I know how hard David's life has been, but I know other men who've been dealt far worse, and they don't take it out on women.

I find I don't have much sympathy for him.

She wipes her nose, but her eyes are dry. They fix out the window, her heavy lids flickering.

"Anyway, fuck David. He's just bitter," she says. "I tried for years. I'm not trying anymore."

There's a dark undercurrent to her voice.

"Do you have siblings?" she asks.

"No," I say firmly.

She can tell by my tone that I'm not willing to talk about my family. There's a short silence, then she shrugs and sits up.

"It's getting on towards dinnertime," she says. "You better go home."

I shift up on the bed and take her face in my hand, kissing her gently. Slowly, so she remembers the way it feels after I'm gone. We don't talk much as we go downstairs. She kisses me again on the step, her fingers hooked in my belt loops.

I light a cigarette and walk back through the field to my truck. Back at Sovereign Mountain, I finish up chores. It's dark when I get back to the gatehouse and start undressing. In my pocket with my keys is the flower I put in her hair. She must have slipped it in when she kissed me goodbye.

That night, I sit staring out my window, the flower in my hand. The moon is big, caught in the spidery branches of the tree outside.

Under my mattress, carved into the wood is a list of names.

Clint Garrison.

Thomas Garrison.

Avery Garrison.

The first name is crossed out. The others are just biding their time. Part of me wishes I had a good enough reason to add one more, one that, once crossed off, would simplify everything.

David Carter.

CHAPTER THIRTEEN

DIANE

It's the haying season before I realize it.

I'm stuck in the kitchen, cooking for all the men working the farm. Our busiest times are when hay comes due. David is gone from dawn to dusk, and he expects me to run everything while he's away.

I get up early for the last full harvesting day of the summer. It's still dark out, and the world is blessedly cool. Back and hands aching, I pull on a simple cotton sundress that reaches my ankles. It's light and flows around my body—perfect for working in the kitchen.

The stairs creak. I make my way to the kitchen and find David sitting at the breakfast bar. He glances up from his phone, black eyes distant.

"I'm heading out," he says. "Make sure lunch is ready by twelve."

I stay quiet as I turn the coffee machine on and go to the fridge. Inside sits a fresh jug of orange juice I made before bed last night. I take it out, pouring a glass.

"Thomas Garrison wants to speak with you," David says.

I glance up, freezing.

He stands, pushing his phone in his back pocket. His plate stays on the table. He won't clean it up—that's my job as the designated maid.

"We're having some issues," he says. "I need you to quit being a bitch to him."

There's something in his voice that makes my stomach churn.

"What issues?" I ask.

He shrugs. "Apparently, we're in the path of the highway that's being put in next summer."

I frown, recalling reading about the project. "That's ten miles southwest of here."

"The state wants to put in an access road," he says. "To cut building costs."

"Where?"

He takes the cup of juice from my hand and drains it. "Through the west side of Carter Farms, through the willow grove."

My blood goes ice cold. The grove is where the cemetery sits. Where everyone I love lies sleeping.

"That's illegal," I say. "They can't do that."

He slams the glass into the sink. "By law, they can do whatever the fuck they want if the state approves it."

My lower lip trembles. I hate when he's angry; it makes me want to curl up and hide. "But it's...our family. They can't build a highway over it."

He walks to the hallway, pausing to look back. "I already spoke with the councilman. The state is offering to exhume all bodies in the path and put them in a government burial ground west of us."

"No," I burst out. "Nana asked to be buried on our family's land. I won't let them touch her."

A crease appears between his brows. "Well, you take your ass to the office of Mr. Corbin Buchanan and see if you can't convince him. Maybe it's the one time you being a girl will be of some use. You're old enough."

My jaw drops. Tears sting my eyes.

"That's disgusting," I manage.

He shrugs. "I'm fine with using any means I can to keep the farm from being destroyed. It's all I have."

My stomach sinks. He didn't say it was all we had. In his mind, the farm is his, and he isn't wrong. Right before Nana died, she told him the land was in his name.

It's so unfair, I want to scream.

He leaves, boots clipping angrily. The door slams, and his engine starts and dies away. My hands shake as I put the orange juice away and gather up his dirty dishes.

What did he mean by that comment?

Is he going to force Thomas Garrison on me to get in good with their family? Does he think that'll save us somehow?

I'm a little sick all morning. Tears a breath from falling, I make lunch and lay it out, taking bread and butter to the back porch while the men eat.

After a while, the back door bangs open. David steps out and takes a cigarette from his pocket and puts it in his lip. He flicks his old metal lighter and sinks down to sit on the stairs beside me.

My body tenses. His bad mood hangs like a rain cloud over his head.

"The councilman is a cousin to the Garrison family by marriage. Second cousin, but they're close," he says. "That's how they get preferential treatment."

His voice is as dry as the dust at our feet.

"So...what?" I manage.

"So get on Thomas Garrison's good side. Better yet, get in Avery's good books."

I shudder. My stomach is too upset to eat. I toss the bread into the yard, and the chickens fight loudly over it.

"Avery is a horrible person," I whisper.

He blows a cloud of smoke out. "So stick with Thomas. He's the one who wants you anyway. He's been nagging me about getting with you for years."

"I don't know that he's any better."

He stands abruptly, brushing past me. David didn't get my blonde hair; he's got dark curls and eyes that are almost black. He's handsome on the surface but ugly underneath. I hope I get a chance to warn any potential girlfriends that he's not above slamming them into the wall if he's angry enough.

I scramble to my feet. He glances over me and takes a drag off his cigarette.

"I've been sacrificing for this farm for years," he says. "It's time you did the same."

"What are you asking me to do?" I snap.

His eyes crackle. "If Thomas Garrison wants you, I don't give a fuck what your excuses are. You say yes to him. You get in that family's good graces. Then I'll see what I can do."

Tears spill over. "Please don't make me do this."

His hand shoots out and he grabs my upper arm. I gasp—God, he's strong. He yanks me closer, and the desperation in his eyes flashes like a thunderclap.

"I was there when she died too," he snaps. "I heard what Nana said. She said bury me here on this land. So you be agreeable for one fucking minute, and you say yes to whatever Thomas Garrison asks. You hear me?"

I shudder. He's got the same expression he had when he slammed me into the hallway wall.

"Yes," I breathe.

"You swear?" His fingers tighten.

"I swear," I sob.

"Good. I'm going to talk to him."

He releases my arm, shoving me back. For a second, I think I've caught my balance. Then, my heel hooks on my skirt. My body plummets. I have a fleeting image of the porch railing hurtling towards my face before pain explodes in my temple.

I hit the ground like a sack of rocks.

The world spins.

Quick as a flash, I roll over, suddenly sick enough to throw up. The dirty floor presses to my face, grit stuck to my lips.

The door slams.

I lay there dazed. Then, a wave of shame moves through me that's stronger. I ease myself onto my hands and knees. I graze my fingertips over my temple, and they come away bloody.

I need to get upstairs before anyone sees.

Holding my hand over my face, I run inside past the dining room door. The men will be done eating soon. I scramble as fast as my spinning head will allow upstairs to my room. There, I dart into my half bath and lock the door, sinking against it.

I lower my hand.

It's not as bad as I feared. There's a cut that broke the skin, but once I get it cleaned up, I can hide it with a bandage. I fumble under the sink and come up with a rag, which I wet with cold water and press to the wound.

My heart pounds, but stronger is the shame.

Why?

Why do I feel so ashamed when someone else hurts me? I should be burning with rage. Instead, I'm trying to figure out how I can conceal what David did.

I swallow past the lump in my throat.

No one can know. I hate when my pain is exposed. It feels like rolling over and showing my belly to the world. I need it to be secret so I can lick my wounds in peace.

Downstairs, boots sound in the hall. The trucks start up again and fade away. I wash myself in the sink and dab the blood until it stops. Then, I cover it with a bandage and brush my hair over it.

My eyes are swollen, but otherwise, I look alright.

This complicates everything. I'll have to conceal this from Westin, because if he sees a bruise on me, put there by David... Well, I don't know what he'll do. The darkness I hear in his voice sometimes promises he's capable of violence.

I'm caught between two awful choices. I can tell Westin and accept whatever he decides to do, or I can make the responsible choice to hide this and help David save the farm from being bulldozed and paved over.

My heart aches.

I've never met anyone like Westin. Since Nana died, I've spent my life rusting away at Carter Farms. At first, I thought he was my way out, but after knowing him longer, I think what I feel is more complex and serious than I expected.

Yes, he could be my freedom. He could also be the first and last man I fall for.

I have to choose, but I'm not ready to.

Responsibility, or Westin?

Miserable, I go to the window and lean my forehead against the glass. Outside, the fields stretch out in a sea of gold. I grew up in this room. I know every knot and chip on the floorboards. I know exactly how the clouds form over the hills before a storm and how they form when they're just rolling through.

I know the farm belongs to David legally, but I always saw myself raising my family here. I saw myself being carried over the front door by my husband. I saw years of breakfasts at the kitchen table and dinners on the back porch, faceless children running in the fields. A faceless man kisses me, smelling like sunshine and horses.

I'm dying to live like that—in charge of my own destiny. I want a home filled with only people I love. I want to sit at my own table come dinnertime.

But there's no hope of that if we lose Carter Farms. It will be pavement, and no one will ever know how much I wanted to be happy here. All the love I want so badly will be just an echo, never brought to life.

There's more hope if I do as David says.

That night, I lay on my side and let the tears flow until they soak my pillow. I hate everything, everything except Westin, and that makes me cry harder. In the dark, I decide I'm going to wait until I'm not bruised anymore and tell him about the access road. Maybe, by some miracle, he'll pull a blank check out of his wallet.

There has to be a hope.

If I don't have hope, I have nothing.

But I'll wait until he can't see what David did. He might be Westin, but he's still a man. I don't want to see what kind of violence he's capable of.

CHAPTER FOURTEEN

WESTIN

The pastures are rotated. The cattle and horses rest in the lower fields, surrounded by shade with access to the river. Everything is just maintenance until we start branding in the fall.

I'm restless because every time I go to see Diane; she has every excuse in the world as to why she can't let me inside. Her face is worried all the time now, but she won't tell me what's going on.

It's killing me.

Finally, one day when I know all the Garrisons and David Carter have gone to West Lancaster, I leave Sovereign Mountain. I've been patient with Diane, and I've never had much patience to start with.

Time to go get what's mine.

Carter Farms is dead quiet when I pull off to the side of the road, hiding the truck behind the trees. On foot, I cut through the field to the house. The chickens are out in the yard, so I know she's home. She always calls the chickens inside the coop when she leaves to keep them safe.

The rooster jumps from the railing, crash-landing in the grass. I sidestep it and climb the back porch, rapping the screen door hard.

Silence.

I knock hard again. Through the screen, I see her lean into the hall.

"That's enough," she hollers. "I heard you."

I lean against the wall. "Open this fucking door, Diane, or I'll break it down. I'm done with this."

She gasps. Then, the door flies wide open, and her eyes narrow on me.

"I didn't invite you here, Westin Quinn," she snaps. "Don't you go beating on my door like you're the damn sheriff."

She's pissed off, but not really, and I'm too distracted by that short yellow dress to care. Quick as a flash, I heft her in my arms and kick the door open. We tumble into the empty kitchen, and I push her up against the hallway wall.

"Westin," she gasps. "Put me down."

I kiss her hard to shut her up. She's got a bite to her, like hard liquor. My forehead creases. It's early in the day to taste like whiskey, but maybe she was just having iced tea with something extra.

I pull back, and that's when I see it: a faint, green bruise on her temple.

My stomach drops. Suddenly, her refusal to see me makes sense.

Someone hit her.

I let her slide to her feet, taking her by the jaw and turning her head. Defeat clouds her eyes. She goes limp, letting me brush her blonde waves back. There's a scab about the size of a quarter and a healing bruise on her hairline.

My blood turns to fire.

"Who did this to you?" I ask, keeping my voice tempered.

I don't want to scare her more than she already is. She shakes her head.

"Nobody. I fell on the back porch and hit the railing."

I study her face and decide she isn't lying; she's just withholding the truth. Right away, I know it won't do any good for me to go after David in front of her. It had to be him. There's no one else, not unless David let those Garrison fuckers mess with her. The thought of him standing there and letting them beat her is somehow worse than if he did it himself.

She tilts her chin. "I fell."

"When?"

"About a week ago."

"You said on the front porch?"

"The back," she says, narrowing her eyes. She's too sharp for me to trip up.

"Did you go to the quick clinic?"

She shakes her head. "No reason to. I put a cold rag on it and patched it up with gauze. Didn't even hurt."

She's lying about that part, I can see it in the way her pupils blow. I make sure my face is unreadable. It's clear she has been abused and she feels ashamed. Getting angry in front of her would be cruel.

I need to make sure she feels safe. Then, I can put a bullet into the motherfucker who did this to her later on. She shouldn't have to see the ugly parts.

I'll get the truth out of her gently. If it was her brother, he'd better find a priest and start confessing, because there's nowhere on this Earth he can hide where I won't find him.

"Come with me," I say.

"Where?"

"Out."

She shakes her head. "I have chores."

I take her by the chin and pull her face up. "Fuck it. Come with me to Sovereign Mountain tonight."

I expect her to refuse right away, but instead, she considers it. Something really has changed since I saw her last.

"The men won't be back until tomorrow," she whispers finally.

"He'll never know."

She bites her lip. Then, she nods, and for the first time in a week, her beautiful face lights up like sunshine. God, I can't resist her. My mouth comes down on hers, and she kisses me through her smile.

I kiss her back, and she tastes like I'm not leaving without her today.

She goes upstairs. I close up the barn, leaving the side door open so the horses can go inside once the sun sets. Then, I lock the chickens in the coop and meet her on the front porch.

She's in her boots and her little yellow dress, her hair loose over her shoulders. My eyes wander over the freckles on her bare nape.

I'm going to taste her there. I'll kiss down her spine, ease her legs apart, and lick between her thighs.

I get her for a night. I feel like the richest man in the world.

Her hand slips in mine, and my heart goes crazy as I lead her over the field and down the short hill to where I parked in the shade. I help her into the truck and toss her bags in the back with a straw bale and a bag of apples I picked up at the convenience store the other day. There's a jug of water, which might be warm, but it'll work.

I lift her by the waist and put her into the passenger side. She glances at me sideways.

"No yellow lily today?" she asks.

"You said to let them grow," I say.

She turns and puts her hand on my face. Our eyes lock, and the hair rises on the back of my neck.

I think I'll marry this girl. She must feel my breath hitch, because she falters, her lips parting. I'm speechless, so I take my hat off and fit it on her head.

"There you go, so the sun doesn't bleach your hair," I say.

She smiles, all the sadness gone.

"Thank you, sir," she whispers.

My brain thrums. My dick twitches. My eyes drag down her bare arms, and the memory of my belt wrapped around her wrists is strong. Maybe we'll take a detour before we get back to the gatehouse.

I settle in the passenger side and turn the key. The windows are down, and her hair whips around her face as I get back on the road. But we don't head towards Sovereign Mountain. Instead, I take a back road paved with loose gravel.

"Where are we going?" she asks, letting one arm hang out the window.

"You want a swim?" I ask. "It's pretty hot out."

She glances sideways. "I didn't bring a suit."

I shrug. "I didn't either."

The tension in the cab crackles like the air before a storm. She bites that full lower lip and her breasts heave. I slide my hand over her knee and grip her bare inner thigh—the soft part, right below her sex.

We're both quiet for a few minutes.

"Where are you from, anyway?" she asks finally. "Did you always live at Sovereign Mountain?"

I don't like talking about my childhood, but today, with the sun shining through the window and her sitting there in a dress that looks like summertime, I feel like I could say a few words.

"The ranch is pretty new," I say. "My family farm sat there before."

"How'd you do that?"

"Build a ranch? One foot in front of the other," I say. "Tell me about your life."

A crease appears between her brows. She stares straight ahead.

"There isn't much to say," she says. "My parents have always been gone. My Nana raised David and I as best she could. I feel like she did a decent job with me, but David's kind of a dick."

I bite back a laugh.

"Sorry," she says quickly.

"No, I like your honesty, Diane," I say. "What kind of woman was your Nana? She from around here?"

She nods, her eyes lighting up like the clouds have parted. I do a double take. It hits me how much her grandmother meant to her. It must have hurt deeply when she passed.

Of course it did. She doesn't have anybody else.

"Carter Farms has been in our family for a long time," she says, shifting to face me. She puts my hat on the seat between us and leans her temple on the headrest. "My Nana was sweet, but she was tough. I wish I could be like her."

I don't tell her that she is; I know she won't believe me.

"What happened to her husband?" I ask.

She shrugged. "Not much. He was a little older than her, so he passed first. I remember him a tiny bit, but it's just flashes from when I was a toddler. They really loved each other."

"That what she said?"

She nods. "And it's in *The Canterbury Tales*."

"What now?"

"You know how some families have a family Bible where they record important dates?" she asks. "Well, all my family had was a copy of *Canterbury Tales*. So we used that. There's a list of all the marriages on the front page. My grandpa left a little note in there, saying he loves her forever. She signed her initials under it, like she was co-signing on it or something."

"That's sweet," I say.

"Yeah," she says, her voice soft. "It is."

"Who's the last couple in there?"

"My parents."

I've got a mind to make sure my name gets written in that family book next to hers someday, but it's too soon to voice that out loud.

"I can't imagine it," she says, "loving somebody that much and having to keep going without them."

My mind goes back to my mother. Sometimes, I wonder if she loved my father at all. Maybe she stayed with him out of resignation, or because she had a son with him.

"What happened to your parents?" she asks.

Her face is innocent, waiting on my answer. The wind tugs at the stray curls around her throat.

"My father's dead," I say.

She studies me. "You look like you didn't care for him."

I shrug. We go over a bend and around a corner, where the road narrows and I pump the brakes a little.

"I liked him fine," I say.

Her lips purse. "No you didn't."

"He was a hard man to get to know," I say, after a short pause. "My mother ia a good one, like your Nana. She made my childhood good."

"Does she look like you?" she asks.

"Not so much," I say. "Tell me something about your family."

Honestly, she could read the phonebook out loud and I'd listen. I just want to hear her soft voice.

"Nana always made me wear a hat in the summer," she says. "My hair used to be white by August. Nana got three straw hats: one for the house, for the barn, and for the pickup so when I forgot, I'd have an extra."

"You have pretty hair," I say, wishing I had more eloquent words.

She bites her lower lip. My eyes drop to her mouth. The truck swerves and I right it, forcing my attention back to the road.

"Watch yourself," she says.

"You got me distracted, darling," I say.

She's blushing, the pink making her handful of summer freckles stand out. "If I didn't know better, I'd think you're taking me out to compromise me, Mr. Quinn."

I slide my hand over her knee, bare skin on my calloused palm.

"Oh, that right?" I say.

She clears her throat, tossing back her flyaway waves. "Does it bother you that you're so much older than me?"

That makes me pause for a second, but I keep my face impassive.

"No, not much," I lie.

She doesn't need to know about my baggage yet. There's a long silence as I pull the truck down the last hill and shift it into park. We're at the edge of the swimming hole, dusty earth around the wheels. The creek trickles, filling up the rounded basin surrounded by brush and trees.

Everything smells like summer. I never want it to end.

I glance over. She glances back. Her throat bobs.

"Why me?" she whispers.

I get out of the truck, circle it, and open her door. She turns sideways, bare legs dangling down. I lean over her, caging her in.

"Because you're so fucking sweet," I say, bending in to kiss her mouth. God, she's soft all over. "And I can't sleep for thinking about you."

She tangles her hands together, picking at her thumbnail. Brown eyes, soft like velvet, fix on me.

"Really?" she whispers.

"Why do you think I keep coming back?"

She shrugs. "I don't know."

"I can't get enough of you, darling."

Her breath hitches. I lift the edge of her skirt, inching it up so I can slide both hands up her thighs. She squeezes her knees together.

"You behave yourself," she whispers.

I laugh. "Diane, I probably won't. Not with you looking like that."

She's so flustered, she can't speak. I bend in and kiss her long and deep. When I pull away, her eyes are glassy. I know if I slip my fingers under her panties, she'll be wet.

"Let's go for a swim," I say.

She gestures at me. "You first. I'm not stripping until you do."

I stand back and reach down. Her eyes drop and her lips part. Slowly, so she gets to watch, I unfasten my belt and strip it off in one go.

"Your turn," I say.

CHAPTER FIFTEEN

DIANE

I shake my head hard. I just want to see him get naked and show me all those hard muscles and scars. He gives me a lopsided smirk and starts unbuttoning his shirt.

He's pulling it off, revealing his tanned torso, the ridges of muscle down his stomach, the dark hair on his chest, and the trail going down to his belt. He starts on his pants. I stare, my jaw slack, as he unzips and pulls them off. He's in just his boxer briefs, tight on his body.

"Come here," he says, holding out his hand.

This time, I kick off my boots and slide down into the dust in my bare feet. He shuts the truck door.

I take a step closer until he's standing over me, looking down at me.

His hand comes up, rough as he slips the straps of my dress down, tugging it until it falls in the dust at our feet.

I'm in my handmade cotton bra and panties. They're blue and white striped with little yellow flowers embroidered on the edges. I swallow hard; he's looking at me like he hasn't eaten in days.

"Jesus—fuck," he says quietly.

"What?" I whisper.

He cocks his head. "Better not say what I'm thinking."

My stomach swoops. His big, hard hands slide up my sides, and I want to moan at how good it is to be held. Then, he's undoing my bra and pulling my panties down until I'm completely bare.

His throat bobs as his gaze drags over my body.

There's something dark about his hunger today. A chill moves down my spine, but it's not stronger than my desire.

I'd do a lot to be looked at like this forever.

"Why are you staring?" I whisper.

"Because you're naked," he says. "And the prettiest thing I've ever seen naked, at that."

"You're not naked yet," I whisper, uncomfortable being the only one fully exposed.

His eyes glitter. "Finish undressing me."

My arms wrap around my breasts, gripping myself tight. The hot wind makes my hair flutter at the small of my back.

"No, sir," I say, cocking my head.

His brows jerks. "You teasing me, darling?"

I nod. I don't tease anyone much, but it's not by choice. I don't like anyone well enough to tease them, but Westin is a different story. He likes it; I can tell by the curve of his mouth as he pulls his underwear off and straightens, fully naked and breathtaking.

I stare, transfixed. Every time we've had sex, we're already tangled up by the time his clothes come off. I've never stood back and gotten a good look at him naked.

I want to look him all over, but what I'm staring at stares at me first. I swallow hard. It's impressive.

"How do you ride with that thing?" I ask before I can stop myself.

He laughs. "I make it work."

I cock my brow, still unable to pull my eyes from his groin. He's big and thick, the dark hair at his base neatly trimmed. It blows my mind that part of him has been inside me, more than once. It's no wonder I'm sore when it's over.

Deep inside, I'm feeling like I have an itch he could scratch with that.

He takes a step back, ripples spilling out around him.

"Come here," he says.

There's a note of authority in his tone. He moves deeper until the water hits the V of muscle at his waist. I obey, making my way down the bank and stepping in. It's lukewarm from baking in the sun.

He cocks his head, watching me as I draw near, until the water is just below my breasts. He looks down at me, and I look up at him.

"Who hit you?" he says, voice low.

I swallow hard, dropping my eyes. A sunfish moves in circles around his body and disappears.

"Look at me, darling," he says. "Who hit your face?"

I drag my gaze back up. He's not going to let this go until I'm truthful.

"David pushed me, and I hit my head on the railing," I whisper.

My heart thuds like a drum. There's a long silence. His face is unreadable, but when I meet his eyes, my stomach goes cold. I've never seen someone look so angry and so calm all at once.

It's chilling.

"Does he push you a lot?" he asks.

I have to clear my throat to get the words out. "Not a lot. He pushed me down the porch stairs a few years ago. He took me by the throat once and slammed me into the hallway wall."

"I see," he says.

"Are you...going to do something bad?" I whisper.

Westin's eyes give me the shivers, like a frost is setting in. He reaches out and touches my face, cradling it. I melt into his touch, desperate for assurance.

"Don't you worry, darling," he says softly. "I handle my business."

"Am I your business?" I whisper.

"Yes," he says without hesitating.

I sink lower in the water until it covers my breasts and my hair floats.

"What is this, Mr. Quinn?" I say.

His brow crooks. "Mr. Quinn? That's Westin to you."

"Or sir," I say daringly. "I can tell you like when I call you that."

I expected him to take my teasing the way he did a moment ago. Instead, he reaches down, taking me by the hair and lifting me to my feet. It doesn't hurt, the way he does it with his fist up against my scalp. I go willingly, too shocked to resist.

Between my legs is a raw heartbeat.

His hand slides down and cradles my head. His mouth brushes mine. I'm frozen, barely breathing.

How is he so gentle and stern all at once?

"I like when you call me sir," he says. "Because you are my business."

"I'm not yours, though," I whisper.

"Diane, I will brand my name onto your ass if I need to. Good luck being anyone's business but mine after that."

What the fuck is wrong with him?

What's wrong with me for not running?

I can't answer. The air between us is thick as a thunderstorm. He drags me even closer, hand on my neck, and he kisses me, but this time it's different. It's scorching hot and tastes like falling hard and hitting the ground fast.

A thunderclap. Heat like lightning in my veins. A storm I can't escape.

My lips open because he forces them, and his tongue swipes over mine. Then, it comes back for more. When he pulls away, the world spins.

"Let me have you," he says, his voice hoarse.

"You have," I gasp.

His eyes narrow. "No, I want all of you. No pulling out, no condoms, no leaving when it's done."

"I don't want—"

"I'm fine with it if you get pregnant." His eyes glitter, narrowed. "I'll take care of you. You come live with me at Sovereign Mountain."

It's not a question. My heart slows. Did he just say that? I shudder in his arms. I'm used to being ignored. I don't know how to be the center of anyone's attention.

But I can't hide from my feelings anymore. My heart is going soft for him. It scares me, even if it's what I want.

"Westin," I stammer. "I'm only twenty-one."

His jaw works. His gaze flicks up and focuses on something far away. He's thinking hard.

"If I leave, you'll end up in some other man's bed," he says grimly. "Either I stake my claim on you, or I lose you. I won't lose you."

My fingers flex. I'm gripping his wrist, although I'm not sure when that happened. My nails dig into his skin. He doesn't react.

I don't know if I can say what I want to say.

Or if I should just be quiet.

Fuck it, I've never been good at keeping my mouth shut. His hand is on my neck, holding me in the water. His rough thumb is dragging over my nipple and making it hard to think. I'm acutely aware of how my body reacts to his absentminded touch.

"You're a bad man," I whisper.

It sounds childish when I say it like that, but it's the kindest way to say what I'm thinking.

He glances down, and he's a little dead behind his eyes.

"What?" he says.

"I thought you were good," I manage. "You seemed so easygoing when I met you, but I think you might be...dangerous."

His jaw twitches, and my mind goes back to when I joked about Avery disappearing at Sovereign Mountain. Westin laughed a little too hard at that.

"Are you a criminal?" I whisper.

The corner of his mouth turns up. "What does me being a criminal have to do with you, darling?"

I frown, confused. "I'm trying to figure out who you are."

"Westin River Quinn," he says.

I pull back, and he lets me go, his palm leaving my breast. My feet sink to the bottom, and I scramble back, out of the water. I fall to the shore, dirt sticking to my naked skin.

He moves towards me, water rippling from his powerful body as he gets closer.

My heart pounds.

I think I fucked up. We're going too fast.

My survival instincts kick in, and I scramble to my feet, not caring that I'm naked. I can find something to cover myself with later. Right now, I need to put some space between myself and this man who lives behind Westin Quinn's mask.

I move past the truck, whirling to look back. He's not pursuing me—he's putting his pants and boots back on. Yes, he's working quickly, but it's giving me the time I need to bolt up ahead.

Right where the dirt road meets the paved one, there's a trailhead that splits north. I know it breaks off and goes up the field. It's a few miles, but eventually, it'll spit me out at the edge of Carter Farms.

I take it, scrambling down the hill. My feet hit the ground at the bottom, and that's when I hear him. I whip around, but it's too late. Somehow, he's right behind me. Then I'm in his arms, lifted off the ground and tossed naked over his shoulder.

I hang there, stunned.

This is the most undignified thing that's ever happened to me. I'm hot, and between my thighs pounds like a drum. I'm unable to speak until he sets me down at the water's edge in the soft mud, cool on my back.

"Run from me again, I'll put you over my knee," he snaps.

My jaw drops, but instead of indignation, heat flows through every part of my body, quickly followed by shame. On the outside, I want to scream, to fight him for catching me and bringing me back, but the other part of me is thrilled. The deep, deep down part I should be ashamed of.

That part basks in being the center of his desire.

And it wants more.

I gasp, pushing myself up on the heels of my hands. He's crouched over me, hazel eyes bright like an animal's stare.

"I'm not leaving, Diane," he says. "And neither are you."

My mind flits back to when he tied me to the steering wheel and fucked me. A dormant part of me woke up that day, a shameful part that wanted him to do something worse, like keep going after I beg him to stop.

My heart skips a beat. My mouth is dry.

Deep, deep down, I like that he's a little dangerous. An outlaw. The kind of man I can see breaking into my bedroom, tying me up, and... No, that's not right.

My head is all mixed up, but my pussy isn't. It's soaked.

"What if I try to leave?" I whisper hoarsely.

He cocks his head. "I would stop you."

"How?" I whisper.

His chest heaves. "I can show you, but you have to promise me that if I hurt you, you'll use a safeword."

"What's that?" My mind whirls. Does he have a term for what we're doing?

He's on his hands and knees over me. All I can see are his hungry eyes.

"Just use red for now," he says. "Say red if you want it to stop."

It hits me that Westin might be into things I'm not aware of, things that I only know about from the few romances I skimmed in the library, hidden behind the shelf out of shame.

He did put a belt around my neck, after all.

"You like rough...things," I whisper. "Different things...than usual."

He hesitates. Sweat etches down between his pecs. "BDSM—I do, but safewords are just common sense, darling."

He's so desperate, it cracks his voice. Distantly, I know what he's saying, but not in a literal sense. My head is telling me to be careful. My body is telling me it might die if I don't let him have me.

I want to give in and meet this new side of Westin.

"Yes," I pant, my hips rising. "I'll say red if I want it to stop."

"Say it," he demands.

"Red." It comes out in a desperate rush.

When I first met him, he was one thing. Now, he's another, darker thing altogether. I can taste it on him, on his breath. I felt it when he tied me to the wheel of his truck.

Those hands are capable of pleasure, but I think they're also capable of so much more, things I want but don't understand yet.

His hand comes up, going for my throat. I strike it back, the sound ringing out. We both know it's a test. He doesn't react for a second. My pulse thrums. Then, quick like a snake, he's on top of me, one hand pulling my thighs apart.

My head spins.

He's so much bigger and heavier than me. He was holding himself back in the kitchen. He was trying to be gentle so he wouldn't scare me—but not anymore.

He takes me by the throat, and his fingers dig into my cheeks, forcing my lips to part.

"Is this what you want? You want me to force you in the dirt like a whore?" His voice is thick with desperation.

I gag on his fingers as he hooks my mouth open. Then, he spits onto my tongue. I choke, shocked. Between my thighs, my sex burns with need.

I wanted to know what it felt like to be alive.

And now, I'm so alive, I might come from it.

I gasp, cough, and swallow. In the time it takes me to get my bearings, he flips me onto my stomach in the dirt. Our filthy bodies come together, and his knee shoves my legs open.

His zipper hisses, and my spine arcs as he pushes the head of his cock into my soaked pussy, forcing it in, inch by inch, until I'm whimpering. My inner muscles tighten and loosen, pulling him in despite how big and heavy his cock is.

I wonder if I'll bleed again.

My brain thrums. My nipples rub against the dirt.

This tastes like life, like a sweet apple bitten by his mouth and put into mine with bloody hands. I flip my head to the side, unwilling to fight him anymore.

He feels too good—all the pain and pleasure rolling through me is too powerful.

His hand braces in the mud by my eyes, hard, lean fingers digging in. Knuckles tense. The veins up his forearm stand out. My eyes roll back at the first thrust. He's big, and he fills me perfectly, like our bodies were always meant to be connected.

He pumps his hips, groaning. I cry out softly. His other hand slides into my hair and closes against my scalp, dragging my head back. His hips slam into me, and I see color for the first time in my life.

Beautiful, like a meadowlark rising dark against the golden sky.

Am I really supposed to give this up for Thomas Garrison?

There has to be another way to protect the farm. I can't walk away now.

I can't leave him.

I'm not the woman I was a month ago, and I never will be again. He made sure of that. I sank my teeth into the forbidden fruit. Now, I'm out of the garden, and I left with the snake.

But I know what it feels like to be alive.

CHAPTER SIXTEEN

WESTIN

My head is empty. The world shakes on its axis.

I pull from her and flip her body. She's muddy, and I drag my fingers over her stomach, drawing patterns in the dirt on her skin. My handprint is on her breast. She cries out softly, her hazy eyes on the blue sky as I push back inside.

Her hips are loose, her legs spread.

She wants it.

And God, I want it too.

I grip her upper thigh, and something in her awakens. Her body tenses and her eyes flash. Her hand comes up, and her fingers dig into the back of my neck.

Her hips rise to meet mine, and they collide in a shower of sparks. We're both panting, rutting our bodies together in the dirt, streaked with mud, desperate to be so close that we can never untangle ourselves.

I slam into the soft resistance of her cervix. I'm too big for her, but I don't care. My hips stay there, grinding. My sweat drips onto her face, but she doesn't brush it away. Her body shakes, and I grind harder.

Then, she comes, crying out loud enough that it scares the birds from the trees above us in a dark flurry. Her cunt tightens, working me from base to tip. Pleasure comes in a rush, and I can't stop it. My head is empty, my dick doing all the talking.

Her eyes widen.

My hips rut harder, fucking, chasing my orgasm. She's soaked, she's willing, but more than that, she's mine.

Now seems like a good time to finally consummate that statement.

The last thrust is the sweetest. It tastes like lightning in my teeth and heaven in my groin. Our bodies meet, and I can't bite back my groan as I'm washed away.

She moans, and I come hard, emptying everything I have into her pussy.

No condom in sight.

We both go still. Breathless, I disengage my hips and fall onto my back, pulling her muddy body into mine. She shakes like a leaf. I run my hand over her back, and the mud that's starting to dry there crumbles.

I kiss her forehead.

"Diane," I whisper.

She pushes herself onto her elbow. Her dark eyes are soft. Her lower lip is a little bloody—she must have bit it at some point. I bend and kiss her, tasting metal.

"Let's wash up," I say.

Before she can protest, I get to my feet and strip my dirty clothes. She lets me pick her up and carry her back into the lukewarm water, and she melts into my arms while I wash her clean.

"You're coming home with me, Diane," I say quietly. She's not going back to that house where David can put his hands on her again.

I turn her around, gathering her hair. It's tangled with mud and brambles. Gently, I start working the little sticks and leaves from it.

"You hear me?"

She nods, releasing a slow sigh. "I hear you."

"I want you to go get your things and meet me on the hill tonight," I say.

She glances back, eyes huge. “You want that?”

I pull her back against me. Her soft ass nestles against my groin beneath the water, and her head falls back into my chest.

“I think I meant to take you home for good that first time we met,” I say, meaning every word.

She inhales sharply and holds it. Then, she whirls, eyes narrowed.

“Do you mean that, Westin Quinn?” she demands.

“I swear it.”

I’ve been unsure of a lot in my life, but I’m dead sure Diane Carter is mine. And if I’m so sure, what’s the point in waiting?

“I mean to marry you,” I say.

She’s shocked, her eyes roving over me as she tries to gather herself. Then, her shoulders straighten.

“Okay, fine.”

“Good,” I say. “You’ll be my wife. I’ll take you to the courthouse, and it won’t matter if I wear a condom or not. You can have as many babies as you want.”

Her dark eyes narrow. She’s thinking so hard, she’s chewing open the scab on her lip. I take her chin in my hands and kiss her forehead.

“You’re my business now,” I say.

“Fine,” she whispers again.

What’s holding her back? There’s something in her eyes that bothers me. She’s not good at being vulnerable, and I can tell there’s something going on that she’s not sharing. It’s the reason she keeps pushing me away.

“What is it?” I press.

She shakes her head. “Do you love me enough that you can handle baggage?”

I nod. “I can handle bullshit, Diane. That doesn’t scare me.”

“Okay, I’m worried we might lose the farm if I go with you,” she blurts out.

“Why?”

“Because they’re building a highway west of Carter Farms,” she says, her voice catching. “The city councilman, Corbin Buchanan, is trying to run a big access road right through our farm, right where my parents and Nana are buried. He's a cousin to the Garrisons, so David thinks if I get in good with them, they'll be willing to stop him."

I turn this over in my head. I knew about the highway west of Carter Farms, but I didn't know about the access road. That land has been in the Carter family for decades. I know Diane will do anything to keep it preserved.

I get it. Both Sovereign and I put our blood, sweat, and tears into our ranch. The land means everything to us.

"Truthfully, Diane, I don't have the kind of cash to buy property. All my shit is tied up in property and investments. Let me talk to Sovereign," I say. "He might be able to help sway the councilman."

She shakes her head. "I know the Garrison-Sovereign feud."

Everyone does. It's well known that the Garrison patriarch, now dead, attacked Sovereign's mother a long time ago. They know his parents were evicted from Garrison land afterwards. But only some people know that Sovereign had a fiancée a long time ago. She died in a car accident with Clint Garrison driving. It's a long, sordid history that has resulted in years of tension between the two ranches.

A cousin to the Garrisons is no friend of ours. If anything, Sovereign Mountain involvement might make the situation worse.

I take her face in my hands. A vein flutters in her throat.

"Diane," I say firmly. "Go get what you need and meet me on the hill over your house."

She swallows. Her lips part. The tip of her tongue wets them.

"Okay," she whispers.

For a fleeting second, she believes me. I see it in her fragile dark eyes. That's all I need—just to get her to believe for one second that I can take care of this, that I can take care of her. I bend down and kiss her mouth.

"Go back, get the things you need, and meet me at the hill overlooking your house," I say, keeping my voice firm and controlled.

"Okay," she whispers again.

She made a choice, but it's delicate. She's not used to trusting anyone. Truthfully, she's not used to trusting men, and that's going to be a struggle for me to overcome. The trust was scared out of her before we even met.

If she'll just let me, I'll do anything to build it back.

CHAPTER SEVENTEEN

DIANE

He drops me off at the bottom of the hill, and I walk up the driveway. The sun is still up, half-hidden by evening clouds, and the yard is bathed in dark gold. My eyes are on my feet.

I almost don't notice the trucks lined up in a row.

My heart sinks as my steps falter. The men were supposed to be gone in the city all night, but here they are. David's truck is in the driveway, as usual.

Parked alongside are two more trucks, stamped with the Garrison Ranch logo.

I'm so scared, I can't breathe. Instead of going through the front door, I veer towards the barn. Maybe I can hide in Sunshine or Gracey's stall until they leave or fall asleep. I'm a foot from the barn door when I hear a sharp whistle.

I turn. David stands on the porch with Avery Garrison at his side. The cherry tips of their cigarettes glitter beneath lowered hats.

"Come here, Diane," David says.

There's something raw in his voice that makes my stomach drop. It sounds a bit like regret. Slowly, boots dragging, I make my way to the front porch and climb the steps. When I glance up, Avery's eyes are on me. He lifts the cigarette to his lips and takes a drag.

I shudder.

"Get inside, girl," he says.

I glance at David. He takes his hat off, smooths his hair, and looks away.

"Who's inside?" I whisper.

Avery stabs his cigarette out and pulls the door open, jerking his head. "I said, get inside."

His voice is sharp like a knife's edge. My heart thumps as I move quietly past him into the dim hall. David follows at my heels with Avery behind.

I falter in the doorway, shrinking back against the wall. Avery brushes past me and takes two shot glasses from the counter. He pours one, passes it to David, and pours another. There are papers on the table. I lean in, trying to see them, but they're turned over.

My throat is a dry lump.

Something bad is happening.

My entire body feels it, like cold water trickling down my spine. Footsteps sound on the porch, and Thomas Garrison steps in, kicking the screen shut behind me. This time, he doesn't look anywhere but right at me, like he owns me already.

My breath comes faster. My palms are wet.

His eyes are darker gray than his brothers, and his short hair is fairer. He's got one arm covered in tattoos, and he's well built, heavy with muscle. By rights, I should be attracted to him, but everything about the Garrison brothers just feels...off.

He takes the cigarette from his lip. I want to tell him not to smoke in my kitchen, but I'm too scared.

"You want to tell her?" Avery says, glancing at David.

David is the only man in this room who won't meet my eyes. He's standing at the sink, staring at his reflection in the dark window. He's still in his work clothes. His shirt is old, and there's a patch on each elbow, hand-sewed by myself.

I did that ages ago, when he was about sixteen, when he was occasionally still kind to me.

"David," I whisper. "What's happening?"

My brother's jaw works. He's only twenty-six, but he looks older. His shoulders slope from carrying too much for too long. Tonight, there's nothing behind his eyes. The last bit of my brother is gone.

My chest aches. My lashes are wet.

"David," I whisper again.

He turns, sending me a poisonous glare. "You're going with Thomas. You'll be his wife," he snaps. "Surely, you're not selfish enough to let them pave over our land? It's time you pulled your weight."

My fists clench.

"No," I breathe. "I'm not doing that."

Thomas snorts. His neck has a drunken flush that scares me. Avery leans on the sink and takes another shot before putting the whiskey up in the cupboard. He runs a hand over his mouth, his eyes lock into mine.

The corner of his mouth jerks up.

I know right then I don't need to be half as scared of Thomas as I should be of Avery.

"It's already done," Avery says.

"No, I don't... I'm not doing that," I gasp.

David pushes off the sink and grabs me roughly by the upper arm. I'm too shocked to do anything but cry out as he drags me into the living room, far from the kitchen.

He lets me go, the way he did on the back porch. But this time, I manage to catch myself.

When I turn, his eyes are burning.

"The Garrisons agreed to stop the access road," he snaps. "But Thomas wanted you, so you're going to fucking go with him. If I have to walk you into that courthouse with a gun to the back of your fucking head, I will. This is my land."

I want to spit in his face.

Instead, I start sobbing so hard, I can barely breathe. David has pushed me, slammed my head in a wall, called me a bitch and a whore. He has shamed me and bullied me any chance he got.

But I never thought he'd do this.

"How could you?" I gasp. "You gave them me for the farm, David."

"You'll be fine. Thomas Garrison is well off."

"Nana would kill you if she was alive," I snap, my chest heaving.

He goes pale and takes me roughly by the arm again. "Nana would have cut her heart out if it meant saving this farm."

He's right, Nana would have done anything to save the farm. And the truth is, if she was in my place, she would have married a man she didn't love to keep the land from being paved over.

I'm a horrible, selfish person.

But all I can think of is the way Avery looks at me. Thomas won't protect me from his brother, even if he himself doesn't hurt me. I'll be stuck on Garrison Ranch.

Easy prey.

"You were what they wanted, so you are what they're getting," David says, his voice like stone.

"Why?" My hands tremble, tangled together.

David's lashes fall. "Thomas has always wanted you. Avery...I don't know. But that's not my problem. I found a way to keep Carter's Farm safe and intact."

I run my hand under my dripping nose. "I won't sleep with him," I snap, not caring that this is an embarrassing subject to bring up to my brother. "I don't care if he's my husband."

David's eyes flicker, but he keeps them down.

"I really don't care what he does with you," he says flatly.

My face is hot and wet with tears. I sink to the couch and clasp my hands.

"If he's expecting me to be a virgin, he's too late," I whisper.

A crease appears between David's eyes. I can see the question on his face as he glances up and, recklessly, I decide to answer it.

"Westin Quinn," I say, my voice small.

His brows rise. "Are you fucking serious?"

I nod.

"From Sovereign Mountain? Jesus—fuck, Diane, don't ever tell any of the Garrisons that," he snaps.

"What? They'll kill me for not keeping my legs closed?" I snap, getting to my feet.

He grabs my elbow, dragging me close. There's real fear in his eyes.

"No, they'll kill you because he's from Sovereign Mountain," he says. "You keep quiet about it. If he asks, say it was one of the wranglers or hired help. Do not say it was Westin Quinn."

"Why do you care?" I spit softly.

"You'll be safe with Thomas," he says, the emotion leaving his voice again. "I'm making a calculated trade. I don't have a choice."

I'm speechless. The entire day was euphoric freedom and pleasure like I never imagined. It was fucking and kissing with the assurance that I would get to go home with a man who makes me feel seen, who listens when I talk, who says I belong to him.

Suddenly, that's gone.

And I'm numb.

I should have known things like Westin Quinn don't just happen to women like me. He's too alive. I'm the girl who dies rusting away at the bottom of a barrel, too small to reach the sun. I'll pack my things tonight and spend the rest of my life rotting away in misery, married to a Garrison.

I want to scream at David, but he's right that we have to do everything we can to preserve the farm. It'll break my heart if the state government comes in and exhumes Nana, taking her from the land where she was born.

If I let that happen, knowing I could have prevented it, I'll live with that regret until I die.

I can't have Westin if it means I lose the land.

"I'll do it," I whisper.

He sighs, leaning back. "Take whatever you want. Nana's dishes and quilts are yours. I just want this done tonight."

"You mean you want me gone tonight," I say, my voice empty.

He goes to the door. "Go pack your things. Anything else you want, I'll have it sent to Thomas' house later this week. He's taking you home tonight, and tomorrow, you go to the courthouse."

He leaves, boots clipping down the hall. I hear their voices in the kitchen, and I close my eyes, leaning against the wall. The front door opens and slams. I wonder who came in from the front porch, but I don't really care. Silence falls.

"Diane."

I open my eyes. Jensen Childress stands in the dark doorway. His face is shadowed beneath his cowboy hat. It occurs to me that he's friendly with Sovereign Mountain. If I recall correctly, he knows Westin well. I lift my chin and wipe my face.

He gestures, helplessly. "I dropped by to pick up a check. Looks like I walked in on something."

"You know Westin," I say.

He nods once. "I do."

My chest constricts.

"Can you tell him that I'm sorry?" I manage.

"You're going with Thomas, aren't you?" he says, stepping into the living room.

"I need the Garrisons' protection to save the farm," I say, squaring my shoulders.

He takes his hat off, releasing a sigh. "You're brave, Diane. I've always thought that about you."

I don't feel brave. I'm so scared, my knees are weak.

"Just tell Westin I'm sorry when you see him next," I say. "He knows about the access road."

He blinks, not moving.

My throat closes. I clear it. "And tell him to stay away, that I'm handling this."

He gazes at me for a long time. Then, he dips his head once.

"And, Jensen," I whisper. "That gun you keep in your belt... Can I have that?"

He doesn't speak. I see his shoulders sink as he takes the pistol from its holster and hands it to me, pointed down. I take it and slip it into the folds of my skirt, the metal warm in my hand.

"It's fully loaded," he says, voice hoarse. "If you're at close range, make sure you have time to flip the safety first."

"Thank you," I whisper.

He puts his hat on his head. "Good luck."

Then, he's gone. I wonder if he's going to Sovereign Mountain tonight. I hope he is. It'll break my heart if Westin waits on the hill for someone who's never coming.

Broken, I climb the stairs and creep down the hallway. My room is sticky with summer heat. My bed isn't made. I pull back the covers and stare down at the faint bloodstain.

I scrubbed it out, but it left a pale mark. It's a reminder of the best afternoon of my life, wrapped up in the heat of his body.

This house has kept me safe for twenty-one years, but tonight, it feels like a museum for the things that could have been.

If my parents had lived, maybe this wouldn't have happened.

If David hadn't turned bitter.

If Thomas Garrison hadn't decided he had to have me.

If Westin Quinn and I ever stood a chance.

Tears streaming down my face, I pack my suitcase, stuffing everything I own into it and zipping it shut. I wrap Jensen's pistol in one of my sundresses and hide it at the very bottom, beneath the worn copy of *Canterbury Tales*.

My entire life is in this bag.

I drag it downstairs. Thomas leans on the counter, talking with Avery. Wordless, I stand in the hallway until Thomas walks by without looking at me and beckons for me to follow. Avery pushes past him. I'm the last one through the door, and I turn, looking back.

David stands in the doorway. A tiny part of me hopes he shows a speck of remorse. Maybe it would make me forgive him for everything he's done.

But he just looks relieved.

CHAPTER EIGHTEEN

WESTIN

All she has to do is get out of the house and make it to the fence. It's a ten-minute walk. From there, I'll meet her, and we'll go back to where I hid the truck in the woods.

Then, I'll take her home.

The sun sinks so slowly, I swear I can hear it etching its way across the skyline. I sit at the top of the hill, elbows on my knees, staring at the straight line of the hill where she'll appear.

Only, she doesn't come.

I glance at my watch.

My stomach turns, and I run a hand over my face to clear the sweat. From the moment we met, I've been able to feel her emotions, like the bare end of a live wire, touching my heart. I know she wouldn't just leave me here waiting for her unless something happened.

Something happened. I know it did.

I cling to that as the sky goes dark and stars glitter white. There's no way in hell she stood me up, not after what happened at the swimming hole. I was with this woman all day, naked inside and out, listening to her spill her fears, her hopes, her pain.

We talked about having babies together, for fuck's sake.

She didn't stand me up. I know she didn't.

The air is cool, and the ground is wet with dew when I go back to my truck. I've waited long enough. I need to drive down and see if I can catch a glimpse of her. I make it halfway there when a pair of headlights appear over the hill. They slow and pull up beside me, window rolling down to reveal Jensen. His jaw is set.

"Diane's gone with the Garrisons," he says, not meeting my eyes.

My stomach sinks. Part of me knew she'd pick the responsible choice. She's practical to a fault. My fingers tighten on the wheel, knuckles aching. Jensen leans out the window, concern in his eyes.

"I'm sorry," he says. "She said to tell you she was sorry. And that she was handling things, so you should...stay away."

I hear myself thank him through the roaring in my ears. I put the truck in reverse and pull onto the gravel shoulder of the road, spinning it around. My foot hits the gas, and I'm going back to Sovereign Mountain, in shambles inside.

For a short hour and a half, I thought I'd talked her into coming back with me, letting me take care of her and the farm.

Maybe I wasn't that convincing after all.

I drive through the dark until Sovereign Mountain appears in my windshield. My chest burns like it has never burned before. I head into the gatehouse and up to my bedroom. Wrathfully, I pull the mattress aside, propping it up against the wall.

On the platform underneath is a long list of names carved into the wood. Most of them are crossed out. The only ones that aren't are Avery and Thomas Garrison. I take out my jackknife to add one more name to the end.

David Carter.

I flip the knife shut and pocket it. I'm going to enjoy killing him. There's no easy death for men like him. He's going to be the unfortunate recipient of all my rage and disappointment that, after thirty-seven years, I fell in love, and he ripped her from me at the eleventh hour.

My father told me to always aim to kill. Men do the job right the first time around. Maybe I'm a hell of a lot more like him than I hoped, because I'm going to make sure there's nothing left when I'm done.

I go to shower the dried mud off. I smell like her, like sweet lemonade. When I dry off, I catch a glimpse of the brand on my back.

Gunslinger.

I stop, eyes dropping down to my hands. I think this might make me into into something far worse than I've ever been.

CHAPTER NINETEEN

DIANE

My nails dig into my arms. I can hear Thomas breathing behind me.

"I won't fuck you," I whisper.

The only thing visible is the light over the stove in Thomas Garrison's kitchen. His keys hit the counter with a clatter. He lets out a long, impatient sigh.

"Fine," he says.

I don't know what I expected, but it wasn't for him to cave so easily. I turn, my arms wrapped around my body. I'm still in the dirty sundress I wore with Westin. I can still feel his hands on me.

As I'm standing here in the kitchen of a Garrison, I can feel another man's cum dripping down my thigh. I press my legs together. It feels like what Westin did to me at the swimming hole was years ago.

I can't let Thomas touch me. He might be benevolent enough not to force himself on me, but I don't know what he'll do if he finds out about Westin. David was right to warn me not to mention his name in a Garrison household.

He watches me, clearly unhappy, but not surprised.

"I want this to be in name only," I breathe. "Non-monogamous. I'll sleep in my room, and you feel free to sleep wherever you want."

"You're going to be my wife," he says flatly.

"Give me time," I whisper, my voice cracking. "Please, Thomas. I don't know you. I'm not ready for this. I didn't choose it."

He takes a step closer, then another, until he's standing over me. His hand comes up. I flinch violently, leaning away. He starts to brush back my hair, but then he sees my reaction. His fist drops.

"Jesus, who beat you?" he snaps.

My eyes start watering. Maybe, if I'm being honest, they're not watering; I'm just crying. I shake my head, unable to answer him. He lets out an impatient sigh and runs a hand over his face.

"Fine, I won't fuck you tonight," he says.

I wipe my nose with the back of my hand. "You can sleep with whoever, just give me some time."

"And you?"

"Me, what?"

His eyes glint. "So you're going to sleep with...whoever too?"

I shrug, nodding, and that's the wrong thing to do. He was tempered a moment ago, but he's angry now. I take a step back, and his hand shoots out, gripping me by the neck. Fear explodes through my body, and my heart goes wild. He drags me in until I'm against his tall body.

"Fine, let's fuck whoever we like. You spread your legs for anyone, see if I care," he snaps. "Good luck with that. There isn't anyone to fuck for twenty miles of this godforsaken ranch."

He lets me go, shoving me the way David does. I spill back against the sink, paralyzed. He goes to where I left my linen purse and yanks it open, taking out my wallet.

My jaw drops. I can't say a word as he takes out my driver's license and my bank card. He hesitates, and then he takes my social security card, the cash too, and shoves them all in his pocket.

"I want you to know that when I'm gone in the evenings, I'm fucking someone else," he says, his voice glacial. "And until you're ready to fuck me, have fun fucking yourself, you whore."

He turns on the heel of his boot. His footsteps are loud as he heads down the hall.

"You sleep in the spare room, off the kitchen," he yells. "I didn't want you anyway."

The front door slams, and I wince. The engine of his truck roars to life, and I see the headlights disappear down the drive.

I'm so relieved he didn't touch me, but my hands still shake as I turn on the light and find my way to the spare room. It's a simple bedroom with a twin bed, a window, a desk, and a dresser.

Dust is thick like snow on the floor. Dead flies litter the windowsill.

I lay my bag down and locate some cleaning supplies in the kitchen. Head spinning, still unable to process, I clean every inch of the room before unpacking my bags. After the sheets and quilt are washed, I make the bed. Then, I tuck Jensen's pistol under the bed, in my mostly empty purse.

I lay on my back, the light still on.

There has to be a way to keep Thomas out if he changes his mind. The door opens outward, and there's no hook and eye lock or deadbolt. I can drag a chair from the dining room, but he'll notice it's gone.

Instead, I find a long coil of rope in the laundry room and a hook under the kitchen sink. Working quickly, I attach one end to the doorknob, screw the hook in the ceiling, and run the rope through it. Laying on the bed, I loop the rope around my wrist and tighten it.

If anyone comes in, I'll wake. The gun is loaded and within reach.

There are some things Nana would have never asked of me. If Thomas forces his way into my room, I don't care if I go to prison for it.

I'll blow his head open.

CHAPTER TWENTY

WESTIN

I'm so fucking angry, and I don't know where to put it all.

Sovereign doesn't notice. He's getting ready to bring Keira Garrison up to the ranch. I've never seen him more determined about anything in his life. His eyes are always distracted. When I speak, he asks me to repeat myself every time.

I wish Sovereign had someone for me to kill, because I need an outlet for the fire burning in my chest. Instead, I lose myself in work. When I'm not doing that, I'm getting drunk at night in the gatehouse.

It's not healthy. I need my girl back.

A week passes. I stay up until midnight, staring out at the tree outside my window. My mother used to say I bottle things up, that I'd be healthier if I just talked to people, but I'm my father's son through and through. I don't want to fucking talk it out.

I want to shoot Garrisons.

Or David Carter, unless I can find something worse to do to him.

Maybe I'm justified in how I feel and what I'm doing about it, maybe not. Maybe I drink too much. Maybe I stay up and replay every time I kissed her in my head. Maybe I touch myself a few too many times a night thinking about some other man's wife.

Maybe I'm all fucked up inside over what could have been.

After the second week, all my bottles are empty, so I clean myself up and get a haircut and shave. When it's bedtime, I lay on my back and stare at the ceiling. I don't sleep, but I pretend I do until I give up and take Rocky from the barn.

We move through the dark, the lantern hanging off his saddle, to the hill that overlooks Thomas Garrison's house. She's inside somewhere. The lights are all off, except for the one that hangs over the barn.

Inside that fucking house, she's in his bed.

My stomach is sour. I'm so angry, I have to argue myself out of walking down that hill and shooting him dead.

The next night, I go a little earlier. The light is on downstairs, and I can make out the outline of someone inside. Then, the light goes off and turns on in the bottom left window. My breath catches as the curtain draws back.

There she is, in a little white slip, like a pale gold ghost.

It feels like someone shot me right through the heart. Even from this distance, she looks so sad as she leans against the glass. Her face turns up to the full moon for a long time.

She pulls the curtains shut. I stand there for another hour before I go home. The night after that, I go at the same time and watch as she turns out what I assume is the kitchen light. Then, the bedroom light goes on, and she sits in the window, staring out.

Looking at nothing at all.

It turns into a routine. I watch her go to bed, and after she pulls the curtain shut, I can go home and get some sleep.

What I thought would be the best summer of my life turns into living hell. Jensen stays at the gatehouse one night. He's on the porch having a cigarette when I head out to get Rocky from the barn.

"Where are you going?" he asks.

I pause on the steps. "Getting some air."

The tip of his cigarette glows. It's dark tonight, and the moon is a sliver in the sky.

"Do you go out every night to get some air?" he asks.

I shrug.

"You're looking a little rough," he says flatly.

I run my hand over my jaw. It's stubbled. I shaved my beard off when I stopped drinking every night, and I've kept it cut back since.

"I look fine. Fuck you," I say.

"Are you sitting on that hill over Thomas Garrison's house?" He cocks his head.

I don't say anything. He lets out a stream of smoke and leans back in his chair.

"It seems to me, the balance of things in Diane's world is...delicate," he says. "But I don't think seeing her would upset it, so long as no one knew."

"I've got no desire to fuck things up for her," I say.

"This isn't what she wants." Jensen's jaw is set.

"I said I'd figure this shit out for her."

Jensen sighs, leaning forward and resting his elbows on his knees. "She's scared, and she has never had anybody to depend on but herself. Go see her. Try to convince her she can trust you."

I hesitate. Jensen doesn't know that Sovereign plans on bringing Clint's widow to Sovereign Mountain. He knows about the Garrison-Sovereign feud—he knows some of the awful particulars, like Sovereign's fiancée being pregnant by Clint the night she died. That Sovereign has a deep loathing for infidelity because of it. But he's unaware that we plan to kill the rest of the Garrison brothers when the time is right.

He doesn't know that I have a delicate balance of my own.

"It's a situation, given who her husband is," I say.

"I get that," Jensen says. "I'm just saying, it wouldn't hurt just to talk. Just make sure the Garrisons don't find out, or she'll be in trouble."

He hands me a cigarette, like he knows how angry I am inside. I take a drag and let it sit for a minute as I think it over. Truth is, if I see Diane again, I'll fuck her.

And I'm trying not to be that kind of man.

My mind goes back to her in my truck, on my lap, wrists tied to the wheel.

Pretty like summertime, flushed and riding me hard.

If I see Diane again, I will step over a line I've never crossed. It doesn't matter to me that it's Thomas she'd be cheating on. I have my doubts he's faithful to her; none of the Garrisons are known for being faithful. No, this has nothing to do with Thomas.

Truth is, as much as he loved my mother, I'm not entirely sure my father played it straight. I don't have any hard evidence, just a few too many nights when he came home late and wouldn't say where he'd been.

I can't go down that road. I won't do it.

I can't visit my mother, sit in her kitchen, and talk to her with the same mouth that touched another man's wife.

I shake my head in the dark, even though Jensen can't see it. "I don't think that's a good idea."

Jensen is quiet for a long time. Then, he sighs and gets to his feet. "Diane is a lot stronger than you're giving her credit for," he says.

Hell, I know that. She walked into the belly of the beast and told me not to follow her. I run my hand over my face. The night is hot, and I'm sweating. Jensen goes to the door and pulls it open. I start down the path to the barn.

"Hey," Jensen calls, and I stop, turning. "You want her back, gunslinger? Get the fuck out of your head and do what you do best."

He doesn't wait for an answer; he just goes inside. My heart thumps like a drum as I take Rocky up to the hill over Diane's house. Her lights are all out tonight, so I sit up there for a while and just look at the stars overhead.

Gunslinger.

He called me that on purpose; he knew what it would do to me. I turn Rocky around and ride him across the ranch to the valley where Jensen and I shot beer cans. In the dark, I dismount and kick through the ground until I find a shard of glass the size of a dollar bill.

It's dark, but my eyes adjust enough so I can see the railing. I walk to it and place the glass in the center. Then, I walk back and take my pistol out. I think I see a faint glimmer as the barely-there moon catches the glass.

The man I wanted to be and the man I am are two different people. I didn't realize that until it was set in stone.

I spin in a circle and take a breath. My finger comes down on the trigger.

Glass shatters.

Goddamn it.

I go home, defeated for days after. Then, things move slowly up at Sovereign Mountain—until they move fast.

One minute, the ranch is quiet as we ready it for winter. The next, I wake abruptly to the sound of gravel spraying beneath pounding hooves. I'm out of bed in a second, pulling on my clothes and boots and heading out the door. Up the path of the gatehouse, I can see the outline of Shadow just inside the barn.

Sovereign slides off. As I approach, I can make out another shape on Shadow's back—a woman.

I enter the barn. "Is that the Garrison girl?"

Sovereign nods. There's a hard set to his jaw. "I need you to cool down Shadow, put him away."

"What happened?"

He lifts the Keira Garrison down. I see a flash of her as she writhes in his grip. She's barely clothed, her curvy body protected only by a thin slip against the early autumn cold. Her brilliant red hair flips back, her wide, scared eyes rolling.

"Someone burned the house," Sovereign grunts. "I have a pretty good idea who. I pulled her out and released her horses."

My stomach sinks. He's implying that Thomas and Avery did this.

"Would they? It's their property," I ask.

Sovereign shrugs. "Can't say. Looks like vandalism to me, but I doubt we'll ever get the truth out of them."

I gather Shadow's reins. "Better take her inside. It's fucking cold out here."

He lifts her, carrying her from the barn and out of sight. I can't help but feel a pang of jealousy at seeing him get his girl. Still more intense is the thought of Diane being in a house with a man who was willing to hurt Keira.

That thought sits in my head all night. By morning, my mind is made up.

I have to, somehow, find a way to see my girl.

CHAPTER TWENTY-ONE

DIANE

My life went from bad to so much worse in a few short weeks. Now, there's no Westin and no hope of getting out.

I wake early, before the men are up, and put on a thin cotton dress to withstand the kitchen's heat. My hair has to be tied up to keep it away from the grease and smoke. Thomas fired the kitchen help when he married me, so I'm the only cook. I think that was his revenge for refusing to sleep with him. He's going to keep me isolated and overworked until I give in.

I can outlast him.

I'll raise him one and hit back too. It's my new goal to torture Thomas every opportunity I get. I'm careful about it. I had a lot of practice with David. Every crime has to be tiny and leave no breadcrumbs that could lead back to me.

I catch a mouse in the barn and release it in his truck. It makes a nest and chews the electrical wiring.

I put a cricket in his bedroom and lay quietly listening to him curse and tear up the closet looking for it.

I can't do anything outright to hurt him, but I can torture him so subtly, he never puts the pieces together. I hope he feels like he's losing his mind.

He fucked up my life, so I'm going to fuck up his until I find some way out of this prison.

It doesn't take long for it to be obvious he regrets picking me. He thought he could bend me, break me, but he didn't expect me to show my teeth.

He won't go back on it. I'm the best free employee he could have. But more than that, he's afraid if he makes a fuss, Avery will find out he hasn't fucked me. I can tell it's embarrassing for him that I won't sleep with him. He's so dependent on what his brother thinks of him that he'd do anything for his approval.

So, we exist, locked in a constant, unspoken standoff.

At night, I sleep with that rope around my wrist. In the morning, I get up and cook for Thomas, sometimes Avery, and all the ranch hands. I clean up and have leftovers in the kitchen, rinse and repeat for every meal, until it's ten at night and I'm still scrubbing pots.

My hands are rough. My back hurts. I'm thinner than ever because I have no time to eat and I'm on my feet all day.

I'm too nervous to eat anyway.

The worst part is the isolation. If it wasn't for Billie, Thomas' sheepdog, I wouldn't say a word to anyone. She belonged to him when I showed up, but he ignored her most of the time. I struck up a friendship with her, and pretty soon, she started sleeping at the foot of my bed. I count myself lucky on long nights she's there. Sometimes, I'm so ruined by what could have been, I can't sleep.

I almost ran off and hitched up with a cowboy from Sovereign Mountain. But I didn't. Now, I have to lie awake and hope that saving Carter Farms is worth it.

Maybe, if I can just get back to the cemetery, I can get some kind of sign to keep me going.

Then, something comes that breaks my bleak world apart. It's late September when I'm standing in the front hallway staring out through the screen door, and a truck with the Sovereign Mountain emblem comes up the drive.

My mouth goes dust dry.

It has been weeks. I haven't seen Westin Quinn in over a month. Truthfully, I never thought I'd see him again.

A thrill moves up my spine.

The driver's side opens, and a big, broad man even taller than Westin steps out. He's got a gun in his open holster. My eyes drag over him, and I get a chill even though it's hot out. There's something about his washed-out blue eyes that seems dangerous, almost foreboding. I know without a doubt this is Gerard Sovereign, the infamous head of Sovereign Mountain Ranch.

Billie bursts past me and starts yapping on the porch. I follow her, keeping my arms crossed tight.

The passenger door opens, and Westin Quinn steps out.

My pulse goes wild—he looks so damn good. His chestnut hair is swept back. He's in a t-shirt that shows off his torso, just as handsome as he was the day I last saw him at the swimming hole.

Blood shoots to my head.

He never came after me, not all summer long, and now, he shows up today, sauntering out of the truck like he barely knows me. My vision flashes red hot, and I stomp to the edge of the porch. Westin circles the truck, and for a second, our gazes lock.

There's a warning in them.

Don't say a word, he's begging.

I remember what David said, about how the Garrisons would hurt me if they found out I'd slept with a man from Sovereign Mountain. I have a split second to make a choice, and in it, he makes it for me.

"Where's your husband?" he drawls.

Like he barely knows me, like he didn't ask me to run away with him and have his babies. My mouth tastes sour. If I get a chance to be alone with him, I'm going to murder him. Or fuck him. I'm not sure which yet.

I jerk my head toward the barn. "He just got in. What do you want?"

Westin tilts his head. "We want to talk to him. Nothing you should worry about...darling."

I inhale sharply. "Don't call me darling," I spit. "Unless you want to lose your fucking balls, Westin Quinn."

His brows shoot to his hairline.

Behind him, Gerard laughs softly and starts walking to the barn. Westin's eyes drag over me, and I can't read them. He stares at me for a second, and that second feels like a lifetime. Then, he turns and follows Gerard around the house and out of sight.

My heart hurts so badly, all I can do is go inside. The kitchen is empty, dust glittering in the shaft of sunlight from the window. I sink down, and Billie slinks over to lay in my lap, begging for me to rub her belly. I wrap my arms around her warm body and push my face in her hair.

Tears seep out. She feels them and shakes her head.

I can't live like this. I'll slowly lose my heart that longs for freedom and my soul that wants to rest on my land.

That night, Thomas is in a horrible mood. He eats in silence and tosses his dish into the sink so hard, it cracks. He has a habit of doing that, and it reminds me of David. Silently, I clean up and go out on the porch where he's smoking.

"I'm going to the cemetery soon," I say.

He shakes his head. "I said you weren't leaving."

I gather my courage. "If you don't let me go, I'll ask Avery to take me, and you know what he'll do to me then."

His throat bobs, sweat glistening on his bare neck. He knows Avery wants to sleep with me, and it would kill Thomas if that happened. This isn't the first time I've subtly threatened him with Avery before. It's incredibly effective.

"Fine," he spits.

I narrow my eyes, triumphant.

"But I won't take you," he snaps, flicking away his cigarette. "You can walk, and you'd better have breakfast, lunch, and dinner done before you leave."

He stomps back inside, and I hear him go upstairs. At some point, Thomas is going to snap. I feel it coming, like the quiet whistle of an oncoming train. He'll snap, and underneath his weakness, I'll find violence. But for now, I'll keep pushing him, because that's the only freedom I have.

I go to my bedroom and lay on my back. The rope is looped around my wrist. The gun is under the pillow.

I'll see Nana, and I can ask her to get me out of this mess.

CHAPTER TWENTY-TWO

DIANE

I put on my yellow sundress, because it's still hot in the middle of the day, and wrap a sweater around my waist for when it gets cold. Then, in my boots, I start down the dirt road that cuts through Garrison Farms. It'll take me two hours of solid walking to get to the cemetery.

Under my skirt, I made a thigh holster out of braided rags and tied the gun to my leg. In a bag over my shoulder is an electric lantern and a knife. It'll be dark when I get home, and I'm not looking forward to it, but I know there's no point in asking Thomas to drive me. This is my punishment for using Avery against him.

Billie goes with me. We plod in silence until the dirt road ends and we get to the edge of Carter Farms. From here, I can see the house. David's truck isn't in the drive, so I don't have to take the long way around.

My heart twinges as I get close enough to make out the porch and front door.

This is my home.

It will be again someday.

Tears push up. I turn away, keeping my head down and continue walking. It's not much further to the wooden gateposts of the Carter family cemetery under the willow tree. The sun is setting, and gold filters through the trees. The grass is long.

My throat is tight.

The gate creaks, and I step through. It's then I notice there's a circle of grass stomped down outside the fence, like someone walks there and stands, waiting for something. It must be an animal, because I know David doesn't visit.

I hold back my skirt and wade through the tall grass to Nana's grave. So much of my life since her death has been spent in this little corner of the world. It's such a simple existence. I feel it should be easier for me to get.

All I want is a home and a family. I want to sleep here when I'm gone.

It shouldn't be so goddamn hard.

Tears in my eyes, I yank the grass up with my bare hands and kneel. Her headstone stares back at me, comforting in its familiarity. A sense of calm settles in me, and I find my body slowly relaxing. All the tension of the last few years eases.

"Hey, Nana," I whisper.

My throat catches. I thought I would have a million things to say, but now that I'm here, I only have one thought in my head.

Get me out. Please, get me out.

I can't break my deal with the Garrisons. This is my home. This is where my family's souls rest. One day, I'll sleep here too, with the stars bright overhead. The thought of their bodies being pulled from the ground, the fences knocked down, and the willow tree uprooted—it's too much to even imagine.

I wipe my cheek. Between my finger and thumb, I rub the tears away until they're gone.

Instead of speaking, I lie down and press my ear to the dirt.

And listen.

No words of wisdom seep up through the ground. Everything is so quiet. There's no pain. I close my eyes and remember what it felt like to curl up in Nana's arms. That was before the world was complicated and filled with men like the Garrisons.

Before I realized how incredibly vulnerable I am.

The sun goes lower. The gold turns to a dusky gray. I push myself up, grass sticking to my cheek, and stand. My unsteady legs tingle with pins and needles.

I have to go back and face reality.

Gathering my things, I leave the cemetery and loop the hook and eye lock down. I'm dreading having to walk back in the dark. Billie waits in the tall grass, but the expression on her face stops me in my tracks. She's crouched, her ears flat, like she's guilty. She's got something in her mouth.

I crouch. "Spit it out, Billie."

She obliges, and I frown, turning my head. It's a half-chewed dog treat.

"Di-ane."

I jump to my feet and whip around and my heart stops.

Standing tall and broad with his hat in his hand is Westin Quinn. He wears a worn shirt with the top buttons undone, showing a triangle of tanned skin and dark hair. Looped through his work pants is the same belt he used to tie me to the truck wheel.

My heart starts working again, picking up speed like a runaway train.

Thump.

Thump.

Thump.

My spine prickles. My body goes hot.

"Come here, Diane," he says, his voice low.

I don't move.

"I said, come here."

I lift my chin. "I know what you said, sir, but that doesn't change me not listening."

He hits his hat against his thigh. "I'm going to spank your perfect ass," he says, but there's no anger in his voice.

No, it's thick and desperate, like if I don't come to him, he might die at my feet.

I go because I asked for answers, and my Nana gave me Westin Quinn. That much is obvious. His eyes follow me, lingering on my mouth. He's giving me that look, the one that comes before a kiss. His hand comes up, rough and warm, on the back of my neck.

He pulls me in, but he doesn't kiss me.

"Fuck," he says. "I've never touched another man's wife."

I can taste the desire on his breath.

"It's not like that," I blurt out. "I made Thomas agree it's in name only. He sleeps with whoever he wants...and I can too."

His eyes narrow. "I don't believe that."

"He did. That's why he won't let me leave Garrison Ranch."

"So he said it, but he doesn't really mean it." His brows are creased.

I nod. "But he said it."

His throat bobs. Sweat trickles down and disappears beneath his shirt. We're so close, I can feel the heat coming off him. I want to feel every inch of him. I want him laid out in this field with his cock between my legs, as deep as he can get it.

I've been dead for weeks, but tonight, I'm alive again.

"He sleeps with other women?" he asks.

I nod. "He does. I thought it was only fair if I wasn't letting him touch me."

His eyes change, like the light sparks back into them. His hands tighten on the nape of my neck, and he drags me another inch towards his body until my breasts brush his upper stomach.

We both inhale sharply.

"He's never touched you?" he rasps.

"No," I whisper. "You're the only person who has."

I can tell he's dying to know how I pulled that off, but I'm not getting into Thomas and Avery's complicated relationship or how I've exploited it to protect myself.

Right now, I don't want to think about the fucking Garrisons.

He steps back, and Billie rises. He gives a low whistle, and she drops back down. Her tail swishes. Apparently, all it takes for her to fall in love is a treat. Westin reaches in his pocket and takes out another, tossing it underhanded so she can snap it from the air.

"Stay put," he orders.

She wriggles her body, like she's promising she will. I scowl, but he doesn't notice. Instead, he picks me up, letting my bag drop to the ground, and slings me over his shoulder. I yelp, but I don't protest.

He carries me several yards away, like he knows I want privacy from the cemetery, and spills me into the grass. His face is hard, his eyes glittering in the dim light. The hands that rip his belt open have more scars than I remember.

I love it. I love his rough body.

He pulls his shirt free of his pants. Then, he falls over me, shoving my thighs apart. My skirt slides back, revealing the gun strapped to my thigh. His brows rise, and his gaze flicks to mine.

"I came here alone, I have to protect myself," I whisper.

He bends in, almost kissing me. "You shouldn't have to. That's my job."

"I've never used it."

"Where did it come from?"

The memory of the night Jensen gave me the gun is so far away tonight. "It's Jensen's. I asked him for it before the Garrisons took me away."

He bends, kissing the inside of my thigh, right between where the twisted rags cut into my skin, above the cold barrel of the gun.

My entire body tingles. Every fiber of me is alight, like warm sunshine runs through my veins.

And I remember why I fell for him—because he feels like a hundred years of living. Dirty, messy, complicated, with lust and joy and grief and the kind of pain that comes from growth. He feels like the life I dream about having.

"Spread your legs," he says.

I hesitate.

"Spread them," he repeats, his voice cracking.

He's desperate, hungry. I obey, startled by this side of him. I tasted it at the swimming hole, when he fucked me on the bank. Now, it's back in full force.

My spine arches as my thighs spread. I wonder distantly if it'll hurt when he pushes inside me, like it did when he took my virginity. It has been so long since he had me last.

His hand slides up my other thigh and pulls my panties down. My legs start to clench, but he stops me with his head, knocking them back.

"No," he says firmly.

Hesitantly, I spread my legs. It's not like he hasn't seen my pussy before. My heart pounds so hard, I feel it in the base of my throat, like the storm in my chest is trying to be let out.

His jaw tightens. His eyes go dark. He falls over me, but this time, he doesn't stop himself when his mouth hovers over mine.

There's a second, a half breath, where we still have time to stop.

Then, his mouth meets mine, kissing me so hard, I can't breathe. The dull sheen over the world that fell into place when I married Thomas evaporates. Our bright colors meld like the northern lights, dancing on my tongue as his taste sparks in my mouth.

He kisses me like he's starved, and I have to pull back to take a breath. He follows my mouth with his until I push him with a hand on his chest. Our gazes lock. He's wearing that intense expression, the one he gets when we're past the point of no return.

"Fuck it, Diane," he says hoarsely.

CHAPTER TWENTY-THREE

WESTIN

Someday, I'll tell this story and explain myself. I'll say she wasn't really his wife. They won't really believe me. Who does when the details are this strange? I'll say I was drunk in love. They'll look at us and say it worked out in the end anyway. At some point, I'll stop trying to justify my sins to my great-grandchildren.

Life doesn't exist in black and white.

Maybe this is adultery.

Maybe it isn't.

God as my witness, I don't know. I'm not the man I hoped I was, not even close, but I think unfortunately I might be the man my father raised.

Tonight, I don't care.

Desire is so much stronger than anything else. In my book, Thomas gave her permission. If he didn't want her fucking around, he should have held himself to the same standard.

It's *not* cheating.

My hands shake. I sat on that hill with her just out of my reach for weeks. I beat myself up. I felt like less of a man for not going after her, and I know now that, whatever it takes, she'll be mine.

Thomas is temporary, a dead man walking.

I'll be the father of her children.

She gasps as I sink over her body, mouth dragging up her throat. Blinded with desire, I shove my zipper down. She cries out when my teeth graze where her neck meets her shoulder.

I waited. I watched. I wanted.

Her pupils blow as I push inside her, and my vision flashes. My lower spine arches as I drive deeper, letting her hot pussy pull me in until our bodies are tangled together on the grass.

Now she's mine.

Her skin tastes just as I remember it: soft, sweet. She's sunshine in human form, like lemons and whiskey and sugar, and I eat her alive with my body, thrusting hard, nothing on my brain.

We spiral together. Desire rolls in waves with my body, crashing into us, taking our breath away.

I roll to my back, holding her hips to straddle me. All hesitancy has faded. Her chin rises and her lips part. Her lids flutter and her eyes roll back as a moan falls from her lips.

It's good—so good, it doesn't feel real.

Her hair falls down her back, rippling as her body rises and falls. I'm buried deep, and she takes me. I wonder if it hurts, but if it does, she loves it. Our bodies are soaked where they meet. She's wetter than she has ever been.

My fingers dig into her hips, making sure she keeps every inch inside as she rides me.

Her palm falls flat on my chest. Her spine arches and her eyes widen.

Her pussy tightens, pulses, and then she comes undone, clenching hard around me. She freezes for a breath before her body starts shaking. I slam her down onto my cock, taking her as she wrings every wave of pleasure out.

"Fuck, you need this," I gasp.

"No," she whimpers, eyes meeting mine, big and brown beneath those heavy lids. "I needed you."

My neck prickles. I flip her again and lift her leg up, slinging it over my elbow. Her eyes roll back as I start pounding as deep as I can get.

But it's not enough.

It's never enough.

Nothing can express what I felt being so close but so far. I can fuck her body for hours, but I really want to fuck her soul. Somehow, that still feels out of reach. My eyes fall, and I see it: a silver wedding band on her finger.

I don't even know what I feel. Anger? Disgust?

Murderous rage.

Without thinking, I pull it from her finger and toss it to where my belt lies. Her naked hand curls, but I grip her wrist and pin it over her head. My hips work, pounding her into the ground.

Mine. My woman.

She drags her nails up my back. I fuck her pussy, my mouth on her throat. I want to eat her alive, consume her until we're so deeply entangled, I can feel her breath in my lungs.

But I can't leave a mark on her body.

I roll onto my back again, taking her with me. She rides me hard, her tits bouncing. Her eyes are glassy as she chases another orgasm. Inner muscles clamp around my cock, growing tighter. The grass around us is beaten down. It'll be obvious to anyone who comes across this patch of land what happened here.

"Good girl," I pant. "Make yourself come on my cock, darling."

"Oh God," she breathes. "Westin."

My hips meet hers, thrusting up into her body.

"Go on, come for me," I urge. "Let it out."

Her hands fly off my chest, fists tight, as pleasure hits her. I grip her wrists to hold her steady and let her lean back as it rolls through her body. I pull her in, propping myself up on the heel of my hand. My arm wraps around her, and I hold her close. She shakes, coming hard in my arms.

I'm on the edge. My brain is blank.

I've never seen her so pretty or so desperate.

She whimpers. I flip her onto her belly, lifting her by the hip. Her cunt is soft and wet, and I slide in easily. My eyes close, just for a breath.

God, I've come home.

Our bodies go still. My mouth brushes the back of her neck.

"Westin," she whispers.

My name coming from her lips is heaven. I tilt her head back and kiss her mouth hard, giving her my tongue. When we break apart, her eyes are big and soft, hazy like the mist settling over the mountains. She's at peace in this brief second.

My hips pick up again. My kisses are messy and chaotic on the nape of her neck and upper spine, imprinting it with all those lonely nights.

They say more than I can with my words.

I feel her glow, her bright heart. I taste her sunshine. Only this time, she's tinged with grief. Her kisses used to taste like innocence.

My heart hurts, but my cock takes over. Desire moves in a rush down my spine. My hips stutter. I'm deep in her, moving in short strokes, unwilling to pull out any further than necessary.

My mouth is by her ear. She's trembling.

"Don't pull out," she moans deliriously. "Come inside me. Please."

All it takes is those words, and I'm tumbling over the edge. Pleasure rips through me, and I jerk my hips back and spill myself over the back of her thigh. My forehead presses into her upper spine. My hips work until I'm done, leaving her drenched in my cum.

"God, girl, you trying to get knocked up?" I say, giving her a sharp slap across the ass.

She moans, wriggling her hips.

"I'm not playing Russian Roulette with my dick while you're married to another man," I say, falling to my back beside her.

She rolls to her side, and I do the same. We're inches apart. I smell the lust between her thighs, mixed with my cum. She reaches up and touches my face, running her finger down my jaw, laying it against my lips.

"I forgot what it's like," she whispers. "I don't want to go back."

"I can't let you go home," I say, voice hard.

Her eyes widen. "You don't have a choice."

I take a beat because she's so fragile, I'm afraid to push back.

"Did you write his name in your family's book?" I ask.

She smiles sadly. "No."

I've had that in the back of my mind for weeks. Her name with his is an abomination.

"Good," I say. "You come home with me today."

She takes a shuddering breath and releases it. I feel her pain on it, sharp like a knife. I already know what she'll say.

"If you have the money to buy this land out from under my brother and the influence to stop them paving it, I'll go home with you tonight, Mr. Westin River Quinn," she says, voice shaking.

I knew what her answer would be—I don't have either of those things, at least not yet. But I'm confident I can get both the land and figure out some way to stop the road. I just don't have a solid plan, and I know she needs that.

I get that, I do.

"I'll figure it out," I say. "I swear."

She offers me a sad smile. I brush her hair back and kiss her mouth because I can't stop. I can't get enough of tasting and touching this woman.

"I like the way you call me Westin River Quinn," I say. "What's your middle name?"

She shakes her head. "Oh no, I'm not telling you that."

I flip her over, laying halfway on top. The grass is warm underneath, and everything smells so good. I prop my chin on her pelvis, gazing up at her like she hung the moon and stars.

"Tell me," I beg.

She bites her lip. "Okay, but don't tell anyone."

"Cross my heart, darling."

"Okay, it's Lemon. It's a family name."

I can't stop smiling, it's too perfect. "I like that. Lemon Carter and River Quinn. Feels like we could be two different people who don't have to deal with all this bullshit."

"Hmm," she says. "I feel like it doesn't fit with Diane, but it's pretty all on its own."

I nod, but all I can think about is how I've been dying for this for so long. She doesn't know and I probably won't tell her how many nights I almost walked across the field and pulled her out of that house.

But everything is so complicated. I promised Sovereign revenge, and he has waited so long for it. The Garrisons' blood belongs to him.

And then, there's the shame of what I've done.

I close my eyes.

I can't just take her home. If she loses her land because of me, she'll never forgive me. I learned pretty quickly Diane isn't the type to give everything up for love. I don't blame her; I'd do anything to save Sovereign Mountain.

I wish I could tell her I can pull a solution out of thin air, but I can't. Instead, I keep my mouth shut and kiss her again. She smiles, and her hand slides through my hair, stroking it with her delicate touch. Her hands are calloused, and I hate that. She shouldn't have to work so hard.

We lay there, hazy. After a while, she stirs and pushes herself upright.

"Do you feel like...I cheated?" she whispers.

I sit up, reaching for my belt. "Do you feel like Thomas cheats when he sleeps around?"

She works her lip then shakes her head.

"That's your answer, darling," I say. "As far as your conscience is concerned, you did nothing wrong. And if you're worried about it, tell that pretty head it wasn't your fault. You were just walking in the field, all alone, and I took advantage of you."

Her lips part. A slow flush creeps over her face.

"You like that," I say.

She shakes her head hard. "No, I don't."

"Do you fantasize about me doing that to you? Being rough?" I say.

Her inhale is sharp. "Sometimes. I've never been scared of you. I think you make me feel safe."

I'm so fucking grateful I make her feel safe enough that she wants me to take control of her body. Now, I just need to find a way to make her trust me with everything else. She's quiet as I kiss down her shoulder.

"I know trust is hard, Diane," I say. "I know you don't believe me, but I'm going to give you everything."

Billie starts growling impatiently at the bottom of the hill, so I pull back from Diane and finish buttoning my shirt. She puts the cheap ring back on her finger, and I look away because I want to kill someone.

I walk her to my truck and drive her a few miles out from Garrison Farms. When I pull off the road to let her out, she wipes her face with her sleeve.

"Goodbye," she says. "This was probably a bad idea."

"I don't regret it," I say.

I take her wrist, and she turns, fixing those big, dark eyes on me. "Swear to God, I will get you out of this. I don't care what the paperwork says. You'll be my wife."

She smiles sadly. "I'm not so sure. But I'm safe for now."

I kiss her mouth, and she tastes like salt. "I'll be back for you."

She doesn't want me to break her heart. I know it's so delicate and bruised already. She slips from the truck, taking her dog. I wait until they're just over the hill, and I park in the woods. Then, I follow her by foot to make sure she gets up the driveway and into the house safely.

It'll take time, patience, and a loaded pistol, but I'm going to fix that heart.

CHAPTER TWENTY-FOUR

WESTIN

"Do you know if Clint ever beat on Keira?"

Sovereign looks up. We're knee deep in the river, pulling mud and branches from the low water. The summer burned up all the deep parts, and we haven't had the autumn rains yet. Now, we're relying on rain barrels for the upper pastures that can't access the pond.

We're both soaked in sweat and creek water. I spit, trying to get the grit from my teeth.

"The fuck?" Sovereign says.

"I said—"

"I heard you," he says. "But why ask that?"

I shrug. Since the night Keira arrived, Sovereign has been distracted. He works, we talk, but he's always up in that room with her, in his head. I don't begrudge him being in love—he deserves it after all this time—but that hasn't stopped me from worrying over the possibility of what the Garrisons are capable of.

"You think Thomas is just as mean as Clint?"

Sovereign's jaw works. "No, Thomas is a pussy. And as far as I know, Clint never hit her. He was always too manipulative to be that straightforward."

"I assumed psychological torture was his preferred method," I say.

Sovereign nods. I can tell he doesn't like talking about this, and I don't blame him. I fall silent, and he goes back to pulling debris and tossing it on the shore. After a while, I feel like enough time has passed to start bothering him with questions again.

"Do you know Corbin Buchanan?"

"What's that?" Sovereign takes his hat off and runs his hand over his hair.

"I said, do you know Corbin Buchanan?"

Sovereign squints. "He's a city official," he says.

"He's in charge of the new highway getting put in west of us," I say. "And the access roads around it."

"Sounds correct," he says.

He turns, dragging a log from the water and rolling it up the bank. I follow him, standing back to watch the river start flowing again. We both sink down, taking off our hats, to get a drink. Sovereign hands me a water bottle and takes out a pack of cigarettes.

"I think he's cousin to the Garrisons, but not blood," he says. "I don't have any direct dealings with him. As long as he's not fucking with Sovereign Mountain, he's fine."

We have a smoke in silence.

Finally, Sovereign lets out a short sigh. "I'd better get back," he says. "I told Keira I wouldn't be late today."

The world didn't change much when he brought Keira to Sovereign Mountain. She's quiet, and I rarely see her except during meals. They spend most of their free time alone. It grates on me that he got his girl and I'm still high and dry, someone else's wedding ring on Diane's hand.

Sovereign has a deep, enduring disgust for infidelity. His first love's faithlessness scarred him so deeply that he wasn't willing to touch Keira until Clint was cold seven months in the ground. If he knew what I did with Diane, he'd never look at me the same.

All my excuses sound like bullshit. He won't believe that Thomas agreed to an open marriage. I barely believe it myself.

I drop my head.

"How long are you expecting to let the Garrison brothers live?" I ask, keeping my voice casual.

"Why?" His forehead creases.

"I don't think it's good to let this go on forever."

Sovereign shrugs, getting to his feet. "It's better to kill them during the winter, but I may wait longer—I don't want heat from the authorities. It hasn't been long enough since we took out Clint."

He has a point, but God, it kills me inside. We don't speak as we gather our things and take Rocky and Shadow back down to the barn. We finish up chores, and I head to the gatehouse.

In my office, I get a cold beer from the fridge and flip my laptop open. I don't know if I have it in me to wait until Thomas is dead. I need to find a way to get Diane out and save her farm now. It seems like locating Corbin Buchanan and seeing if he's willing to talk business is the best idea.

Three days later, I put on my good hat, the one where the SMR logo still shines gunmetal gray, and take the truck into the city. It's not my favorite place; maybe I like it even less than Sovereign does. It takes me an hour to find parking, then another hour to get into the city building. The streets are more crowded than I remember, but then, I haven't come into the city in months.

A woman with neat blonde hair tucked into a bun sits at the front desk. Before I can say why I'm here, she points me through the scanners. I go through security and head up to where the stairs are split. At the top is the room where they hear city meetings. I've been here once or twice for zoning hearings and the like.

It's quiet when I push open the door and slip in. Right at the front of the room is a long table with four men and a woman seated at it. My eyes flick over the name plates until I get to the one I'm looking for—Mr. Corbin Buchanan.

I sink into the back seat and study him. He's older than Sovereign and me, by maybe five years. His hair is black and his skin light beige, some salt and pepper in his beard. I can't tell if he's from around here, but if I had to guess, he is. I make a mental note to start sorting through his past.

The meeting isn't anything I'm interested in—parking meters, city parks, that kind of thing—but I wait until the end, watching Mr. Buchanan talk.

He's confident; I can tell he's got money. There's an aura of assurance around men who've never wondered where their next meal was coming from. He has a little bit of the Garrisons in his face, even though he's not blood. Maybe it's my bias talking, but I see it in the hint of arrogance.

I flick my eyes over his body. His suit is tailored. His boots are leather. The hat that sits on the table before him is a fine, dark material.

I narrow my gaze. I think I might not like Corbin Buchanan too well.

The meeting concludes. I wait until the room is cleared and the last person follows Corbin out. Then, I put on my hat and follow him out into the hall.

"Mr. Buchanan," I say.

He turns, a line appearing between his brows. "Hello. Can I help you with something, sir?"

I hold out my hand. He shakes it.

"Westin Quinn," I say. "I'd like to talk to you."

He glances over his shoulder. His assistant waits at the end of the hall.

"Do you want to make an appointment?" he asks.

"I'm from Sovereign Mountain," I say. "I wanted to talk to you."

He freezes. "Oh, is that right?"

"Yeah, that's right."

He goes from being a friendly stranger to eyeing me with distrust. "Sovereign Mountain, huh? Did your boss send you down here?"

I shake my head, taking a step in. We're about the same height.

"The access road you had planned to put through Carter Farms—are you putting a stop to it?" I ask.

The open, easy aura dries up fast. Of course it does; he's part of the Garrison family. I square up to him, our eyes meeting. His jaw ripples as he grits his teeth.

"That's not anything I'm talking about with you," he says.

"I'm not here for trouble," I say, keeping my voice low.

He shrugs. "You know who I am. Hell will freeze over before I do business with Sovereign Mountain, but you give your regards to your boss. I don't have anything against him personally."

When he says that, his face is a little less grim. I see my opening, and I take it.

"Look, I don't have anything against you," I say. "The Sovereign-Garrison feud doesn't have anything to do with me."

"Doesn't have much to do with me either," he says. "But they're family."

"I get it," I say. "My business is separate. I just want to know what you intend to do with Carter Farms in regard to the access road."

He shifts his weight, crossing his arms. He doesn't trust me, but I wouldn't either.

"I can't tell you anything about Carter Farms," he says. "That's private business."

"I just want to know if stopping the road is a done deal," I say.

His eyes narrow. "How do you know so much?"

"I know David Carter."

"Then you should ask him."

I bite back my retort. It's clear I won't get anywhere with Corbin today. He has already got a built-in distrust of me, so I take a step back.

"I'd be happy to talk again, Mr. Buchanan," I say.

His forehead creases with annoyance. "I don't take bribes."

We both know that's not true. He's not telling me he doesn't take bribes, he's saying he won't take them from Sovereign Mountain.

"I wouldn't dream of thinking you would," I say. "Thanks for your time, Mr. Buchanan. I look forward to speaking to you again."

There's a gentle threat in those last words. He'll see me again, like or not. He gives me a quick nod. His brow is knitted like he's confused, but he's soon swept away into the other room by his assistant. I head outside and move down the street towards my truck.

Come hell or high water, I'm getting Diane that farm.

If Corbin doesn't take bribes, maybe he needs to go the way of Clint Garrison. A hand extended in a white flag. An unexpected meeting. An unexplained accident.

A gunslinger who doesn't miss.

A problem solved.

CHAPTER TWENTY-FIVE

DIANE

It's not uncommon that Avery comes up to Thomas' house and they leave for the night. I know they go into the city and lose themselves in whiskey, women, and poker tables.

I'm not sure if Avery knows how much Thomas gambles when he goes. I'm the one who has to drag him up to his bedroom when he returns. I see the I-owe-yous in his wallet and the distinct lack of cash.

I'm not sure how much he owes, but it's a lot.

Thomas' drinking has some advantages, the primary one being that I can rob him for spare change while he's passed out. I take any cash he has left after I haul him to bed. Sometimes it's a dollar, sometimes more. I cut a slit in the mattress and stuff it deep inside.

I'm not sure what I'm going to do with it, but I know that whoever has money has power. It doesn't matter that I have the same legal rights to own land and go where I want.

They have the money, so they have the power.

There's an unusual burst of warmth in late September that lets in the frost by night but holds off the snow during the day. One evening, when Avery and Thomas are gone, I open my bedroom window and sit by it. It's chilly, but the fresh air smells so good.

In the distance, dogs yap from Avery's farm over the hill. My heart hurts. I'm lonely and tired of sitting in this room, hoping that the world changes.

It's then that I hear it: a faint tread on the grass outside.

My eyes snap open.

The constant tension I live with at Garrison Ranch is gone instantly. Warmth rushes through my veins. Westin Quinn stands on the other side of the screen. He's shadowed, but when he tilts his head up, his hazel eyes glitter.

I want to cry with relief.

"Westin," I whisper. "What are you doing here?"

He comes close, so close until there's nothing separating us but the wire screen. I reach out, and he spreads his hand so I can press my palm to his. His fingers are big and square, rough from work. My hands look small and cold in comparison.

"Came to see my girl," he says.

My lips quiver like I might smile. Instead, I sniff.

"How'd you know I was alone?" I whisper.

"I was leaving town, and I saw the Garrisons at the bar," he says. "I reckon they'll be gone all night with the way they were drinking."

I hesitate, unsure what I want. Maybe I should invite him in, but this house feels like death, and Westin burns like the sun. I part my dry mouth and clear my throat.

"Take me to Sovereign Mountain," I burst out.

Those are the words he's waited for—I see relief hit him. He nods once.

"Go get your boots on, darling," he says.

I nod, my pulse racing. He melts into the darkness as I pull the window shut. Billie is sleeping on my bed. She lifts her head as I draw a thick, oversized sweater atop my dress and wriggle into my boots. I kiss her head, running my fingers through her coarse hair.

"I'm leaving the bedroom door open," I tell her. "If you need to leave, the dog door is unfastened. Okay?"

She licks my face. I kiss her one more time and dart from the bedroom and out the back door. I lock it securely, and I'm halfway down the steps before Westin appears. Without thinking, I jump into his arms, and he catches me easily.

Our mouths meet. All the pain in my chest is gone, replaced by golden warmth. He's good at kissing, takes his time warming me up, and then he goes in with his tongue and makes my stomach flip.

When we break apart, I'm dizzy.

"Did you drive here?" I ask.

He nods. "I'm parked off the road."

He sets me down and takes my hand. I follow him blindly, my brain turned off. All I want is to put all my fear into his capable hands and lose myself in him for tonight.

We get to his truck, parked halfway in the woods. He pulls open the door and lifts me inside. Our eyes meet, and he takes his hat off and fits it on my head.

My throat tightens. I want to speak, but I can't. He closes the door, and there's a second of silence while he circles the truck. Then, he gets in, filling the cab with his presence, warm like a fireplace on a cold night.

I inhale, closing my eyes. For the next few hours, I'm safe.

He's big, rough, but not the way the Garrisons are, not the way that will hurt me.

I don't know how I know. I just do.

Maybe that's why I bend to him when I've never bent to any man.

We drive in silence. He reaches over, shoves his hand up under my skirt, and grips my thigh, right below my panties. I'm soaked, tingling with desire. Part of me wants him to pull over and tie me to the wheel the way he did before. The rest of me knows how much better it will be if I can just wait until we get to his bed.

The driveway up to Sovereign Mountain is long. A sign looms overhead, stark against the night sky. There's a huge, sprawling ranch house that sits by a glittering lake, blue in the moonlight. To the right, I see all the lights of the employee housing. Beyond that, stars dance over the trees and dark mountains.

The air feels pure up here. It reminds me of being home at Carter Farms.

Westin pulls around the house and down the side driveway. Not far from the ranch house sits what was likely a guardhouse once upon a time. It's large, two stories, shaded by two huge trees on either side of the door.

He cuts the engine. I take off his hat and lay it on the dashboard.

"Is this where you live?" I whisper.

He nods. "I prefer it. People come through the ranch house all day, but the gatehouse is quiet."

"Can anyone see us?" I turn and look back at the light on in the upper level of the ranch house.

"It's possible," he says, opening the door. "But not likely."

I wait until he comes to lift me out. It's amazing how fast my brain went from survival mode to letting him manage everything. He sets me on my feet, takes my hand, and leads me to the front door. He pulls it open, guiding me through with a hand on my back.

The light flickers on. We're standing in an open concept living room. Everything is clean and neat, the furniture dark wood and leather. The rug is a deep blue plaid, and it matches the curtains in the kitchen on the far end of the space.

It's exactly as I thought Westin Quinn would live. Clean, no frills. Everything is in its place, all the dishes in the sink washed and towels folded on the counter.

"Are you hungry?" he asks.

I shake my head. How can I be hungry at a time like this?

He jerks his head up to the ceiling. "Let's go upstairs, darling."

Maybe this is as simple as it was when he took me upstairs to my bed; when, between my sheets, I learned what it felt like to be alive. But it doesn't feel that way. Maybe because we both have more scars this time around.

I know my heart is broken and tied together with nothing but a string called Westin Quinn. If I had to guess, I'd say his heart was already broken when we met.

He holds out his palm. I slip mine over it.

Then, we go upstairs.

His bed is just like the rest of the house—clean and neat, white sheets and a plaid blue quilt, turned down. Everything smells like laundry soap. There's a wooden cart in the corner by the fireplace. On it sits a glass and a bottle of whiskey.

"Turn around."

I obey. He shuts the door. Now that we're in full light, my eyes roam over him hungrily. His deep chestnut hair is slicked back, like he ran his fingers through it. I'm so close, I can see the faint lines around his eyes. I wonder if they're from wearing that pleasant mask everywhere, the one he takes off when we're alone.

His shirt sticks to his chest. The top few buttons are open, and my toes curl as I sneak a quick peek at the hair between his pecs.

I take a step closer.

He stays still, and I feel like I'm approaching a big animal in the wild, like any sudden movement will make him throw me down on the bed.

My eyes go lower. Down to the belt he used to tie me up. Down to where his shirt isn't properly tucked in. I pull the fabric free, and my fingertips graze the warm skin of his lower stomach. His chest tightens in a quick inhale. His eyes burn like fire.

I know he feels that touch in his groin.

I lift my eyes. "I want it the way you like it to be."

The words come out wrong, all jumbled. His brow creases.

"What do you mean?"

I worry my lip. "By the swimming hole, you mentioned being into...things."

"You mean BDSM," he says flatly, like it's nothing.

I nod. "I'd like...to know what that means."

He takes me by the chin. He turns my face up so I have to crane my neck. I forgot how tall he is. He's serious, his eyes having quieted down to glimmering coals.

"Do you really?"

"I do," I whisper.

His other hand slides behind me, and I feel it in my hair, gathering the tangled curls into his grip, wrapping it twice around his fist. My pulse stumbles, speeding up. He wraps it around one more time until his grip is at the nape of my neck.

Our bodies are close. I feel the heat of his groin against my belly.

"Is that what you really want?" he breathes.

"Yes," I gasp.

His eyelids flicker. "You will call me sir tonight."

Arousal pours through my veins. "Yes, sir."

Something clicks in my brain. All the fear and pain I carry around like a burden on my back falls away. There's nothing but his big, broad body, his hand in my hair, and the bed where I know he's going to ruin me.

I glance sideways. It's so neat, the sheets tucked flat.

He drags my head back. His head dips, his mouth brushing my forehead. I've never felt more grounded than right now. Somehow, he knows how to pull me back in, to make me feel like home is a real place, not just something I wish for at night.

He lets my hair go and pushes the sweater off my shoulders. It falls with a soft thump. He sinks to his knees and starts unbuttoning my dress.

This feels new, different.

"Pick a word for me, darling," he says, eyes down as he undresses me. "Any word you feel comfortable using as a safeword."

I think it over, suddenly self-conscious. My mind drifts to the safest thing I know—the willow tree at Carter Farms.

"Willow," I whisper.

He slides my dress down around my ankles. His head dips, and his hot mouth brushes my panties right over my sex, warmth seeping through to my clit.

"Perfect," he says. "If you need me to stop, say that. Understood?"

"Yes, sir," I say.

It's funny how easily I call him that. He hums low in approval. Then, with one finger, he hooks my panties and draws them aside. I shaved, maybe out of the vain hope this would happen. My pussy is smooth, and it feels delicious when his hot tongue pushes into the crease of my sex and finds my clit.

His tongue dips out and then in again, like he didn't get enough the first time.

He groans. My knees sway. He pulls back, and my panties drop to the ground. Then, he rises, towering over me, and unhooks my bra. My breasts fall free, and my nipples go hard.

He picks me up and carries me to the bed.

CHAPTER TWENTY-SIX

WESTIN

The night she told me she wasn't sleeping with Thomas Garrison was the night I went out and bought everything I needed to make her mine: toys, implements, and a diamond ring.

The toys can come out tonight.

The ring should probably wait until her husband is six feet under.

She falls onto her back, naked and breathtaking. Her blonde hair is the longest it has ever been. It tumbles over my bed, like yellow flowers in the summer fields.

I kneel between her spread thighs. Her pussy is dusky pink and laced with arousal. She gasps as I lift her further up so I can bend and lick between her legs. Her spine arches. Her toes curl, and I grip her ankle, loving how small it feels in my fist.

My cock throbs. I want to be inside her so badly, but not until she's ready.

Not until she's broken.

"Do you want a shot, darling?" I ask, my voice hoarse.

She nods. I feel her eyes on me as I go to the cart and pour the bourbon. When I return, she's on her knees, her feet tucked under her body. She's breathtaking like this, sitting naked on my bed.

"Stay there," I say.

I set the shot glass aside and go to the closet. Hanging on the wall is a collar. I take it down, running my fingers over the soft leather. I bought this for her and had the inside engraved with her name.

Diane Quinn.

Her eyes widen as I leave the closet. Her body shivers as I brush her hair back and clasp the collar around her throat. It's black leather, and the inside is lemon yellow silk.

"Does it feel good, darling?" I ask.

She nods once. "It feels...secure."

"Good girl," I praise. Her body is relaxed, and she has those big brown eyes locked on me intently. I bend and kiss the nape of her neck, holding her hair aside.

"Is my hair in the way?" she whispers, lifting her wrist to show me the band around it.

I slip it from her hand and kneel beside her. She keeps still as I gather up her hair and braid it loosely. Her breasts heave, her dusky pink nipples tight. When I lean in, I swear I can smell the wetness between her legs, and it makes me want to push my face into her pussy again.

But not yet.

She stays perfectly still, watching as I retrieve the whiskey glass from the table. I circle the bed until I'm standing at the foot of it and beckon her closer.

She obeys, wriggling until she's right before me.

"Open your mouth," I order.

Her lids droop, and arousal makes her cheeks flush. Her lips part, and her pink tongue extends.

"Tilt back," I say. "Wider for me."

She opens her mouth as far as she can and pushes her tongue all the way out. My mind goes right back to that day in her kitchen, when she took my cum in her mouth and showed it to me on her tongue.

Fuck, she's so perfect.

I shoot the whiskey and bend over, letting it stream from my mouth to hers. There's a common theme here. From my lips to my love's, our tastes mingling. Apples, whiskey, anything else.

I just want her to taste me, to know I'm stained in and on her body.

She swallows, whiskey dripping down her chin. I let it slip lower until it's between her breasts. Then, I lick it off and sink my teeth into the side of her neck until she moans and her hips writhe.

I tear my mouth from her skin. "Did that make you wet, you slut?" I breathe.

She moans, shaking. Her nails bite into her thighs.

"Get on the floor, on your knees."

I step back and start unbuttoning my shirt. She scrambles up and sinks to the floor by the bed, sitting back on her heels. Those dark eyes follow my every move as I unfasten my belt and strip naked. Her breasts heave, her gaze dragging over my body.

I take her by the jaw and force her lips apart. Her eyes widen, but she doesn't resist me. I grip my cock at the base and push the head into her soft, hot mouth. Then, carefully, I let the whiskey flow down my stomach. It gathers in the ridge down the center of my abs, down over my groin, and follows the curve of my cock until it spills into her mouth. Her throat bobs as she drinks it down.

I give her a little more.

She swallows like a good slut. The excess spills from her lips and down the valley between her breasts.

My head goes blank. I pick her up with one arm and flip her back onto the bed. Her thighs fall open, and I kneel between them. Her eyes flash as I lift the bottle over her belly and pour it into the little dip of her navel. Her gasp turns to a moan. I set the bottle aside and lap the whiskey from her belly. kissing her, nipping her soft skin, drinking from her body.

This isn't enough. I'm fucking selfish; I want everything.

My mouth lowers until it finds what it wants—her soft, drenched cunt.

She moans, and her hips lift. It takes me a second to realize she's coming. Then I taste it as wetness spatters my chin and stains my bed. Pleasure rips through her in waves, shaking her and leaving her weak when it goes.

Those pretty eyes are dreamy, fixed on the ceiling.

She's slipping into submission until she's sweet, until she's free of any burdens. That's where I find her, limp beneath my body. I pull her up against the pillows and shove her thigh up, hooking it over my elbow.

She shakes as the head of my cock slips into her cunt. A tear etches from beneath her lashes.

"Oh my God," she breathes.

Our bodies shudder together, and my mouth grazes her forehead, like kissing an ember. My hips sink close, and we're fused, both breathless. Then, I drag my length from her body. Wait a beat. And slam inside.

The bed hits the wall. She cries out, her eyes flying open. Her hand comes up and plants on my chest.

"What the fuck," she gasps.

I nip her breast. "What? Did you really think I'd given you everything?"

"I did," she whimpers.

I flip her over, cradling her with my hand on her lower stomach. She cries out, nails tearing at my quilt as I guide my cock into her pussy. She stretches, scratching at the headboard, writhing in my grip as she tries to get away.

But she doesn't safeword me.

I grip her braid, wrapping it in my fist. Her head yanks back and her spine arches beautifully, giving me more space inside her cunt. I steady her hipbone against my forearm and slip my fingers between her legs. Her clit is swollen. She's so wet, it runs down my wrist.

"You're my whore," I pant. "You've always been my whore, from the fucking first moment I met you."

She cries out as our bodies meet. Rough, hard. Almost violent.

"You left the first time we met," she cries out.

I slam into her again, pulling her head back to look down into her eyes. "I should have stayed. I should have taken you upstairs and let them all hear me fuck you."

My fingers work her clit, and she comes again. It's so easy together, pleasure tumbling out without even trying. This time, her orgasm is short and quick, pumping around my cock.

I fuck her through it, holding her down by the hair. My own orgasm draws closer and closer until I can't hold it back anymore.

I thrust to the hilt and come hard as my brain explodes in full color. There's nothing in the world that feels as good as coming inside her. Once she's mine, I'm going to keep her up all night.

We collapse, my body over hers. It takes a second for me to realize what I did.

"No," I rasp. "When is your period due?"

"Three days," she says, forehead creased. "It's fine, I think. I shouldn't get pregnant."

We're playing with fire. She's married, but she's not sleeping with her husband, so if she gets pregnant, he'll know it was by another man. I highly doubt their agreement to not be monogamous will keep him from losing his shit.

She wriggles under me, turning over. Her fingertips graze my face.

"It's okay, Westin," she whispers.

What does it matter anyway? If she gets pregnant, I'll take her away before she shows. Tonight, drunk off whiskey and Diane, that seems like a real plan.

"How do you feel?" I ask.

"Good. Really relaxed," she murmurs, eyes hazy. "I could sleep for days."

"I'm not done, darling. Get on your knees," I say, rising to my feet. "We're just getting started."

CHAPTER TWENTY-SEVEN

DIANE

I'm tender from his cock. He feels big and hard and hungry inside me. It scratches an itch I've had since we first slept together. He can do whatever he wants with me; I just want to ache tomorrow.

"Go on, get on your knees," he says. "I thought you were a good girl."

Those words in that deep voice make me scramble to my knees on the bed. The corner of his mouth jerks up.

"I can't put my name on you," he says, cocking his head. "If I could, I'd make good on my threat to brand your ass. But that doesn't mean I can't put my name in you."

I do a double take, wide eyes following him as he goes to the closet. When he returns, he carries a box that he places on the dresser. He takes something out and tosses it onto the quilt.

A little bottle of lube. A glass bulb with a silver flared top.

My stomach swoops. I know what that is, and I know where it goes. My mouth is dry as I lick my lips, watching him closely. He uncaps the bottle, spills the lube into his palm, and rubs it over the plug.

"On your knees, darling," he says. "Face in the bed, ass up."

"Is your...name on that?" I whisper, hesitating.

He flips it over, revealing the top. It's silver and adorned with what looks like a brand. The letters are in black: WRQ.

"You made that for me." I look up at him.

"All of it was made for you," he says, kneeling one leg on the bed. "There seems to be some dispute over who you belong to, and I intend to put that to rest."

I'm hot all over, unable to speak. No one has ever wanted me the way Westin does. It leaves me breathless.

"Palms on the bed," he says.

I obey, spreading them and sinking down to my elbows.

"That's a good girl," he rumbles. His fingers work the lube over my asshole, making my face burn.

He doesn't have any shame when it comes to sex. I'm sure tonight is just the tip of the iceberg.

I shiver. Deep inside, I want to know just how far he's willing to go.

His fingers work over my sensitive opening. The tip dips in. I bite my tongue and close my eyes. His other hand rests on my hip, holding me in place as he works the tip of the plug against my opening.

"Relax, darling," he says, kneading me with his fingers.

I focus, trying to obey. He pushes, and there's a split second of pain, and then it's inside me, bigger than his finger, but less intrusive. Maybe it's because it's smooth and he's rough. Experimentally, I wriggle my hips, and the plug rubs against all the right places.

He bends over me. "Does it feel good?"

I nod. He nuzzles his face into the back of my neck.

"Sit back on your heels," he says, moving off me.

I obey and he rumbles his approval. "Now, put your palms on your thighs, upward facing. Good girl. Open your mouth."

Tentatively, I obey. He took something else from the closet—a little velvet bag. From it, he pulls a strip of leather with a metal buckle.

It's a ball gag.

My thighs tense. My pussy responds, already dripping from the plug. He kneels one leg against the edge of the bed, brushing back my flyaway hairs.

"If you need out, you hit my arm or leg," he says. "I'm going to ease you in, so no hand restraints this time."

So it gets worse?

My mouth is open, but somehow, my jaw drops as he dips the ball gag between my thighs. I feel it, round and smooth, against my pussy. He drags it up over my clit, back and forth. His head dips, and he captures my nipple between his teeth and flicks it with his tongue.

Oh God. My body quivers.

"Keep your mouth open." He moves to my other nipple. "It's alright to drip a little."

His voice is hoarse, sitting low in his chest. The ball gag moves over my clit in slow circles. My mouth starts salivating as soon as I start thinking about it, but I don't pull my tongue back. It drips down between my breasts. He licks it off my skin.

His eyes dart up, intense, impossible to read.

The gag moves faster. The pressure increases.

"Come for me, you pretty slut," he breathes. "You can do it. Give me one more."

He takes my nipple in his mouth and grazes it with his teeth. Heat plummets through my veins. My body coils and releases so fast, all I can do is let out a sharp cry as I come. He moans, pushing the gag up against my pussy so I can ride it.

I can hear how soaked I am.

Pleasure ebbs, leaving me hot and shaky. He lifts his head and sits up, pulling the gag from between my legs.

"Good girl," he says.

I nod, but before I can speak, he slips the gag between my lips and fastens it beneath my hair. The taste of what he did to me blossoms over my tongue: sweet, with a slight tang and a hint of his cum. I try to swallow as I start salivating, but the gag blocks me. Wetness slips from the corner of my mouth and etches down my neck.

His eyes drag over me, drunk with lust. "Fuck, you're such a sweet girl. Look at you."

I blink my wet lashes, tongue pinned down by the gag.

"Do you want to see yourself?" he asks.

I feel my eyes widen. Before I can nod or shake my head, he picks me up and carries me to the far side of the room. I didn't notice it before, but there's a full-length mirror with a wooden frame in the corner. He sets me down and locks an arm around my chest to hold me steady.

My cheeks flush dark pink.

I've never seen myself like this...so raw and vulnerable.

He takes me by the braid and drags my head up to look into his eyes. "It's no fucking wonder I'm obsessed with you, darling."

My chest aches, but in a way that I hope it never stops. His fingers close at the base of my neck. His mouth brushes my forehead.

"I want you to be mine," he says. "I'm going to get you back, Diane, and then I'm going to put a collar around your neck and keep you forever."

My eyes go wide. I'm not positive what that means, but I get the sentiment behind it. It somehow feels more life altering than when he said he wanted to marry me.

I wonder if he put a gag in my mouth to keep me from protesting.

I don't have time to mull it over, though, because he picks me up and carries me back to the bed, spilling me onto my hands and knees. His weight sinks the mattress. His tongue, hot and demanding, slides over my pussy, eating it from behind like he's starving.

The world shifts. This man is altering my brain chemistry.

My toes curl, and I'm whimpering around the gag as I come again, my breath stolen by the wave of pleasure that moves through my hips. His hungry tongue pushes into my pussy before stroking down to my clit. I waver, unable to hold myself up anymore.

His fingers work at the base of my neck. The ball gag falls from my lips.

"I want to hear you fucking scream," he rasps.

He digs both hands into my hips, and I have a second to brace myself before his cock slams into my pussy. It's tight, so tight that I do exactly as he says and scream, shocked by the intrusion.

"Fuck, that's right," he pants.

He slams the bed against the wall, and I cry out again, vision flashing. God, he's going to break me into a thousand pieces. There's no room; it's too much.

Something buzzes down below. Did he have a vibrator on the bed? I can't remember. All I know is it's on my clit and I'm shaking. He fucks hard and slow, using all the strength in his powerful body.

"Good girl. Come for me," he breathes. "You come on my cock, come until you can't come anymore."

Obediently, I come because I can't hold back. He fucks me through it, breath hot on my shoulder. The vibrator stays on my clit. When I try to squirm away, he spanks my thigh.

That only makes me come harder. I'm wrung out like a dishrag when another orgasm starts. This time, it builds so fast, it's all I can do to take a breath before he's riding me through it.

"Good fucking girl," he moans.

He doesn't reward me with a break. I'm so weak, I might faint in his arms. I'm just now realizing that every deep thrust makes me scream out loud. I can't bite it back, can't help it.

I hope they can't hear me at the ranch house.

My body hits a breaking point. I can't tell when I'm coming and when I'm not. I'm just a wet mess of pleasure and pain, held up by his iron forearm locked over my breasts. At some point, he dropped the vibrator, and he's using his fingers on my clit.

Circling as he fucks me. Rubbing from side to side. Punctuating his touch with a light spank here and there. Tears slip down my cheeks. A sob fights its way out.

Through all of this, he's careful not to leave a single mark behind.

CHAPTER TWENTY-EIGHT

WESTIN

She doesn't safeword me, not even when she goes limp in my arms. Her cries turn to moans as she hits her breaking point. Her tears taste like defeat.

The good kind, the sweet kind.

This isn't about our bodies. No, this is about the barrier she keeps up between us. Maybe it's about the barrier I keep up too. Her heart is so soft, her mind so beautiful, but she protects it behind a wall. I know all about building walls, and I know how hard they are to break down.

Touching her body isn't enough. I need to touch her heart.

I want her to touch mine too.

My hips stutter, and I realize I can't hold back. Her eyes are rolling, but she won't safeword me. She's so fucking stubborn, she's going to force me into making that choice.

If she was mine, I'd push her all night. But I can't leave marks.

So, I thrust deep and come, filling her up for the second time tonight. What's done is done. She gives a soft moan and sinks onto her belly. My body eases over hers, still hungry for her bare skin against mine.

She whimpers. I brush her hair back and kiss her temple.

"Are you hungry, darling?" I whisper.

"Yes, sir." Her lips barely move.

I ease my cock from her pussy, and she lets out a groan when I slip the plug from her ass. I lift her, draping her arm around my neck, and carry her to the bathroom just down the hall. It's spacious with a large tub, big enough for both of us. I turn on the water and set her on the sink.

She lifts her eyes to mine.

"That was...."

I brush her hair back and pull it free from the braid. "You were perfect," I tell her.

She bites her lip. "I was loud," she whispers.

"Of course you were," I say. "You were getting put through my mattress. I'd be disappointed if you weren't."

She smiles weakly. I tilt her chin up and kiss her mouth. When I pull back, she looks a little more grounded.

"Go use the toilet," I say. "Do you need me to lift you?"

She shakes her head hard. "Can you leave?"

"You want me to leave so you can pee?" I ask, unable to keep from smiling.

She nods. I shake my head.

"No. Get used to me never leaving you alone," I say.

She blushes, but she goes to do as she's told. I wash my face with cold water, mostly so she doesn't feel like she's in my spotlight. The toilet flushes, and she's pushing me out of the way so she can wash her hands. I grip her waist and nuzzle my nose against her neck.

She smells like my wife.

I help her into the tub so I can wash her hair. It's soft like silk in my fingers. She moans as I work shampoo into her scalp. This is less about her needing to be clean and more about giving her physical closeness while she unwinds.

She eases into my body as I run warm water through her hair to clear the suds. When I'm done, I turn her around and pull her into my lap to rub her hair dry.

"How do you feel?" I ask.

She nods. "Really good. There's this...never mind."

Her chin dips, but I lift it. "Tell me."

"There's this...knot that I always have in my chest. Maybe it's anxiety, maybe just from being all tensed up, but I don't feel it tonight. Maybe I don't feel it when I'm with you at all."

She doesn't want to look me in the eyes. I hold her against my chest so she can hear how my heart is beating for her tonight.

"I have you," I say quietly. "And I'm not letting you go home."

She goes rigid and pulls back. I said the wrong thing. I should have just locked her in my bedroom, but I know that would break her heart.

"I have to go back," she says. "Carter Farms is mine, and I'm getting it back."

I shake my head. "No."

Fire blazes in her eyes. "You can't tell me shit, Westin."

I want to laugh, but she's dead serious. Instead, I do something incredibly reckless and decide to tell her the truth, maybe because I'm at the end of my fucking rope.

She's my wife, not his.

She shouldn't be in his house. She should be in my bed where she belongs.

"We're going to kill them," I say.

Her entire body goes stiff. Her lips tremble. "What?"

"Sovereign is going to kill the Garrison brothers," I say. "We've planned on it for a while now. It was just never the right time, but I think it'll be soon."

She mouths silently, then she shakes her head.

"No, no, he can't do that," she says. "They're the only thing keeping my farm safe. He can't do that."

I grip her waist, keeping her in my lap.

"His family has feuded with theirs for decades," I say. "Abel Garrison, your dead father-in-law, tried to rape Sovereign's mother. He evicted their family when they fought back. And Clint fucked Sovereign's fiancée, back when they were young, right before he got in a car wreck that killed her."

She rears back, shocked.

The clock in the hall ticks. Her throat bobs. I see the gears working in her head.

"I understand why he might want revenge," she whispers. "But please, let me talk to him."

"No," I say. "No, I have this handled. I won't have you begging anyone but me for mercy or for the lives of the Garrison brothers. They're not worth your breath."

"No," she says, her nails digging into my chest. "But my land is worth everything."

She jerks herself from my grasp and steps from the tub. I follow her, water dripping on the floor as she heads back to the bedroom. Her hands shake. She starts tearing up the room, looking for her clothes.

"Diane," I say.

She ignores me.

"Diane Carter," I say. "I will tie you to my bed if I have to."

She freezes, glancing up. I mean it, and she can tell. Tears rush into her eyes, and she sinks down onto the bed, cradling her hands.

"It's all I have of her," she whispers.

I kneel before her. She's rubbing her knuckles so hard, I have to grip her wrists to get her to stop. Her hands were warm when I fucked her. Now, they're ice cold.

God, I'd do anything to keep her from feeling like this ever again.

This isn't just about land or a family cemetery for her. This is her last lifeline to the woman who raised her, and she's clinging to it with both hands.

I know her heart aches, but if she wants her farm, she has to trust me.

"Darling," I say, weaving my fingers through hers. "I swear to God, I will not kill the Garrison brothers. Your farm will be safe."

Her chin trembles, and she inhales sharply, blinking back tears. She's distraught enough that she clearly didn't catch the only thing I promised was that I, personally, wouldn't kill Thomas and Avery.

"Really?" she whispers.

I kiss her hands. "Really."

She sniffs, her shoulders easing. I feel guilty for twisting the truth, but it doesn't matter, because I'm going to do whatever it takes to get her through this alive.

The Garrisons will end up six feet under. Carter Farms will go to her; I'll make sure it's her name on the deed if it's the last thing I do.

Maybe I'm a bastard, but I'm the bastard she's got. I won't kill the Garrison brothers. I'll keep my promise in a technical sense.

Sovereign will pull the trigger.

It's his blood to spill, not mine.

All I can do is make sure he does it soon. Her arms slip around my neck. She kisses my mouth, and I feel her fingers on my upper back, tracing the raised brand.

"Take me home, gunslinger," she whispers.

That word has always haunted me, but from her lips, it tastes like sweet, whiskey-laced tea. So, I do as she asks, and I watch her while she puts her clothes on. We drive through the darkness, and I walk her up the hill to the empty house.

When I return, I take Rocky from the barn and ride out into the dark. At the crest of the hill, I dismount and let him graze nearby in the moonlight. Far away, I see the light from her barn glitter.

I stay up watching it all night.

CHAPTER TWENTY-NINE

DIANE

Even though I was confident, it's still a relief when my period comes. The day it makes an appearance, I see him, standing at a gas station talking to a group of men. While Thomas fills the truck, I duck inside to grab him a case of beer.

Westin walks up behind me, scanning the fridge.

"Excuse me, ma'am," he says. "I'm just going to get that case behind you."

I step aside, and he leans over to grab an eight-pack.

"Are you in the clear?" he says, lips barely moving.

I know what he's talking about. I keep my head down, pretending to fuss with my purse.

"Yes," I whisper. "I just got my period."

He pushes the fridge door shut, tipping his hat like he doesn't know me, and disappears. I'm dying to follow him out, just to see him give me that look. The one that makes my knees weak.

But I just go pay for the beer, like I don't know him either. My stomach is sick because I know this can't go on for much longer.

I've felt the storm rolling up over the hills for years now.

It's coming sooner than I think.

A few days later, I'm standing in the kitchen, washing the dishes. It's what I'm usually doing at this time of night on a Tuesday. The house is clean, the men are in town, and no doubt my husband is getting laid or gambling again. The house is pleasantly quiet, so it's a shock when I see lights come up the drive.

I frown, drying my hands. I'm in just my slip. I wasn't prepared for anyone to be home. The truck moves fast and comes to a quick halt. My heart jumps, and I back away from the window.

Footsteps crunch over the gravel. I barely have time to whip around before the door bangs open and Avery comes through like a bull breaking through a gate, his face dark.

I stumble back, hitting the sink.

Behind him is Thomas, and a few steps behind him comes my brother. I haven't seen David since that horrible night he gave me to the Garrisons. He looks the same, and the sight of him is like a knife to my fluttering heart.

I open my mouth, but before I can speak, Avery has me by the throat. My entire body seizes, and my legs scramble against the floor as he lifts me, just enough so I'm on my toes. My head spins. I can't breathe, my vision flashes black.

"You fucked one of them," he snarls.

Behind him, Thomas stands with his fists clenched. His face is deathly pale, and his gray eyes glitter. Time slows, and I see it, what I've dreaded for years.

This is his breaking point.

The low whistle of the oncoming train is here, and it's hitting me. Maybe it'll kill me.

My vision flickers. All I can think about is how good it felt to lay in the warm grass with Westin by the cemetery, how he was like sunshine on my tongue. Then, Avery lets me go, and I tumble to the ground, cracking the back of my head on the cabinet. Dizzy, I lay on my side, trying to get my breath back.

Avery's shoes move away. They're replaced by Thomas's brown work boots.

I wonder distantly what horrible alignment of planets led to my birth. I could have been anyone. Even being David would be better than this. But no, I was born a woman with nothing to her name.

I never stood a chance.

The toe of his boot strikes my ribs on my right side. I've never felt pain like this; it leaves me breathless, almost unable to register it.

Then, it happens again and again.

The world fades from dull colors to nothing at all, but before it does, I see my brother standing in the doorway. One more time, I wish for an ounce of remorse on my brother's face.

But he's just watching me, hands tucked behind his back, eyes like dark ice.

It hits me at the same time as Thomas' boot when David started hating me. Once upon a time, he was a sweet, little boy. But now, he's a man. He drinks with men, he talks like other men, and he sees me the way they do—as just a little less than human.

It's not clear to me that he even knows it.

The world flickers in and out. Eventually, the men are all gone. My broken body is on its side, and I'm somewhere overhead, watching it. I've never been beaten before, so I didn't realize how badly it would hurt. My stomach aches. My swollen, bruised skin is tender. I want to vomit, but I can't; my stomach muscles are loose, and I can't clench them.

My nose drips crimson on the floor. Using everything I have left, I crawl from the kitchen and make it to the bedroom. My body is bruised, but as I pull my clothes off and run my fingertips over it, I find it's not broken.

Maybe that's the best I can hope for.

Bruised, but still unbroken.

The men don't come back for two days. Patched together with rags and bandages from under the sink, I keep the ranch running as best I can. We'll need groceries in a few days. Finally, on Saturday morning, after I've put dinner into the slow cooker, I hear the door to Thomas' truck slam.

Quietly, I limp towards the back of the kitchen. A doorstop jams the back door ajar—it has since that night. I can't do that again; I need a quick escape. Boots move down the hallway, but they trip and stumble. I curl back, glancing into the sink to locate the nearest knife.

It's dirty, serrated, but within reach.

Thomas appears. He's unwashed and his face is swollen. He's drunk, with that flush men get when they have too many beers and their skin goes deep red.

Our eyes meet. He runs his hand over his face, wiping the sweat.

"I loved you," he says.

I freeze.

He spits, and I flinch. I just washed this floor.

"I saw you when you were in eighth grade and I fell in love with you," he says, fighting not to slur his words. "You're lucky it was me who got you. My brother would have torn you apart. You'd have deserved it, fucking bitch."

All my sympathy dissipates. He doesn't love me. He wants to own me just so he can crush me slowly. I've seen what men like him do to women like me.

He'll keep me in hell just to say he got what he wanted.

A fly buzzes on the screen. He sways, and the floorboards creak.

"I don't love you, Thomas," I whisper.

He blows out a breath from between his teeth. "Why? Because I'm not Westin fucking Quinn from Sovereign Mountain? Because I'm not a piece of criminal trash?"

I can't speak.

"I know it's him. Someone saw you two going up to Sovereign Mountain."

I swallow past my dry throat. Whoever that person was, they'd better die quickly before Westin finds them.

"No," I whisper. "I don't love you because you beat me."

He tries to speak, but he stumbles over his words. It doesn't really matter what he has to say. It's what he did that made all the difference.

In the last three days, I've become a different woman. The little bit of pity I had for Thomas and his weakness is gone.

There are some transgressions that can never be forgiven.

Thomas takes a step closer.

"Stay back," I whisper.

For a second, I can't tell if he's going to hit me again or burst into tears. I'm past the point where his tears would have any effect on me. Luckily, he pulls it together and clears his throat.

There's a painfully long silence.

"Fuck you," he says flatly.

I want to say that right back, but I know better. He hits the countertop, hard enough that it shudders. I flinch, drawing back.

"Please," he snaps. "You're not hurt, and you never were."

He seems to have sobered up a little, because when he stomps back to his office, his steps clip evenly. The door slams, and my heart is the only sound in the empty kitchen.

Until another car door shuts outside. Boots crunch in the driveway, but no one comes inside. My pulse races. I'm raw from fear, from the bruises on my ribs. I listen to my blood pump through my veins. In the distance, the cattle low. A nightbird cries over the field.

On my bare feet, I move down the hall. I should go to Thomas and tell him someone is here, but I'm too afraid to ask for his help.

Maybe whatever is outside isn't as bad as what's inside.

I lean against the wall and crack the door. The porch light casts a golden glow over the walkway leading up to the house. Avery stands with his hat pulled low over his face. He's dragging on a cigarette. The smoke moves in a lazy trail from his lips.

I draw back, but his gaze flicks up. His steel eyes glint in the dark.

"Come here," he says.

I can't move.

He releases a stream of smoke from his nose. "Don't make me say it twice."

Distantly, I wonder if tonight is going to be just as awful as when Thomas beat me, just awful in a different way. Shaking like a leaf in the wind, I step barefoot out on the porch. I'm in just my slip—I didn't have time to change when Thomas came back.

The straps hang off my collarbones like I'm nothing but a coat hanger. There's never any time to eat at Garrison Ranch. The days slip by like water through my fingers.

I live off scraps and a dream of going home.

He stands at the bottom of the stairs. Carefully, he takes his hat off, and I remember when Westin took his off and put it on my head, on that hot day when he drove me to the river and kissed me on the bank.

I want to live. God, I just want to live.

My dry lips part. "Whatever you do, just do it quick," I whisper.

He laughs, his teeth glinting. "You wish you were dead, huh?"

He says it like my misery is a joke. I don't answer, because the truth isn't simple. The only way I'd wish I could sleep forever is if it was in the quiet of the cemetery with Nana at my side, the silvery willow blowing above my head.

No road, no pavement to block the stars out.

Still, even if the farm was safe, I can't wish that. I know what life tastes like now.

It's sweet apple, from Westin Quinn's tongue to mine. It's the incredible, glorious pleasure of his hard, hot body. On me, inside me. It's the dirty things he says. The way he makes me want to marry him and have his babies.

No, Westin makes me want to live, even if Thomas makes me want to die.

And that's enough for me to take a step back.

"I'm going inside," I gasp out.

I spin on my heel and run, locking the door behind me. I have a faint impression of his glittering eyes as he puts his hat back on. I pull the bolt down. His boots crunch, fading away. His truck revs and skids down the driveway.

I taste his anger like smoke on the wind.

And I know I'll be burnt by its fire before too long.

I see Westin not long after. He's in town, at the grocery store. Thomas drops me off to do the shopping. I'm standing by the bakery, waiting for them to wrap up my things, when I feel him, like sunshine on my back.

I turn. He's a few yards away in the produce department. He looks good, startlingly real, the edges of his blue shirt stained with sweat where they touch his neck. His hair is brushed back. His bright hazel eyes are fixed on me like he's been watching me for some time now.

He's got an apple in his hand. Round, half red.

Our eyes meet. My body tingles, and he flexes his shoulders like something's bothering him. I get the impression of strength I only see when he's naked: warm, thick muscle, scarred by cruelty.

My lips part.

Heat floods my body.

He bites the apple, and I'm back in that bed with my head in his lap. By the glitter in his eyes that he knows what he's doing. It's no accident that I'm thinking about him naked just from the flex of his shoulders. I know how strong he is between the sheets, like a beast of burden.

Like a man who has no problem reminding some other man's wife, in the middle of the grocery store, no less, just how he took her virginity.

My toes curl in my boots.

"Here you go, ma'am," the deli clerk says.

I take the bread and sliced cheese. When I turn back around, he's gone. On the drive home, I'm silent, pressed to the door.

I wish I could just tell Westin what Thomas did to me, but I can't. If he finds out they hurt me like that, he won't wait to make sure Carter Farms is safe.

He'll do something terrible, I know it.

CHAPTER THIRTY

WESTIN

It feels like I'll be stuck like this forever, sitting up all night with the branches of the oak outside my window blurry in my vision. It was risky bringing her to Sovereign Mountain. I don't regret the sex, but I'm ashamed of putting her in potential danger.

I had no business bringing her back to my bed.

So, I stay back, waiting out every agonizing second until Thomas Garrison is gone. The only solace I find in our separation is that at least she's safe, even if it is in another man's house.

The ranch is quiet for a few days in late fall. Sovereign took Keira to the hunting cabin to round up a few stray horses that escaped during the barn fire at her old farm. Jensen is busy doing construction work in South Platte. I don't have anything to occupy my mind, so I start drinking again.

Not heavily, just a shot when I get in from chores. Then another, maybe two, before I can close my eyes.

It's evening when someone knocks on my door. I'm halfway undressed, but I go and pull it open.

Keira stands outside. Hastily, I button my shirt, mind turning.

Something is wrong, I can feel it. It curls in on the cold wind swirling around her body. It smells like...death. The hair on the back of my neck stands on end.

"What are you doing here?" I murmur, leaning past her to look for Sovereign.

"Gerard left," she whispers.

Her pale, freckled face is blotchy. I don't spend much time with Keira—when she's not up in her room at the ranch house, she's out with the horses or Sovereign—but I know her well enough to see she's been crying hard.

"Okay?" I press.

Her lip quivers. "I was going through a box of Clint's things. There was a black card with a silver dog on it, and...he got really quiet when he saw it and left."

My brows reach my hairline.

Jack fucking Russell.

I snag her elbow and pull her into the gatehouse, shutting the door. She stands in the kitchen, looking so lost that it hurts my chest. When she turns to sit at the table, her hair falls back. My eyes drop to the discreet necklace at the base of her throat. Sovereign put a collar on her.

We stare at each other. I gesture, unsure how to respond. We barely know each other, but for some reason, she came to me for help.

"You want something?" I ask.

"Whiskey," she whispers, voice fragile.

I pour two glasses and sit opposite her. Her eyes are huge, her fingers barely gripping her glass. Her jaw shakes as she takes a drink. Then, she looks at me and, God, I hate myself and I hate Sovereign in this moment. She doesn't deserve all this heartache. Neither does Diane.

"What did the card mean?" she asks.

"That's Jack Russell's calling card," I say.

If Sovereign wants to keep secrets from her, maybe he should have been here tonight. I'm no good when it comes to crying women. I can't refuse her the truth when she has tears rolling down her face.

"Who's Jack Russell?"

"A hitman," I say flatly.

Her chin trembles. Her eyes are like saucers. "Like...an assassin?"

I nod. "Just like that. When you hire Jack to take someone out, he gives you a calling card. When the job's done, he brings a finger, maybe a tooth, as a receipt. Then, he takes the calling card back."

Her eyes dart over the table. I can tell we're both thinking the same thing.

"So my husband paid Jack Russell to kill someone?"

"You don't get a calling card unless Jack gives it to you," I say. "He had a deal. Looks like it didn't pan out. Stroke of good luck for the bastard he paid to kill that he happened to die first."

Her eyes narrow. "I know Gerard killed Clint and forged the will."

It's right then that I decide it isn't my fucking business to keep Sovereign's secrets anymore. Whatever she knows, it's far more than I thought. Sovereign went to go see Jack Russell, which means Clint was going to have someone killed.

My eyes fall on the woman sitting before me.

My stomach goes ice cold. I keep my body relaxed, my face impassive. I've spent enough time lying with my mouth; I can do it with everything else at this point.

If I had to guess, Clint was going to ask Jack to kill his wife, which begs the question—is Diane as safe as I thought?

My ears roar. Keira's asking me something about Gerard, and suddenly, I'm spilling everything onto the table. About his first fiancée, how she was cheating with Clint, the man who may well have been responsible for her death. About his mother dying, his father drinking himself to sleep in a ditch and never waking up.

It all floods out, ugly, like an open wound. All the secrets we hide at Sovereign Mountain.

All except mine. She doesn't ask about mine because nobody does.

Through it all, my knuckles are white, but I keep my fucking composure, because that's what I do best. I sit down, I shut up, I clean up other people's messes. I sit with their crying women while my own heart is breaking.

If the Garrisons were willing to try to kill Keira, what will they do to Diane?

A door slams, and boots crunch over gravel outside. I jerk my head up.

"He's back."

Keira goes pale, nodding. I stand, putting my hand on her shoulder. "Just...trust Sovereign. You'll be safe."

I don't mean to sound dismissive, but I have places to be tonight. The knob turns and the door swings in. Sovereign enters, bringing in the cold on his coat. At his heels is a tall, broad shouldered man with black hair beneath his cowboy hat. His clothes are dark, a gun strapped to his thigh. When he lifts his head, two green eyes glitter back at me.

Jack Russell.

He hangs back. Sovereign's eyes rake over Keira, drunk, at the table. "What are you doing here?" he asks.

Her lip quivers. "I came to talk to Westin."

Sovereign's jaw grits. He jerks his head to the corner, and I step aside with him.

"You let her drink?" he says.

Right now, I'm pissed, and I don't have a good reason. Nobody in this room knows about Diane, but I'm still so fucking angry that they're all wrapped up in their problems without a thought for mine. I know it's not rational, but I want to put my fist into Sovereign's face.

"She was fucked up already," I say pointedly. "She knows everything."

Sovereign's shoulders hunch. "I need to talk to her alone."

"She's hurting," I say. "I hope you don't contribute to that."

He gives me a confused look, stepping away to take Keira by the elbow. They move upstairs, and I'm left with Jack Russell. I swing around, facing him.

"You were going to kill Keira?" I say.

He takes his hat off, running a hand over his hair. "No. I don't kill women or kids, you know that."

"So why give Clint the fucking calling card?" I spit.

"Curiosity," he says, silky voice low. "What's it to you?"

My head is spinning—I need a fucking cigarette. Pushing past him, I pull on my coat and take a pack out of the breast pocket. He follows me out onto the porch and plucks the cigarette I light from my fingers. I'm so strung out, it's all I can do not to take it back and knock him the fuck out.

I need to calm down.

I light up and start pacing back and forth. Jack watches me coolly.

"Sovereign is angry," I say. "He brought you back, which means he's planning on doing it tonight."

"Killing the Garrison brothers?" Jack says. "Seems so."

I stop, turning on him. "There's a woman at Thomas' house. I want her out of there, safe."

The corner of Jack's mouth turns up in a tempered smile.

"There's always a woman," he says.

"I mean it," I say, voice flat. "If anything happens to her, I will hold you and Sovereign responsible. You leave her to me."

"I'm here to kill Garrisons," he says. "I'm not responsible for anything else."

My blood is boiling. Maybe I'm not angry with Sovereign; maybe I'm angry with myself. I swore to keep Diane safe, and I let her sit in that house for months. I should have ignored her pleas to let her save Carter Farms. I should have walked in there the day they took her and put a bullet in both Garrisons.

"What's she to you?" Jack asks.

I take a step closer. "She's mine."

His brows rise at the aggression in my voice, but I don't wait around for him to answer. My boots carry me back through the front door and into my office. Above the mantel is my gun rack. I pull two pistols and a rifle down, take my hat from the hall, and go back out to where Jack stands.

His eyes follow me, watchful.

I shove the rifle into his hand as I walk by, heading down the front steps. Jack's silky voice cuts through, like a gossamer thread.

"Where are you going, gunslinger?"

My steps falter. I look down at the pistol in my hand and on my belt. I'm holding the magazine in my other hand, full of bullets. My eyes rise to the cold sky overhead, the branches of the oak like cracked ice across the gathering clouds.

I waited. I watched. I wanted.

I'm done. It's not my fucking business what happens to anybody else. I don't care if Sovereign knows I've been fucking another man's wife. My pride is irrelevant. My patience is at an end.

I slide the magazine into the pistol, clicking it in place.

"Where I should have gone a long time ago," I say savagely. "I'm going to get my girl back."

I go to the barn and prepare the horses for a hard run. My heart is empty save for blind anger. All I know is that for all his faults, my father would never have waited this long to take what he wanted.

When Sovereign and Jack finally appear, I don't have a fucking word to say as we mount up and ride out into the night.

CHAPTER THIRTY-ONE

DIANE

I haven't heard from Westin in a few weeks.

My heart isn't broken, but it's crumbling.

Soon, there will be nothing left.

Ever since the day Thomas beat me and Avery and David let him, things have been worse. Avery doesn't stop by anymore. I wonder if it's because Thomas is keeping him away.

I know how much he dreads the day his brother finds out the truth about his marriage. As much as he doesn't care what happens to me, he'll do anything to make sure the outside world thinks he's man enough.

Thomas' fatal flaw isn't cruelty: it's weakness. He's a puppet of whoever he desires the good opinion of. In this case, it's Avery.

It's a cold evening in November when Avery finally comes back to the house. I'm cleaning up dinner when his truck rolls up the drive. The headlights flash and the engine dies. He walks in through the front door, and I shrink back against the stove.

In my heart, I know it was him. He somehow saw Westin take me to Sovereign Mountain.

My stomach burns.

He spares me a brief glance as he walks through the kitchen and into Thomas' office, where he's working at his computer. The door closes, and I hear their voices rise and fall. After a while, they start rising more than falling.

Hands shaky, I finish the dishes and wipe my hands. I haven't had a break in hours, and I need the bathroom. Quietly, I tell Billie to stay on the floor before I take off my boots and tiptoe barefoot down the hall. The bathroom shares a wall with Thomas' office, so I'm careful as I close it.

I use the toilet and go to wash my hands. My reflection stares back at me. I'm in jeans and a thin t-shirt. Carefully, I slip the shirt off and touch my ribs. The bruises are almost completely healed. I got lucky; Thomas didn't kick me as hard as he made it look.

The knob jiggles.

My breath catches.

"One moment," I say, but the sound doesn't come out.

The knob turns. I forgot to lock it. The door opens, and Avery walks into the bathroom and shuts the door behind him.

My body tingles with fear. He's in a Henley, sleeves rolled up to his elbows, an unlit cigarette behind his ear. The entire room smells like whiskey, and it makes me wonder if he's sober. It's hard to tell with Avery.

"What are you doing?" I whisper, backing up.

He's positioned so I can't get around him to the door. It hits me just how big the Garrison brothers are. I'm used to seeing them from an arm's length—I try not to get close—but Avery is easily as tall as Westin.

"I don't know how a little bitch like you got my brother so tied up in knots," he drawls, his voice soft.

My mouth is dry. I couldn't talk even if I had the words to counter that.

He reaches up, and I flinch. It feels like he was going to touch my face...but he stops himself.

"You know what they say: thou shalt not covet thy brother's wife," he says. "But are you really my brother's wife if he can't even fuck you?"

I can't get back any further. The towel rack digs into my upper spine.

"Can't?" He mulls over the words. "Or won't because he's got a manipulative little cunt in his ear?"

I wonder distantly if Avery really wants me, or if he just wants to crush the little spirit I have left.

His hand comes out and wraps around my neck. It's not sweet the way it was with Westin. The pressure doesn't spark heat in my body. Instead, it makes me wonder how many breaths I have before his grip goes too tight to draw more.

He pulls me closer. The shirt drops from my hands.

"If he doesn't fuck you, I will," he says. "I made that deal with Corbin to save your farm. Someone's getting your pussy out of it."

He lets me go, and I stumble back. My vision flashes as he turns on his heel and the door slams.

My grace period is done. I crumple to the floor. I don't know who told Avery, if it was Thomas or if he just guessed, but my time is up. I'm surprised I held them off for this long.

I take a moment to cry myself out. Then, I put my shirt back on and leave the bathroom, ignoring Avery and Thomas' stares from the kitchen. They burn on my back as I duck into my bedroom and shut the door. I lean against it and listen until their footsteps fade out the back door.

Heart pounding, I creep to the window, the same one I saw Westin through. They're standing on the porch, smoking.

I'm on my knees on the hard, wooden floor. My hands are weak, but my body is strong. I know Thomas, and if I go as willingly as I can, he won't hurt me. I have my doubts it will be pleasurable, but I don't think he's violent like that.

Avery, on the other hand...I know he is.

Heart in my throat, I wash in the little half bath off my room. My slip hangs on the back of the door. I strip naked and pull it on. Then,

I brush my hair out and dig through my clothes to find my dressing gown. There's no way I'm leaving this room and walking upstairs to Thomas' bed in just a slip. It was bad enough that Avery saw me in my bra a moment ago.

I square my shoulders.

I can do this.

My eyes close. My mind fills with the soft scent of field grass, the cool of Nana's headstone, the silvery willow blowing overhead. Someday, I'll go home, and when my life is done, I'll sleep forever beside the people I loved most.

That and Westin Quinn are the only things I've ever wanted.

I take a deep breath. They took my freedom, but they'll never take my pride. I'm the only granddaughter of the strongest woman I've ever known.

Hands unsteady but heart brave enough to carry me through the night, I walk out to meet them.

Thomas and Avery are still on the back porch, the door hanging open even though it's cold. I wonder where Billie went, maybe out the back to get away from Avery. She hates him.

The front door is unlatched. I turn to head down the front hall and freeze.

Why is the knob turning?

I stumble back, the hair on the back of my neck rising. It swings open, and Gerard Sovereign strides into the hallway, like the first vengeful horse of the apocalypse. Behind him comes Westin, his face hard as stone. Bringing up the rear is a tall man with his face half covered by a dark bandana, his narrowed green eyes zero in on me.

My heart goes crazy.

No, no.

He promised he wouldn't do this until Carter Farms was secure. He promised he wouldn't kill Thomas. My mind goes into overdrive, racking my brain until it starts to sink in.

No, Westin said *he* wouldn't kill Thomas.

He never said Sovereign wouldn't.

Before I can speak, Westin skirts around Sovereign and takes hold of me, dragging me back against his body. I open my mouth, unsure if I want to scream at him or scream to give the Garrisons a fighting chance. I'm so fucking angry right now, I can't see straight.

I don't want death and bloodshed. I just want freedom.

"Hush, darling," Westin breathes against my neck. "We're not here for you."

I kick back, hitting him hard in the shin with a crack. My chest seizes and my vision tunnels. Darkness creeps in like frost.

I can't control my panic. I'm so tired from everything that's happened since that day at the swimming hole. Every fiber of my being is raw and bruised. I think my heart that has been crumbling at the edges for weeks is shattering into a million pieces.

I'm at my breaking point.

"Fuck," Westin snaps.

"Where's your husband?" Sovereign says, his voice low.

My eyes widen, darting back down the hall to the open back door before I can stop myself.

Sovereign nods once. "Take her to the kitchen."

Westin pulls me back, and I let him, because I know his strength intimately. We duck out of view as Sovereign and the man with the covered face disappear down the hall. As soon as they're gone, I expect Westin to release me.

But he doesn't.

White hot rage floods me. I wriggle hard, the terry cloth robe slipping to the floor. I'm in just my slip, nothing underneath.

His hand moves up under my clothes, though not on purpose, and I lose it. Maybe it's how tense my body is from being shut in the bathroom with Avery, but I'm primed for a touch that isn't his, and his skin on mine triggers my survival instinct.

I lash out, hitting him with my nails and leaving bright red scratch marks down his face.

He rears back, shocked.

"Jesus, Diane," he breathes.

My face crumples. "Get away from me," I beg.

We both hear footsteps in the hall. Westin snaps into action, but he doesn't take hold of me again. Instead, he takes his belt off and carries me to the chair, using it to lash me down. I'm too stunned to fight when he forces the tie of the terrycloth robe into my mouth and knots it around my neck.

The same way he did in his bed, with the ball gag.

My heart hurts. My body aches.

This reckoning, right here in the same kitchen Thomas beat me in, is the oncoming train. It's derailed. The impact is shredding my remaining sanity. I don't know how I can come back from tonight.

I feel like I'm drowning.

Distantly, I see Sovereign walk Thomas and Avery into the kitchen and tie them to the remaining chairs. He and the man with green eyes have their guns out. Their voices sound garbled, like I'm listening through water. Avery is running his mouth. Thomas is quiet. I can hear that much.

They're not going to make it through tonight.

Which means, when morning comes, I lose everything.

Everything is hazy, but suddenly, I hear words I understand. Sovereign is talking to me, looking at me. I fix my eyes on him, still so angry, I can hardly breathe.

He circles the table and crouches beside me. He's a lot more frightening up close than I realized—pale eyes cold, lip curled like he tasted blood and he's starving for more.

He pulls the gag from my mouth.

"Diane," he says, his voice a soft rumble, "have you ever fucked another man while married to Thomas?"

I don't know how, but I feel every fiber in Westin's body go tense. He's not even touching my chair, but he crackles like a live wire.

"Come on, Diane," he says, looking up at Thomas. "You can tell Thomas all the dirty things you did. He won't live long enough for it to matter."

The room is so quiet, the little sob that escapes me echoes. Thomas shakes, like this pours salt right into his open wound, the one he thinks I gave him, the one that Avery likes to work away at so it's always oozing blood.

Hurt people hurt people, and Thomas has hurt me deeply. I'd still want him dead if it wasn't for the farm.

I can't look at him. My eyes drop.

"No," Sovereign says, his voice splitting the room. "You look at Thomas and tell him that Westin fucks you so hard, I can hear you scream all the way from the gatehouse."

My breath catches. This time, I glance over my shoulder, and Westin is staring at Thomas and Avery. His neck is flushed, like he's having trouble holding himself back. The veins on his forehead stand out.

Thomas loses his shit. "Just shut the fuck up!" he screams.

"I thought you were interested in the topic of infidelity," Sovereign snaps, rising and circling the table.

My eyes are watering so badly, I have tears etching down my face. My breath comes in short, wheezing gasps. The rope around my body cuts into my breasts.

"Tell me who you paid Jack to kill?" Sovereign orders.

He's talking to Avery and Thomas, but I don't know what the fuck he means. All I know is if I don't get out of these ropes and out of this room, I'm going to die. My chest is so tight, the world spins, my head aches. My vision flickers.

"Just tell him," I beg.

I don't know what's going on, but I want to go home. I want to be back in my little bed with a wire frame and worn sheets.

I want to be rescued.

I want my quilt, my Nana, the sweet scent of hay coming through my window as I fall asleep.

The garbled voices in my ears are split by a sound so loud, it makes me bite down on my tongue. A gunshot, so close to my head that it splinters my ears with pain. Avery is screaming, I'm sobbing, snot and spit running down my chin. Someone is talking, on and on.

Then, it happens again—bang. My head burns from the sound. My eyes flicker into focus. Avery is slumped to the side, blood dripping from his temple. It's thick as it drizzles into his lap.

Everything goes still. My body shakes. I think I screamed, but my body is far below me. Inside, I'm curled up in my bed. Nana holds my head, running her ivory comb through my hair as she hums.

"Revenge belongs to God," she whispers. "But sometimes, God is just a man who loves you enough to save you."

I have to give in.

I have to let go.

These burdens I carry are too heavy for my shoulders.

My head falls back. Nana's face blurs, and I'm being carried. The scent of Westin fills my nose and cold air bites my face. A horse snorts, white mist floating to the black sky.

I'm lifted up, up, up until I wonder if I've died.

But no, I feel the warm sides of a horse against my bare legs. It prances as Westin swings up to sit behind me. His breath burns through my hair, and his arm locks over my body.

"I have you, darling," he says. "And this time, I'm keeping you."

CHAPTER THIRTY-TWO

DIANE

I'm out for two days.

In the periphery of my eyes, I catch glimpses of Westin as I move in and out of sleep. He sits on the bed, smoothing back my hair. He gives me water. Once, he asks me to eat. I can't get any words past my cracked lips. Inside, it feels like I've been stripped raw enough to bleed.

Nana visits me. She sits in the corner in a rocking chair. She doesn't speak, but it feels like she's telling me she's pleased.

She just hums that tune, sweet and low.

It's early morning some days later when I finally surface and stay conscious. The bedroom is empty, and the curtains are pulled back. Through them, the world is covered in a thick blanket of glittering white, so intense that I have to squint.

My mouth tastes like dust. My head is light, but the sense of impending doom in my chest I've had since I married Thomas is gone.

Every joint in my body protests as I push myself up to sit against the pillows. I'm in a man's t-shirt, and it smells like Westin. The faint scent of coffee tinges the air. My stomach tightens in response. For the first time in weeks, I think I might have an appetite.

I want to get up, but I don't trust my legs to hold me.

Instead, I lean back and pull the quilt up around my waist. My chest is empty, like it was scooped out with a big spoon. I'm raw and so tired. My head tells me I must have slept for days. My body is begging for me to curl back up and sleep a few more.

I hear boots on the step.

My mind goes into overdrive. It's Thomas or Avery.

I have to get up and run.

The door opens, and Westin leans in the doorway. He's in one of his worn blue button downs, work pants, and boots. I can tell he was outside—he smells like winter.

He fixes those bright hazel eyes on me, and my chest heaves.

"I have to go back, don't I?" I whisper, tears welling up.

He's at my side in a second, pulling me into his arms. My cheek presses into his firm shoulder, and I sink deep into his embrace.

"No, darling," he says. "You never have to go back."

"But what about Thomas? What about the farm?" I gasp, tears slipping down.

"Thomas is dead, and you're safe," he says.

I hear his voice, feel it rumble in his chest, but I can't absorb it.

"My farm?"

"I promise, I'll handle it."

The little bit of strength I have left wants to get dressed and go down to Carter Farms. My brain tells me that makes no sense. There's several feet of snow outside right now. It's the dead of winter. David could sell, but no one will try to build a road through my farm until spring.

Mercifully, I have time. I pull back. Westin brushes my hair from my face.

"I want you to eat something," he says.

"Avery? What happened to Avery?" my voice cracks.

"Sovereign shot him," Westin says.

It hits me like a wall of bricks crashing down. I never have to go back. No more nights with a rope around my wrist and a gun under my bed. No more living on high alert, waiting for the sound of tires on the driveway. No more trying to guess if Avery and Thomas are drunk enough to hurt me, or if they'll just fall asleep.

"What happens now?" I whisper.

He brushes his lips over my forehead. "Nothing until the winter breaks."

A sob claws up my throat. I cover my mouth, but it's too late. He turns me in his arms, forehead knitted. I cover my mouth with my other hand too. Tears break free and spill down my cheeks.

"Darling." His voice is so gentle.

No man has ever spoken to me as gently as Westin does.

He pries my hands away, and the sobs release like a dam crashing down. My body shakes. I can't breathe. I'm a limp mess against his chest, crying so hard, I can't tell what's snot or tears or saliva. His shirt is soaked. His hand is on the back of my neck, his arm around me.

"I was so scared," I burst out, my words slurred.

"I know, I know, baby girl. I'm so fucking sorry," he says, his voice a hoarse rumble. "You're never leaving me again. You're safe."

He doesn't tell me to stop crying. He's the first person to let me sob it all out.

I'm so deeply hurt. Marrying Thomas, living in fear of Avery, laying awake and longing for home in the dark, watching Sovereign blow a hole in Avery's head—it changed me.

I'm not the girl Westin met all those months ago. I think I might have too many wounds to ever be that girl again.

My sobs quiet down. Finally, I can breathe evenly. I touch my puffy face, the skin tender. Westin shifts me in his lap and turns my chin up. The gaze he fixes on me is sober, the lines of his face around it stern.

"You've been fighting against giving up control for a long time, Diane," he says. "That's done."

"Westin—"

"I said, it's done."

My voice falters, and I fix him with a teary stare.

"You let me handle this situation from now on," he says, not unkindly. "It's not your job anymore. I fucked up. I never should have let you stay in that house. From now on, you let me keep you safe. Understood?"

I don't know how to be taken care of. Numbly, I shake my head, but I can't come up with the words to tell him that. He studies my face for a moment before picking me up and taking me to the bathroom. I sit in the chair by the door while he runs a bath.

My head is fuzzy, my eyes sticky. My fight is all used up, washed away by my tears. When he takes my shirt off and lifts me into the tub, I let him move me like I'm a doll. I just lay with my head against the porcelain edge of the tub while he untangles my hair.

My heart is numb. His touch is the only thing holding me together.

"I tried," I whisper. "I did try, Westin."

His fingers go still, and then his lips graze the top of my head.

"I wish I knew how bad it was, darling," he says. "I'm taking this out of your hands now. Understood?"

I swallow, throat dry.

"Say it," he urges gently.

My lips part, my eyes close, and all I can see are the branches of the willow tree moving in the breeze over Nana's grave. I hear the hum of cicadas in the afternoon, the soft chirp of crickets at night. Through it all runs the soft current of the river where he kissed me for the first time, the swimming hole where he caught me in his arms and made me his in the dirt.

Slowly, I sit up and turn. Our eyes meet.

"Are you really a bad man?" I ask.

I still sound so childish. He clears his throat.

"I don't know, darling," he says. "But even if I am, I'm in your corner."

I touch his shoulder, moving my hand under his shirt, over skin warm like sunshine. The hard ridges of his scarred brand brush my fingertips.

Gunslinger.

I think that, even if Westin is a dangerous man, he might be a good one. The world hasn't been kind to him, but he's not like Thomas or David. His shoulders might be heavy, his body scarred, but he's not bitter.

No, he's bright, like the sun—pure and lethal.

My dry lips part. "I understand."

He doesn't speak after that. I'm exhausted enough to let him do whatever he wants. His mouth is set in a grim line as he washes my body and dries it. Then, he pulls a clean shirt over my head and puts me back in bed.

He wants me to eat. I'm starving, so I obediently let him feed me broth and toast. One spoonful, one bite, at a time. When I'm done, he pulls the covers up to my chin.

"You sleep," he says firmly.

He moves back, but I take his hand. When he crouches down, I'm acutely aware of him in a way I haven't been before. He's big, his presence filling the room. It's warm skin, rough fabric.

It's home.

I look down at his hand in mine. He's always had so many scars. I assumed they were from barbed wire, but now, I'm not so sure.

"Promise?" I whisper.

He doesn't ask what he's promising; he just nods. I release his hand and burrow down under the covers. The world is cold and frightening, but I'm safe here with him.

Hazily, I see him across the room in the chair by the fireplace. He's sitting with his long legs stretched out, just watching me until I finally close my eyes.

CHAPTER THIRTY-THREE

WESTIN

I'm eaten alive by guilt.

She was never safe there. I should never have listened to her. I should have paid attention instead and acted, regardless of what she wanted. But I was so consumed by what I wanted—her—that I didn't realize how much she was willing to endure to save her land.

I'll regret that until I die.

And I'm going to do everything I can to fix it.

I take Rocky, and we retrieve Thomas' body. It's frozen solid, which makes it easier to pull behind as I ride back out to his house. Avery still sits at the table, his body bound. Before I left, I took a second to turn off the heat. He's frozen too.

My breath rises in white puffs as I drag Thomas' body into the kitchen and drop it on the floor. Then, I move to the bedroom, a thick bandana over my face, to where Diane slept.

Hanging from the ceiling is a rope, looped through a metal hook. It's tied to the door, and there's a knotted end laying on the bed. It takes me a second, but I realize it's an alarm system.

I pull back the pillow. Underneath is Jensen's gun.

It's no wonder she slept for days. She lived in a prison of fear, never knowing when the Garrisons would turn on her. Guilt, now familiar, floods my chest. If I had known it was this bad, I would have shot them all and taken her home, to hell with what she or Sovereign wanted.

I'd have dragged her kicking and screaming out of here.

Her things are ice cold in the dresser drawer. I gather them up, but she barely has anything of worth. Her toiletries consist of a bar of soap, a plastic razor, and two pads in a plastic bag.

In the end, I take only her copy of *Canterbury Tales* and the gun. Then, I retrieve a container of gas from the barn and douse the lower floor of the house. With another jug of gas, I soak the second level until it's dripping through the floorboards.

At the front door, I light a match. I want this house and the bodies in it burnt to ash.

I move to the barn, which still has electricity, and refill the horse's food and water. They all have access to a round hay bale, so they're not starving, and their water has a heating unit.

Someone from South Platte will see the smoke before sundown. Animal control will be out here to gather the horses before they run out of food.

I'm almost out the door when I hear a low whine. From the corner of my eye, I see a white and gray shape crouched in the dark, far corner.

It's Billie.

Crouching, I click my fingers. "Come here, Billie."

At the sound of her name, she crawls out on her belly and slinks to me. I rub behind her ears, her long hair matted with ice and dirt. I know she's starving, probably not in any fit shape to run back to Sovereign Mountain.

Rising, I find some rope and call Billie out to the yard. Rocky stands while I hoist her up and swing into the saddle behind her. Surprisingly, Billie lets me secure her with crisscrossed ropes to my torso. She probably would have held still on her own, but I don't want to risk hurting her. She means a lot to Diane.

We head back up to Sovereign Mountain. The sun is higher, and it's almost noon when I get back to the gatehouse. Normally, I'd go to Sovereign and let him know that the house is burning, but he's inside with Keira, and I don't want to disturb them.

After Rocky is dried and put away in his warm stall, I walk the plowed path to the gatehouse. Billie follows me without prompting. When we get to the door, she pushes her nose in the crack while I'm unlocking it and inhales. Her tail swishes.

"She's inside," I say.

Billie whines.

I unlock the door, and Billie cranes her neck around the corner, clearly hesitant. My eyes roam over the room and fall on a sight I wasn't expecting.

Diane is out of bed. Her golden hair is braided over her shoulder. Her body is engulfed in one of my red flannels that falls to her knees. The house smells of coffee, and something crackles on the stove.

I pause. This is it—my home, right here.

"Diane," I say.

She looks up, and Billie lets out a yelp before she propels through the door. Their bodies collide so hard, Diane lands on her ass. Billie whines and whips back and forth so hard, I fear she's going to crack in half.

"I think she missed you," I say, kicking my boots free of snow and shutting the door.

Diane scrambles to her feet. "Do you have any dog food?"

"There's some up at the house," I say.

She bites her lip. I know she's not ready to go up to the house where everyone else lives. I go to the fridge and pull out some chicken breast left over from a few nights ago. Diane takes the bag from me and tears it into shreds, reaching for a bowl.

"Give her a handful and see if it stays down," I say. "She hasn't been fed in a few days so her stomach is sensitive. I'll get the dog food later."

She nods, obeying. Billie shoves down the chicken and starts rummaging for more. I click my fingers once, making a sharp noise. She backs up and sits.

"Good girl," I say. "You lay down."

She slinks to the living room and curls up on the rug before the fire. Diane watches her with a strange look on her face, almost wistful.

"Thank you for finding her," she says. "I know you probably didn't want to go out in the cold."

I decide not to mention I actually went out to burn the Garrisons and their home. Instead, I take her by the waist and pull her against me. She's too thin; she needs to rest and recover.

"I wish you'd told me how bad it was at the Garrisons'," I say.

She shakes her head. "You wouldn't have let me stay."

"No, I wouldn't have." My voice is tinged with cold.

She shakes back her flyaway hairs and, for the first time in a year, I see a tiny flicker of the girl I met before all the sweetness and hope was taken from her eyes.

Right then and there, I swear to myself I'll do anything I can so she can be soft again. When summer comes, she'll be sun-kissed, in the passenger side of my truck, my hat on her blonde head, not a single care in the world.

"Diane," I say. "What can I do to fix this?"

Her brows draw together. "You mean when you lied to me?"

I shake my head. "No, I don't regret that. You're hardheaded, darling. You'd have let them kill you to save your land, I see that now. I'm so fucking sorry."

She touches my chin. "It's not your fault."

My mind flashes with a single image: my father, standing at the edge of the woods by our house. He takes two bullets from his pocket and fits them into the shotgun. I stare up at him, the sun making my eyes stream. He's big and strong, my father.

"Let me tell you something, son," he says. "We're just complicated animals. At the end of the day, it's survival of the fittest."

I don't understand what that means, but I remember the silhouette of my father as he clicks the gun into place and lifts it. A shot rings out.

He ejects the casing with a savage snap. "Now, go on, let me teach you how to gut an animal."

Diane is saying something. I jerk back to the present. Maybe my father was right to raise me the way he did. Maybe if I'd been more like him, Diane would never have endured so much pain at the hands of the Garrisons.

My father shot first and took what he wanted.

I hesitated. I waited.

And now, her light is dimmed.

I put her hand in mine and kiss her forehead. She gives me a little smile. I sit down at the head of the table with the ghost of my father hanging over my head. Diane makes up my plate and sets it before me. When she turns to leave, I catch her arm and pull her into my lap.

"I need you to know that I'm never leaving you alone again," I say quietly.

Her eyes are big, staring up at me. "It's okay."

"No," I say. "It will *never* happen again."

She purses her mouth, startled by something in my face. Then, she nods.

"I understand," she whispers.

She wriggles out of my grasp, and I let her go for the price of another kiss. Then, she brings her plate and sits beside me. We eat in silence and have coffee, steam rising from our silent table.

It feels like the beginning of peace.

CHAPTER THIRTY-FOUR

DIANE

The snow is so deep, the entire ranch hunkers down to wait it out. That means I'm in Westin's house, alone with him.

He doesn't sleep in the bed with me. He stretches his long body out in the chair by the fireplace and closes his eyes. For the first few nights, I wake in a panic, see him in the chair, and my heart slows.

The firelight flickers on his face, and I'm safe again.

For the first time since Nana died, I'm safe.

I'm not sure if it has been a few days or over a week, but one morning, I wake early feeling more normal than I have in months. I shower, using his shampoo because I don't have any. It's the cheap kind, from the gas station, but it feels like luxury after what I've been using. After I'm dried and in his flannel, I go downstairs.

He only has bacon and eggs in the fridge. I'm learning that Westin doesn't care for luxuries. As long as it's functional and neat, he's pleased.

I put the cast iron pan on the stove and start frying. The house is so quiet. He must have taken Billie with him, because she's nowhere to be found.

Quietly, I pad back upstairs. In his room, I open the closet.

This is my first look into the little things that make up Westin Quinn. My stomach flips. Everything smells good, like him.

Inside are a half dozen button down shirts, mostly blue, but one green and the other tan. He wears plain dark blue work pants, and it looks like he has one good belt. It hangs on the back of the door, next to a black hat with less wear and tear than the one he uses every day.

There's a cabinet at the back of the closet. I prop the door open and step inside. My jaw drops.

On one side of the cabinet are several pistols and rifles, all glossy and clean. The other side are...things that make my brows rise to my hairline. A black leather crop that looks like it's never been touched. The collar he put on me, the one I never had a chance to look at that night. My hand shakes as I pick it up, turning it over in my hands.

Soft black leather. Yellow silk inside.

I turn it over, and heat floods my body.

Diane Quinn.

My heart picks up, going wild. Quickly, I put the collar back in the exact place I found it. There are other items—a jumble of silver, black, and the scent of expensive leather—but I shut the cabinet door fast.

I don't think I was supposed to see those words.

At least, not yet.

That's what I get for not minding my own business. I feel like I should be sorry, but I'm not. Instead, I'm warm and restless between my legs.

Maybe I finally feel safe enough for desire again.

I think I hear boots on the walkway outside. I shut the closet door and hurry down the hall. In the kitchen, the bacon is sizzling on low. I run to the cupboard and start taking two mugs out. The doorknob turns, and Westin fills the house with his presence, Billie at his heels.

I turn, offering him a smile. He kicks his boots clean and shuts the door, joining me in the kitchen.

"Come here, darling," he says.

I let him take me by the arm and pull me near. For the first time, I'm in a kitchen where a man's touch doesn't mean something bad.

God, it feels so good.

He kisses me, and then he brushes my hair back, his eyes lingering on my face.

"What?" I whisper.

He shakes his head. "Nothing. You just look pretty."

My mind goes back to his cupboard of guns and sex toys. Diane Quinn—that's what he put on that collar. He really does mean to marry me.

"Want some coffee?" I whisper.

He nods. I make coffee, and he takes his coat off and feeds Billie. He sits at the head of the kitchen table, knees spread, and watches me cook. I find I don't mind cooking for just us. It's cozy.

I set a plate of bacon, eggs, and toast before him. Then, I sit down with my own plate, even though it feels so strange to eat at the main table instead of my room or the back porch.

He takes a sip of coffee. I watch him steadily.

"It's good," he says. "But everything you make is good."

I smile, and it feels so natural, like when he used to visit me at Carter Farms. We eat in silence, just the gas fireplace burning in the living room. Billie lays down at my feet and sighs.

There's a lump in my throat, the good kind.

He sets his plate aside. "What do you like?"

I falter, unsure what he means.

"You like books, flowers," he says. "You like being outside, but out of those, all I can get for you is books. What else do you like?"

I stare at him. "I don't know."

He puts his hand on his thigh. "Come here, Diane."

The way he says it—it's like warm sunshine and whiskey. I go like I'm being drawn by a magnet. He pulls me into his lap and tucks a bit of hair behind my ear.

"Just pick something. Any little thing you like," he says.

I wrack my brain. "In the general store, they have a row of candy on the cash register. I used to get a piece every time I did the shopping for Nana."

His lids flicker. "The general store on main?"

I nod. He clears his throat, like that means something. "What kind?"

I consider it. "I like the Lemon Chews."

His throat bobs. He keeps looking at me like he can't believe I'm here. It's blinding, being at the center of his attention.

"What do you like, Mr. Quinn?" I ask.

The corner of his mouth jerks up. "You, mostly."

I can't bite back my smile. His hand goes around the back of my neck, and he pulls me in, kissing me hard, the way he used to. This time, it's so sweet because I know he doesn't have to leave before the end of the day.

I get him all to myself.

Neither of us feel like talking. Instead, he kisses me until I'm hot under my flannel. His hands are gentle on my waist and neck. His mouth starts out soft, but then it gets harder until I feel his need in every touch.

He has to do some repair work on the barn. I clean up breakfast, and he goes upstairs for a bit. It's a minute later, and he comes back down to kiss me before going out. When I head back to the bathroom in the hall, I find a little bag of toiletries: a bottle of women's shampoo, a bar of flowery soap, a metal razor, a pack of tampons, a nail file. It's not much, but I know he'll get me more when the snow melts.

I take a luxurious bath. I finally have time to kill and nothing to do.

No dishes to wash. No floors to scrub.

It's heaven.

Instead, I take my time scrubbing my skin until it's soft. I shave and file my nails until they're smooth and oval. I haven't felt this kempt before in my life.

Maybe when he goes into town, he can get me a little bit of makeup.

I dry off and stand before the mirror in the bedroom. My body is thin. There are oven burns on my forearms. That's not the worst part, though.

The worst part is how hollow my eyes are.

I wrap my arms around my body. It's fragile, but inside, I think I could be strong again. If he keeps me safe like this for a few months, I can bounce back.

I know I can.

Thomas beat me down, but he didn't break me.

I still want to live.

In the bathroom, I find some lotion. I take my time rubbing it into my skin. Then, I pull on his flannel again and go downstairs to find a distraction.

I rummage in his pantry and freezer. I find canned chicken and vegetables, enough to make soup. While it simmers, I start rolling out pie crust. The butter is frozen solid, but I manage to warm it enough to use. By the time he comes in, smelling like ice and horses, there's a canned cherry pie on the counter.

He stops short, his jacket in his hand.

"You don't have to cook, darling," he says.

I nod once. "I know."

He kisses me. We don't talk during dinner, but I swear he doesn't take his eyes off me the entire time. The soup is thin because I couldn't find everything we needed, but it's warm and the broth is good. Afterwards, he sends me upstairs and tells me he'll clean the kitchen.

In the bedroom, I have to take a moment. The air in the house is thick with tension. When I sat across from him, it crackled like a summer storm.

It's only going to get worse when he comes up to sleep in the chair.

I brush my teeth then crawl into bed in just his flannel. I don't have anything else to wear. After a while, he comes up and goes into the bathroom. I curl up on my side and pretend to close my eyes, but I watch the strip of light under the door.

My heart beats—*thump, thump, thump.*

The gas fireplace is on low. Through the window, stars hang low in the velvet sky. I swear, there's a little bit of old, dark magic at Sovereign Mountain. Sometimes, at night, it feels like something out of a storybook.

The bathroom light turns off. The door opens.

Fuck, he looks good.

Oblivious, he goes to the chair and sits, stretching his legs out and leaning back. My eyes trail over the line of hair, the V of his lower abs, down to the band of his sweatpants.

Between my thighs, I ache, empty and sensitive and wet. I shift my hips, squeezing my legs. Pleasure ripples.

I think I might need him.

I push the covers back and swing my legs over the edge of the bed. He turns his head, but it's too dark to make out his expression.

"Darling?" he says.

Instead of answering, I climb onto his lap in the chair and straddle him. He inhales sharply, his hands sliding over my hips.

I pull the flannel over my head and toss it to the floor.

"Goddamn," he says reverently.

Up until now, sex with him was a guilty pleasure. We did it quickly, knowing he had to leave or with the heavy cloud of Thomas over our heads. For the first time, our bodies touch, and there's no one but us in the room.

No guilt, no fear, no shame.

"Do you remember when you said you like when I called you sir?" I whisper.

"Yes." The words are hoarse.

I slip my hand down over his naked chest, scarred, with short, coarse hair. Warm and so safe.

"Please, fuck me," I say aloud. "Sir."

I can't see his face, just the glint of his eyes. He spits into his hand and slips it between my thighs. Rough fingertips touch where I ache. My head falls back, and a moan works its way out. Then, he pushes down the front of his sweatpants.

He's hot and hard against my sex. I wrap my hand over his, around his length.

He feels like life.

Together, we guide his cock between my legs. I gasp, and he swears under his breath as the head slips inside. I'm soaked, but it still twinges as he stretches me to take him.

"Take me, darling," he says, voice dropping to a rasp.

My hands move to his chest, nails digging in. He takes me by the waist and fucks up into me until every inch of his cock is buried in my pussy, until I swear I feel the head of his cock stroking against my cervix, giving me a hint of pain with my pleasure.

He makes me want that edge.

"What does it feel like for you?" I gasp.

He rocks me on his length. "Inside you? You feel like velvet. Warm, tight, so wet."

My head falls back, and the ceiling swims.

"Grip me, darling," he tells me.

I obey, tightening my muscles around him. He groans, fucking harder. High with pleasure, I reach between our bodies. He slows, letting me explore where we join together.

My pussy is soft, and it wraps around his hard, veined cock. Our heartbeats thump as one. My fingers come away wet. He catches my wrist, licking them clean.

"You taste so sweet," he rasps.

He takes me around the waist and lifts me. Still inside, we move to the floor before the fire and sink down. There's a soft rug beneath my body, Westin over it. To my left, the fire flickers.

Maybe I could find pure happiness with him right here, on the floor by the fire, in a world where it's too cold for anything bad to happen. Deliriously, I believe it.

"Please," I beg.

My reservations are gone. I want it the way it used to be—intoxicating and new. He pulls from me and kicks off his pants. Then, he kneels, drawing my hips onto his thighs. In the firelight, I can see his eyes roll back as he pushes his cock into me. Warmth seeps deep into my veins.

"Mine," he says. "My girl."

There's no room for argument. I don't want to protest tonight. Tomorrow, we can figure out the farm and our future. Tonight, our bodies are finding each other again.

He fucks me hard, hips rising and falling, sweat etching down his chest and stomach, head back and eyes heavy.

"Please, sir," I gasp.

He grips my breast, teasing my nipple with his thumb. "Do you want to come?"

I nod hard.

He pulls out and rolls to the ground beside me. I shift back, unsure what he wants until he moves me to straddle his face.

"Grind yourself," he orders.

"What?"

He lifts me up, bringing me up to his chest. "Grind that sweet, wet pussy on my face, darling. Get yourself off into my mouth."

Arousal rushes through me like I did a shot of whiskey. I don't know how to do this, but he's already pulling me over his face. He's already groaning and dragging his tongue over my sex in hungry strokes.

The heat of the fire on my side is nothing on the inferno between my legs. He holds me steady. Slowly, I start riding him the way I did in the chair. It must be right, because when I look over my shoulder, he's rock hard.

Pleasure builds quickly. It starts like a little itch, and I have to grind on his mouth to scratch it. Then, it's warmth, it's fire. It's a flood and he's licking me like he's starving while I come against his face.

My body goes weak as my orgasm ebbs. I push myself down until I straddle his hips. His cock twitches beneath my thigh.

He runs a hand over his face. "Fuck, girl, I could drink you neat."

He's so filthy, and I melt for it every time. My nails drag down his chest, marking him.

"Take me the way you like," I whisper.

There's no argument. He carries me to the bed, and I fall to my back. Then, he's between my legs and buried so deep inside me, I cry out from the shock.

The bed slams into the wall. I feel everything in his body crashing into mine. All the heartache. The separation. His frustration. Pounding into me again and again.

He thrusts into me one last time, and inside, where I'm tender from his roughness, I feel him twitch. His lids flicker, his spine arches. Then he lets out a soft "fuck" and goes still.

There's a sharp twinge in my stomach as he pulls out. I try to bite back my gasp, but he hears it.

"You alright?" he asks.

"Yes," I whisper.

He leans over and turns on the lamp. I look down and freeze. Red streaks his lower abdominals and my thighs. We both go quiet, shocked by the sudden scent of metal.

"Oh," I say.

"Well, you won't get pregnant," he says.

Is that a note of disappointment? He gets up and disappears into the bathroom, coming back with a dark towel.

"I haven't had my period since right after we slept together last," I say.

"That was weeks ago."

I nod. "I think...I think my body feels safe now."

He looks at me with an unreadable expression. Then, he leans in and kisses me hard, like he wants to sear my mouth to his forever. I fall back as he eases me down, kissing my neck, moving lower to trace it around my navel and kiss each hip bone. Then, he goes lower, and I jerk back.

"What are you doing?"

He looks up, cocking his head. "Eating you out."

"What?" I whisper, horrified.

He just gives me a look and disappears under the quilt. It's sinking in that Westin isn't the sort of man I can tame or bend to my will.

He's hungry, and he'll do what it takes to satisfy it. He's not interested in hearing the word no from me or anybody else.

He makes me come until I'm begging him to stop. Then, he flips me onto my stomach, pushing a sacrificial pillow under my hips. I'm tender as he eases himself deep inside.

"Whore," he breathes. "Beautiful whore, my whore."

He fucks me, holding me by the nape of the neck, and I'm weak when he's done. I lay on my back while he catches his breath, and I count the crimson kisses he left on my body.

Then, we go again. The bed is going to be a mess in the morning, but neither of us care.

Our bodies move under the sheets. The bed frame creaks. Outside, the world is frozen, but beneath the quilt, we plant seeds that will bloom into flowers when spring comes.

CHAPTER THIRTY-FIVE

WESTIN

I'm shaken by the sex we had last night, so shaken that I go into the office downstairs and take out the contract I drew up around the time I bought that ring. I think it's time to come clean with her and talk about what I want this relationship to look like. She told me what she wants. It's time for me to do the same.

Working quickly, I rewrite it, keeping it simple, straightforward, making sure it focuses on giving her what she needs most.

She's still sleeping when I find her. I lay it on the bedside table and shut the door behind me.

When I come in from morning chores, she's in the kitchen. Our eyes meet, and her cheeks go pink.

"Come here," I say.

She dries her hands and obeys. I take her by the back of the neck and kiss her mouth, tasting the coffee on her tongue. I move my kiss from her lips to her neck. She moans, and her hand grips the front of my open coat.

"Westin," she whispers.

I pull back. "What is it, darling?"

"I need some real clothes."

I shrug out of my coat and lay it aside. "I like you naked."

She gives me a look, her lips pressed together. "I'm being serious."

I watch her body, covered in just my t-shirt, sway to the sink. The stove crackles, and the house smells like breakfast. I haven't asked her to make food—I don't mind making it myself, but she does it anyway. She's a good cook, better than the Garrisons deserved.

"Sovereign and I should have the drive cleared by the end of today," I say. "The roads are clear enough to get to South Platte."

"Can I make a list?"

I sink down at the table. "I thought you liked calling me sir. You don't do it outside of sex much."

Her forehead creases. "I didn't agree to anything yet, despite the...papers you left in the bedroom."

"You saw those?"

"They were a bit of a shock."

I cock my head. "So you read the part where I said I'd like you to address me properly."

Her mouth is doing that thing again, that little twist, like she's fighting against herself. She's balking at the idea of being submissive. Her pride appears to have decided that desire isn't enough.

I push my chair out and pat my thigh once. "Come here."

She sits. The shirt hitches up, and I'm acutely aware of her bare pussy against my work pants.

"Do you want to give up control to me?" I ask.

Her brows knit. "What does that mean?"

"It means you let me be the Dominant in this relationship, and I'll care for you," I say. "But you're still in control. Your submission is always voluntary, darling."

Her eyes are round. "What's the purpose of that?"

I brush her hair back and touch her chin. "You're afraid of losing control, Diane, but you want to know how good it feels to give it up. I want that too."

Her breasts heave. Under my shirt, her nipples harden. She's at war with herself, but I know I'll win out. I won last night when I went down under the sheets. I saw her give in. Maybe she doesn't know it yet, but her armor is cracked.

"It's a deal, Mr. Quinn," she says hoarsely.

"I'll hold you to that, Miss Carter. Now, go on upstairs and get the contract. We're going over it while we eat."

She obeys. I wash up in the sink and fill two plates with sausage and eggs before setting them on the table. The coffee is poured, and I'm waiting with a pen when she returns. Her eyes move over me, like she wants to hesitate, but she sinks down in the chair beside me.

"Open it up," I say. "Show me any questions you have."

She flips through. The contract is short and contains the usual things—safewords, honorifics, aftercare, indicators of consent. There's one page at the beginning with specifics. She flips to it and points.

"That. What is the point of that?"

I have to bite back a smile.

The submissive agrees to be used freely by the Dominant, before and during the night, two days a week, on Tuesdays and Thursdays. These sessions will be followed by aftercare, as per usual. An anklet will be worn to indicate consent.

"Oh, that's just for fun," I say.

Her brows arch. "Maybe I don't want fun."

I slip my hand between her thighs and find her clit. A little gasp escapes her as my fingertip works it.

"You're holding so tightly to control with both hands, darling," I say.

Her eyes are round, her lips are parted. I've struck a chord. She drags her gaze back down to the second page, and her shoulders sink as she releases a long breath.

"I don't even want what I'm holding onto," she whispers.

"Diane," I say quietly, "this contract gives us a space that's just for us. You want to heal, to be safe and let go. This is the safety net that lets you do that."

There's a long silence. She wraps her arms around her body. I reach across and pick her up, putting her in my lap.

"You read the contract front to back upstairs?" I ask.

She nods, eyes down, like she's guilty about something. I take the pen, put it in her fingers, and flip to the last page.

"Sign it," I say.

Her lips part as she glances over her shoulder. I bury my face into her neck and inhale. She smells like soft sunshine. My hand slips into her lap and slides beneath the hem of my shirt.

"Spread your legs, darling," I whisper.

She does as she's told. Her eyes flutter shut.

"No, keep your eyes open," I correct, finding her clit between her thighs. It's warm, and her pulse thrums beneath my fingers. My halfway hard cock hardens the rest of the way.

"Pick up the pen," I say.

My touch goes faster, ghosting over where she's most sensitive. She hovers the pen over the paper.

Her muscles flutter around me, soft like velvet.

The ink touches the paper. She has a beautiful signature, laced across the page. The pen hits the table, and her head falls back. Her soft mouth parts, and a moan slips out.

"Good girl."

My hand leaves her pussy, and her eyes open. She turns and fixes me with a crestfallen gaze.

"I'll give it to you when you're ready," I say. "Now, go eat."

She sinks back into her seat. She's a little drunk with arousal, but not too drunk to finish her breakfast. I'm quiet as I clean my plate.

"What happened to Thomas?" she asks, after a while.

I set my fork down and take a sip of coffee. "He got shot," I say.

Her face stays the same. "How?"

"Keira shot him," I say. "Sovereign's woman. She used to be Clint's wife."

"I know who Keira is." Her brows rise. "How did that happen?"

"Well, I brought you back and went out to find Sovereign," I say. Part of me wishes I could keep ugliness away from her, but she deserves to know. "Thomas broke free after Avery was shot, ran out and took a horse from the barn. Sovereign and Jack went after him."

"Is Jack the man with the covered face?"

"He is."

"How do you know Jack?"

I work my jaw, unsure if I'm ready to tell her that. Truthfully, the day I had my back branded, one person showed up to help, and that was Jack Russell. He appeared as quickly as he did when we killed the Garrisons, and he was gone as soon as the action was over—the antithesis of a fair weather friend.

"I just do," I say.

She purses her lips. I take another sip of coffee.

"Keira went after Sovereign in the morning and found him up by the river," I say. "Thomas was there; he shot Sovereign, just grazed him, so Keira shot him."

I can tell she's thinking this over. Her dark eyes are hard like stone.

"I wish I was brave like that," she says finally.

"What you did to save your farm was brave."

She shakes her head. "But I didn't save it."

I take her hand. "You've carried this long enough. I'm carrying it the rest of the way."

Her eyes flick to mine, big and sad. "What are you going to do?"

"Trust me," I say.

She looks away. Truthfully, when the snow has melted from the mountains, I'm going to find David Carter and finish him. When he's done, I'm moving on to Corbin Buchanan and putting a stop to the road. If I have to do that with a bullet, I will.

The gunslinger will do what he does best.

CHAPTER THIRTY-SIX

DIANE

Later in the week, Westin comes back from the store with two large bags of clothing. It takes a while to do a run into town, so I was alone most of the day. I thought about venturing to the ranch house in hopes of some female companionship, but it turns out being locked up by Thomas made me shy. I'm not sure how to make friends.

I climb down the stairs when I hear the door. Westin sets the bags on the table and takes me by the wrist to pull me in. When he kisses me, he tastes cold.

"How was going into town?" I ask.

"The roads are clear," he says. "Bring your things upstairs and make sure I got what you wanted."

I turn to go, and he spanks me across the ass. My entire body freezes, and then it remembers his touch is good. His touch is safe.

"Go on," he says.

Face warm, I bring my bags upstairs and shut the door. I hear Westin whistle for Billie in the yard. She likes Westin; he's the first man she seems to care about.

I spill the first bag out onto the bed. There are jeans, leggings, t-shirts, and more in three different sizes. I sort through and pull all the correct sizes out and bag the rest back up. The second bag is loungewear, like sweatsuits. At the bottom are bras and panties. It figures that he got those sizes exactly right.

His boots ring out on the stairs. I gather everything up and put it in the laundry basket. The door opens, and he enters, filling the room with his big presence.

"Thank you," I say.

His lids flicker. "Thank you, *sir*."

"Do you really expect me to use that all the time when we're alone?" I frown.

He taps my chin once. "Really, I do."

"Why are you trying to break me?" The words slip out before I can stop them.

"What gave you that idea? Darling, I don't want you to change, but I need you to understand that I'm all in and this is the language that makes the most sense to me. All I want is for you to work on feeling safe."

I hesitate, gnawing my lip. What he describes sounds heavenly. I'm tired; I want to be taken care of for a while.

"Are you sure you just don't want kinky sex?" I whisper.

The corner of his mouth turns up. "Of course I do, but only with you."

He draws near, turning my head with his jaw so he can kiss my mouth. A strand of hair falls over his forehead. I reach out and brush it away.

"Why are you like this?" I whisper.

He sobers, quick as a flash. "Like what?" he asks, warily.

Maybe I should stop talking, but I don't.

"I don't know you, Westin," I say. "You seemed like one thing when we met, but then you felt so dark...like I should be afraid of you. Maybe I should have listened, because...I fantasized about killing Thomas, but I would have never done it. You don't seem to care that you just walked in and shot everyone."

His hazel eyes are guarded. "I didn't shoot anyone," he says.

"You know you played a big part," I say. "And...I sort of wonder how many times you've done it."

My tone goes up, like it's a question. His gaze narrows, but he's tight lipped.

"Tell me about the brand on your back," I say. The aura in the room is cold. I take his jaw in my fingers, holding him lightly. "You can't make me sign something like that and not be truthful with me," I whisper.

He wets his lips. A muscle in his cheek twitches.

"When my father gave Sovereign and me a plot of land, we divided the labor according to who was best at what," he says. "I've always been able to shoot, fight, and defend myself. So, I became that for us, for this land. Sovereign is good at running things; he's a sharp businessman."

"So what does that make you?"

"An asshole with a god complex," he says.

"I'm being serious," I say.

He rises, taking off his coat. "I'm the housekeeper."

"Westin."

He drops the jacket. I can tell he's bothered, because he starts rolling up his sleeves.

"I can shoot a tin can from the back of a moving horse with the sun in my eyes, Diane. What do you think you do with a skill like that?"

He kills people, probably anyone who stands in the way of Sovereign Mountain. Of course, I know what that word branded into his back means. I just hadn't realized it was so literal. I curl my cold hands tight.

"So...how many of those tin cans have you shot?" I ask quietly.

"Quite a few." He might be agitated, but his voice is calm. His body is restrained.

After being so afraid of Thomas and Avery, it's a relief that he doesn't let his emotions get the better of him. One thing I'm confident of is that Westin Quinn will never hurt me. I might be one of the few people immune to that.

“Am I too much for you?” he asks.

Maybe he is too much, but I shake my head.

“How does the brand come into all this?” I whisper.

“I was on a job, two men who came for Sovereign after he acquired their land,” he says. “I miscalculated for the first time in my life. I took a risky shot and missed the motherfuckers. He hit me hard enough I passed out. When I came to, they had me tied to a chair, and they used a branding iron to carve that into my back.”

My stomach turns. My head is light.

“How did you survive that?” I whisper.

“Getting branded won’t kill you, in most cases,” he says. “I broke a molar gritting my teeth, but I didn’t make a sound.”

I slip my fingers under his shirt. The top buttons pop open, giving me access to the brand on his back. My fingertips stroke over the hard, twisted lines of scar tissue.

His eyelids flicker, like I’m touching an open wound.

“Why that word?” I ask.

He snorts. “When Sovereign and I were working our way up, we had a lot of opposition. They’d call us the King and the Gunslinger as a way to mock us, like we’d never amount to anything. After a while, Sovereign gained a lot of respect, but I don’t do much in the spotlight. They kept calling me Gunslinger. They still do, maybe as a way of saying I’m an accessory. Less important, like all I am is a gun for hire, at Sovereign’s disposal.”

“I’m sorry.” My lips crack, and I wet them.

He shrugs one shoulder. “Honestly, it could have been something a lot worse. I got off easy.”

“They branded your back. That’s horrifying.”

His jaw works. My brows rise.

“What did you do to them?” I ask hoarsely.

“Someone came in at the last minute, got me untied,” he says. “They fled, and I took a horse and went after them. Ran them halfway to South Platte before shooting them off the backs of their horses.”

There’s a long silence.

"What...what happened to the horses?"

He laughs once, taking my hand and leading me to the bed. He sits, pulling me into his lap as his rough fingertips brush back my hair.

"You know, for all your fight, you're so fucking sweet, Diane," he says. "The horses were fine. I took them both back, and one of them is my gelding, Rocky. The other is retired."

My fingers tighten on his shoulders. He uses his insistent head to push mine to the side again and kisses the dip beneath my ear.

"I don't feel sweet," I whisper.

"You are," he murmurs. "You're like sugar, darling. Especially between your legs."

He needs to stop kissing me so I can think straight.

"So...what happened to Clint on Sovereign Mountain?" I gasp. My mind races, trying to remember the details. "Did you and Sovereign kill him too?"

"Now, why would I care about Clint?"

"I don't know. Why would you?" I say. "Tell me."

He's got my shirt pulled down from my naked shoulder. His mouth drags over it, kissing down to the swell of my cleavage. Against my thigh, his desire is hot and barely restrained.

I wriggle. He keeps me still with hard hands.

"I'm asking a serious question," I press.

"Goddamn it, Diane," he says under his breath.

My nails come out, piercing his skin. "Do you think I want to be fucked by a man who kills anyone who crosses him and lies about it?"

He goes still. Then, he pulls back, and his eyes are narrowed. "I told you that I shoot tin cans for a living, and you know what that means."

"I wish you'd say the words out loud."

"Why? So God and Diane Carter can judge me?"

I pull my hands back, but he grabs them and holds them steady.

"Because you're asking me to give up control," I burst out, my voice shaking. "You want my body and my heart and everything, but you didn't tell me the truth."

He sets me on the bed and rises. "I kill people," he says. "I killed Clint, I helped kill Thomas and Avery, and I'll kill anyone who gets in the way of me again. That's how it's been and always will be. How do you think this ranch got where it is?"

Everything clicks into place, and it's making me sick. He laughed a little too long when I said I wished that Avery would go up to Sovereign Mountain and die. I was joking—apparently, he wasn't.

Now, his reaction makes sense. I should have realized they killed Clint the minute I saw them break in and shoot Avery.

"You and Sovereign killed Clint," I say slowly. "Because of the feud?"

"Yes," he says. "And because Sovereign met Keira and wanted her."

My head spins. What the fuck is wrong with the men on Sovereign Mountain? It seems they're both in the habit of walking into other people's lives with the decorum of a bull in a china shop, just bursting in and taking what they want. I know Westin, despite pretending like he had a conscience, never intended to give me up.

"Did you ever stop to think about any of it?" I breathe.

"What does that mean?"

I stand, pacing to the other side of the room. He hurt me; not the way Thomas or David or Avery did, but he hurt me all the same.

"I'm so young," I burst out. "And you just took everything in one day. You knew who you were then, and I didn't...I didn't know who I was sleeping with. I'd never even been kissed before that day."

He's quiet.

For the first time in my life, I see a man admit to his failure. A little part of me heals in his silence. He's not defending himself or blaming me. He could easily say I was more than willing, but he shoulders the blame even though we both know it's not fair.

"Now, you're different than I thought back then," I manage.

His eyelids flicker, hurt behind them.

"This is all I've ever been," he says hoarsely. "Take it, because there won't be any leaving, darling."

There never was—I want to scream, but I can't even figure out what I feel. He's so bullheaded. The odds were always against him, but he showed up anyway. Bullheadedness is his best and worst trait—it saved me. I can't hate him for it.

"You're it for me, Diane," he says. "I watched you from the hill almost every night. I went to the cemetery every week hoping to see you there. I might have fucked you too soon, but I never left you."

My heart aches in my chest. All those nights when I sat alone in my room and stared out the window, he was watching me.

His eyes glitter. "I swore to myself you'd be mine," he says.

A tear slips down my cheek, leaving a hot trail behind.

His throat bobs. "I'm all in for the long haul, darling. Get used to it."

He takes me by the nape of the neck and pulls me in. His mouth finds mine, and then it finds the top of my head as his arms wrap around my body.

I've learned quickly that Westin needs touch to connect. I think I might be the same. It feels like borrowing his courage and the slow beat of his heart to lay against his body.

"I don't mind fighting," he says, voice low. "You can break my shit, throw my plates, but you can't leave."

I sniff, wiping my face on the front of his shirt. "I think I give up," I whisper.

"That's alright too, darling."

We might both be more broken than I thought. Maybe he's right that we need structure to build our relationship. Maybe I should have actually read the contract. It was overwhelming at the time, and I'd wanted an out to think things over.

Guiltily, I pull back and wipe my face. He tilts my chin up.

"You alright?" he asks.

I nod. "Yeah, let's talk more later."

He kisses my forehead. Then, he leaves me, and I stand in the window that overlooks the back side of the barn. After a while, Sovereign and Westin appear on their horses, moving through the snow until they disappear.

CHAPTER THIRTY-SEVEN

WESTIN

Sovereign and I stand at the top of the hill overlooking the charred foundation of the Garrison home. The police came and went. Animal control showed up with trailers and took the horses and cattle away. Now, the ranch is cold and quiet, still stained with ash.

"How's your girl?" Sovereign says.

He glances at me, pale eyes narrowed. Now that the snow is cleared, we've been busy cleaning up our mess. Sovereign has a bandage on the side of his head where Thomas shot at him, but otherwise, he's unharmed. I've seen Keira up at the house once or twice. She's pretty well adjusted for someone who took a life for the first time.

But then, it's hard to know what goes on behind closed doors. I barely know what goes on in Diane's head, and I sleep in her bed.

"She's...alright." I shrug.

His jaw works. When we were up in the mountains, he apologized to me for airing my shit out to everyone. I forgave him, because now that I have Diane, everything else seems unimportant. Maybe we'll talk about it more. More likely, we'll crack open a bottle and forget the whole thing. That's how we've operated for years.

I clear my throat. Killing the Garrison brothers was something we had planned for years; I just didn't expect the world to feel so ordinary now that it's done.

Everyone talks about justice. No one says what to do the day after.

"You told me up in the mountains that you and Diane weren't reconciled," he says.

My mind goes back to that conversation and how quickly I shut it down after he apologized. I'm happy to tell others that I'm sorry, but I'm not good at receiving it.

"Honestly, I didn't know. I thought she was going to be fighting mad when she woke up. I did lie to her about us killing the Garrisons, but she forgave me for a lot, and truthfully, I wasn't expecting it," I say.

His throat bobs. I know he's thinking that Keira did the same for him.

"So what's really going on with Diane?" he says gruffly. "Turns out, I don't know shit about what you've been doing."

"Early last summer, I went to David Carter's house and met Diane there," I say, shrugging. "I thought she was pretty young, so I went home. But the next day, I went back and...well, all the men were gone, so we went upstairs."

He stays as he is, both hands stacked on the saddle horn. "I remember you saying something about a girl last summer. I got confused, thinking she was someone else you used to run around with."

"You make me sound like more of a whore than I was," I say.

He shrugs. "Anyway, go on."

I narrow my eyes at the burnt ranch house. "I kept going back. One day, I asked her to run off with me. She was supposed to meet me that night, on the hill over Carter Farms...but she never showed."

His jaw twitches.

"The highway they're putting in west of us, they need an access road through Carter Farms. The Garrisons agreed to stop it, but only if Thomas could have Diane. So, the night I was waiting for her, they picked her up and took her away."

My chest hurts with regret at the memory.

A crease appears on Sovereign's forehead. "I always wondered why she ended up with him. She didn't seem happy when I saw her that day we went to Garrison Ranch."

I clear my throat.

"She hasn't said a word about what happened during that time," I say. "I haven't pushed her, but she's different than she was before she married him."

Sovereign's eyes are unreadable. I know what he's thinking. When he brought Keira here, she was timid from being with Clint. All I know is that she wasn't physically abused.

"What does she do?" he asks.

"She fights," I say. "She's safe, but she still fights."

"It's possible it was just from living with Thomas," he says, "but...it's likely someone did something to her."

It's not what I want to hear, but I know he's right. We stare out over the white fields for a while longer.

"I wish I could kill them again," I say.

Sovereign nods. "I'd dig Clint up and shoot him every day if I could."

He shifts his weight, and his horse starts moving up the hill along the property line. Rocky and I fall into step beside him. The wind whips through the mountain pass in the distance, shrieking and dying away, only to cry out again.

"I need to get her farm back and keep the access road from being built," I say.

"They won't build shit until spring," he says. "I just put in an offer on Garrison Ranch. If they don't accept, it'll be auctioned, and I'll buy it then. But they'll accept."

That doesn't surprise me. It has been our plan all along to get ahold of the Garrison land once the family was gone.

"I'd like to make Kiera a shared partner on my portion of the ranch," he says. "We need to talk about where that leaves you."

"I'm thinking of liquidating," I say. "Selling to you and putting my cash in the bank. Maybe using it for my own home."

He blinks twice. For him, that's a lot of emotion. "What?"

I shrug. "I can't live in the gatehouse forever, Sovereign. I want a family, kids, same as you."

He gives me a slow stare, the gears in his head turning. "You're thinking of buying Carter Farms for Diane and living there?"

"The thought crossed my mind," I say. "It runs along Garrison Farms. I can liquidate the shares I have, buy some of the Garrison land to the west, and we'll be living on two ranches, side by side."

His mouth twitches in a short smile. He shakes his head once.

"Who would've thought," he says. "Just don't liquidate yet. I can't buy any shares for a while longer if I'm buying up that much Garrison land. I'm fresh out of free cash until we move through the season."

"I can hold out for a little while. I still have to figure out how to get David Carter off the land."

"We'll talk more."

We're both quiet for a while. The fence line is strong, and there's little to no storm damage. We ride back down to the barn, and by then, it's the middle of the afternoon. I stop inside the dining hall to bring some food for Diane and feel someone tapping my arm.

I turn. Keira stands behind me, twisting her hands. We've barely spoken since that night at the gatehouse. She looks the best she's ever been—whatever Sovereign is doing is working.

"I wanted to ask about Diane," she says, chewing her lip.

"She's fine," I say. "I think she's feeling a little overwhelmed. Me and her are on good terms, though. She's just resting."

"That's okay," Keira says. "I just hoped...maybe she'd like to help Maddie and I cook something later in the week. Maddie helped me come out of my shell; maybe she'd be good for Diane."

I smile, putting my hat back on. "I'll let her know."

Sovereign appears. He steals her attention with a hand around her waist, and I leave out the side exit via the porch.

The sun is already starting to sink. I'm halfway to the gatehouse when I hear a shot in the distance, down the south end of the farm.

It sounds like a shotgun, perhaps a poacher or someone clearing wild hogs away.

Maybe it's the conversation I had with Diane about my past, but the walls that keep back all my least favorite memories are fragile. That gunshot stops me in my tracks. The discomfort of revealing the past is still fresh. It bursts out, hitting me like a rush of water.

I freeze, and suddenly, I'm a child again.

BEFORE

I'm twelve, standing on the curb outside the hardware store. My father said he would be back in a minute. He gave me two dollars and told me to get a pack of bubble gum. I got some from the gas station. It's crushed between my back teeth, the sweet taste sickly in the summer heat.

There's a faint screech at the end of the road. I squint, but the sun burns my eyes. From behind me, I hear my father leave the general store a few blocks down. The bell rings, and I hear his heavy tread. I know he's got a bag full of cigarettes, some flour and butter, and a little gift for my mother.

Usually lemon candy from the cash register.

The screech gets closer. I turn, and a car peels around the corner. It comes to a quick halt before the door flies open, and a man with pale blue eyes and a bandana pulled over his nose appears. He's screaming something, but it makes no sense.

I stumble back. He pulls a gun out, yelling someone else's name.

I've practiced at the range for as long as I can remember, but I don't have a gun. My heart feels like it's laying on my tongue. My vision is blurred.

"Get back!" my father yells, stepping in front of me.

My father has a gun on his belt. The man's eyes drop, and my father's hand moves to the pistol. A sharp crack rings out over the street. I see my strong, tall father collapse like a sack of bricks into the gutter. Blood trickles from his thigh.

Something flips in my brain.

Everything goes completely still, the way it does after a heavy snowfall. The man with the pale eyes backs up. Two other men jump from the back seat and round the car, their pistols up. I drop to my knees, pick up the gun, and shoot the way I was taught.

Intuitively, trusting that my heart knows where the bullet needs to go.

Bang.

Bang.

Bang.

They go down, one after the other. In the distance, police sirens wail. They pull around me in a circle, and an officer carries me off the scene. My father is on his back, blood soaking his jeans. His eyes are open, so I can tell he's alive.

I should be screaming. I'm twelve years old.

But, as my mother tells it, I don't make a sound. I don't say a word for a week until my father gets out of the hospital and comes home. In true fashion, my father never speaks about it after the police let us know what happened. It was a freak accident, a dispute over drugs. We were in the wrong place at the wrong time.

A one in a million mistake. One that leaves me forever altered.

I learn something that day: my father is the biggest, strongest man I know, and he can't protect me. No one can. So, I practice, in the heat, in the cold. I learn to fight with a knife, a gun, and my bare hands.

Most of all, I learn to keep it all behind a mask. Because if those men had thought I was capable of killing them, they'd have shot me too.

NOW

Gunslinger.

The word moves like a whisper on the wind. It's still a mockery. The gunslinger can shoot a tin can with the sun in his eyes, off the back of a running horse.

But he can't keep his woman safe.

Rage at myself courses through my veins. I'm my father's son; I'm not an angry man. I don't raise my voice or leave broken things in my wake.

No, my rage is precise. It hits its mark.

I've fucked around long enough, and Diane was hurt because I can't accept who I am. It's time to start taking what I want, consequences be damned.

CHAPTER THIRTY-EIGHT

DIANE

I move our things into the primary bedroom. It's enormous, and the bathroom off the side has a big, round tub. The best part about it is the window seat that looks out over the back field. I climb into it, wrap myself in a blanket, and watch a group of deer scavenge in the snow as the sun sets.

Maybe tomorrow, I can bring them hay.

Westin went back out after a quiet lunch at the kitchen table. We haven't spoken much since our conversation the other day. I hope I didn't cross a line we can't come back from.

Downstairs, the door opens, and Billie's nails click on the floor as Westin tells her to go lay down and his steps move up the stairs. The primary bedroom is at the top, and he pauses just outside the door. It pushes open, and he steps inside.

My stomach flips. He looks especially good today, maybe because he just got a haircut. I like how the edges are shorter. It makes me want to run my fingertips through them.

"Are we sleeping here now?" he asks.

"I like that the bathroom is right off the bedroom," I say.

He nods distractedly and starts unfastening his shirt. Maybe I went too far moving his things into the dresser. I didn't touch the closet, though. I follow him with my eyes, and his face doesn't change as he puts his clothes in the basket and goes to shower.

I curl up against the pillow. This bed has red flannel sheets, and they're cozy enough that I'm in just a blue slip. He bought it for me, and I wear it because...because I want him to look at me and be pleased.

Maybe I'm too prideful to admit it, but I want to please him.

It makes me feel good.

My mind drifts back to the contract I signed. I stretched the truth when I said I read it, but before he finds out, I'll go over every word.

The shower turns off. Then, he appears in those sweatpants, the ones that look like sin on him. My thighs clench. I think I might be ovulating, because I want to jump him despite all the confusing thoughts in my head. It hasn't been that long since I had my period, so it's possible.

He circles the bed.

"You didn't read that contract when I left it out for you, did you?" he says.

My brows rise. Did he just read my mind?

"Answer me, darling," he says, his voice low.

I shrink. "I read the first few pages. I was going to read the rest later, I promise. You were just...annoying me, so I said I read it."

He looks down at the bedspread. There's a long silence, and finally, he crosses the room to the pair of armchairs on either side of the gas fireplace.

He sinks down, his knees spread.

"Go get the contract," he says.

He's not fucking around tonight. Cowed, I get up and pull it from his bedside drawer where I moved it. His eyes rake over me, but I can't read them.

"Come here," he says.

My bare feet pad over the floor. I dig one into the other, waiting for him to speak again.

"You will sit here, at my feet, and read every word of it," he says.

Something shifted. We're past the point where I can wriggle out of doing as he asks. All I have now is a safeword. Flushed, I sink to the floor. He beckons me closer until I'm facing him, down between his knees.

"Read it," he says. "I'll wait."

Heart pounding, I flip to where I left off.

The submissive agrees to a system of punishment and reward as part of the 24/7 dynamic and must use her safeword to halt it.

The submissive agrees to sexual overstimulation, including forced orgasms and edging as punishment.

The submissive agrees to impact play as punishment and stress relief.

The submissive—

I have to stop and take a breath. He's right, I should have read this before signing it. I glance up. He points at the papers.

I lower my gaze.

—agrees to the use of aids during sexual punishment, such as toys, props, etc. The submissive may always veto any items.

The next portion is separated by a line. I hope it's less overwhelming.

The Dominant takes on full responsibility for the emotional, physical, and mental wellbeing of the submissive during and outside of sexual encounters.

The Dominant and the submissive will communicate clearly and directly with each other. Bratting is allowed and encouraged, but all serious discussions must be held outside of the dynamic in a neutral environment.

The Dominant will provide aftercare in all circumstances, regardless of the scene.

The Dominant will provide weekly stress relief for the submissive.

I'm at a loss. Is this what he was talking about when he begged me to let go and allow him to care for me? I lift my eyes.

"Is this all...necessary?" I whisper.

He nods once. "I'm not always kind in-scene. I need to know you feel safe."

I give him my best pleading, bedroom eyes, the big, round ones that usually break him down. His face stays hard like stone.

"Finish the contract," he says.

My pussy tingles, but I manage to pull my attention back down. I think I like when he's stern—it's distractingly sexy. The contract goes on and on, alluding to every possible scenario. He's thorough, and it does make me feel safe. I don't have to guess what he wants or if I'm going to get what I need.

At the very end is an amendment.

The submissive will take birth control of her choosing. The Dominant may not finish on or inside the submissive's vagina until she is sufficiently protected against pregnancy.

That's the last thing, right above my signature. I know he added that for me. He's outspoken about how he feels about having children with me, but I'm not ready. I stare down at it, and everything feels so final.

How did we get here?

Was this where he'd planned on bringing us all along?

I don't have to ask that aloud. I already know his answer. I close the papers and hold them out. He sets them aside and shifts, spreading his legs.

"Get on your knees," he says, his tone smooth, devoid of emotion.

My body tingles as my toes curl. I do as he asks.

"Good girl."

My mind goes completely quiet. His praise falls into me like a drop in a pool, spreading warm ripples through my veins.

"Put your hands on your knees, palms up."

I obey, laying my upturned hands on my thighs. They're pale in the firelight. He takes something from his pocket wrapped in a handkerchief.

"Eyes on me," he says.

I force my gaze up. He's half shadowed by the fire and cut like stone, from the V of his lower abdominals all the way to his heavy nose and lowered brows.

"What did you do?" he asks.

My dry mouth parts. I lick my lips.

"I lied," I whisper.

My nipples poke through my slip. Tonight, I'm acutely aware of my body and how different it is from his. He's hard and big and takes up space. I fit perfectly between his thighs, and that makes me feel so small.

It's all part of his design. I see that now.

"Give me your hair band," he orders.

I obey. Carefully, he smooths my hair into a high ponytail. Then, he uses it to tilt my chin up.

"You're not going to use your teeth. Just hold this on your tongue."

He reaches into his lap, and I wait for the hiss of his zipper. Instead, he takes something from the handkerchief.

"Open, darling."

My head empty, I open. Something cool and...oh God, it's soap. He's using soap in my mouth because I lied to him. I might burn up into dust from the shame. It barely fits between my lips and lays on my tongue. He adjusts my jaw so my saliva won't drip down my throat and tucks a flyaway curl behind my ear.

"You weren't good," he says gently. "Were you?"

Humiliated, I shake my head. Something trickles down my inner thigh.

"You will not lie to me, especially where your safety and consent are concerned. Understood?"

I nod. My heart pounds.

I can't tell if I want to cry or come or both.

He waits for several humiliating minutes. My jaw aches, but I keep perfectly still. Finally, he leans in and takes the soap from my mouth and sets it aside. My mouth tastes sharp. I don't want to swallow. A tear slips out and etches to my jaw.

"Spit into my hand," he says.

He cups it under my chin. I'm already embarrassed, so I lean in and spit into his hand until the taste subsides. He wipes his fingers on his handkerchief and lays it over his thigh.

"Do you need to rinse now, or can you continue your punishment?"

His tone is even, like he's not angry, just disappointed. It's so stern, it makes my toes curl. Deep inside, I ache. All I want is for him to pick me up and slide me down over his cock.

"I can continue, sir," I whisper.

He strokes my cheek with his thumb. "That's my girl."

I open my mouth to speak again, but the faint taste of soap gags me. His brows crease, and he leans back.

"Run to the bathroom and rinse," he orders.

My legs are weak as I stand. I'm dizzy and flushed in the bathroom mirror as I rinse my mouth until the taste is gone. Then, I do as he says and return to where he sits, waiting in the armchair.

"Do you want me to kneel, sir?" My whisper cracks.

He shakes his head once. "No, lay yourself across my right knee."

My pussy has a heartbeat like a drum. He could get me off with a single touch. His thigh looks thick and hard, like it would be paradise to ride myself against it.

"Focus, darling," he says.

I shake my head once. "How...do I do this, sir?"

He takes my hand, guiding me between his thighs. His other hand rests on my lower back as he drapes me over his arm and lowers me over his knee. My cheek lays on the armrest, and my toes dig into the floor.

"You're not ready for the crop or the belt, not for punishment," he says. "I prefer to use my hand anyway."

I shiver—maybe not yet, but I think I might like to try them soon. He lifts the short hem of my slip, and warmth from the fire washes over my pussy. I'm so wet, it's sticky on my inner thighs. His fingertips trail over my ass and dip down, sliding to my clit.

"Oh God," I burst out.

He hasn't let me come since the night he ate me out on my period. I'm not brave enough to touch myself without his permission. My hips wriggle, desperate for friction.

"No. You made your bed, darling. You lay in it," he says.

He's so cruel, but he's so kind about it. I go still, tilting my head to lay my cheek on the chair. One of his big, rough hands goes to the back of my neck, and the other starts rubbing slow circles over my ass.

Then, he spanks me, hard enough that I yelp.

"Do not struggle," he says. "Hold still and be a good girl for me. You may cry if you need to."

I'm slipping down through sweet, warm darkness, into a gentle space where there's nothing but the sensations moving through my body. I have no memories of the last few years. All I know is he's holding me. He's in control, and I'm safe in his arms.

It's euphoric.

His palm strikes me over and over again. My skin heats up, and I drip down the inside of my thighs. I moan, whimpering, but I sound so far away. It hurts, but the way it does when he fucks me hard, only this is less frantic. It's like a purging of my emotions.

All the fucked-up things in my head and chest ebb away. There's no anxiety, no fear, just sweet release.

My ass burns by the time he decides I've been sufficiently punished. I'm a wet mess, my eyes dripping, my pussy soaked. He lifts me into his lap and brushes my hair back.

I sniffle. He wipes my tears with his thumb.

"Good girl," he says. "Are you going to be truthful with me moving forward?"

My heart is raw, but he's the safest place in the world. Nobody has ever held me the way Westin does. Here, in his arms, I can be honest.

My throat tightens. I squeeze my eyes shut, and tears slip down fast, etching hot trails down my neck. He cradles my face.

"Diane," he says. "Tell me what they did to you."

My eyes fly open. His face is gentle, his brows drawn together. My nose runs, my lips shake, but he waits, holding me until I'm ready to speak.

"Avery found out about you, the night I came to Sovereign Mountain," I gasp. "He came to the house with Thomas and David. Avery pushed me on the floor and Thomas just...beat me. I don't know how else to say it. He used his boot...and David, he just watched."

It all pours out, ugly and jumbled, right into Westin's lap.

He doesn't flinch. He listens without lowering his eyes. It feels good to have a witness.

"I don't know why David just watched," I whisper. "He must hate me so much."

His jaw tightens.

"He's a coward," he says.

I wipe my face. "I don't want sympathy. I just want to forget it ever happened."

That's the truth, laid out before him so there are no more secrets between us. Now, maybe all the horrific memories of my time as Thomas' wife can just fade away. I want to scrub them from my mind. I want to lose myself in the warm summer sun that is Westin and pretend Thomas was nothing but a bad dream.

"Please don't ask me to talk more about it," I blurt out. "That's all that happened. He beat me, then he left. The night you and Sovereign showed up, I was going to sleep with him for the first time because I was afraid Avery would hurt me. But you saved me. I never want to think or talk about them ever again."

He's quiet, his hand moving in slow circles on my back.

"I'm done," I say, louder. "I'm free and I'm safe with you."

He narrows his eyes, like he's thinking deeply. "Is this dynamic what you need to heal? Be honest with me, darling."

"I think so. It's different," I say. "You were right. I felt safe tonight."

He pulls me in, holding me to his chest. I close my eyes, and I'm back in his truck, untouched by misery. In my mind's eye, I turn and see him, so handsome in the driver's seat.

We were so alive for that summer. He brought me to life.

I know he can do it again.

"You saved me, Westin," I whisper. "I'm hoping you can do it one more time."

"Darling," he says, mouth moving in my hair. "Of course."

He carries me to bed. A warm washcloth runs over my body before he brings cold water and holds the glass for me. He puts me in one of his flannel shirts and tucks me into bed.

I lay with my back against him, spent from crying.

"What do you need to sleep?" he asks.

"Touch me," I whisper. "Sir."

He slides his hand down my thighs, beneath the sheets and flannel. His touch finds my clit, and he pleasures me slowly in the dark. Outside, the world is harsh. Outside is where all the memories of the past live. Inside, there's just me and Westin, buried beneath the quilt, skin on skin, voices hushed, little sighs of pleasure drowned out by the rush of the fireplace.

Both wrapped up in each other, trying to keep the cold out.

CHAPTER THIRTY-NINE

WESTIN

The morning comes late, as it does in the dead of winter. Outside, the world is frozen in brutal cold. Inside, my bedroom is warm, but the floor is covered in shrapnel from the night before.

I sit on the edge of the bed, shoulders tense. She sleeps, nothing visible but her blonde hair. The edges of my brand itch. It hasn't itched in years.

My head is a mess.

The gunslinger is quick.

The gunslinger can kill without hesitation.

The gunslinger can't protect his woman.

My head drops, my shoulders hunch. I've never felt such rage. All the things she said to me echo in my ears, all the clues I missed.

I should have killed them a long time ago. I should have burned their homes to the ground and shot them while they fled.

I didn't.

Now, God as my witness, I will make sure there's nothing left of David Carter when I'm done.

I want him in fucking pieces, but I have to be smart about it.

There are too many bodies already. When I kill him, it has to be untraceable.

She sleeps. The only thing I can think of to do is get her horses back from Carter Farms. If luck is on my side, David won't be there by the time I arrive. I can't think of anything else to help put her heart back together. So, I go out and put the trailer on my truck and get on the road.

First, I make a detour and head to the capitol building. Corbin Buchanan will be there, and I plan to have a more honest talk with him this time around, maybe let him know I'm not above threats.

There's a gathering of men outside the meeting room doors upstairs. They stand around, hats on their heads, thick coats pulled over their suit jackets.

Corbin Buchanan is by the open door, leaning on the wall. There's a tall man in a dark cowboy hat and work clothes standing with his back to me, to Corbin's left. They're talking like they're friendly, but I taste friction in the air. As I draw near, Corbin looks up and narrows his eyes.

They both turn. My eyes fall on the second man, and my stomach sinks.

Jesus Christ, it's Deacon Ryder.

It has been a while since that motherfucker came this far east. At least, that I know of; I haven't heard his name lately. Deacon is the only man who makes Sovereign begrudgingly stop and listen when he talks. They're not so dissimilar, him and Deacon. They're both rough sons of bitches, with heads so hard they could break rocks with them.

Deacon glances over once. His jaw works. His broad body, as big as Sovereign but with more grace, takes up space with purpose. His dark hair is shorn with a little left on top. His features are harsh, his jaw square, his thick nose crooked in the middle. Over every visible inch of his body are scars and ink, faded from working in the sun.

He's a mean motherfucker, and I pity the woman who ends up in his bed.

Black eyes fall on me. Deacon extends his hand, and I shake it.

"Why are you here, Ryder?" I say.

He shrugs. "I'm not banned from Montana. Yet."

"That's a fucking shame."

Corbin's eyes bounce back and forth. "You two know each other?"

He's refined when I see him like this, alongside Deacon. I open my mouth to answer but stop short.

I'm so fucking angry. My brain tells me to try to find a way this can be solved without a bullet. My heart tells me that Deacon Ryder might be here for a reason, and I should speak with him first.

"Excuse us," I tell Corbin.

I step back, jerking my head. Deacon lifts his brows, but he follows me as I head down to the second landing on the steps

"Why are you in the city?" I ask.

He shrugs. "I got some business."

"You want to go steal some horses?" I ask.

Deacon shakes back his sleeves, exposing a chipped silver watch with a leather band. "I don't have shit to do until noon, so yeah."

We head out, but Deacon has to stop at a street vender for a coffee. Then, we get into my truck with the trailer attached and pull back onto the highway. It's thirty minutes to Carter Farms, and we're both quiet. The cab smells like black coffee and boot oil. My mouth tastes bitter..

The silence is loud. The last time we ran into each other was at a BDSM club in Wyoming. I was on a trip and had time to kill, so I went to blow off some steam. Deacon was there, and we made uncomfortable eye contact before I decided to head out early.

I cleared my throat. "You still with that blonde girl?"

He shook his head. "She was a redhead, but no."

There's another silence. Deacon finishes his coffee and crushes the cup in his fist. I turn off the highway onto the state route.

"You got anybody?" Deacon asks.

"Yeah," I say. "The owner of the horses I'm about to steal."

His forehead creases. "You stealing your own girl's horses?"

"Her brother has them."

"And the brother won't be at the house?"

"Not this time of day."

"Makes sense. Too bad. I was hoping we could fuck somebody up."

My mind goes back to last night, to the memory of her broken body in my arms, shaking as she told me what they did to her. My knuckles tighten. Deacon glances over, and his brow rises.

"Oh, the brother's in for it, huh?" he says. "What'd he do?"

I run a hand through my hair. My eyes stay on the road.

"She was married to Thomas Garrison. He beat her, and her brother stood there and watched."

Deacon shakes his head. "Sounds like you should fuck him up."

I nod, jaw tight. "Yeah, I plan on it."

"I'll help. Sounds like fun." Deacon rolls his jaw again. "You said she was married to a Garrison? The younger one?"

I nod again.

"Well, those motherfuckers are dead," he says. "Everyone heard, everyone knows who did it, but I'd guess with the gunslinger on his payroll, they won't catch nobody."

I pull off the state route to a gravel lane. The road leading to Carter's Farm is clear of snow, and I push my foot down a little harder.

"I didn't do it," I say.

"Sovereign?"

I shrug.

Deacon grins, rubbing a hand over his jaw. "And you both got their women. Not suspicious."

"You know about Keira?" I ask.

"Yeah, everyone knows he fucks her," Deacon says, stretching his legs out. "That story spread up and around like wildfire. All the church ladies had their panties all knotted up over that shit."

I wasn't aware Sovereign Mountain had made it into the town's gossip column. We pull up on the road that overlooks Carter Farms. I get out, and he does the same, circling the truck.

"You don't go to church, Ryder," I say.

He cocks his head. "Maybe I do."

"Do you get hit by lightning every time you walk in?"

He laughs, taking a cigarette from his pocket. "Surprisingly, no."

"What? You going because you're pussy whipped for a some church girl?" I say, not meaning it seriously.

His jaw works again. He drags his cigarette but doesn't answer. I put mine in my lip and circle the truck to take the rifle out of the back. I pull the hard cover over the truck's bed, bracing the weapon on top.

"You shooting somebody?" Deacon asks.

I settle my eye up to the scope, but my hat bumps into it, so I take it off, setting it aside.

"Checking for cameras," I say.

We're both silent. Carter Farms is quiet, the snow tamped down by footprints. Through the scope, I scour the sides of the barn and the edges of the house. It takes a second, but I find it: a security camera pointing at the house. It looks brand new.

I shift an inch to the side, take a quick breath, and squeeze the trigger. It kicks into my shoulder, and the camera explodes through the lens.

"Fuckin' hell, gunslinger," Deacon says. "I need to hire you next time I need a motherfucker gone. It's unsettling what you can do."

That word is a punch to the gut, but I brush it off and lift my head.

"I'm not for hire," I say.

"You ever need work, though, call me."

I put my eye to the scope and keep looking. Just as I'm about to lift my head, I see a sliver of another camera. David must have put those in after Diane left, probably realizing how easy it was for someone to just walk in. I shift everything an inch over.

The camera is barely traceable, even with the scope.

I inhale and let it seep out. I think I feel the sun on the back of my neck. Cicadas trill. My father's eyes are narrowed, his arms crossed. He's watching me, telling me that men don't miss.

My heart knows where the bullet needs to go.

I squeeze. The camera shatters.

"Jesus," Deacon mutters.

I comb over the house and barn, but there's nothing else. Deacon stubs out his cigarette and stands in the open truck door, waiting as I pack up the gun and scope. He puts his hat on.

"Let's go get your woman's horses," he says.

I nod, swinging back into the truck. We're both quiet as we head around the access road that leads to the driveway. After a while, Deacon clears his throat.

"That girl you got... Does she get it?" he asks.

"Get what?"

"Does she like what you like?"

I know right away what he means. Surprised, I glance over at him and find his eyes fixed out the window. We've never talked about our sex lives before.

"Is this about the church girl?" I say, deflecting.

He shrugs.

There's a short silence. I laugh, shaking my head.

"So you're not pussy whipped, huh?" I say.

"Can't be if I haven't had it," he says.

"How long have you been waiting on it?" My interest is piqued.

"Not important," he says, and I know it has probably been weeks.

We pull up, and I circle the trailer so the end is closer to the barn door. There's no one home that I can see, so it seems best we get in and out without causing a fuss. I step out, and Deacon does the same. He squints over at the house.

"Does the brother have a woman here?" he asks.

I scan the yard and house. "Maybe, but it doesn't look like anyone's home now."

Deacon takes out his gun, checking the chamber. He pushes it in his belt and puts his hat on. I circle the truck and head to the barn, pulling the door open. It takes a second for my eyes to adjust to the dim interior, but when they do, I see what we've come for.

Gracey and Sunshine lean out of their stalls, staring with wide, glassy eyes.

"That there's the horses," I say, jerking my head.

Deacon follows me in, grabbing two halters and lead ropes from the bin by the door. The horses are wary, but they come as we usher them from the barn and into the trailer. For a second, I consider letting the rest of the horses out and lighting a match.

But no, that would break Diane's heart. As much as I hate David and want to hurt him, I have to remember that she's the most important thing in all of this.

Back in the passenger seat, Deacon is having another cigarette. I scan the barn and house one more time, but everything is eerily quiet as I swing back into the truck. I turn the key, the engine revs, and we're headed back down the drive and onto the road.

But my heart is pounding slow and heavy.

I wanted him to be there.

I wanted to kill him, to hurt him the way he hurt her—with my bare hands. A bullet in the head is too neat and merciful. David Carter doesn't deserve my mercy.

He deserves my rage.

Deacon and I go back into the city. He wants to talk, so I park, leaving the horses waiting with hay from the back of the truck. We end up in a diner, at the street corner. We both have black coffee and breakfast. I wait until he finishes his food and brushes off his hands.

"I got a problem," he says. "Corbin Buchanan and Vince Cassidy are pushing at the border of my land."

"Vince Cassidy the real estate developer?" I ask.

He nods. "They're gonna try to price me out."

"So don't sell."

He sighs. "He's got oil guys with him."

I take a beat. Real estate developers are one thing. Big oil and gas is a many-headed beast we don't have the resources to take on.

"What's your plan?" I say.

He shrugs. "It appears to me that Vince Cassidy is the one pushing this, and Corbin Buchanan is his puppet in the government. He's trying to run a highway through the South Platte area to get access to everything west of it—my land."

I lean forward. "Corbin Buchanan is planning on putting an access road through Carter Farms so he can bring materials up to build the highway. I need to find a way to stop him. It sounds like we could work on this together."

He thinks it over. "What's your plan?"

"I don't have one," I say. "The snow will hold off any construction, but when it gets warm and they approve the permits, they'll start."

"You want Carter Farms?"

"My girl wants it," I say. "It's hers."

He laughs once, shaking his head. "Talk about pussy whipped, huh?"

I don't answer. He's not wrong.

"Her brother lives there now," I say. "He'll have to sell now that the Garrisons are dead. He's in a corner; he's got no other alternative. I'm not sure why he hasn't sold yet."

"Want me to have a word with the lady in the permit office?" Deacon says.

I consider it. "Sure. I've got a feeling she'd take a check for kicking the can down the road. Give us a few more months of time."

"They always do."

I think back to how Sovereign and I pulled off Clint Garrison's death so cleanly, all the bribes and threats handed out to the lawyer, the coroner, the judge. It worked, and he got his girl. Maybe I can get mine that way too.

"We gotta cut off the people who are facilitating this shit at the source," Deacon says.

He's right, but I need time to figure out how. I sit back and put some bills on the table, picking up my hat.

"I don't want to leave the horses long," I say. "You come up to Sovereign Mountain, and we'll talk about this with Sovereign."

He nods. "Will do."

I leave him there and head back to the truck. My mind whirls all the way to the general store, where I go to get some necessities. I know Deacon is right, but adding someone like Vince Cassidy to the mix will make this hard to pull off. Bodies like his are hard to hide.

I stand by the checkout with bread, milk, and eggs. The register is lined with plastic buckets of candy wrapped in white wax paper. My eyes fall on the closest bucket, one labeled Lemon Chews.

My father used to get those for my mother, maybe as an apology for everything. It was a kick to the stomach when Diane said they were her favorite.

I pick up a handful and set them on the counter before I take out my card. Then, when I get back in the truck, I shove them in my pocket.

Anything for my girl.

CHAPTER FORTY

DIANE

For the first time, I see someone other than Westin. Not because I have the courage, but because I hear a faint knock at my door around noon. I'm in a thick sweatsuit and socks because the floor is always cold this time of year. I brush my hair back into a ponytail and pad to the door, cracking it open.

Keira stands outside, a shawl wrapped around her shoulders. Behind her is a graying woman with a kind but stern face. That must be Maddie, the woman who runs the kitchen up at the ranch.

My mind goes right back to when Westin told me Keira killed Thomas. Maybe I should feel differently, but part of me wants to thank her for that. Instead, I just offer a little smile.

"Hello," Keira says. "Could...we come in?"

I nod shyly. I've never had a friend before. I'm not sure how this works. I step aside and let them in, trying not to stare. Maddie has a basket under her arm, and Keira has a plastic bag. She sets it down and dusts her hands off, offering me a smile.

I feel small and drab. Keira is one of the most beautiful women I've ever seen. Her hair is deep red, her light beige skin covered with little freckles, and her brilliant blue eyes are shaded by heavy lashes.

Her body is curvy, with an hourglass waist and full breasts I can't help but be jealous of.

I wrap my arms around myself. I miss when my body was soft instead of stressed.

I miss everything about myself before Thomas.

"I'm going to make some food," Maddie says.

I can tell she's a no-nonsense sort, and it intimidates me. I used to be so fiery, but somewhere along the way, I lost that. Silently, I watch as she starts unloading the basket and piling food on the table.

"I brought some things for you," Kiera says softly. She has a sweet, low voice.

I try to speak, but nothing comes out. Flushing, I clear my throat.

"Thank you," I say. "You didn't have to do that."

Keira waves her hand, taking up the bag. "Do you want to go upstairs?"

Confused, I nod. She carries the bag upstairs, and I follow her until we stop in the hall. I push open our bedroom door. I cleaned it this morning, even washed the sheets, so there's no evidence of the things he did to me the other night.

Everything is neat and scrubbed. The surfaces shine.

Keira hesitates. "Is it alright if I go in?"

I nod, and she slips through, setting the bag on the end of the bed. I follow and wait with my hands tucked behind my back. Finally, she clears her throat and tucks her hair behind her ear.

"I was married to Clint," she says. "I know it's...hard going through that and feeling normal afterwards. I just wanted to make sure you had the things you needed."

Warmth sparks in my chest. "Thank you," I whisper.

She sits, folding her hands in her lap. "I know Westin has probably gotten you some clothes and things, but I wanted to make sure you had items like pads and tampons."

My cheeks feel warm. I've never talked to anyone about my cycle other than Nana and Westin.

"I don't have any left," I say. "And...um..."

I bite my lip, unsure how to say the rest. She waits.

"Um...I've never taken anything before," I manage. "I don't really know how to go about getting it. Westin...um, he hasn't mentioned what to do in that area."

Her brows knit. "Do you...sorry, what?"

"I need the pill," I whisper.

Her brows rise. "Oh, I see," she says. Her mouth twists like she's annoyed. "Westin should have...what...I don't mean to pry, but are you sleeping with him already?"

I nod.

"And...it was just unprotected?" she asks. "Is that what you want?"

"No, I mean, he pulls out...most of the time," I say in a rush. "And he did mention birth control, but not any steps to getting it."

Keira sighs, like she's disappointed in Westin. "When I was married to Clint, I just went to the clinic in South Platte. Now you can have it sent to Sovereign Mountain because we're so remote. I'll help you with it."

"Okay, I think that should be fine," I say, sinking down to sit on the armchair by the fire.

Keira dumps the bag out onto the bed. Inside are pads, tampons, painkillers, an electric heating pad, and two pregnancy tests. The knot in my chest that only eases with Westin lessens. I never had access to these things freely while living with Thomas. He didn't like me spending money on anything that wasn't for the house.

"Is there anything else I can get you?" she asks, offering a smile.

Already, I like Keira. She's soft and feels trustworthy.

"How do I get over it?" I whisper, dropping my eyes.

My thumbnail is peeling. I pick it.

She sighs. "Westin is a good man; you can lean on him. And I'm here, Maddie is here. She helped me a lot. It just takes time to learn to trust people again."

My eyes blur. Maybe I was hoping for a different answer.

"Let's go downstairs," she says. The bed creaks, and I hear her open the door. "Maddie is making lunch. I think everything seems better when your belly is full."

I wipe my nose and offer a brave smile, following her back downstairs. The kitchen is warm and smells like chicken broth. My mind drifts back to being sick as a child and watching my Nana make chicken soup with homemade noodles.

"What are you making?" I ask.

Maddie rinses out the coffee pot and starts making a fresh batch. "Chicken and dumplings. I hope you like it," she says. "It's my family recipe."

I nod, sinking down at the table beside Keira, who has her chin on her folded hands. "Thank you."

The coffee pot bubbles. The dumplings smell so good, they make my stomach twist. Maddie starts talking about something to do with the spring calving season. Keira answers her. I'm focused on the realization that I could have friends. Other women. It's like a dream.

A bowl hits the table in front of me. It's huge, piled with thick, dark chunks of chicken and fluffy dumplings. On the plate beside it is a stack of biscuits covered in blackberry jam.

"Dumplings and biscuits?" I ask.

Maddie opens her mouth, and I see Keira shake her head from the corner of my eye.

"I had leftover biscuits," Maddie says quickly. "Eat up."

I'm getting tunnel vision. Yes, I've eaten since I came here, but not like this, and it has always been just enough for two. Westin eats a lot of lean meat and eggs, and they don't fill me up.

Keira pours coffee. I start eating, and suddenly, my eyes are wet.

"Are you okay?" Keira asks.

I nod, sniffing. "I'm just a lot happier than I was."

"Well, don't let it get in the way of you having hot food," Maddie says. "Go on, girl, eat."

Keira and I laugh. Obediently, I start eating and keep going until I can't fit anything else in my stomach. The dumplings are perfect, savory and soft, melting on my tongue. The chicken is hearty, the vegetables fresh, the broth thick. When my bowl is empty, Maddie takes it and gives me an approving nod.

"Good," she says. "I'll have a chat with Westin about getting some things from the grocery store."

We have coffee, and I relax enough to ask some questions about the ranch. Maddie lives in employee housing with her husband while Keira lives with Sovereign in the ranch house. I'm dying to ask her about that, because I can't see someone as sweet as her with a man like him.

We have coffee. Maddie unwraps a sticky chocolate cake drenched with canned cherries, and we eat it slathered in fresh whipped cream.

Then, Maddie pulls out a little bottle of red wine. We have a glass each, even though it's only three in the afternoon.

The room is warm. I'm safe. My heart doesn't hurt.

Is this what the rest of my life could feel like?

"We'll do this again next week," Maddie says as she gathers up the empty dishes.

I don't say a word in protest. We clean up, and I stand in the door and wave as they head back to the ranch house. Then, I call Billie in from the barn over the hill and feed her by the fire.

She stretches out. I'm so sleepy, all I can do is put a bowl of leftover chicken and dumplings in the microwave for Westin and head upstairs to bed.

It's dark when I wake to his boots on the bedroom floor. He sinks down on the edge of the bed and sighs. Sleepily, I roll over to touch his lower back, and he turns.

"I didn't mean to wake you, darling," he says.

I push myself up on my elbow. "Where were you all day?"

He turns his body, looking down at me. He's a shadow, but I know by the lines of his profile that he's serious.

"In the city," he says.

"Why?"

"I had business," he says. His hand slips in the pocket of his work pants. I hear change, his keys, then a crinkle. He takes out a candy and holds it out. I open my lips and let him put it on my tongue.

Sweet, chewy lemon—he remembered my favorite.

He clears his throat. “My father always brought my mother candy when he came back from town,” he says, his voice low.

I swallow. “That’s sweet.”

He looks down at the wrapper in his palm. “Yeah, it was.”

Something is going on with him. Usually, he hides behind his barricade. Tonight, he feels naked. He shifts, sinking down to his side so our faces are inches apart.

“I went to Carter Farms,” he says.

“What? Really?”

“Really.”

“Why?”

He bends in, and his lips brush mine. “So that when you wake up, you can go down to the barn and find two horses named Sunshine and Gracey waiting there for you.”

My heart melts. It falls right out of my chest and into his hands. I wrap my arms around his neck and he laughs softly, lifting me into his lap.

“You got my horses,” I whisper, trying not to cry.

“Stole them,” he says. “But yes.”

A broken part of me shifts into place. His beard is rough on my temple. His broad arms encircle me like a fortress, his hands steady as they hold me.

“Are they okay?” I whisper.

“Safe and sound.”

I wipe my face and lift it, stretching to kiss him. The kiss deepens, and my eyes close, a little moan working its way up. He gives me a hint of tongue, and I let him know I want more, parting my mouth so he can consume me. When we break apart, we’re both breathless.

“Have me,” he says, voice low and urgent.

The words are mostly a demand. Maybe if he wasn’t hard beneath my thigh, there’d be some question in them.

“What does that mean?” I whisper.

He slides down my body and uses his head to shove my thighs apart. My slip falls back, exposing my sex. He touches the lace trim, turning it in his rough fingers.

"So pretty," he murmurs.

My mouth is dry. I'm not sure what's going on with him, but it scares me a little. He glances up from between my legs, and his eyes are bright but distracted. One hand slides up my belly, and I weave my fingers through his. In the dark, I run my fingertips over his scars.

Sometimes, I feel much older than twenty-one. Other times, I feel just that.

Tonight is the latter.

I forget that he has thirty-seven years hidden away behind those bright eyes. If I had to guess, there's a lot of heartache in him. I think a little bit of it came in on him with the cold tonight.

I close my eyes. His grip tightens, and his tongue slides on my pussy. He licks it—not like he's trying to get me off, but like he wants the intimacy of oral. I must be right, because with his other hand, he pushes up my thighs so they close around his head. Then, he uses his tongue to touch me, his lips to kiss me, and his breath to tease.

It feels like hours later when he resurfaces, but it's only a few minutes.

I'm drenched from his tongue and my own arousal. He moves up and pushes my legs open. Silently, I let them fall slack, giving him access. He braces his knee, I feel him reach between us. Then, his cock slides in, stretching me slowly as he pushes to the hilt.

I moan, biting my lip.

"Good girl," he says.

He pushes himself up on the heel of his hand. In the shadows, his hard abdominal muscles ripple. I wince, savoring the little twinge as he bottoms out.

Jaw gritted, he pulls out and thrusts hard and slow back inside me. He's still in his pants, pushed just below his groin. A handful of white wrapped candies fall from his pocket.

He keeps fucking, hard and slow. My body tightens at first, but then it loosens, and my pussy takes him easily. I'm soaked now. I hear it, feel it as he fucks. I can't bite back the soft moans. Maybe I love him like this, stern and holding back his natural violence.

He sweeps the candies aside with one hand. They clatter on the floorboards.

Before I realize what's happening, he pulls from me and flips me to my knees.

"Hands on the headboard," he says.

Obediently, I grip the leather and wood with both hands. He takes hold of it too and lifts my hips with his other hand. His hot, hard chest presses to my back, and I feel his groin against my ass. Then, his blunt cock pushes into my pussy, and I let my head fall back against his shoulder.

He pumps, deep.

"I'm not what you want," he gasps. "I'm selfish...destructive."

My stomach goes cold.

"But I'm just selfish enough not to give a fuck," he breathes. "Goddamn it, darling, have me anyway."

I'm frightened now. His hand comes up and grips my throat, holding me as he fucks. Something changed.

I cling to him, cowed. I don't understand men, don't know why they do what they do, how they can be so cold and rough but so driven by their desires. So hard on the surface. So soft under their armor.

My eyes flutter shut.

The gunslinger is deadly, but the gunslinger begs for me in the dark.

He takes a branding without saying a word. He shoots men off their horses, blood running down his back. Then, all it takes is the little lace slip he likes best, and he's desperate.

Maybe he's not the one with the power in this contract.

I'm drunk off that thought. His pace picks up, his grip firm around my neck. His cock drives hard into me, stroking up against my G-spot.

"God, I can't get enough of you, you pretty whore," he pants. "You drive me insane."

His teeth score my shoulder, his hand tightening on my throat. My head spins.

"The first time I met you, I could see those pretty tits under your dress," he pants. "If it had been one day later, I'd have fucked you up against the hallway wall."

I moan, my pussy clenching around his cock.

"What you did...wasn't much better," I manage.

"And you liked it," he breathes. "You loved what I did to you."

Pleasure lights up like a match.

He's right; I loved it.

I loved that he was older and dangerous, that he hung his pistol on the bedpost before fucking me, even though he had no business doing that. I used to close my eyes, spread my thighs, and touch myself to the memory of him taking my virginity.

God, I'm just as bad as him.

I orgasm hard, wetness slipping down my thighs, lips parted, shaking in his arms.

"That's a good girl," he says. "Come, you beautiful slut."

He's close, I can feel his pleasure approaching. I can hear it in his quickening breath, the way it hurts when he bottoms out, in his narrowed gaze. He loses a bit of his humanity when all he can think about is his own desire.

I reach back to push him off me, but he grips my wrist.

"Westin," I pant. "Please, pull out."

He falls over me so we're both on our hands and knees.

But he doesn't stop.

My stomach goes cold.

"Trust me," he says, his voice a low growl in my ear.

His hand covers my mouth. My heart pounds. I'm not sure I should trust a man who admitted he wants to get me pregnant. Then, my mind goes back to the amendment.

He promised.

High off fear, I let him ride that edge, knowing if he doesn't remember his humanity, we'll be broken in the morning.

He takes me hard, his hand over my protests. I'm moaning, maybe as aroused as he is by the prospect of breaking the rules.

But then, at the very end, he comes back to me. His body leaves mine as he turns me on my back. Then, he falls over me and his mouth captures mine. Warmth spills between our bodies, pooling on my stomach. He groans against my tongue, and when our kiss ends, he stays close, like he wants to breathe my air right from my lungs.

"Have me, darling," he whispers. "Trust me."

I don't know what he means.

"Yes, sir," I whisper.

CHAPTER FORTY-ONE

WESTIN

The next morning, bright and early, I head down the mountain in my truck. I stop in town and get a dozen red roses. Then, mind blank, I drive until I pull up outside a two-story house with blue shutters at the edge of South Platte. It's nine in the morning. All the lights are on, and I can see the fireplace burning through the window.

I step out and head up the front porch. A familiar cinnamon scent wafts through the door. It always smells like that.

My knuckles rap on the door. There's a short silence, and the blue front door opens as my mother's pale, oval face appears. She pulls back, shocked that I'm finally visiting. Then, she recovers and pushes open the screen.

"Westin," she whispers. "Come inside, baby."

I'm thirty-seven and six and a half feet tall, but I don't tell her I'm not her baby. I just kiss the top of her head and follow her into the front hall. She's in leggings and a big sweatshirt, her gray and brown hair piled on her head and skewered with a pin. Everything is exactly how I remember.

"Can I get you coffee?" she asks once we're in the kitchen.

I nod, sinking down. She has tiny chairs, and I always feel them groan beneath me. She busies herself making coffee. The room is thick with the unspoken months since my last visit. I clear my throat.

"Sorry I haven't been around," I say. "The ranch has been busy."

She waves a hand. "I understand. How's it been?"

"It's good. We turn a decent profit," I say.

She sets the coffee down before me and gets a cup for herself. I take mine black; she likes lots of sugar. Her eyes fall on my hand on the mug, and she frowns.

"You get so many scars from the barbed wire, baby," she says. "Make sure you wear gloves."

I nod, clearing my throat.

She chews on her lower lip. There's a faint light in her eyes that hasn't been there in a while.

"Something going on?" I ask.

She smiles, tapping her mug. "I'm seeing someone."

My brow arches. "Oh? What's his name?"

"Matthew Hewitt," she says, blushing a little. "He's very kind, quiet and...gentle."

I know the Hewitt family; they own a chain of banks in South Platte. Matthew is about my mother's age, and he has always been respectful towards me, but I don't know him well.

"I'll drop by and see him sometime," I say.

Horror creeps over her face. "Don't you dare, Westin."

I reach out and take her hand. "I won't fuck this up for you. You deserve to be happy."

"Don't swear, baby," she says, her eyes going soft. "And thank you. He's very different from your father, but we're happy."

My mind goes back to this morning. My hand loosens, and I withdraw it. My mother's eyes follow me, her brow creased.

"You came here to ask me something," she says quietly.

I nod. I'm not sure how to say the words.

"Ask me anything," she urges.

"Was my father a good man?" I say, looking her in the eyes.

She's taken aback. Her nails clink on her mug as she thinks.

"He wasn't," she says finally. "He was gentle but very stern and bullheaded. There was a reason my father ran him off with a gun."

I cough, clearing my throat. "What?"

She shrugs. "My father ran him off with a gun the first time he came to our door. He was too old for me, but I was just so...young, I guess. I couldn't see all the reasons why a cattle farmer who'd already been married twice was a bad match for an eighteen-year-old girl."

Quietly, I pick my jaw off the floor.

"You were his third wife?"

She nods. "The first died, the second ran off. He was a distant, hard person. Maybe he was difficult to love."

I'm not sure how I feel about all this new information.

"So how did you end up marrying him?" I press.

Her cheeks flush, and she tucks a wisp of graying hair behind her ear. "Oh, you know."

"No, I don't know."

She waves a hand. "There was a situation."

My brows rise, and I lean back, stretching my legs under the table.

"You were pregnant," I say. "With me."

She shrugs, waving her hand, like everything that's coming out can be shooed away like a fly. "Things were different then. I couldn't have had a baby without a husband."

My mouth is dry. "Did you want to marry him?"

She shrugs. "I mean, he loved me. He was kind to me, kind to you. That's all that mattered. But love...that's a strong word for what I felt."

"Did...he know you didn't love him?" I ask.

She shrugs again, so flustered that her words shake, even though she's trying to be casual.

"He didn't care. That wasn't his way," she says. "He just...willed the world to obey him, and it did."

She stands up, clearly unable to handle the discomfort, and starts clearing the coffee mugs, even though mine is still full. Her back is to me, and maybe that's good, because it gives me the courage to ask what I need to know.

"Am I like him?"

She turns, leaning on the counter. Her eyes are haunted, like she's been dreading this question for years.

The silence speaks volumes. Then, she shakes her head once.

"Yes, but no," she whispers. "You and Sovereign always seemed like the two sides of him."

"So together...we were a lot like him," I say flatly. "That's why we got the farmland."

She nods. "He knew you'd do well going into business together. He wanted to make sure you were taken care of and that you'd take care of me."

Silence falls. The past feels heavy in the kitchen I bought her with the money from the land my father gave me, from one hardheaded man to another, willing into existence by blood, sweat, and calculated violence.

"And ruthless," she says suddenly.

"What?"

Her lids flutter. "Your father was in awe of that part of you. He used to tell me the world wasn't ready for you to take it on, that you were...ruthless."

My heart sinks.

Her lips purse. "It was a compliment, coming from him."

I can't speak.

Her eyes are soft. "I don't want to lie to you, baby. You are so much like your father."

My head isn't on straight right now. Maybe I came here wanting her to tell me I was nothing like him, that all my self-perceptions were wrong. But my mother has always been honest. She told me the truth I already knew.

Now, I just have to live with it.

Neither of us feel like talking about my father anymore after that. It occurs to me that I want to ask if she thinks he was faithful, but I don't have the courage. I don't think it matters matter anymore.

I stay for lunch and have more coffee as she cuts the roses and sets them on the table. When I leave, she hugs me goodbye, and I feel a tremor in her arms.

"I won't take so long to visit," I say.

She steps back. "Bring your girl next time."

I pause, in the doorway of my truck. "What?"

She taps her neck. "You've got a hickey there, Westin."

I swing inside. "Listen, Mom, I need a little time."

Her face falls. "Okay. I won't rush you."

"It's not you," I say firmly so she knows I mean it. "This is about me and...all the bullshit I have in my head. Just give me a little time, and I promise you'll meet her when I've sorted myself out."

She nods, her smile fragile. I get out of the truck again and go to hug her. When she pulls back, she pats me on the cheek and gives me a teary kiss.

"I've never been able to guess what's going on in that head, baby," she says. "But I can be patient."

I pull her in one last time. "I want you to know, nothing was ever your fault. Nothing."

"Oh, darling," she whispers.

"I mean that. I want you to tear it up, go out with all the bankers you want, alright?"

She laughs as she lets me go. I touch her face before heading back to the truck. My head won't straighten itself out. I do a grocery run, trying to get anything I think Diane might want, and pack it into the cold back of the truck. Then, I go to the general store and head to the fabric counter, because if I can't use my words, gifts will have to do.

I stop short, floor creaking under my boots. There's somebody already there, leaning on the counter, chatting up the lady at the register.

"Deacon," I say.

He swivels. "What are you doing here?"

I shrug and lean on the other side of the counter. The lady stands between us, glancing back and forth. She's got a bolt of pink dotted cotton rolled out. Deacon and I look down at it and then back at each other.

"That looks like church girl fabric to me," I say.

"Aw, shut the fuck up," he says.

I laugh, and some of the tension eases in my shoulders. "Listen, you want to get some coffee? I've got something I want to talk to you about."

He shrugs. "Sure. Let me finish up here."

The lady folds the pink cloth and puts it in a bag for him. Then, I pick out several bolts of fabric I think Diane will like. Just as I'm being rung up, my eye falls on a soft, glossy cloth edged with lace. It's creamy white, and the lace is pale yellow.

"What kind is that?" I ask.

The cashier pulls the bolt down. I can feel Deacon smirking behind me.

"It's a satin blend," she says.

That doesn't mean anything to me, but it would look pretty on Diane, so I get a few yards of it. Deacon and I take our tickets and head up to the front register. There's a short line. I glance back at him, but he's checked out, staring up at the ceiling.

"Long night?"

He nods, blinking. "I need to figure this shit out. I had people from the gas company on my porch yesterday."

"What did you tell them?"

"I said they're either getting hit with a shotgun now or with a lawyer later," he says. "I don't have time for this. The summer is shaping up to be as hot and dry as last year. I need to work on my ranch, not fuck around in a courtroom this year."

"I get it." I put my things down.

The Lemon Chews stare at me from their bucket. I take a handful and add it to the pile, even though my stomach is queasy.

"She's got you whipped," Deacon says.

"Maybe they're for me."

"You don't like candy."

"Shut up."

I pay for my things and wait while he does the same, smirking. Then, we head across the street to drop them off in our trucks. The cafe is a block down, and it's empty. I sink into the corner with a cup of black coffee. Deacon sits opposite me in the booth.

"Alright, what's your plan, gunslinger?" Deacon says.

"I don't have a plan," I say. "At least, not a full one. But if I can figure out how to get David Carter, Vince Cassidy, and Corbin Buchanan out to Sovereign Mountain, I can take care of them all in one go."

"I'm all ears," he says.

I lean forward. "The bridge over the river is very high. If you forced a vehicle off there, it'd be hard to get evidence."

His eyes narrow as he thinks. "You're going to force three cars off a bridge? I don't know."

"No, we need to get both men in the car."

"You mean all three."

I shake my head. "David Carter gets something else. I don't know what, but if we can get him up to Sovereign Mountain, I'll take him out before that."

He cocks his head. "You really hate him."

I nod. "I really do."

He leans back, crossing one leg. "So what you need is an event, one big enough that you could invite friends and business associates, one people feel like they can't say no to. Sovereign Mountain isn't well liked, but you have half the town in your pockets."

We sit in silence for a while. He shrugs.

"Maybe a funeral."

I raise an eyebrow. "Would you like to volunteer to play the role of dead body?"

"Alright, no funeral. A wedding."

We both look at each other.

"You're the one with a girl," he says.

"So are you. I'm not getting engaged just so I can invite people over and murder them."

Deacon's jaw works, brows creased. "Were you going to get engaged anyway?"

"Of course," I say. "But it would break Diane's heart if she thought it wasn't sincere."

He lets out a deep sigh and sinks into the seat. "You're right. And she probably wouldn't want her brother at her wedding if he's as bad as you say. Let me think on this. I'll come up with something."

I put my hat on and empty my mug. "I'll start working out the particulars."

We head out the door, and Deacon looks out over the snowy street.

"What's your plan for today?" he asks.

"I got some more errands," I say, taking out a pack of cigarettes.

He takes one. "I'll come with you. I got a meeting in town early tomorrow, so I'm not driving all the way home. You got a couch I can crash on?"

I sigh, shoving the package into my breast pocket. "Yeah, but you better not embarrass me in front of Diane. You act like a gentleman, okay?"

He pulls his hat lower. "I'll be a saint."

CHAPTER FORTY-TWO

DIANE

The door downstairs crashes open. In a second, I'm bolt upright in bed, heart in my mouth.

There are men downstairs. Their boots clatter, and they're talking loudly. It takes a moment, but I pick Westin's voice out of the conversation, and my tight muscles ease. Whoever is downstairs, he has it handled.

I wait, my arms wrapped around myself. After a bit, his boots move up the stairs and the door opens. He looks like he's been busy, and he has a paper bag under his arm.

"Where've you been?" I whisper.

He sets the bag down and leans over the bed. His hand goes around my throat, and he kisses me almost savagely. Excitement runs through him like a current and makes my scalp prickle. He pulls back, eyes glittering. Something is different about him tonight, but I don't know what.

"Goddamn, you're pretty, Diane," he says.

"Are you drunk?" I whisper, my heart sinking.

He shakes his head, kissing me again and swiping his tongue against mine. He doesn't taste like whiskey, just Westin. Then, he puts the paper bag into my hands and starts taking his shirt off.

"What's this?"

"Way back, I saw you wear a dress made from curtains," he says, shrugging out of his shirt and starting on his belt. "I told myself I'd get you some real fabric."

My chest warms. It always takes me aback when he notices little things. Overwhelmed, I open the bag, and out spills cloth of all different colors. At the bottom is a stretchy, silky fabric that's buttery smooth and edged with yellow lace.

"Westin," I say, giving him a watery smile.

He touches the cloth in his calloused fingertips. "You'd look pretty in this, darling."

"I think this is for lingerie," I say.

"Even better. I'll ask Keira for a sewing machine, and you can make something that'll stay on for less than a minute."

My eyes fall. He's horny; I can see his arousal under his zipper. That doesn't surprise me—he's always turned on when we're alone, always touching me, kissing me.

I tear my eyes from his groin. "Who's downstairs?"

"Deacon Ryder. He's a friend," he says. "Sort of."

I frown. "Is he safe?"

He nods, picking up the bag of candy and dropping it on the bedside table. "We had some business together, and he's staying the night because he lives pretty far out."

I nod, burrowing down against the pillows. "Okay, that's alright."

He goes to the bathroom, flicking on the light. "Join me in the shower?"

I shake my head, and his brows rise.

"No, thank you, sir," I say sleepily.

His throat bobs. He's just a shadow in the doorway, but I detect an undercurrent in him. I halfway expect him to tell me to shower anyway, but he just looks at me with his eyes shadowed.

The room goes from warm to uncertain. I pull back the covers, leaving only my blue slip between us. He comes close and kneels over me on the bed.

"I want to know the truth about something, darling," he says, his voice low.

"Yes?" I whisper.

"In twenty, thirty years, will you regret staying?" he asks.

My heart melts. Suddenly, I'm back in his truck, sunshine spilling through the windshield. It's hot and his hand is on my thigh.

"No," I say, voice quivering. "A lot happened that I wish hadn't, but I'll never regret you."

He kisses my mouth then, slow and deep. I don't think he'll ever question my feelings again. There's something final about the way he gets up and goes into the bathroom, shutting the door. I'm still awake when he finishes his shower and gets into bed.

He's still hard, his cock digging into my ass. His breath is hot on the back of my neck, kisses burning down my nape.

"Face down," he says, lifting my thigh. "Be a good girl and don't make a sound."

Heart pounding, I obey. He pushes into me, and I can't bite back my whimper. His hand comes up and covers my mouth. His cock starts pumping, rubbing up against my G-spot. He keeps that position, every stroke sending me a little closer to shouting against his hand.

With his other hand, he touches me, back and forth until I tighten. When I come, arousal spills out around his cock, staining the sheets. He pulls out, dips under the covers, and I feel his tongue on the insides of my thighs.

When he resurfaces, he's biting up my stomach and breasts.

"Fuck, darling, I could drink you neat," he moans, shoving his cock roughly into me.

Exhaustion washes over my satisfied body. He lifts me, putting his back against the headboard, and fucks me in his lap. Sweat etches down his face, dripping on his chest. I let him grip my wrists.

Our eyes are locked.

His body ripples. My body takes every thrust. The only reaction he has when his orgasm hits him is to pull out and grit his jaw. Warmth spills between our bodies, and then everything goes quiet.

I shift. Something crinkles under my leg. He glances down and picks something up from the flannel sheet.

A wax paper-wrapped candy.

He stares at it like he's seen a ghost. His expression is unreadable.

"Westin?"

He tears his gaze to my face. His lips part.

"I love you, darling," he says, voice cracking.

Dead silence. The gas fire rushes. His heart thumps. My body is floating and falling all at once.

"Of course you do," I manage.

His fingers clench, rubbing the candy to peel back the wax paper. It falls aside, and he bites it in half.

"Huh," he says. "I thought it would taste different."

I take the other half, so stunned that I'm not sure what to say. Sweet lemon spreads over my tongue. His eyes are fixed to my mouth, like he can't look away.

He scares me when he's intense like this.

"Are you gonna fucking say it back?" he asks softly.

I bend, kissing his mouth then his chin where his short beard prickles. Then, I kiss down his chest, the salt of his sweat on my lips. His body ripples with tension as my lips brush his upper abdominals, and my nails pierce his sides.

"I love you, Westin," I whisper into his warm body, into the heart of him. "I choose you."

All the suffering I didn't know was in his body drains away. His muscles relax, and he lets out a soft sigh. Then, he pulls my face back up to his and kisses me, sweat and Westin and lemon candy mingling on our tongues.

We fuck again, this time not caring if it's loud.

And, God, it's some of the best sex we've ever had.

When I wake the next morning, I hear men's voices downstairs, and it jerks me out of my euphoria. My heart patters as I pull on my dressing gown and move barefoot down the stairs, pausing at the landing to survey the room.

Westin leans on the counter, talking quietly to a man with dark hair sitting at the table. I freeze. I don't like having men who aren't Westin in my kitchen. It reminds me too much of David and the Garrisons.

I consider going back to the bedroom, but Westin looks up. The other man turns, and I shrink back. He's got a mean face, a crooked nose, and a hard mouth. His skin is covered in tattoos, some recognizable, some not. Somehow, all those parts that shouldn't be pretty make up a handsome man.

"Come here, darling," Westin says.

Holding my dressing gown tight, I creep down to him. Westin slides his arm around my waist.

"This is Deacon Ryder. He's helping me with some work," he says.

"It's nice to meet you," Deacon says. He's got a hard, rough voice. "You must be Diane."

He holds out his hand. I hesitate then shake it. I'm surprised that he does it lightly, letting my fingers just rest on his, like somewhere along the way, someone taught him to be a gentleman.

"You're a knockout," he says, leaning back. "What are you doing with this ugly motherfucker?"

I gasp, and Westin starts laughing.

"You stay for breakfast, Ryder," he says. "Then get the fuck out."

Westin is already making breakfast, but I feel awkward standing there, so I shoo him out of the way and start cooking. He sits with Deacon, and they talk at the table for a while, about the ranch, about business. Then, they go outside, and I see them through the window over the sink, standing at the edge of the snow, smoking with serious expressions.

They didn't go outside for cigarettes. They went out so they could talk about things they don't want me to hear.

I set three plates of food out.

They're planning to do something bad. I can just tell.

I knock on the window and wave them in. We sit at the table and talk about nothing important. Westin and Deacon communicate mostly with lighthearted insults. When the meal is done, I pour Deacon some coffee in a thermos and hand it to him.

"You watch that one," he says, jerking his head at Westin.

Westin flips him off and puts his hat on to walk him out. I stay inside, still in my dressing gown, and clear the table. When he returns, everything is tidied, and the floor is swept. I head upstairs to shower, but Westin takes my elbow on the landing.

"Thank you," he says.

"For what?"

"Rolling with the punches," he says. "Now, run along, or I might just fuck you before work."

I cock my head. His eyes narrow. Carefully, I tug the tie of my dressing gown open, and he gives me that look, the hungry one.

"I'm already late for chores," he says, voice low.

He looks so handsome, all desperate to have me. I push my dressing gown and the strap of my slip down then turn to climb the steps.

I glance over my bare shoulder. He's watching me from the landing, chest heaving.

"Goddamn it, Diane," he says as he comes after me.

CHAPTER FORTY-THREE

WESTIN

We move through our rituals. She keeps to the rules in our contract as best she can. I tie her up and eat her out until she cries from coming so hard. Then, I rub her back, tell her she's a good girl, and put lemon candy on her tongue until she melts into me.

She blossoms.

Her face fills out first, and then her body follows. At some point, she went from being underweight to soft with gentle curves. Her breasts are full and teardrop shaped. They fit so well in my hands. Her hips and thighs fill out until they shake when I fuck her on her hands and knees.

I eat those curves up. Her skin is soft like flowers, her mouth sweet, her pussy like heaven.

I thought I was in love before, but it had nothing on what I feel now.

We race through winter, both too distracted and drunk on each other to do more than work and fuck. Then, suddenly, I go out to do chores, and the air smells like spring. The soggy snow pulls back to reveal dark earth. I have to leave my muddy boots in the hallway before going upstairs.

Sovereign and I planned for an early calving season, following the trend of last year. We bring in the expectant cows and keep an eye on them. More often than not, I wake to a knock on the door and end up digging a breech calf out. It's unpleasant, but that's business on a cattle ranch.

The cows don't birth easy this year. They struggle, and the calving season is full of bloody nights. I tell Sovereign it's on account of the mothers born during the drought being small.

He says he thinks that's true. Maddie washes the windows of the barn with Florida Water and says she'll pray about it.

The losses hit hard. It's thankless work. The ranch hands and wranglers assist where they can. Whoever is awake helps, but usually, it's Sovereign, Jensen, and I who end up with the midwifery.

Sovereign wakes me at three one night, and we head to the barn. There's a dappled shorthorn cow in the back stall. I check the brand and flip her tag. This is her first year having a calf. I run my hand down her nose, shushing her as her sides heave.

"She's gone on too long," Sovereign says, stripping off his shirt. "She needs help."

I unlatch the gate and enter the warm, dark stall. He runs his hand down her spine, and I hold her head while he checks her progress. I hear his heavy sigh as he straightens.

"Fucking breech," he says.

"I'll get the shit," I say, leaving the stall.

We work quickly and silently. The cow is quiet, which I don't like. A loud cow is a fighting cow. Silent means all the strength has leached out of her. We work hard, and it's thirty minutes later when we get the calf out and cleaned up. I mix a bucket of sweet molasses with hot water and urge her to drink it, but she just watches me with glassy eyes.

Sovereign stands in front of her, his hands on his hips. His head drops, and I hear him swear under his breath. I've never seen him like this before.

"She's alright," I say.

He shakes his head once. "Keira and I are going to start trying for a baby when I get unsnipped. This shit gets me now, feels real."

The pieces fall into place.

"Keira will be fine," I say. "She's strong."

He nods. "I've always liked being so far out, away from town. But now, I wish the hospital was closer."

I clap my hand on his shoulder, giving him a shake.

"I'll get this cow fixed up," I say. "You go to bed."

He nods, finding his shirt and leaving. In the quiet of the barn, I ease the cow into the back of the stall and dip my fingers into the water. Slowly, I get her to taste it, then to drink. Then, just as the morning sun cracks through the window, she starts eating. Her eyes go from glassy to watching her calf with interest.

Relieved, I settle with my back against the wall and close my eyes. For right now, the world is right.

"Westin."

I crack my eyes open to find Diane leaning on the door. A shaft of sunlight cuts through the window and makes her golden hair glow.

"Good morning," I say wearily.

"Long night?" she asks. "Keira said Sovereign left at three and didn't come back till five."

I nod, rising. I'm streaked with iodine and afterbirth, but my heart is light. I kiss her, and she unlatches the door to let me out.

"Want breakfast at the ranch house?" she asks.

"Let me shower. I'm filthy."

She cocks her head as we head back to the gatehouse. "Want company?"

My dick twitches. "I'd never turn that down, darling."

Nothing feels better than stepping into the hot shower after a night like that. I stand under the water with my head back and just let it beat down on my chest. She takes her time pinning her hair up. It's gotten so long, it hangs to her waist. Then, she slips in beside me and grabs the soap.

Her hands are soft and careful as she lathers it over my torso.

"Sorry I have to keep leaving you at night," I say.

She shrugs. "I grew up on a farm. I know how it is."

"This spring has been hard."

Her face sobers, her soapy palm stilling on my upper abdomen.

"Spring is here," she whispers, "which means, they'll start building the road soon if no one stops them."

I lift her chin. "Deacon and I are going to take care of it," I say. "It's in his interest to stop the people doing this as much as it's mine."

Her forehead scrunches. "Is that what you talk about with him?"

"It's some of it."

"Can I know what you're planning to do?"

I shake my head, using my thumb to smooth the worry wrinkles from her brow. "Trust me, darling, I'll always come through for you."

"I'd bet a lot on you two," she manages.

"That's my girl." I kiss her forehead.

Her eyes close. She takes a deep breath, and they open again.

"You're both wild cards," she said. "Please get my farm back, but don't do anything that will kill you. I need you. If I have to pick, I'll take you."

I'm speechless. I know how much that land means to her, and I never thought I'd hear those words from her lips.

"You won't have to pick," I promise.

She sniffs and starts rubbing soap into my skin again. "I just want you to know that."

I pull her into me and rest my chin on her head. "I know it, darling."

We end up fucking in the shower, as usual. She wraps her legs around my waist, and I take her hard against the wall. Then, we dry off and get dressed, walking hand in hand to the ranch house.

The main hall is full. Everything smells like sausage gravy and biscuits. Diane goes to find us a seat and I head to the table to fill our plates.

I sink down at Sovereign's side, Diane on my right, and take a sip of black coffee. He has dark circles under his eyes. I doubt he went back to sleep.

"Cow's fine," I say. "She just needed a little patience."

His shoulders sink, and he nods. "Fucking hate this time of year sometimes," he says.

"It's not all bad," Keira says softly, linking her arm through his elbow. "Some good things are happening."

For a second, I think she's implying she's pregnant, but that would be strange, given that Sovereign has been snipped for almost two decades and he hasn't gotten it reversed yet.

"We thought we'd get married soon," Keira says. "Here, at the ranch."

Diane's face lights up. "Really? That's exciting."

It's a relief to me that Diane gets along so well with Keira and Maddie. She needs the companionship of other women. I have my doubts that David ever let her go anywhere, and I know Thomas only let her out to shop, so it's good to see her warming up to having friends.

Sovereign clears his throat and leans back.

"I was hoping you'd marry us, Westin," he says.

"Polygamy's not legal in Montana," I say. "You'll have to take turns."

He gives me a withering stare, but I see a muscle in his cheek twitch. Keira smirks over her coffee, and Diane elbows me in the ribs and rolls her eyes. For the first time in a while, the mood is light.

It feels so fucking good.

"Sure," I say. "I'd be honored to officiate."

Sovereign sits back, reaching in his pocket. He comes up with a crushed pack of cigarettes and gets to his feet. "I hope you know what you're doing, Westin."

I glance up, unsure what he means.

"Deacon Ryder just walked his ass into my house," he says.

I turn, and sure enough, Deacon Ryder stands by the door talking with Jensen. Sovereign and Deacon aren't enemies, but they're natural competitors. We do business together when we need to and go our separate ways.

I follow Sovereign across the room, leaving Diane with Keira. I'm glad to see they're both talking, their heads together. I hate leaving her alone sometimes, especially on days when I know all she wants to do is lay in bed and turn over her worst memories in her head.

"Let's talk outside," Sovereign says.

We leave the hall and head out to the barn. The ground is thick with mud in the yard, but it dries up as we circle to the back pasture. It's warmer now that the sun has risen, and it feels good through the fabric of my shirt. Deacon stops and lights a cigarette, offering one to each of us.

"The road got the green light," Deacon says.

"I assumed it would," Sovereign says.

"How much time before they start building?" I ask.

Deacon shrugs. "Maybe a month or two. There are still building permits being processed. David Carter got an offer on the land from the gas company."

Fuck.

"Alright," I say grimly. "He hasn't signed it."

"No," Deacon says. "I'd say he's reluctant."

I'm sure it's a bitter pill for David to swallow that his farm is being forced out from under him. He didn't want the road put through, but now that the Garrisons are gone, he has no choice. I know him well enough to guess that he'll reap all the money he can from the farm as it goes down.

His heart's not soft, not like Diane's.

"I can't buy it," Sovereign says. "Like I said, I'm cash poor until the season is through."

Deacon shakes his head. "Don't think it's for sale for anyone but Vince Cassidy and Corbin Buchanan."

Sovereign takes a slow drag on his cigarette. The smoke drifts to the sky.

"It sounds to me like you two have a problem," he says. "A joint problem. Maybe one that could be solved the way I solved my last one."

I glance sideways at Deacon. "We've talked about that."

Deacon relates our conversation in the cafe to Sovereign. I stand there struggling not to let my anger get the best of me. Ever since she told me what David did, rage has sat in my chest like a barely-contained wild animal.

Head down, but ears alert, waiting for a chance to lash out.

"You think you can get Cassidy and Buchanan into a car together and force them off the bridge?" Sovereign asks slowly.

I shake my head once, jerking out of my reverie. "Yeah. We need to find an excuse to invite a shit ton of people up here. Everybody knows you carpool so you don't have fifty odd trucks parked on the hill."

"What if that doesn't work?" Sovereign asks.

"I guess we can always slice a few tires."

He thinks about it for a minute and then shrugs. "If that's what you want. But just know, if I die and go to hell, it'll just be me waking up to a shit ton of people on my ranch."

"I know," I say. "But I helped you get your girl."

He stabs out his cigarette. "And I'll help you get yours."

We part ways, and I go back to the gatehouse. Diane is in the bath when I return. I pause in the doorway, just taking in how pretty my girl is. For a moment, the heaviness of what I have to do weighs me down. Then she turns, offering me a smile, and my head goes empty.

I lean over the tub, bending her head back, and kiss her mouth.

"Hello, sir," she whispers.

"Hello, darling."

Her gaze is sober as it lingers on me.

"What's wrong?" I ask.

She chews her lip. "Do you still want...to marry me?" she whispers.

I crouch down, taking her chin between my fingers. Her big eyes with their sexy droop are soft. My chest is tender; I just want to take her to the bed and fuck her gently and kiss her mouth, to try to get her to understand how deep my feelings for her go.

"Of course," I say, my voice hoarse. "I wanted to give you time, but I'd marry you tomorrow if I could."

Her lips tremble. "Really?"

"Anytime, anywhere."

She stands, and I rise with her. Her wet body presses to mine, and her hands wrap around my neck. She's so soft now; not just her body, but in the way she touches me, the way she trusts me. I carry her out to the bed. In the top drawer of the dresser, where I keep our toys, is the ring I bought her in the winter. I take it out and cross the room.

"Hold out your hand," I say.

She does, her brows rising when I slip it on her finger. Her breasts heave and her throat bobs as the ring glitters in the dim light.

"It's beautiful," she whispers. "How long have you had it?"

"A while," I murmur, kissing between her breasts. "When can I marry you?"

"The summer," she says. "I want Keira to have her moment."

"Do you want to just go to the courthouse?"

She shakes her head. "No, I want a real wedding. Everyone at the ranch, anyone else you want there, can come. And I want David there as well."

Shock ripples through me. Did she just say that? I lift my head. "What?"

She purses her mouth. "I want him to see that he didn't break me. Maybe I'll never have Carter Farms, but I will be happy. Fuck him."

I hesitate. She gives me a sharp look.

"I am that petty, Westin," she says.

My heart thumps as I bend down and kiss her deeply. "It's not pettiness, darling. He deserves it."

I let her go back to bathing, and I head downstairs. The wild animal in my chest is jerking at its leash, raring to go. Time to let Deacon know I just got my opportunity to invite a shit ton of people up to Sovereign Mountain.

Now, all I have to do is decide what I feel like doing to David Carter. Fuck figuring anything else out. Getting Carter Farms in Diane's name can wait.

I want blood.

CHAPTER FORTY-FOUR

DIANE

Keira and Sovereign get married at the ranch. Westin looks so handsome officiating that he's all I pay attention to. Keira wanted a small, private wedding, so it's just the ranch hands, the wranglers, and Sovereign's close friends. It's a balmy spring day, the sun is warm, and the grass is a rich, dark green carpet under our feet.

The wedding is small, but the celebration afterwards feels huge. Everything goes hazy at the end. Sovereign and Keira disappear just as the sun starts to set. Everyone else stays in the tent where the alcohol keeps flowing.

Someone sets up fireworks down in the valley, across the road. The beer runs out, and whiskey is pulled from back rooms and poured. My yellow sundress sticks to my body. Westin keeps trying to put his hands up under it, kissing my neck in front of everyone so I have to give him a look to make him behave.

At some point, Deacon and Jensen start shooting tin cans in the field. Sovereign leans out of his window and hollers at them to cut it out.

Westin shakes his head and mutters something I can't hear. Then, he puts his hat on my head, and we slow dance, both too drunk to do anything else.

Around three in the morning, I'm in bed with a glass of water and Tylenol. Then, it's morning, and I'm so hungover, I can't do anything but sleep it off for the next twenty-four hours.

Westin brings me some toast on Sunday morning when I'm finally feeling better. He looks good, but his body tolerates alcohol better than mine. I brush back his wavy chestnut hair and let him kiss me. He tastes minty, like he just brushed his teeth.

"No alcohol at our wedding," I say.

He laughs. "I think it'll be alright," he says. "Just no whiskey for you, darling."

I sigh, feeling a little messy. "Okay, no whiskey for me."

His mouth trails down the side of my neck. "I'll have better things to do than drink on my wedding night."

"I have a feeling I'm one of those things," I murmur.

He pulls back, face sober. "Now that we're engaged, I want you to wear your collar."

My face warms. I wondered when he'd decide to put it around my neck. It's exciting that he feels like we're at that point.

"I thought you'd never ask," I say.

He rises and goes to the dresser. When he returns, he has a thin gold chain with a tiny knot at the center.

"Turn around and lift your hair."

I obey, gathering my hair and tying it into a high ponytail. This feels important, maybe more so than when he put my engagement ring on. It takes him a second to latch the clasp, and then it falls to the base of my neck.

"Look at you," he says, his voice rough.

I touch the clasp. It feels like a little metal bead. "What is that?"

"It's permanent," he says. "I can cut it off, but I'd prefer not to."

I swallow. Maybe that's why this feels different than a ring. Warmth stirs in my lower belly as my toes curl.

I brush my ass back against him., and he slides his hand over my throat.

"You're beautiful," he says.

He lets me go, and I scramble out of bed to inspect myself in the bathroom mirror. He joins me, rolling up his sleeves to wash his hands. I glance over, enjoying the way he looks, all windswept with his forearms out.

"What are your plans for today?" I ask lightly.

He leans on the sink. "I have a meeting, then some chores."

"What's the meeting about?"

I step between his boots and lean forward, resting my chin on his chest. He tugs my ponytail, gripping it by the base.

"Nothing."

I narrow my eyes. "Carter Farms?"

He shrugs. "Wouldn't you rather I handle that on my own?"

I let out a sigh. "I just... We've been waiting so long. I'm worried something is going to happen."

"Deacon paid off some people in the city to push the paperwork back," he says. "We've got time. I'm handling it."

I hate that he won't talk about what's going on with my farm. I wriggle out of his arms and flick my ponytail over my shoulder as I leave the bathroom to let him know I'm annoyed.

He leans in the doorway, arms crossed. "Diane."

I rub my eyes, blinking hard. I was in such a good mood this morning, and thinking about Carter Farms ruined it. It's a dark cloud in the back of my mind. Sovereign Mountain is beautiful, but I want to be back on my land.

"I just want...to go home," I say, and my voice cracks.

He holds out his arms. I go to him and let him cradle me against his chest.

"I know," he says. "I promise, I'll get you everything you want. Just trust me a little longer."

CHAPTER FORTY-FIVE

WESTIN

The next morning, I set out a pair of jeans, boots, and a shirt for her before I head to the barn. When chores are done, I take Rocky and Gracey out, brush them down, and saddle them up.

The sky overhead is dotted with puffy clouds. The air smells like spring.

She comes up the path from the gatehouse. Her blonde hair falls down her back in a braid. Her jeans hug her hips and thighs, highlighting her beautiful curves. The only thing she doesn't have is a hat.

"Come here, darling," I call.

She enters the barn, hands in her back pockets, like she's nervous. "What's this?"

"Let's ride," I say. "We could both use some time out of the house."

She looks confused, but then her face breaks into a smile. God, we've both been so caught up in our problems, I forgot how pretty she is when she's happy. I leave the horses by the hitching post and put my arm around her waist.

I take my hat off, she stands on her toes, and I kiss her. When I withdraw, I settle my hat on her head. It's a little big.

"There you go," I say. "So your hair doesn't bleach."

"What about you?" she asks.

I shrug. "I'll be alright today. It's not hot."

She follows me back into the barn, and I hold Gracey so she can mount up. Then, I swing onto Rocky, and we head out around to the back trail that goes up the hill. It runs along the old divide between Garrison Farms and Sovereign Mountain Ranch. Now, it all belongs to us.

She rides easily, hand rested on her thigh. The light breeze teases her hair. Now, seeing her in the sun, I realize she's pale. She needs to get out more. Being locked up by Thomas made her afraid to go back out into the world.

"I'm surprised you didn't spank me yesterday," she says, a little sass in her voice. "For doubting you."

"Sometimes, people don't need correction, Diane," I say. "Sometimes, they just need somebody to love them."

Her throat bobs, her lips parting.

"What do you think I need, sir?" she asks.

I take a beat. Rocky and Gracey bring us up the hill, through the growing spring grass to the crest that overlooks where Clint Garrison used to live. Now, it's just a burnt patch and a barn. Sovereign will tear it down soon and turn everything into pasture.

"I think you've always needed someone to love you, Diane," I say.

Her eyes are wet, fixed on the horizon. "Thank you," she says, her voice raspy.

I stack my hands on the saddle horn. "I think sometimes, I get wrapped up in my own head."

She nods. "I think I get wrapped up in...all this." She makes a gesture at her heart and drops her hand.

I nudge Rocky closer until I can reach out and touch her thigh. She looks over and offers a watery smile.

"Sovereign Mountain is beautiful," she says. "It makes me feel better."

"I'm glad."

"And you make me feel safe."

I touch her face, pushing her hat back. "All I want is for you to be happy and safe, darling."

There's a faint screech from the trees, like a bird of prey. Crows rise, swirling. I know there's a hawk somewhere in there. Diane lifts her eyes to the mountains. Her shoulders sink, and her face clears as she looks up at them. I know she must have spent a lot of time as a child, watching those mountains, wanting more.

She's hungry. She wants to bite deep into life, to taste it thoroughly.

Rocky paces sideways. Gracey throws her head.

"Do you want to run the horses?" I ask.

Her eyes light up, and she nods.

"Good. Let's take them up, then down. The river cuts across, but we can ford it where it's shallow. We'll keep going until you want to stop."

I click my tongue, and Rocky slips from a walk to a trot, then a canter. His hooves pound the earth, drowning out Gracey approaching until she's passing me by. I wonder if Gracey has a little thoroughbred in her; she's got a long gait and gives Rocky a run for his money.

She keeps a half-length ahead. The wind is warm, the sun is pleasant. My head goes blissfully empty, and all I see is my girl, wild and free, the way she was born to be.

Golden waves tug free of her braid and whip around her face. She rides easily, one hand up with the reins, the other out for balance.

We eat up land, our horses flying until we reach the river. The ground levels out and is littered with flat, white rocks. The river bubbles over little dips and valleys. It's shallow, barely reaching Rocky's knee in the deepest parts. On the other side is a grove of Ponderosa Pines. We urge our horses up the bank and into the woods, sticking to the trail.

The trees provide heavy shade. The air is cool and green in the forest.

"Where do you want to live?" she asks. "Here at Sovereign Mountain forever?"

I shrug. "I don't mind where I live, just as long as I've got land under my feet and sky over my head."

She smiles. "I love that about you."

"You're the same," I say.

She's quiet, her face sober. We pass through the pines, and the world opens up. We take the shortcut through the thinnest portion of old Garrison land, and now we're at the ridge that overlooks Carter Farms.

The sight brings sudden stillness over her face.

Her throat bobs.

"That's my home," she says, her voice husky. "I'd like to think I'd be fine anywhere, but that's my home. I want to live and die there."

I hate that I can't hold her. She's so small, wind whipping her hair over her face.

"You'll get it back. Swear it."

"I believe you," she says. Her voice is so soft, I barely hear. "I spent so much time looking up at these mountains, riding through them. I never thought I'd be on the other side, locked out. I never imagined it would be because David traded me off."

Anger flickers through me. I temper it down.

"I should move on," she says. "I just mourn the person he could have been. I'm not making excuses for what he did."

"Did your grandmother give the farm to David when she died?"

She nods. "I was pissed about that when David told me, but it makes sense. He ran it as soon as he was old enough to hold a pitchfork and drive a tractor. I wouldn't have known what to do with it."

I nod. "It's a lot of work."

Her eyes narrow. "I could have done it if anyone took the time to teach me. But after Nana died, David made me stay in the kitchen. He said it was cheaper if I did all the housework."

I keep my mouth shut. She opens up so rarely; I don't want to scare her off.

Birds sing in the brush at the edge of the pines. Rocky shakes his head, bridle rattling. She looks up, jerked from her reverie.

"Do you want to ride around to the cemetery?" I ask.

Her eyes light up. "Yes, please."

I jerk my head. "Let's go then."

We stick to the edge of the pasture, keeping far enough away we're not visible from the house. Then, we dip below the hill and ride down the deepest point of the valley. At the bottom sits the willow tree, the overgrown cemetery underneath.

She slides to the ground, tucking Gracey's reins back. I dismount and go after her, but she's already through the gate when I catch up.

"No one took care of it but me," she says, an edge of frustration to her voice.

Her grandmother's grave is overgrown. She drops to her knees and starts tearing up the grass. I kneel down and join her. Overhead, the sun is getting hotter. We work silently, pulling back the long grass. I take a jackknife from my pocket and let her use it to cut it away.

When we're done, her parents and her grandmother's graves are exposed.

She rises, dusting off her dirty hands. I slip my arm around her waist and pull her against my side.

"They're proud of you, darling," I say. "You're a strong woman."

She sniffs. "You better not make me cry, Westin."

I lean in and kiss the top of her head. We stand together for a long time, on the patch of earth she cleared. When this farm is ours, I'll come out here every morning and cut it back for her if that's what she wants.

"Nana used to hum this song to me before bed. She'd brush my hair and hum it. I never knew the words." Hoarsely, she hums a few bars. "It's a hymn, I think."

I nod. "I know that one."

She glances at me, smiling. "You going to tell me you're a church-going man now?"

"I went when I was a kid," I say. "My mother thought she was going to raise a gentleman."

Her brow arches. "And she didn't?"

"Not with the man she picked to be my father," I say.

The mood goes from nostalgic to having an edge of tension. The conversation we had the other night hangs over us.

"I get the feeling he did a number on you," she says quietly.

I don't answer. The pain I carry from the start of my life isn't violent, not in the way not the way she experienced it with Thomas. It's complex, and falling for her has made me realize I'm the result of generations of toxicity in the veins of the man who raised me.

Here I am, at the end of it, trying to sort myself out so I don't hurt the woman I love.

Trying to be a whole man, not just a gunslinger.

The sun climbs higher. Cicadas start to buzz. She keeps rubbing her fingers, trying to get the grass stain off them. They go faster until I catch them in mine.

"It's alright, darling," I say. "Let's get you home."

She nods, and I lead her from the cemetery. She goes to Gracey and waits while I latch the gate and go to help her on. I mount Rocky and look up to find her holding out my hat.

"You wear it, gunslinger," she says, smiling.

When she calls me that, it doesn't hurt. I fit the hat on my head. The horses prance, ready for a chance to tear through the fields.

"Let's go, darling," I say.

"Race you back."

The wind tosses her hair and her dark eyes glitter. She doesn't give me a chance to respond; she just digs her heels in, and Gracey takes to the field. Rocky goes without urging, eating up the distance.

Neither of us care if we can be seen from the house anymore. We race through the field that will belong to her someday, sooner rather than later. The ground is hard, the rainy season is over, and nothing trips up the horses. We fly, not urging them, just letting them run.

I let her get the best of me. She already has anyway.

CHAPTER FORTY-SIX

DIANE

We announce we're engaged a few weeks after Keira and Sovereign's wedding. I invite them over for dinner and make a roast for everyone. Over dessert, coffee, and whiskey, Westin tells them he'd like to have a big wedding on the ranch.

"I never thought you were the big wedding type," Sovereign says.

I stare, confused by the ghost of a smirk on his face. Westin gives him a look and pours more whiskey.

Afterwards, Keira and I clear the table, and the men disappear abruptly into the office at the front of the gatehouse. I rarely go in there; it's where Westin works on business contracts for the ranch. Still, I'm curious, so I crane my neck as they disappear behind the door.

"Sometimes, it's better not to know," Keira says quietly.

I frown. "Does Sovereign talk to you about business?"

She nods. "He tries to. When my first husband left the farm to me, I had to run everything, and it soured me on it. Sovereign gave me equal ownership of his shares of Sovereign Mountain and wants me involved, though, so I try to listen to him about it."

That strikes me as unexpectedly sweet. I didn't expect that of Sovereign; he's so gruff and cold.

Keira tucks her hair behind her ear. "Honestly, I have other things to worry about this year."

Her cheeks go pink, and she shuts the dishwasher. I put the teakettle on.

"What's going on?" I ask.

She leans against the table, squirming slightly. It's interesting to me that Kiera's incredibly shy about anything sex related but wears a submissive's collar. She must not be very shy in other circumstances.

"We're going to try for a baby," she says.

"Really?"

She nods. "Not yet, but soon."

I think about her and Sovereign—how rough and dangerous he looks and how sweet Keira is.

"Does he ever scare you?" I ask.

Her blush recedes. It takes her a moment, but she shakes her head. "Not anymore, but he did. Why?"

I shrug, struggling for words. "I just... Sometimes, I feel like I should be afraid of Westin, but I'm not. And I wonder what's wrong with me for that. I was terrified of Avery and Thomas. What makes him different?"

I've never said that aloud, and I regret it right away.

"I didn't mean it like that," I rush.

She smiles, shaking her head. "I know what you mean. I guess if you think about it, you and I are a lot alike on paper, but we're so different in person."

I nod slowly. Maybe on paper, Westin is just as frightening as the Garrison brothers, but...I've seen him on his knees, promising to give me everything.

It is so different.

"You know Sovereign best," I whisper.

She smiles, nodding. "I do. And I don't mind a little roughness around the edges. I don't think you do either."

There's a twinkle in her eye and a dimple on her cheek.

"It's kept me safe," I admit, trying not to blush. I wonder how much she knows about Westin and me.

The kettle whistles, and Keira pours two cups of chamomile. I accept one and sink down at the table.

"Westin is a good person," Keira says. "He's always helped me when I needed it, and he saved Sovereign over and over again. If he's decided he's in your corner...well, too bad for anyone who does you wrong."

"Sort of like a guard dog," I say, meaning for it to be a joke.

Keira shrugs, taking leftover cake from the fridge and unwrapping the wax paper. She cuts a slice for me and sets it on the table.

"You don't question the morality of a guard dog," she says. "You just let it do what it does."

That drives past all my anxiety and hits me deep inside. Keira and I don't talk much after that; we have our tea and cake. Then, Sovereign appears and takes her back to the ranch house. Westin stays in the office for a while longer, and I go upstairs and get ready for bed.

I'm in the bathroom, rubbing cream into my face, when he walks in and starts stripping.

"Everything okay?" I ask lightly.

He kisses the top of my head. "Everything's good, darling."

Tonight is a free use night; they come every Tuesday and Thursday now that I'm on the pill. I put the little silver anklet on and curl up in the bed. He's in the bathroom for a while, the shower running. My lids flutter, soothed by the rush of water.

What Keira said hits home.

He promised to save my farm. He's already saved me. I don't care anymore to question his methods. He's going to do what he does best regardless of what I want.

My eyes slip closed.

It's late in the morning when I wake, feeling rested for the first time in a while. I turn, and the little anklet is laying on the bedside table. My heart skips a beat, my face flushing. I slide my fingers down to my pussy and part myself, dipping the tip of one inside me.

He was there last night.

I clench, and his cum leaks down my thigh and stains the bed. My muscles are so relaxed, I know he made me finish in my sleep. I wonder what it was like for him, if I'm quiet when it happens.

I stretch.

Every day, little by little, he's building me back up. I never thought I could trust a man enough to let him have my body while I sleep.

As I'm braiding my hair after my shower, my ring catches the light, and I can't wipe the smile off my face for the rest of the morning.

Keira and I convince Jensen to take us into town. He shows up to drop off some wire, and we hitch a ride with him to South Platte to get some shopping done for the wedding.

I'm glad we decided to have a big wedding. I don't like the idea of all that attention, but I love the excitement. I've never had anything that feels so untainted. Everyone is happy for us, wanting to help. It's so pure after the last few years of misery.

In South Platte, I pick out white satin fabric. That night, back at the gatehouse, Keira and Maddie measure me and start making a pattern for my wedding dress. Part of me feels like this can't be real. I'll pinch myself and wake up, curled up in that little room off Thomas Garrison's kitchen again.

After Keira leaves, Westin returns. He was up at the ranch house, banned from our kitchen while Keira and I worked on my dress. My stomach flips as he steps through the door and sets his hat aside.

His eyes are sober.

"Come here, darling," he says.

I go to him, standing on my tiptoes so he can kiss me. His hand rests in my hair, his thumb on my cheek.

"What's wrong?" I ask.

He shakes his head once. "Nothing."

He's holding something back, but I don't push him yet. Instead, we eat dinner, and he asks about wedding preparations.

"Do you want any groomsmen?" I ask as I clear away the plates.

"Sovereign will be the best man and walk you up. Deacon will stand up with me."

I frown. It's a little strange he picked Deacon. It's my understanding they're on good terms when it comes to business but not close friends.

"Will Keira stand up with you?" he asks.

It's a touchy subject. Other than Keira and Maddie, I don't have any friends. I've started making casual conversation with some of the women who live in the employee housing, but they're all too busy for more than that.

I nod. "She said she'd like to."

"Good," he says.

I start boiling water for coffee. It's part of our ritual on Wednesdays. He sits at the table, and we talk about our week. At the end, he reviews where we are with each other, and we talk about what needs improvement. But first, I make coffee the way he likes it: fresh ground, patted into a pour over filter, set in the glass funnel.

Hot water swirls. Foam rises to the surface. I fill his thick, stoneware cup and place it on the table before him. For a second, I see his hands just as they were that first day: scarred from wire, big, capable.

"Good girl," he says. "Go undress and come sit on my lap."

He doesn't have to give specific instructions anymore. I go upstairs, wash quickly, and put on his favorite slip. Then, I come back downstairs and balance on his knee, enjoying the feel on his hand on my waist.

"I want to talk about something first," he said.

There's a sober note to his voice. I nod.

"My mother is still alive; she lives in town," he says. "I'd like her at the wedding."

My brows rise. "I had no idea."

"I saw her a while back, told her you exist," he says. "But I've been putting off bringing you to meet her for a couple of reasons."

I wonder if I did something wrong, but when I look into his eyes, I know it's something else. He's a million miles away.

"My father was a lot older than my mother," he says, voice gruff. "He wasn't a violent man. He loved her, but he got her pregnant when she was too young and...maybe her life could have been different. I worry sometimes that...I'm too much like him."

My stomach sinks.

"How old was he?" I whisper.

"When they married? Early fifties."

It's obvious that Westin and I are not the same as his parents, but he won't even look at me. I can tell it's taking everything he has to be this vulnerable. I can't dismiss his feelings. Gently, I take his hands in mine.

"We're different. I chose you, Westin."

"My father wasn't abusive," he says. "I idolized him. I thought he was everything a man should be. When I was old enough to know better, the damage was already done."

I think his voice cracks, but maybe that's just the sound of my heart breaking for him.

"I thought if I gave you a contract, it would make it better. That way, I can see your consent written out." His voice is flat, like he's had some time to think this through. "It felt more real. I can take it out, look at it."

I turn on his knee and lift his head, his beard prickly beneath my fingers.

"I love you, Westin," I whisper.

His grip intensifies. "I'll give you everything, darling," he says. "Anything you want."

I believe him; I'm just wondering how scorched the earth will be in his wake. He doesn't give me time to overthink. He turns me so I'm straddling him and brushes a flyaway curl back. His forehead presses to mine, his eyes close.

"Love me," he says.

His grip is tight. Hands steady, I unfasten his shirt until his chest and stomach are bare. His belt clinks as I pull it open and push his pants aside. He's hot and hard when I wrap my hand around him and guide his cock between my legs.

We both gasp. Our eyes connect. He's like magic. One touch, and my body is wide awake.

I wrap my arms around his neck. He buries his face in my shoulder. Our hips rise and fall together, not chasing anything, just trying our best to fix all the broken pieces that surround us. After a while, he carries me upstairs with his cock still inside me, my arms and legs wrapped around him. We fall into bed, and our eyes lock in the dark.

"Whatever I do," his voice is gruff, sitting deep in his chest, "whoever I become, love me still, darling."

Deep inside, I know he's planning to do something terrible. My nails rake gently up his back, touching the scar tissue of his brand, tracing it with my fingertips.

He's not a good man, but he's the one I want.

CHAPTER FORTY-SEVEN

WESTIN

It's summer now, and I'm getting married next month.

I can't wrap my head around how quickly things have changed. For years, I had an empty home and cold bed waiting for me at night. Then, one day, I decided to attend a business meeting concerning some cattle feed, and now, I'm whipped for a little blonde woman who keeps rearranging my house.

I didn't go down to Carter Farms that day looking for a bride, but here I am, waking up to the prettiest bride-to-be every morning.

"Do you feel like it's not real?" I ask Sovereign one day as we watch some of the wranglers bring in rogue cattle from the eastern pasture.

Sovereign sits on Shadow, eyes narrowed against the dust. His hat is pulled low, his hands stacked on the saddle horn. He's more relaxed now that he's married. It looks good on him.

"What's that?" He doesn't take his eyes from the cattle.

"Do you feel like you'll just wake up and Keira's not real?"

Between his brows creases. "No. Why would I think that?"

I shake my head. Sometimes I forget that, despite how he's changed since meeting Keira, he's still himself. We sit in silence for a while. Last summer and during the winter, we drifted apart, both consumed by our own problems. Now, we're back to how we've always been—companionable silence unless something needs saying.

"Did you ever ask Diane what the Garrisons did to her?" Sovereign says after a while.

I nod. "Thomas Garrison beat her. David Carter watched and let him."

A muscle in Sovereign's jaw twitches. "What's your plan then?"

"I can't think of anything bad enough," I say. "If I'd known what Thomas did, I would have done a lot worse than what he got. David deserves the worst. I want to catapult that motherfucker off a cliff."

There's a long silence. Sovereign clears his throat. "You could...do that," he says. "It's a viable option."

I glance over—he has my interest. "How's that?"

He shrugs. "I'm not the executioner—you are. But pitching somebody off a cliff at high velocity...that would make it hard to put the pieces together. Literally and figuratively."

My mind clicks into high gear. I've thought over the problem of how to kill David quickly and cleanly without traumatizing Diane. She can't know what's happening. He'll just disappear, and if she asks, I'll tell her only what she has to know.

For the first time, a plan forms in my head.

Sovereign and I don't discuss it again. We finish moving the runaway cattle back into the right pasture, and then we head back to the ranch and leave the horses standing by the watering trough in the barn. The lunch bell rings. Sovereign pauses on his way to the house, noticing I'm not following him.

"Not hungry?" he asks.

"I've got something to take care of," I say.

He nods, taking off his hat, and heading back to the house. I go to the blacksmith shop and shut the door. There's a stack of paper and a carpenter pencil by the wall. I take them out and lean my elbows on the table, thinking.

I'll need a lot of tension, which means some kind of pulley system so I can manage it by myself, something that can be drawn back and hooked into place in advance.

My pencil hovers over the paper. My brain sits empty for several minutes. Then, it hits me, and my hand starts moving over the paper. This is what I do best. It's the way I got our ranch to the untouchable position it's in now. Sovereign lets me know what needs done. I work out how to do it.

I spend the rest of the lunch hour sketching prototypes. After a while, I have a pretty good idea of what I'll need. It'll just take some time to work out the kinks and make sure it functions.

I'll have one chance.

And, God, it'll be so satisfying.

I stow the papers and go to the house to wash up. Sovereign is in the living room, leaning on the wall with his arms crossed, talking to Jensen. Beyond them, I see Keira and Diane sitting on the couch. They have several bolts of fabric piled on the floor, and they're doing something with pale pink ribbons.

I pause in the doorway. Diane sees me and smiles.

"I didn't see you at lunch," she says.

"I was busy."

Sovereign glances at me, but his expression doesn't change. "We need to check the pond in the south pasture. Jensen says we've got some shit jamming up the river again."

"We need to reroute that section of the river someday," I say. "Are we clearing that out this afternoon?"

"Yeah, let's get it done."

I nod again, and Diane gives me a wistful look, like she wishes I didn't have to work so much. Jensen reaches for his hat, and Sovereign goes to say something under his breath to Keira. Then, they head back down the hall, and I follow them, grabbing a roll from the dining table. I'm on the porch when I hear Diane's feet pattering after me.

I turn. The door slams as Jensen and Sovereign disappear on the porch. I catch the faint scent of cigarettes, so I know I have a second.

"We sent out the invites," Diane says. "Everyone said yes from the list you gave me."

"Even Vince Cassidy?" I'm surprised by that one. He knows Sovereign, but not me.

She nods. "He did. Keira asked Sovereign to put in a good word."

"Good," I say, jerking my head towards the living room. "What are you two doing in there?"

"Making decorations," she says.

She smiles, and I see her like she's a photograph. Golden hair soft and loose down her back. Body relaxed, beautiful curves filled out because she has plenty to eat now. She's not afraid of anything.

I did this by doing what I do best.

Taking my hat off, I beckon her closer. "Give me a kiss, darling," I say. "I've got to get back to work."

She smiles, coming close until her curves meld into me. I slide my fingers in her hair and lean down to kiss her, making sure she tastes how much I can't wait for the day to be over so we can be alone. When we break apart, she smiles and bites her lower lip.

"You better go, sir, or we might have to take a detour," she says.

"If I wasn't in a hurry, I might."

She slips from my arms and heads back to the living room, making sure I see her skirt twitch and her hips sway. I shake my head, put my hat on, and go back to work.

My mind is occupied the rest of the day. Jensen needs a ride back to his house, so I drive him and swing by the home improvement store. In the back aisle, I spend a long time picking out wire rope cables. They have to be hard enough to propel properly when they meet a solid object, but buoyant enough that they can be drawn back for sufficient tension.

I pay for everything with cash and leave the store with the bed of my truck full. When I get back to Sovereign Mountain, it's late. The air is warm, and the moon glows full over the tree by the gatehouse.

Diane is at the table in her slip. I go and kiss the top of her head, and she looks up, offering her mouth for another.

"What's that?" I ask, tapping the paper.

"Guest list," she says, biting her lip. "David didn't accept earlier, and that makes me mad."

I sink down. She has her lips pursed, the way she does when something pisses her off.

"I'll go talk to him and smooth things over," I promise.

She turns in her seat. "No, I asked Sovereign. He did something, and now David is coming, apparently."

"That's the easy way out," I say. "No one wants to be in his bad graces."

She studies me for a moment. "Does Sovereign know what Thomas did?"

I nod. "He was the one who told me to ask what happened."

She looks down, picking at her nails. "Keira told me they're trying to have a baby. I think they'd both make really good parents."

I nod, staying silent. She offers me a tired smile, reaching out to touch my hand.

"I'm going to bed," she says.

We go upstairs and shower. After we're both in bed, my arm tucked over her body, she lets out a little sigh.

"Did they build the road yet?" she whispers.

"No," I say. "Not yet. But don't worry, I have the entire thing handled."

"I wish you'd tell me what you're going to do," she whispers. "I saw you talking to Deacon. I see you having secret discussions with Sovereign. You have a plan."

"I have a plan, darling."

"Is it horrible?" Her voice is fragile, like a spider's web.

"Not for you," I say. "It'll be the best day of your life. You'll wake up with everything you've ever wanted."

"My land," she says sleepily. "My gunslinger."

"Is that enough?"

"It's more than enough."

Her breathing deepens, and her body goes limp. She'd hate it if I said anything, but she snores when she's all worn out. Not a lot, just faint snorts I can hear when the house is silent. She also mumbles in her sleep and frowns a lot, like she's mad at somebody in her dream. Maybe me. I love it; sometimes, I stay up just to watch her sleep.

Someday soon, we'll be in bed like this in our new home at Carter Farms.

Not too long now.

CHAPTER FORTY-EIGHT

DIANE

I wake with a start.

It's Saturday, July Seventeenth.

I sit upright in our empty bed, the sheet falling back. I'm not at the gatehouse; I stayed in one of the spare bedrooms at the ranch house. Westin slept at Jensen's house. He's not supposed to see me until Sovereign walks me down the aisle.

Someone knocks timidly on my door.

"Come on in," I call, reaching for my dressing gown.

Keira steps inside, a tray in her hand. She's still in her lace robe wrapped around her stunning curves. Her red hair is piled on her head and tied with a headscarf.

"Good morning," she says, smiling. "Happy wedding day."

She sets the tray down. It's wheat toast, black coffee, and two slices of orange.

"I thought you might have a little bit of an upset stomach," she says. "You know, from the nerves."

I get up, taking inventory of how I feel. "I am nervous," I admit.

"Better eat something," she says. "Even if it's just fruit."

Obediently, I eat the orange and take a sip of coffee. Keira goes to the closet and takes out my dress. She made the pattern for me, and we worked on it with Maddie. It's pure white satin with a corset bodice, balconette cups that give me beautiful cleavage, and a flared waist with a skirt that falls to my ankles.

"It's so pretty," Keira says, hanging it on the back of the door. Her eyes sparkle.

"I feel like you're more excited for this than your wedding," I say.

"I was nervous for mine," she says. "I don't do well with that kind of thing."

"Enjoy yourself today," I say. "You did a lot to help me get ready, and I never thanked you properly. I do really appreciate it."

"Of course," she says, her voice soft.

"I mean it. I never had a friend before you," I say, feeling awkward.

She swallows, crystal blue eyes wet. "I know what that's like."

My lashes are damp too, and I swipe them with the back of my hand. Keira laughs, shaking her head back to keep the tears from falling.

"So, any wedding advice?" I say, sitting down on the bed.

She crosses her arms. "I haven't been married long."

I know Keira is shy when it comes to talking about sex—I am too—but just this once, I push her buttons.

"How about wedding night advice, then?" I say, smirking.

She blushes, rolling her eyes. "Oh, I think you know what to do."

There's a knock on the door. Keira frowns, leaning over and pulling the curtain back. I look over her shoulder, and everything seems normal. Sovereign's truck is in the drive. Cattle low in the fields. The horses stand in their paddocks, flicking away flies.

Keira jumps up and peeks into the hall. I hear her husband's voice rumble, and then she pulls the door ajar.

There's a beautiful woman, maybe in her fifties, standing in the hall. Her hair is tucked in a soft bun behind her ear, and she's in a fitted, dove gray dress. She gives off a soft, cozy aura that I gravitate towards.

Right away, I know who she is.

Keira steps aside, letting her into the room. Her eyes dart from the woman and back to me. "This is Mrs. Quinn," she says. "Sovereign picked her up from town this morning."

I can't stop staring. She's beautiful, so elegant. There isn't a hint of roughness, chestnut hair, or hazel eyes about her. Westin must have gotten everything from his father, because he looks nothing like his mother.

"Hi," I whisper.

"Hello, Diane," she says, her smile as soft as her voice. "I'm Eve, Westin's mother. He sent me over early to help you."

It's just like him to wait for our wedding day to introduce me to his mother. I'm not good with feelings, but suddenly, my chest is warm, like a dam burst. My lashes flutter, trying to keep back more tears. Keira appears beside me in a moment, her hand rubbing circles on my back.

"What's wrong?" she breathes.

I shake my head. "Nothing," I say, refusing to cry. "I just...don't have any family."

Eva steps forward and pulls me in, wrapping her arms around me. She smells good, like what I imagine mothers smell like. Cinnamon, like a warm hearth in autumn. I bury my face against her shoulder and wonder if my mother would have smelled like this too.

She holds me for a minute and pulls back, tucking my hair behind my ear. I see a hint of Westin then. Her kindness reminds me of him.

"You're beautiful," she says. "Westin is very lucky."

I smile, wiping my face. "I'm glad you think so. I'm lucky to have Westin."

"Oh, just you wait until he stirs up trouble," she says, her tone light. "Then you'll be trying to pack him up and send him back."

I laugh, glad she's changing the subject. I don't want my eyes to be puffy on my wedding day. Keira goes to the bathroom and turns on the tub. She leans in the doorway and crosses her arms.

"All these men are trouble," she says. "But they're worth it."

"Sovereign spent so much time at our house when they were younger," Eve says reflectively. "He was a good influence on Westin, especially when he got sober."

"What was Westin doing?" I ask curiously.

She sighs, waving a hand. "Oh, drinking, getting in trouble, you name it. They were both rowdy, fighting each other and eating us out of house and home. It cost me a fortune to feed those boys."

Keira nods, smiling. "I've noticed. Luckily, they pay their own bills now."

"Anyway, Westin's a good one, just a bit like his father," Eve says. "He'll always treat you right, Diane."

"Does...he look like him?" I ask.

She nods. "He looks a bit like my father, but mostly like my first husband. So, yes. Anyway, show me your ring, honey."

She's trying to change the subject again—I can tell she doesn't like talking about Westin's father. I hold out my hand, and she inspects the diamond against the light.

"It's beautiful. He did a good job." She nods, pride in her eyes.

"Better have something more to eat," Keira says. "I'm running a bath, and then we'll do your hair."

I shake my head. "My stomach is a little unsettled."

Eve sets her purse down and sits on the edge of the bed. "Are you sick?"

"No, just nervous."

Truthfully, it's the fact that we're throwing the biggest wedding of the year today, and I'm the centerpiece. And David will be there. As much as I want him to see that everything he did to me was in vain, I'm starting to regret having invited him. I don't want to see his face.

Maybe I should have let the past lie.

Keira takes my elbow and pulls me into the bathroom. Bobby pins in her teeth, she gets to work fastening my hair up in curlers. Eve starts working on the other side, following after Keira to spray it into place. It feels nice that she's here, even though I don't know her well.

My stomach rumbles, and I put a hand over it, hoping it settles soon.

"Are you sure you're not...you know?" Keira asks quietly.

"Pregnant?" I say. "No, it's not that."

I don't want to explain about David, or that my husband-to-be is planning to do something terrible but I don't know what.

"I was pregnant with Westin on my wedding day," Eve says casually.

"Really?" Keira says.

She nods. "I wore my mother's dress, but it had the waistline lifted to cover my bump."

"I'll bet you looked beautiful," I say.

She shrugs. "I was scared. But that's a story for another day. Let's get you ready and into that beautiful dress, Miss Diane. We don't want to be late."

I'm dying to know more, but she's right, so I bathe and sit on the bed and let her and Keira brush out my curls and do my makeup. It's soft, with a hint of blue on my lids and a touch of pink on my lips. They pin my waves at the nape of my neck and weave daisies from the field into them.

I slip on the satin dress Keira and I labored over for the last few months. It settles over my body like a cloud, soft, hugging my curves in all the right places. Keira turns the mirror around.

I'm quiet, just taking in my reflection.

The gunslinger's bride looks back at me in shades of white, pink, and gold.

Beautiful. Ready for her wedding day.

"Westin won't know what to do when he sees you," Keira says, her eyes wet.

"He probably will," I say.

Keira giggles. "At least he will...later on."

Eve pretends she doesn't hear us. "We don't have much time. We should go."

Outside, there's a tent set up that's shielded from view. The aisle runs behind the ranch house, with what will serve as the altar beneath two trees by the lake. The day is warming quickly, but everyone will be shaded and cool by the water. I sink down and fold my hands in my lap. The chatter of distant voices wafts up the drive.

I was shocked by how many people Sovereign and Westin know. But then, they've lived in the South Platte area for their entire lives. I just assumed their reputations would scare people away from attending. More likely, their reputations made everyone too afraid to refuse.

My mouth is dry. I wonder what Westin is doing right now.

"Here are your flowers," Keira says, appearing at my elbow.

She puts a bouquet of yellow lilies in my lap, tied with a blue ribbon. From somewhere far away, I hear a violin. It's isolated, but the hills echo it back in a chorus. My heart aches, in the sweetest way.

"Is everyone here?" I ask.

"Everyone but Westin," she says, chewing her lip. "He's a little late, but I'm sure it's okay."

"He's late?" I ask, standing up. "What time is it?"

"He's late to being early," she says. "Sovereign went after him."

My heart jumps in my chest. If this had happened months ago, I would assume it was all a dream, but I know he won't walk away. I close my eyes, standing at the edge of the tent, and turn my face up to the warm sun. He'll be here; I feel it deep in my heart.

He'll always be here.

We wait a few more minutes, then Keira disappears and returns in a flurry. She seems more out of breath than usual, but she's brimming with excitement.

"He's here," she says. "Everything's ready."

Time slows down as I turn and look out over the lake. The row of trees shelter the guests from my view. I know there's at least two hundred people, and at the front of the aisle, Westin is waiting for me.

"You okay?" Keira whispers.

I nod. "I'm just...happy."

She hugs me gently so she doesn't crush my dress. Then, she tugs a little curl free by my ear, adjusts my neckline, and takes my arm to lead me out to where Sovereign waits. I stand alone, my palms sweating against the flower stalks while he walks his wife up and seats her. Then, he's back, and it's time.

I swallow, mouth dry. In the distance, cicadas buzz. The cattle low in the fields as they search for shade before the sun blisters the earth.

Sovereign glances me over, eyes sober. "Are you ready?"

I hesitate.

"Sovereign, what is Westin doing?" It comes out in a rush.

He cocks his head. "He's planning on marrying you—if you'll get up there and do it."

I shake my head. "No, he's going to do something. I hope it's not today."

Sovereign doesn't have an expressive face, but as soon as I say it, I know I'm right. There's a flicker in his stare. Then, he blinks, and his eyes go back to being ice.

"I've known Westin almost my whole life," he says. "You can trust him."

I nod, swallowing. "I know," I whisper.

He holds out his arm. I take it, and he leads me down the little hill and under the trees into the shaded, green grove. We pause, and the violinist to our left begins playing softly. My throat catches as I recognize the melody. It's the hymn my grandmother used to hum to put me to sleep.

My heart clears. My anxiety vanishes, leaving me with nothing but warm, summer sunshine.

Like the day he walked into my life.

I look up to find him standing there, dressed in his good pants and vest, shirt rolled up to his forearms, exposing all those barbed wire scars. The sun glints off his chestnut hair, making his eyes glitter like deep water. He's got a scratch on his cheek and two Band-Aids on his forearm.

Oh God, what did he do now?

There's nothing to do about that now, though. I'm walking up the aisle, and everyone is silent, watching me. Maybe they wonder because we don't look like we should be together.

He's hard, I'm soft.

I'm twenty-two, he's thirty-eight.

I've only ever wanted to live. He's in the business of killing.

But all they need to do is look at the way he's watching me to know, by some trick of fate, that this is meant to be.

Sovereign guides me to the front until I stand before Westin. He shakes his hand like he barely knows him, but then Westin leans in, and they say something to each other, their voices too low to hear. Whatever it is, they exchange a glance that lets me know it meant something before pulling back.

Sovereign takes my fingertips and hands me over to Westin. His hazel eyes catch mine, bright as the day we met. I smile and my mouth shakes.

Gently, he turns us to face the preacher. He stands before us in his starched black shirt and pants, rifling through his book. His glasses stick out of his breast pocket, and it takes a minute for him to find them.

He doesn't know my name, and Westin has to whisper it to him. I look sideways at Westin as we recite our vows, but he stares resolutely ahead.

He forgot to book the preacher. I know a rush job when I see one.

I'm exasperated, but just for a fleeting moment. Then, everything fades, because nothing but Westin matters anymore. The past rushes away, like the current of the river where he first kissed me, carried away like silt after heavy rain.

Tomorrow, the world will be right.

I know because he promised it would be.

CHAPTER FORTY-NINE

WESTIN

Keira and Diane tasked Sovereign and I with getting a preacher for the ceremony. In the excitement of our other plans, we all forgot. I was up in the hills, making sure everything was ready at the edge of the ravine. Sovereign was getting my mother from the city. Jensen was in the blacksmith shop, taking inventory of the weapons. Deacon was bringing in the horses from the pasture.

It was eight-thirty on my wedding day when I realized we didn't have an officiant.

Deacon and I went into South Platte to the nondenominational church beside the bank. Luckily, someone answered the door. Unfortunately, it was the same preacher from back when my mother made me attend.

"Westin," he said, brows rising. "I haven't seen you in years."

"I'm getting married today," I said. "I need a preacher."

He frowned. "Well, I can't leave today. I've got service tomorrow."

"How about for a check?"

He shook his head.

"I've got a gun," said Deacon. He leaned against the truck, cigarette in his lip. "Which is it gonna be? Check or gun?"

The preacher's eyes widened. "I'll get my book."

I handed him a check, put him in the back seat, and we got back to Sovereign Mountain as fast as possible.

We made it back in the nick of time.

Everything worked out. Now, I'm standing here, waiting on the prettiest woman in the world to walk down that aisle. Deacon stands to my right, hands folded, and opposite is Keira, standing up for Diane. I'm at the front between them, looking out over the congregation. Everyone who works the ranch is here, alongside everyone we're friendly with in South Platte. My mother gives me a soft smile from the front row.

The only person I don't see is Jack Russell. We sent him an invitation, but who knows if it found him. No one knows where he lives. I addressed it to his bar in hopes it would find its way to his doorstep.

At the very back, I spot Vince Cassidy. Corbin Buchanan. David Carter. They all look out of place, lined up in a row.

Bang.

Bang.

Bang.

I cock my head, distracted by the thought of what will happen later tonight.

The music goes still.

The wind picks up, a breeze that smells dark and sweet, like the pines on the mountains. Then, the music starts up again, and everyone goes quiet.

My bride floats down the aisle on Sovereign's arm. The world fades out around her, and I forget everything—how to breathe, how to exist.

I've seen some of the most beautiful sunrises in the world out here in rural Montana. I've seen sweeping mountains carpeted in bluebells. I've seen lakes so placid, they reflect the sky like a painting. I've seen beauty in its most breathtaking forms.

But I've never seen anything as beautiful as Diane.

Any shred of doubt I have over what I'm going to do tonight vanishes. I'm willing to have more blood on my hands if it means I get to marry this woman. I'll find heaven growing old at Carter Farms, Diane at my side and our children playing in the backyard.

She halts a few steps away. Sovereign shakes my hand, and I lean closer to speak into his ear.

"Thank you," I say. "For everything."

Sovereign doesn't talk much. He never has. We've never had a heart to heart in our lives—that's not our way.

He gives me a firm nod. "Thank you," he says. "For everything."

We draw back, and he holds Diane's hand out to me. Captivated, I take it, and she offers me a little smile. The breeze flutters flyway waves around her slender throat. At the base sits her simple, gold collar, a sweet afterthought.

Mine in every way she can be.

Her mouth quivers, and I have to keep myself from bending to kiss it. I take her other hand, and we face forward. If I'm honest with myself, I stumble on my vows. They're short, from the black book the preacher carries, but I'm so undone, I can barely get to the end.

All I can think about is what happens when I'm alone with her—when we're married, when my job is done, and it's just me and my wife.

I just have a few things to do first.

CHAPTER FIFTY

DIANE

It's getting late. Slowly, the sun etches arcs overhead and sinks until the edges of the sky bleed dark blue. I'm shocked by just how many people Westin ended up inviting to the wedding. The tent is bustling. It's hard to get from one end to the other or carry on a conversation without shouting.

I end up spending most of my time in my chair. Westin stays at my side as much as he can, but he keeps getting pulled away. Everyone wants to talk and congratulate him.

I'm dizzy from everything. In my heart, I just want to go back to the gatehouse.

Keira comes to sit with me after a group of wranglers from the ranch abscond with Westin again. She brings me a glass of champagne but doesn't drink any herself. I don't want to be presumptuous and ask, so I stay quiet. It's obvious something is going on, whether she knows for certain or not. Her skin is glowing, her red hair somehow more vibrant, and she can't catch her breath.

I focus on her, listening as she talks, because now that things are settling down, I'm painfully aware that David is among the guests.

I don't regret having him here, but now that he can see he didn't crush me after all, I wish he was gone.

“Darling.”

We both look up. Westin stands on the other side of the table. He’s so handsome, his shirt rolled to his elbows and collar open, that I blush. Keira excuses herself, giving me a little squeeze on the elbow.

“It’s time to dance,” he says.

My stomach flutters. He takes my hand and pulls me around the table. Everyone steps back, and I hear the band switch to a quieter melody on a single violin.

I look up at my husband, surrounded by the glittering lights and the crowd, bright like the sun.

“May I have this dance, Mrs. Quinn?” he says, so low that only we can hear.

I nod, swallowing the lump in my throat. He takes my hand and pulls me into his chest, his other palm on my lower back. The world melts away, and all I can see are his fingers woven into mine. All I can smell is Westin. All I can feel is his warm, hard body holding me up.

I’m safe.

I never have to fear again.

Squeezing my eyes shut, I listen to his slow heartbeat and let it regulate mine. Thump, thump, thump. Moving in time with our bodies.

When I manage to peel back my lids, my gaze falls to the other side of the tent. Standing in the doorway, arms crossed, is David, watching me, his face half shadowed.

My throat closes. In a second, everything floods back—the bitterness, the years of cruel words, the many times he put his hands on me out of anger. I regret so much, and it was never mine to regret. A long time ago, he let himself slip into hopelessness.

He never looked out of his window, waiting for the meadowlarks to rise the way I did every night.

He chose his path.

I chose mine.

I meet his gaze head on. The hair on the back of my neck stands up. His dark eyes are dead, no sign of life left.

No regret.

Maybe just a little disgust.

Even now, looking at me in my happiest moment, he can't find it in him to regret.

I turn, burying my face in Westin's chest. Maybe it was a mistake to invite him here tonight, but it also feels good to get this closure. The little part of me that always wanted to hit back when he put his hands on me is satisfied.

I hit back. Not with my fists, but I did all the same.

CHAPTER FIFTY-ONE

WESTIN

It's almost time.

My wife throws her bouquet into the crowd. It bounces off the back of a chair, and Maddie catches it. She has been married for ages, so it causes a ripple of laughter that livens the room. The bartender starts pouring another round of drinks. The music picks up again.

I have to take a piss.

Diane sits with Maddie and Keira, happy and occupied. I dip out of the tent, a whiskey in one hand, and make my way to the edge of the woods several yards away. I have my belt open and my dick out when I hear a branch crack. There are a half a dozen other men out here, doing the same as me, so I ignore it.

Then, I hear someone relieving themselves, too close for comfort. I glance to the side, and I see David's profile to my left, maybe two yards over.

My blood boils. It's all I can do to finish and close my pants. His zipper hisses, and I turn around, pretending I didn't see him.

No—fuck that. I pivot abruptly. His collar is open, tie over his shoulder, whiskey in one hand, same as me.

"Quinn," he says before I can speak. "I want to talk to you."

I lift my glass. "I'm all ears."

He comes closer, and I can see the sweat staining his shirt. His black eyes glitter in the light from the tent. He takes a deep breath.

"I never meant for all the shit to happen that happened," he says.

I work my jaw, not trusting myself to speak.

"We were in a desperate situation," he says. "I made the only choice. She was fine. She came out of it fine."

I'm so red-hot inside, it's a miracle I don't break. I can't. If he senses something is up, he won't go with Deacon and Jensen. He'll just flee. He needs to think I forgive him when this conversation is done.

God, that's a bitter pill to swallow.

"My sister is fine," David says.

I take a sip of whiskey and a step closer. We're eye to eye.

"My wife is fine," I say carefully.

He sputters. "Yes, Diane's fine. I'd like to let bygones be bygones. Our farms are right up against each other now that the Garrisons are gone."

"I thought you were selling."

"I'm hoping this could change that. Maybe Sovereign could have a word about it. He owns the biggest farm around here."

"Ranch," I say. "You have a farm. I have a ranch."

His brow creases. "Whatever it is, we're neighbors, and this marriage makes us brothers too. I'd like to build a bridge and let the past go."

It hits me that David's not only a true coward but a narcissist as well. He can't conceptualize the damage he did to my wife, but I know it intimately. I know how broken and scared she was when I stole her from Garrison Ranch. All he knows is how to save his own neck.

I take a deep breath. "I agree."

"Really?" He cocks his head.

"Some things are so broken," I say carefully, "that it's better to just let the water wash all the pieces away and forget the past completely."

He holds out his hand. I shake it. Our chests are inches apart, our eyes locked. Then, he releases me and steps back. Neither of us speak for a moment.

He turns on his heel and goes back to the tent. Through the doorway, I see Jensen and Deacon appear at his side. They sweep him up and head to the bar. The next part of our plan is in motion. I need to get Diane somewhere safe so I can take care of business.

In the tent, I find my wife and take a seat, pulling her to sit on my knee. She can tell I'm tense, but she doesn't ask why. I think, at this point, she knows better. She asks me if I had any cake, and I say I didn't, so she feeds me a piece off her fork.

Safe in my arms, I let her have her moment. She's smiling, lighter than she's been in months, but from the corner of my eye, I'm watching Jensen and Deacon lead a drunk David out of the tent.

Like an animal to slaughter.

They disappear into the dark, talking, laughing. I beckon Keira from the corner of the room to come and collect Diane. Her brow is furrowed, and I know that Sovereign told her where we're headed.

"Where are you going?" Diane asks as we leave the tent.

I kiss her forehead. The moon is so full overhead, it's as light as the early morning. I can see her face clearly. Her blonde hair is curled in the humidity, flowers tangled in her waves, cheeks flushed and eyes bright.

God, I can't wait to get back to her tonight.

"I have a few things to tie up tonight," I say. "Then I'll be back to tie *you* up."

She blushes. Keira looks away.

"When?"

"Soon."

She kisses me hard, hands tangled in the front of my shirt. Then, Keira takes her away, down to the gatehouse. They disappear around the bend, and I turn on my heel, unwilling to waste a second.

I saw Deacon and Jensen leave with David ten minutes ago under the guise of going for a ride and talking business now that our ranches are neighbors. That means I need to tear up the side of the mountain or risk fucking everything up. Tonight has to be perfectly timed, or we're shit out of luck.

Rocky is already saddled up. In the hayloft, I brush aside the blanket and pull up my rifle, slinging it over my shoulder. Then, I drop to the ground beside Rocky. He shies away, and I soothe him, clicking my tongue. We need to get in and out quietly.

Music thrums from the tent. Everyone is so fucking drunk, it'll be a miracle if they hear anything.

I strip off my vest and roll my sleeves up, undoing my top button to free my collar. The gun and scope goes over my shoulder. I tighten the straps to keep it firm on my back. Then, I take my hat from where it hangs by Rocky's stall door and swing up on him. He senses my quick pulse and prances to the side.

"Down boy," I say. "All you have to do is run tonight."

I click my tongue, and he shoots forward, hooves clattering, gravel spraying. We skid from the barn, and he spins hard as I turn the reins. The cliffs take an hour or so to reach on a good day. I have to make it in thirty minutes.

Rocky runs like he has never run before. I should have taken Gracey because she's quick, fast, but this feels like something my horse and I should do together.

The trees are a dark shadow. Down below, the tent glows. Overhead, the moon is a white ball in the sky. Stars hang heavy, burning pale gold. Everything is bathed in deep blue.

Thump.

Thump.

Thump.

Thump.

Rocky's uneven gait pounds with my heart, alongside the blood in my veins.

My mind calms. This is what I'm good at, what I've done for years, but this is the first time it was all for me. Normally, I hunt and kill for Sovereign and the ranch.

I've never hunted my own prey before.

My hands are numb when we pause at the bottom of the cliff on the other side of the woods. I slow Rocky, letting him cool. His sides are lathered. He huffs under his breath as I slide down and sling the reins back over his neck.

We climb, quickly and quietly. About halfway up, I tell Rocky to wait, and he does. His ears prick forward, his glossy eyes following me as I walk away. I know he doesn't like that we're parting.

For his safety, he needs to stay back.

In the dark, I move on, one foot in front of the other, until I'm deep in the woods, retracing my footsteps from early this morning.

I find the rope and follow it.

Hand over hand.

Step over step.

The woods are so quiet. I see the single wire thread running through the trees, barely visible in the moonlight, like a spider's web.

My heart slows. Overhead, a nightbird cries. The further I follow the rope towards the cliff's edge, the less isolated I am. In the distance, the trees start to open up, and I catch the low rumble of voices.

I crouch down. The trigger point is a foot before me.

A metal lever glints. All I have to do is pull, and the tension will release. The panel of fencing made of wire rope will throw David's body into the ravine, into the river, where the hungry current will take the parts far away.

No reasonable trace left.

I rise to a standing position. Through the gap, I see Deacon and Jensen are making sure to stand on either side of the danger zone. David stands in it, but a little too far to the left for comfort.

I need him to shift.

I need to do this right. No chance David doesn't fall.

I clench my jaw, waiting. There's no poetic justice to this. No, this is pure, messy vengeance. I want him gone in the messiest, darkest way I can get. Thomas got his punishment; now it's time for David to have his so I can let go of this burning rage.

He took the woman I love and forced her into misery. He's so fucking small, and he's about to be smaller still.

Little pieces for the water to wash away, just like I told him.

My mouth goes dry as an eerie but familiar sensation settles over me. I'm not alone anymore. My father prickles my spine with his presence—a ghost I just can't kick. It's so strong, I have to turn around to make sure it's just my mind playing tricks on me.

Swear to God, it feels like he's breathing down my neck.

Every word he spoke to me echoes in my ears.

For the first time, they don't disturb me. My father was a softly broken man—not cruel, just in pieces all the time on the floor of his iron fortress. Maybe someday, I'll know why he was the way he was. Maybe I spent too long knocking on his door to care why he kept it closed.

I had to be a scourge to give Diane the life she deserves. In his hardness, his coldness, my father made me the gunslinger. He pushed me to be relentless, to be what he thought a man should be.

A man who shoots. Who takes. Who kills.

That was the only gift he passed on, and now, it has given me everything. In her darkest hour, the gunslinger was who she needed.

That era is over; that pain stops with me. Tonight, I put the warring sides of my heart to rest. I'm already molded, but I don't want my son to be a killer, finally finding love after decades of hard existence.

I am my father's son, but my son will be so much more.

I lift my eyes. My father's ghost is quiet.

Up ahead, David steps back. I take a beat, and my vision narrows, putting him at the center of everything. My mind goes back to what Diane told me, that he stood there and watched while Thomas used the steel toe of his boot on her ribs.

Anger pours through my veins. My hand closes around the level, and I pull it down.

Click.

The spring engages. The taut wire releases with a soft hiss.

It's not spectacular. One second, David is there, the next, he's gone. The panel of fencing springs back, wobbling with a colossal sound that echoes off the ravine. Deacon swears and falls back in shock. Jensen runs to the cliff's edge and peers down.

I run up through the trees and burst out into the open grass. Deacon holds his arm, but he's not bleeding. I move past him and come to a halt beside Jensen.

In the swirling water, I see everything I need to see.

Leftovers.

From behind me comes the thunder of hoofbeats. My heart picks up, and I spin around. Jensen scrambles back from the cliff's edge and pulls his pistol from its holster. Deacon reaches for his as well, but it's Sovereign who bursts over the hill astride Shadow and skids to a halt.

"Is he gone?" he asks.

"He's gone," I say.

Shadow prances, spraying up dry grass and dirt. "It's too late for Corbin and Vince. They got in the truck and left by way of the state route. I tried to hold them back."

My mind works fast. I've done plenty of jobs where the target didn't behave properly. It always comes with a moment where I have to think on my feet. I'm used to it.

"We were going to force them off the bridge," I say. "The one below the cliffs across the state route."

Jensen nods. "We can't make it back and get to the trucks in time."

My brain races. "No, but I can make it there on horseback. The trail cuts straight there."

Sovereign frowns. "And run them off the road on a horse?"

I shake my head. "No. I can shoot them off the bridge."

Deacon comes up behind me. "That'd be an impossible shot in broad daylight. You can't make that."

I glance up at Sovereign. He's quiet, heavy brow furrowed. I know what that means, and it bolsters my confidence. Distantly, I hear Jensen's boots fade as he goes to retrieve the horses from where they stand a few yards away.

"You couldn't make the shot, Deacon," Sovereign says. "But Westin can."

I'm grateful. When I doubt myself, he's always come through to pick up the slack. Our eyes meet, and he jerks his head.

"I need a lighter horse than Rocky," I say.

Jensen returns, his black mare in tow. She's half thoroughbred with long legs. She's restless, ready to run. Wordlessly, Jensen holds out the reins, and I take them.

"What's her name?" I ask.

"Godspeed," he says. "I brought her out here with me when I came to Montana, so you better bring her back, gunslinger."

I nod, running my hand over her neck. She's prancing sideways. I know she won't like leaving Jensen, but she's aching to run. I check the strap of my rifle and sight and swing up on her, standing to adjust the stirrups.

"Get Rocky from the woods," I say. "He'll take you back."

Jensen nods. I glance up and meet Sovereign's eyes. Shadow fidgets, restless from the nervous energy.

"Go get them," Sovereign says. "Don't fucking miss."

I can't miss. This will be the riskiest shot I've ever taken with no room for error. If Corbin and Vince leave our ranch alive, we'll be in for a world of trouble. No, I have one bullet, and it has to go through that windshield and strike the driver, or we're fucked.

I nod, tensing my legs. Godspeed kicks off, spraying dirt as she heads down the hill.

It takes a moment to get adjusted. I'm not used to riding a horse with such long strides. Godspeed eats up distance, her body soaring cleanly over the ground, hooves tearing up grass in her wake.

We fly through the dark, our bodies just a shadow beneath the blue moon.

CHAPTER FIFTY-TWO

DIANE

I stand in the kitchen. Keira is by the stove, her arms wrapped around her body. The tea kettle whistles in a thin shriek.

"He's killing David," I say, my voice cracking, "isn't he?"

She nods, her eyes big. "That doesn't mean he's bad. I killed your husband, but he deserved it."

I swallow. "He did deserve it."

The kettle gets louder until Keira reaches over and turns it off. She pours two cups, and I sink down opposite her at the table. The scent of chamomile and lemon wafts up in curls of steam. My throat is lumpy, and a heavy weight crushes my chest.

"I want them to come home safe," I whisper.

"They will," Keira says. "Sovereign promised."

We're both quiet, staring down at the table. She reaches out and takes my hand. Outside, the wind picks up, wailing like a banshee swooping over the ranch.

This isn't how I dreamed my wedding night would be.

CHAPTER FIFTY-THREE

WESTIN

Hooves skid to a halt. My boots hit the ground.

In the distance, lights glimmer.

The valley is laid out at my feet. Far to my left, I see the cliffs where Sovereign killed Clint. Down below, the road is a coal gray snake through the mountains. I sling the rifle from my back and hang Godspeed's reins around her saddle horn.

At the edge, I set up my rifle. The sky is clear, and it's light enough I see the truck from a mile away. I sink down onto my belly and fit my eye to the scope.

The road curves. The truck eases closer.

Sweat etches down my forehead. I blink it away. My body is soaked with sweat from riding hard.

I take a breath and release slowly. An owl screeches, and the wind picks up in the trees. Lifting my head, I assess it. Fuck, there's more breeze than I anticipated up here. Sweat stings my eyes, and I wipe it away with my palm and look through the scope.

I have less than a minute.

The river glitters. Everything is so silent now.

This time, as I lay in wait, I don't feel my father looking over my shoulder. I don't see the stern line of his mouth in my mind's eye. My head is just blank, and I'm fully honed in on my target.

Sweat slips down through my hair, and I flick it back, repositioning my eye.

Thirty seconds.

I breathe in, my finger hovering over the trigger. The truck is close enough that I can make out the windshield. Then, it hits the curve before the bridge, and I see that the side window is open.

That's a harder shot to take, but it's cleaner.

I blink hard. My eyes sting, but I barely feel them. The world is gone around me, nothing but the tiny space inside my scope. The truck moves closer, on the bridge now.

I'm so quiet inside.

This is, without a doubt, the hardest shot I've ever taken, and it has the highest stakes. I can't miss. I promised my girl she'd have everything, and I intend to make good on that.

Their vehicle is almost at the center of the bridge. I recognize it as the truck Corbin Buchanan showed up in, his company logo a pale smear on the side.

I have no time left.

Everything clicks into place at the last second, the product of years of practice. I see the sliver of the window. I know where the driver sits. I think I see a glimpse of his face, like a pale half-moon. The truck window comes into full view, going fifty miles an hour at least.

My finger comes down on the trigger, and I account for the kick.

I account for everything, the way he trained me to.

The wind.

The dark.

The miles.

I swear, I feel the mechanics of the pistol click into motion.

In fifty years, this bullet will be nothing but a story, just like the rest of it—the hot summer day I fed her apple from my mouth, the pining, the secret tryst by the cemetery, the bullet in Avery's head, and now, the greatest shot I'll ever take.

The world is so tranquil, it's hard to believe it's still spinning. I lift my head, heart steady, eyes fixed on the truck. It keeps on in a straight line for a few seconds, not wavering.

My stomach sinks. Fuck, I missed.

Then, it veers, grazing the guardrail and sending up sparks. The wheels spin out of control, and it flips. A crash echoes through the valley before it rolls over the edge and falls.

And falls.

There's a second explosion as it collides with the water. I know there's nothing left, not from that height. The two men and their truck are in shreds, rolling down the current.

My shoulders sink. I rise until I'm on my knees, looking out over the empty road.

Hot wind ruffles my hair. The moon glimmers overhead.

They're gone.

I sling the rifle up over my shoulder. Tonight is my wedding night, and my work here is done.

CHAPTER FIFTY-FOUR

DIANE

Keira left after sitting with me in silence. We finished our tea, and I swore I was fine as she gave me a hug before going back to the ranch house.

I sit, staring at the wedding present she left, custom-made and gifted by the Sovereigns: two fine crystal glasses with Mr. and Mrs. Quinn engraved in gold on the rims and a bottle of expensive whiskey to go with them.

Reality has sunk in.

My husband killed my brother tonight—the man who hurt me beyond repair.

I don't know how I should feel.

Is it wrong to be a bit relieved? After everything David did to me, maybe it's better he can't inflict anymore hurt on the world. I get up, taking the glasses and the bottle upstairs to the bedroom. I pull the curtain open, letting blue moonlight pour through. It's soft, like a velvet pool across our bed.

I strip and replace the sheets with fine, dark ones that smell faintly of the vanilla sticks and lemon waxed paper I keep in the dresser drawer. Then, I go to the closet and take everything from the cabinet.

Handcuffs. A crop. A gag. A plug. Rope. Vibrators. A few things I don't recognize.

I lay them all out. Tonight, I think I'll let him do whatever he wants to me.

I go to shut the cabinet, and the door catches. A roll of cloth is jamming the hinges. I tug it, and something heavy falls in my hands. Jensen's gun. Westin must have taken it from Thomas Garrison's house when he retrieved Billie.

My heart is tender. In my wedding dress, I sink down on the end of the bed and turn the gun over in my hands.

For weeks, this was the only defense I had. Then Westin came, and I haven't thought about it once.

Eyes stinging, I lift my head just as hoofbeats thunder by the barn, echoing off the mountains. The men have returned, tearing up over the hill on horseback, hollering, hooves clattering over the gravel, high off the euphoria of what they did in the mountains.

God, I hope I never have to hear the details.

I rise, the gun in my hand, and grip the hem of my skirt so I can hurry down the stairs and out the front door. My bare feet pound up the walkway and over the dusty path through the gravel.

Their horses are towering shadows in the moonlight. Sovereign swings off just as Westin comes around the corner. He's on Jensen's horse, flecked with sweat. There's a rifle strapped to his back. Jensen is at his heels on Rocky, and they're kicking up rocks and dust as they peel around the corner. Deacon pulls up beside Sovereign and slides to his feet.

"I need a fucking drink," he says. "I'm going back to the tent. Jensen, you coming?"

"I'm going," Jensen drawls, dismounting.

"Jensen!" I blurt out.

My voice cracks, but it's loud enough everyone stops. Westin takes his hat off, and sweat glitters on his face in the moonlight. Nobody moves. I feel Sovereign's eyes on us both, waiting to see what happens.

"Jensen, can I talk to you?" I manage.

He glances at Westin, who jerks his head. I turn and lead the way to the barn door where we can't be overheard. He wipes the sweat off his face and takes his hat off.

"Don't be upset with Westin," he says in a rush. "He's just taking care of you."

I shake my head. "I'm not upset."

"Then what?"

I pull the gun from my skirt. His brows rise, and he reaches out to take it.

"Thank you," I say, voice cracking. "This kept me safe when I had no one to care for me."

He sniffs and pretends he didn't as he pushes the pistol under his belt.

"I reckon you don't need that anymore, Mrs. Quinn," he says.

I smile, tears slipping down my face. "I reckon I don't."

He clears his throat. "Thanks for giving it back. It's the only thing I brought from Kentucky, other than my horse."

My heart is full, despite everything. Briefly, I hug him, and he pulls back in surprise before he lets me. I let go quickly because he needs a shower. I tell him that, and he starts laughing, shaking his head as we head back to the others.

My throat has a lump in it.

I think I'm moving on. I think I'm living.

Everyone goes quiet, and the atmosphere goes from adrenaline drenched to hesitant when I return. Sovereign has Rocky and Shadow by the reins. Jensen swings up on his horse and rides off with Deacon. In the distance, I hear laughter and music from the tent.

"Did Keira go to the ranch house?" Sovereign asks.

I nod, wordless, my eyes locked with Westin's. Distantly, I hear Sovereign say he'll put both horses away. Then, I'm alone with my husband.

He draws close. He smells like sweat and horses. I slide my hands over his good shirt, soaked and scuffed with dirt. His clothes are ruined, but I don't care.

"Do we need to talk?" he says, voice strained.

We should, but I don't want to tonight. I shake my head, and he takes my hand, leading me barefoot to the gatehouse. He pauses before the door, unlatching it and pushing it open.

He takes his hat off and fits it on my head. Then, he picks me up and carries me over the threshold. My bare feet curl, and a delicious shiver moves through my body.

He sets me down and kisses me, forehead bumping against his hat. I take it off and set it on the table. He's panting when he pulls back.

"Upstairs," he says, spinning me around. "Now."

Heart pounding, I pull my skirts out of the way and scramble up the stairs. I hear him lock the doors. Outside, the party is still going on. It'll last as long as the liquor does. I go to the window and pull the curtain aside. At the crest of the hill, a bonfire crackles orange.

"Darling, shut that window."

He's in the doorway. It's strange, but sometimes, I forget how handsome he is, and then it strikes me out of nowhere—glittering hazel eyes, deep chestnut hair, strong, muscled body. The other parts of him eclipse it, especially now that I know him.

His fire, his persistence, his fierce loyalty to the people he loves, his anger—for being such a calm man, he has a deep sense of justice. He's so angry deep in his soul that the world doesn't live up to it.

I think I love that about him.

I cross the room and put my hand on his chest. Maybe now that he has me, now that he has killed his enemies, he can be at peace. I want to see Westin happy, the way he was the summer we met.

"Darling," he says, voice low and husky.

I take him by the shirt and push him back until he collapses in the armchair. His chest heaves as I straddle him and score his neck with my teeth.

"Do you know?"

"Know what?" I run the tip of my tongue up his neck. He tastes like salt and gunpowder.

"What I did tonight."

I take his collar in both hands and rip it open, revealing the rough hair, the hard muscles. I rake my nails over the ridges.

"I know what you did," I breathe.

His brows rise. "And you don't care?"

His belt clinks under my fingers. "It's not about caring, Westin," I say, pausing with the leather gripped in my hands. Our eyes lock, and the air crackles. "I married you."

He just looks at me.

"I never asked you to change," I say, meaning every word. "I fell in love with the man you are, not the man you could be."

Something shifts in him, like a heavy weight moves from his body. He leans forward abruptly and takes me by the throat, like I'm made of glass. His eyes roam over my face before he bends in. Our mouths brush, and I inhale the breath from his lungs.

Mine. My gunslinger.

"You go downstairs and shower in the bathroom there," I say. "I need the bathroom up here for a minute."

He groans under his breath. "I want you now."

He pushes my skirt up, and his fingers graze my naked pussy. I didn't wear underwear because my dress is so thin. His pupils blow in the firelight. I snatch his wrist to pull his hand out, but he resists me.

He cocks his head. "Don't forget who you are to me."

Arousal throbs down below, his fingers pushing into my pussy.

"I know who I am," I whisper. "Take your hand out."

He leans in, fingers still inside. "Are you using your safeword tonight, darling?" he breathes.

His mouth brushes my throat. I nod.

"Out loud," he orders.

"Yes, sir," I moan. "I'll use my safeword if I need to."

His eyes flash dark. My spine prickles. His fingers plunge into me, finding my G-spot. My hips roll as his other hand pushes up the skirt of my wedding gown. Right at the top of my thigh is a delicate garter made from white lace and little yellow ribbons.

His mouth parts, distracted.

"Jesus Christ," he says hoarsely. "Go—go get ready and leave that on."

He pulls his fingers free, and I scramble down, ducking into the bathroom and shutting the door. I hear his boots go down the stairs. Hands shaking, I peel my dress off and get into the shower. When I'm scrubbed and dried, I slide the garter back on, settling it on my upper thigh.

In a little box on the chair is the lingerie I made from the silk he bought for me, a slip with ruffled, off-the-shoulder straps and matching panties. Mouth dry, I put them on.

Then, I pull out my makeup and do my hair up in curlers. Everything has to be perfect. I color my lips and apply a little blush, finishing with mascara that I know will end up running down my face. I dry my hair and arrange it in soft waves.

He's back; I hear him in the bedroom.

My stomach flips.

His steps move around the room. I know he sees the toys I laid out. My toes curl, and my eyes catch my reflection. I'm beautiful, sexy in the soft way he likes, perfect to lay back and let him do whatever dirty thing he wants to do tonight.

I don't want to make a single choice.

He's in charge.

CHAPTER FIFTY-FIVE

WESTIN

I see her plan. My cock is so hard under my sweatpants, I wonder how long I can wait.

The door creaks open, and I'm speechless.

She's beautiful, maybe even more so than when she walked up the aisle, because this is all for me. Her golden hair falls in soft waves around her face. Her mouth is pale pink, her lashes heavy and dark. And she made herself a slip and panties out of the fabric I bought her at the general store.

"Come here," I say.

She comes, hands tucked behind her back, her big, dark eyes fix on mine. I lift her hand, glittering with my rings. I touch her throat where she's collared.

My girl. This is my girl.

"Sir," she whispers.

"Darling?"

"I'd like you to do whatever you like," she whispers. "I have my safeword."

"I plan on it."

She gasps as I turn her around, pulling her back against my body. I slide my hand down and into her ruffled panties, finding her naked pussy and playing with the silky arousal gathered on it.

"Are you wet for me?" I breathe.

Her head lolls. "Yes, sir."

"Tell me."

"I'm so wet for you, sir," she gasps as my fingers cup her sex.

I'm still high on the adrenaline of killing David and the others. My baser instincts are at the forefront. It has taken everything I have to be civilized so far, but that shuts off as she arches her back and pushes her perfectly round ass against me, begging for it.

I want her to come. I want to drown in her pussy.

"Go sit on the bed," I order.

She obeys, crossing her ankles. Her eyes follow me as I leave the room, and they widen when I return with a padded chair with wooden arms. I put it at the end of the bed, facing the fireplace.

"Take your panties down," I say firmly.

She doesn't hesitate. Her hips wriggle as she hooks her thumbs in them, and they fall around her ankles.

"Sit," I order.

She does as she's told. I lift her and arrange her body so she's sitting on her heels. I take the handcuffs from the dresser and fasten her wrists to the arms of the chair. She shudders when the collar goes around her throat, the soft silk and her new name resting against her skin.

She stays quiet, watching me with wide eyes.

I go into the closet and pull the bottom drawer in the cabinet out. She hasn't found these toys yet, which is probably for the best. I spill the bag out onto the bed and pick up a little leather harness.

"This fits over your hips," I say, kneeling before her.

Her brow creases, but she doesn't protest. I slide the delicate straps over her ass. Then, I press a curved vibrator inside her pussy and settle the flattened upper end over her clit. It clips into the harness tightly enough that she can't wriggle it off.

Her lips part. Her big eyes follow mine as I go to the dresser.

"Where did the whiskey come from?" I ask.

"Wedding gift," she says softly.

I pour a glass, neat, and turn to face her. The air crackles. I flick the remote in my pants pocket on low and have a sip of whiskey. It's very good.

She moans softly, body shuddering. Her lashes flutter.

I turn it up, and her eyes roll. She's soaked; I felt it when she was in my lap. It doesn't take long for her first orgasm to roll through. Her breasts heave as it ebbs, and her eyes open, big and desperate.

"Sir," she gasps.

"You're alright, darling," I say gently. "Be a good girl and have another."

Her hips jerk, and her hands fist as I turn the vibrator a notch higher. I take a slow sip of whiskey, rolling it on my tongue.

Her eyes flutter shut.

"No. Eyes on me while you come," I order.

Her soft brown eyes snap open and fix on me.

"I can't hold it back, sir," she whimpers.

"Don't then," I say, taking a step closer.

Her spine goes stiff. Her body shakes, and her soft, golden waves fall over her bare shoulders. My eyes fall to her cleavage, swelling over her bodice. God, she's so beautiful, it's hard to believe she's real.

Her head falls back. Her body shakes.

My cock throbs, desperate to be inside her, but the rest of me wants to savor this, to torture her until she's so pleasured and spent, all she can do is whimper.

"Sir, I can't," she gasps.

I turn off the vibrator before I cross the room and crouch, looking up into her face. "What are you, Diane?" I ask.

I feel myself slipping deep into our dynamic. She's already there, big eyes glassy.

"I don't know, sir," she gasps.

"You're a toy," I say flatly. "For me to play with."

Her lips tremble.

"Say it," I order, tapping my finger on the edge of the glass. "Repeat what I said. All of it."

I rise, towering over her, and tilt her chin up. Her eyes are wet, her mouth swollen from being bitten.

"I'm a toy for you to play with," she whispers, face flushing.

I grip her chin. "Good toys shut their little mouths and do as they're told. If I want you to come until you pass out, you will. Understood?"

Her throat bobs. "Yes, sir."

My thumb plays with her lower lip. "What are you good for?"

"Taking your cock, sir," she whispers.

"Good girl," I praise. "You're all for me. Your mouth, your pussy, your ass... I haven't fucked you there yet. I think I will tonight."

Her lips part to protest, and I push my thumb between them, choking her briefly. Then, I withdraw and turn the vibrator back on, flipping it to the highest setting.

Her body twists. Her knuckles are white, straining against her bonds. I rise, ignoring her, and go back to the bed where I left the toys. She moans, whimpering and panting. I take a thin silver chain with two clamps on either end and return to the chair.

"Open your fucking mouth," I say.

She obeys, lips shaking. Tears etch down her cheeks, dragging her makeup in gray streaks. I push two fingers into her soft, wet mouth.

"Suck while you come," I order.

Her eyes roll back, and she moans around my fingers. Her body shudders and seizes as another orgasm rips through it. I pull my hand back and glance down between her thighs, but the chair is dry. Setting aside my glass, I loll her head back and tug her slip down to expose her breasts.

"Sir," she gasps.

Her breasts are tight and flushed, her nipples hard. Working quickly, I fasten the clamps on them. The tips flush dark pink, and she twists against the sensation.

She's such a beautiful whore. Perfect, wet, hungry to be used.

I lick over the clamps, sucking on her pinched nipples, one after the other. She moans like she's broken. I stand and take a step back, picking up my glass.

"I want two more orgasms, fucktoy," I say, voice hard. "Then you get a break from the vibrator."

Her eyes widen. I turn the vibrator back on and sink into the armchair by the fireplace to watch. She's so beautiful, my wife—soft body bound to the chair, hair falling down her back, a trickle of sweat between her breasts as she strains against her bonds.

I could fuck her every day and never feel like I've had enough.

She comes again, crying out in desperation as her orgasms hit her, one after the other. I stand, heart pounding, and drain my glass. She peels her eyes open as I stand over her, reaching between her legs to remove the harness.

"Oh God," she gasps as the vibrator slips from her body.

I don't speak. Eyes glued to her ruined face, I put my middle and ring fingers into my wife's tight little cunt. She sobs, tears slipping fast down her cheeks.

But she doesn't safeword me.

Her pussy is tight and soaked around me. Entranced, I rub my fingers over her inner muscles until I find it, that swollen place I know she wants to release. Our eyes meet, hers desperate, mine hard and empty.

"One more," I say firmly.

"I don't know, sir," she whimpers, shaking her head.

"One more for me, baby girl," I say softly. "This time, let go of everything. Alright?"

She sniffs. "Yes, sir."

Her voice is fragile. She's hanging on by a thread. I take a sip from my glass with one hand, and with the other, I stroke where it hurts, where she needs to come. Her lips tremble, her thighs shiver.

"I can feel...it, sir," she whispers. "You...touching me, inside."

"I know, baby. I know you feel it," I urge. "Let your hips relax...like that. Good girl."

She gasps, breasts heaving, making the chain rattle. I slide my thumb up and rub her clit back and forth.

"Fuck," she moans.

"One more, darling," I urge. "Just give me one more."

Her hips tighten and relax, ebbing with the wave of impending orgasm. I see it like a storm in the spring, soft, smelling faintly of arousal and her sweet, flowery perfume.

I dig my fingers deeper like she's ripe fruit. I need to get to her center.

My cock is so hard it aches. It's hot and heavy, so sensitive, I feel every little movement.

I need her to come.

Then, she does, unwinding as it hits her from head to toe. I drain the glass as her pussy tightens. My eyes fall to my wet knuckles, to the wasted arousal soaking the chair.

Such a waste.

She's so sweet, I could drink her neat.

Her head falls back as she comes so hard, she stops breathing. It's distracting enough that she doesn't see me slip the crystal glass between her thighs. She doesn't know she releases in a short gush that fills it a third of the way. My brain buzzes. My entire body tingles.

My head is empty.

She collapses, only held up by the cuffs. I rise, taking the glass and bolting the first half, letting the taste of my wife spread over my tongue, drip down my throat, course through my veins.

My hands wind in her hair at the nape of her neck. Her lips part, and I drain the rest of the glass. Her eyes flash as it disappears into my mouth. Realization dawns on her, but she doesn't stop.

She doesn't safeword me.

I set the glass aside, take her jaw in my hand to part her lips, and spit her into her own mouth. Our eyes lock. She knows what I did. Then, her throat bobs, and she swallows everything I gave her.

"Fuck, darling," I say. "That's my good girl."

She moans in response—it's all she has left. I unfasten the cuffs and lift her, tossing her gently to the bed. Her body softens, her thighs spreading. I push the toys off the side and tug her slip down until she's naked except for the clamps on her nipples and that silk garter.

I drag my mouth over her belly. My cock throbs against my lower abs.

"You're being such a good girl," I murmur. "But I want to make sure you keep behaving. I made you feel good, so now it's time to remind you you're mine."

CHAPTER FIFTY-SIX

DIANE

I'm ruined.

He's dark and dominating tonight. It's everything I wanted from him, but it's also new, and my nerves buzz. He's never been this harsh, this rough, with me, and I can't let go of the knowledge that the hands that fill my pussy killed someone tonight.

God, I shouldn't be alright with this, but I am.

He flips me onto my belly. My nipples ache from the clamps, my pussy is raw from the vibrator, and I'm humiliated that he spat my release into my own mouth.

He's filthy, and I'm addicted to him.

He runs his hand down my back to my ass, squeezing it. "I'm going to gag you," he says. "If you need out, you shake your head hard. Understood?"

"Yes, sir," I whisper.

His weight disappears for a minute, and then he kneels over my body. His hand guides the ball gag between my lips and fastens it under my hair. Then, he drags my head back so he can look at me.

"Fucking beautiful," he breathes.

All I can do is blink. He bites my shoulder, though not enough to hurt, and presses kisses into my skin, down to the middle of my back. I'm sensitive there. His mouth is hungry, his beard rough.

My toes curl. I'm belly down on the bed, the nipple clamps crushed beneath me. He slides his arm under my hips.

"Your ass is so fucking perfect, darling," he rasps, gripping it and digging his fingertips in. He spreads me, and my heart pounds. It's humiliating, being pinned on my belly while he inspects me.

"Perfect," he murmurs, kissing where the underside of my ass meets my thigh.

Oh God, it's sensitive there. I moan around my gag.

"That tight little cunt," he murmurs. "Tucked between your thighs. Fucking Christ, it's my weakness. You're just so pretty, so soft. Every part of you."

He spreads me open, and my eyes roll back as his tongue drags over my asshole.

Oh God, it's too much.

He's too much, but not too soon. His obsession overwhelms me, always has, but I've never been able to resist him.

It's why we're here, husband and wife tonight. He's obsessed with me, and I'm obsessed with him. He knows he became a man he didn't want to be, but that's who I fell in love with. Somehow, none of that matters. I think we're healing—slowly, one night at a time.

We're imperfect, but that's what I wanted—I wanted to love hard and messy, to live so fast, I don't have a single regret when my life is done.

I moan, shaking my head. He stops everything right away, flicking the gag out of my mouth.

"What's wrong, darling?" he asks.

I roll over under him, gripping his sides. "Nothing. I just want you, face to face. Please. I want you inside me, sir."

His pupils blow as he pushes off his pants and lifts me by the thigh, thrusting, shoving the hard length of his veined cock into my pussy, stretching me with enough force that I have to breathe through the pain as my body adjusts.

He slides one lean hand up, dragging mine with it, intertwining our fingers.

Our eyes meet, and in the dim light, I see him as he is: a man with flaws, with scars. A gunslinger who loves me with everything he is.

"Mine," I whisper.

He bends, capturing my mouth in a deep kiss. When he breaks away, his eyes glitter in deep hunger.

"My girl," he says. "You've always been my girl."

He braces his other hand and takes me hard, rutting his hips with hungry strokes, slamming into me until I feel it up against my cervix, pleasure and pain washing through me. I feel everything tonight, and every part of it is good.

His hips stutter, right as I'm on the edge of tapping out. Deep inside, he spills with a low groan.

He pumps twice, wringing out the last drops, and pulls his cock from me. We fall onto the bed together, and he draws me close to his warm chest.

"Good girl," he breathes.

We lay in silence for a while before he stirs.

"Do you feel married?" he asks.

I nod. I do—I feel blissfully married. Drunk on him, I push my face into his chest and inhale. He smells so good, like forever.

"Tired?"

"No," I murmur.

"Good." His voice is a low rumble overhead. "I'm not done with you, darling."

I sit up shakily. "My pussy is sore."

He stands. "I'm not using your pussy," he says. "You stay there. I'll get you some water. I've got a few more rounds in me. All you have to do is take it."

CHAPTER FIFTY-SEVEN

WESTIN

I get her a glass of cold water and wipe her from head to foot with a warm washcloth while she sips it. Then, I retrieve the plug with my initials engraved on it and kneel on the bed.

She looks up at me, pupils blown.

"Turn around and get on your hands and knees," I tell her.

Shakily, she obeys. I shift to kneel behind her body and reach up to run my hand down her back. She's beautifully curvy. I run my palm back up and press on her spine until she sinks to her elbows.

"Westin," she whispers.

"Trust me, darling," I say.

She buries her face into the bed, and I bend and run my tongue over her asshole. She interrupted me last time, but I'm going to eat her the way I've fantasized about, licking her until her thighs quiver, then using the tip of my tongue to tease in circles before pushing it in, just a trace.

"Oh fuck," she gasps, voice muffled.

I pull back, drunk, and dip the plug into her soaked cunt before dragging it up to her asshole. Her knuckles go white as I push, working it slowly around and around.

"Bear down for me, darling," I breathe.

She obeys, and it slips into her body. I lick around the plug, tasting traces of her pussy. Then, I move over her until my mouth is by her ear.

"We're going to let that sit for a moment," I say. "Then, I'll help you prep in the bathroom before I fuck your ass."

Her body shudders, but like the obedient slut she is, she nods.

"Does it hurt?" I ask.

She shakes her head, looking back at me through wet lashes.

"No, sir," she whispers. "It feels good. I feel full."

"Good girl," I praise, sliding my hand down her stomach to her clit. She stays still as I play with her, making sure not to touch the most sensitive point. I know she's exhausted. She doesn't have many more orgasms in her, and I want her last to be when I'm inside her ass.

"Tell me you want it," I murmur.

She hiccups, moaning into the bed. I take her hair and pull her face up.

"Go on, darling," I order.

"I want it, sir," she gasps.

"No, say it all."

I pinch her clit, and her hips jump.

"I want you to fuck my ass, sir," she gasps.

"Good girl. Get up and go to the bathroom."

I follow her in, turning on the low light. Even in the dimness, her cheeks burn as I hand her everything she needs and explain briefly what she should do. Then, I bend her over the sink and remove the plug, leaving it on the counter for her to put back in. The door shuts, and I sink down on the edge of the bed.

This is the last part of her I haven't fucked. I could have done it earlier. She was willing, but I want some kind of consummation now that the killing is over. Now it's happening, and I'm honored.

She's letting me have power over her body, to use her so intimately.

I don't deserve this, but I'll never turn it down.

The bathroom light clicks off. The door opens, and she appears, hands tucked behind her back. I beckon her, and she comes to stand between my knees.

"I'm going to restrain you," I say.

She nods, humiliated eyes on mine. "Yes, sir."

I kiss her mouth. "Good girl. Lay on your back."

She crawls onto the bed, flashing the plug in her ass, and settles on her back. I fetch the restraints and attach them to her upper thighs and calves. There's a tension tie between them, so when I pull it tight, her legs are bound, spread and bent at the knee.

Cuffs go around her wrists. Those I tie to the two top posts of the bed with a length of rope.

Her eyes follow me as I work. They're big, and completely submissive.

I retrieve the lube and kneel between her legs. "Are you my pretty slut, darling?"

She nods.

I push one finger deep into her warm cunt. "Words."

"Yes, sir," she gasps. "I'm your pretty slut, sir."

I pull my finger out and stroke her thigh, painting her desire across her skin. Her eyelids flicker. I drag my touch down to the plug and start working it, around and around until her eyes roll back.

"You like your ass played with," I murmur. "You filthy girl."

I ease the plug out. She moans, breasts heaving. Her toes curl on either side of me. Tossing it aside, I douse my two fingers in lube and circle her asshole, stroking the soft skin several times before easing my fingertips into her warmth.

"Oh, fuck!" It comes out of her in a rush.

I push my fingers to the middle knuckle. She's soft, hot, and tight around them. A tear slips from her eye and etches towards her temple. Her pussy contracts, the entrance drenched.

Gently, I finger her, making sure I don't hurt the sensitive muscle gripping me. She's writhing against her bonds. I can tell the feeling is overwhelming. Her lips tremble, but her ass is loosening, ready for me to push inside it.

I pull my fingers free and reach for the lube again. This time, I pour even more into my palm and stroke my cock, getting it soaked. Her eyes meet mine as I kneel over her, dipping my hips down to line my cock up with her asshole.

"Please," she whispers.

"I'll be gentle, darling," I say.

She nods. "I meant please fuck me there, sir."

Jesus Christ, it takes everything I have not to thrust hard. One hand between us to guide me, I grit my teeth and press against her ass. She's relaxed, but I've always been a little too big for her to take.

"Bear down the way you did with the plug, darling," I gasp.

She obeys as I press, and the head of my cock slips into her tight opening. My vision stutters as a little cry slips from her mouth. I bend, catching it on my tongue, easing my hips. The tight ring of muscle strokes down the length of my cock as I push to the hilt.

"God fucking damn it," I gasp. "I love you."

She writhes in response, knuckles white, toes curled. Her body is spread open and restrained under mine. Beautiful, receptive. I kiss her, nipping her soft lower lip.

"Can you take it?"

She nods. "Yes, sir, I can."

I brace myself over my wife and pull out halfway, giving her a smooth stroke back in. She bucks her hips. I give her another thrust, and she moans out loud, letting me know I can pick up the pace. In less than a minute, we're both panting, bodies colliding as the bed slams into the wall.

This is all I've ever wanted: to be hers and for her to be mine.

In the dim light, our eyes lock, and something like magic tingles between us. I dip down, kissing her mouth, consuming her breath, letting her beg for more as I pull back. She puts out her tongue, and I spit on it and lick it off, my hips still working with lazy strokes.

I'll spend the rest of my life trying to find more ways to touch her more deeply. To feel her from the inside. To know her. To love her.

I touch her clit, stroking it softly. She comes in a rush, in a swell. Her head falls back, and in that moment, I have nothing to hold back.

My pleasure is a wave that washes over us both and leaves me weak against her body.

"I love you too," she whispers.

I kiss her throat. Then, I get up and pull my cock from her body and unfasten her restraints. She's quiet and pliant in my arms as I carry her to the bathroom. She lets me take off her leather collar before I lift her into the shower naked, save the little gold necklace. I press my lips to her wet hair, my body against hers, our arms wrapped around each other.

I clean her gently, and she cleans me too. I carry her to the bed and tuck her in before disappearing downstairs to get her more water.

On the kitchen table, in the fruit bowl, is an apple.

I stare at it for a long moment before I pick it up and go back upstairs. She offers me a shy smile when I sink down on the edge of the bed. I set the water down and lift the apple to my face.

It smells like summertime, like the day I took her virginity, like something beautiful is just beginning.

I take a bite and put it on her tongue. She closes her lips over it, crushing the crisp fruit between her teeth. Her lashes flutter and close as her breasts heave.

"Now I really do feel married," she whispers.

I have no words. Instead, I bend in and kiss her mouth.

Sweet like Diane.

Sweet like the beginning of forever.

Her eyes are getting so heavy, she can barely hold them up. I set aside the apple core and ease her down, laying her cheek against the pillow. Her lashes flutter, and I stroke my fingers through her hair until they fall against her cheek as her breathing deepens.

She's all worn out. I kiss her temple and ease my body from the bed. In the dark, I leave our bedroom and move down the hall to my old room. It's empty now. A bit of pale moonlight falls across the stripped bed.

Quietly, I lift the mattress and prop it against the wall. The wooden platform stares up at me with all the names I've accumulated in a neat row. Tonight, only one matters.

David Carter.

My jackknife is tucked behind the bedpost. I take it out, flipping it open, and kneel on the edge of the frame.

He hurt her, my darling bride. Now he's gone, and she has her entire future waiting for her with a man who will give her everything. Golden, like the sunrise. The gunslinger did what he does best.

Carefully, I drag the knife over his name, etching it out. Then, I flip the knife closed and set it aside.

I think I'll burn this fucking bedframe. I'm done with it.

CHAPTER FIFTY-EIGHT

DIANE

TWO MONTHS LATER

It takes weeks for Westin to find the deed to Carter Farms. There's little to no professional record of the land. The entire thing will need to be surveyed again to make sure the original property lines are correct. Westin explains what he's doing to get it in our name. It's complicated, and he has Sovereign's lawyer working with him to locate the proper documentation.

All I know is, every day I wake up, and I wish I was home.

I'm alone at the gatehouse a lot during the early fall. Keira is pregnant and exhausted, so I help her when she needs it. When she doesn't, I ask Westin to pick up boxes in town, and I start packing the gatehouse up, one room at a time, fantasizing about when we'll have our own place together.

It's early October one night when Westin comes home for dinner. I'm setting out bowls of stew and fresh bread. Billie lays by the fire, gnawing on a toy Westin brought her from the general store.

Everything feels so cozy and perfect, but in my heart, something is off.

"Come here, darling," he says.

He's standing in the door, cool air swirling. I go to him, and he kisses me deeply. Something is going on.

I pull back, and he presses something into my hand. My pulse rises as I realize it's a piece of paper, faded, yellowed with age, like it was kept somewhere damp.

"What is this?" I whisper.

"Open it."

Hands weak, I unfold it. It's the deed to Carter Farms, all seven hundred acres of it. And at the bottom, typed out in neat script, it lists the legal owner:

David Carter and Diane Carter.

My head is empty. I'm in the meadow, and a meadowlark rises from the tall grass.

All this time, my name was on the deed. David lied. Maybe it wouldn't have mattered—I never had the freedom to act anyway—but it explains why he was never able to sell to the Garrisons.

Maybe it explains why Avery wanted me married into their family in the first place. I wasn't just a woman Thomas wanted. I was also seven hundred acres of debt free land.

My head spins.

It doesn't matter anymore. None of it matters.

The darkness of the past fades, like misty dew dissipating under warm sun. I lick my dry lips and lift my eyes to my husband. He's looking at me with a faint smile, like he's never been prouder.

"Where was it?" I whisper.

"Nailed under the floorboards of David's room," he says.

My throat is lumpy and dry. I swallow as hot tears slip from my lashes. Westin catches me in his arms and carries me to his chair at the head of the table. I push my forehead against his collarbone, letting tears slip silently down and wet the front of his shirt.

"Can I go home now?" I whisper.

His arms tighten, broad and strong, always there when I crumple.

"Of course, darling," he says. "Let's go home."

The next morning, we go into town to buy fabric and lumber. Westin says he wants to do some repairs on the house that will take a couple of weeks. I'm going to start making new curtains for him to hang up. He leaves me in the general store at the fabric counter while he loads the truck with two-by-fours.

As I'm paying, I look down. There's a newspaper stand at my elbow. The top line, in bold, black ink, reads: *Remains Found in River Finally Identified.*

I look up quickly to avoid reading the rest. The cashier offers me a smile, and I smile back, like I never saw a thing.

Westin comes in as I'm bagging my purchases up. He leans across to set his ticket for the lumber down and takes out his wallet.

"Get a couple of those candies you like, darling," he says.

Obediently, I take a handful and set it beside his ticket. The cashier finishes ringing us up, and Westin pays, gathering up our bags. He takes my hand, and we step out onto the street.

Everything is sunny, but it smells crisp like winter is on its way. I hold his hand tight on the drive home. We don't talk much, and the silence is so comfortable. I can see how at peace he is, how relaxed his shoulders are now.

He has everything he wants.

And so do I.

It's a month later, deep in October, when he comes home at three in the afternoon. I'm out on the porch, tying up bundles of cedar to burn in the winter. He stands at the bottom of the steps, his hat hanging by his leg, sun streaming behind him and the air smelling like dead leaves and moss from the forest.

"Let's go home," he says quietly.

My heart hammers the entire drive down the mountain. He packed an overnight bag. Billie sits on my right, head hanging out the window. There's the remainder of the bottle of whiskey Keira and Gerard gave us jammed between the seats. My book sits up on the dashboard. My hands are clasped in my skirt, knuckles white.

When we pull up, I roll the window down and sit there, staring at the house. I'm dimly aware of him getting out and circling the truck. My door opens, and Billie scrambles over me, jumping to the ground. I tear my eyes off the house and fix them on my husband.

Westin takes his hat off and fits it on my head. "There you go," he says. "So the sun doesn't bleach your hair."

My chin quivers. His strong hands circle my waist, and he lifts me down and takes my hand. The house swims in my vision. He cleaned everything— the siding, the walkway, even the flowerbeds so they're ready in the spring. There's a whitewashed swing on the porch and a sapling planted in the front lawn.

He turns me around, puts me in front of the door, and takes a step back.

"You look good," he says.

I smile shakily. He looks at me for a minute longer, and then he takes a set of brand-new keys out of his pocket and opens the front door. It swings in, and he lets me go first, his hand on my lower back.

Everything smells like I remember, but clean and empty. My boots are loud on the floor. I look down, seeing the faint lines where he replaced creaky boards. The wallpaper is torn down, and the walls are painted cream. In the kitchen, he put in new cabinets and countertops. The walls here are lemon yellow, and he hung the curtains I made.

I stop, arms wrapped around my body.

He did this.

I turn on my heel, and he's standing over me, taking his hat off my head.

"Give me a kiss, darling," he says huskily.

I'd give him anything he wanted right now. He kisses me, slow and deep. Then, he takes my hand and leads me through the dining room. The big table is gone, replaced by a pale pine table big enough for four. On the far side, he opens the office door. I lean in, and my jaw drops.

He stripped David's office bare and knocked down the wall to the adjoining storage closet to make more room. The floorboards are all replaced with pale, glossy wood. There's a big bed made up with creamy sheets and a quilt. Gauzy curtains hang over the big window that looks out over the back yard. There's a soft, braided rug in the center of the room and a pine dresser.

"It's beautiful," I whisper.

"This is our room," he says, arm around my waist.

"What about the bedrooms upstairs?" I ask, turning to look up at him.

The corner of his mouth jerks up.

"Those rooms are for the babies," he says.

My brows shoot up. "What babies are those, Mr. Quinn?"

He picks me up and tosses me onto the bed before he climbs on top of me. "The babies we're about to make in this bed," he says, burying his face in my neck. "Goddamn, you smell so sweet, darling."

After we break in the bed, he gets the overnight bag from the truck. I chase Billie to the barn. Somehow, Westin found time to bring Gracey and Sunshine back to their stalls. They're settled in with clean water and hay. I take a minute to scratch their ears. Then, I'm headed over the field to the willow grove.

He doesn't follow me.

The gate is brand new. There's a real latch that closes when it swings shut. The grass is cut back and...he bought headstones for my parents. They're modest, but they match my Nana's perfectly.

I stand there, arms around my body, staring up at the sky with tears streaming down my face.

I don't need to close my eyes and see my Nana's face to know she's smiling. It's in the soft, autumn wind in the willow branches. It's in the sun creeping towards the dusky blue mountains. It winds through the shadows at the edge of the woods. It ripples through the golden grass, and it follows me like a whisper as I take the path back home.

I did my share of waiting, of talking to the dead.

It's time to get to living.

Westin is on the front porch, sitting in the same chair from the day he took me out on our first date. His long legs are sprawled out, his hat pulled low. I step between his boots and take his hands.

"Thank you," I say, my voice fragile. "For everything."

He just gives me that slow smile. "Anything for you, darling."

Over the next few days, we slowly move our things from the gatehouse. Then suddenly, we're waving goodbye to the ranch. Sovereign stands on the porch with Keira at his side, her hand on her growing stomach. I watch as they fade away down the driveway.

Then, it's just us. It feels incredibly significant, and not only for me. Westin went from living with his father to spending every day with Sovereign. This will be his first home that belongs to him. I've never had a choice where and how I want to live. Now, we're striking out on our own.

The future is big and full of possibilities, and there's no one I'd rather discover it with than Westin.

Three days after moving in, I get up one morning and go to brush my teeth. Westin is already out in the barn. I hear him calling Billie and Red, the border collie who used to belong to David. I lean over and look through the bathroom window to see him leading Sunshine and Rocky out to the back pasture.

I crack the window. The air smells like winter.

I'm ready to settle down until spring comes. The house is cozy, the barn full.

I go to put my toothbrush back and pick up my birth control. My hands falter. A strange feeling creeps over me that takes me a minute to identify.

I think I'm ready for a baby. Westin has been ready since the day he met me, and he's not shy about voicing it. My body never felt safe enough to entertain the thought. Now, I think it does. Quietly, I put the packet away in the drawer and fold a washcloth over it.

He comes in, bringing crisp air on his clothes. It's free-use night. Somehow, it's so much more exciting knowing I didn't take my pill. We eat in the dining room. He goes out to lock up the barn. I clean the kitchen and shower before bed.

When he comes back in, I'm in the slip he likes, waiting at the foot of the bed. He doesn't look at me; he just walks right past. I stay perfectly still, back straight, hands folded in my lap.

He comes out looking like sin in those sweatpants. I keep my eyes on my hands. I hear him sliding the little compartment on the bed frame open and taking my restraints out.

My heart hammers.

"Come here, darling," he says.

I go to him, letting him help me up on the bed. He fastens my wrists above my head before he kneels between my legs and slips a blindfold over my eyes.

Every sense comes alive.

Hot breath on my inner thighs. The gentle scratch of his beard on my skin. His hot tongue sliding over my clit, dipping down to push inside me.

My toes curl.

Oh God, so it's going to be that kind of night.

He makes me come until I'm gasping and shaking. Then, he takes the blindfold off, kisses me, and puts me over his knee. He doesn't spank me very often. Most of the time if I break a rule, I get tied up with a vibrator on my clit until I sob. But tonight, he spanks me until I feel heat rise from my skin. Then, he fucks me, limp and tingling, into the new mattress.

We're both exhausted but satisfied when we're done. He wipes my body clean, rubs lotion into my reddened skin, and holds me until my eyes close.

The sex is rougher, harder, in the following week. Every night, I sleep soundly, my body so relaxed that I wake up feeling brand new in the morning. I think I know what he's doing, but we don't talk about it. This time, I let him have control.

My body slowly works its way out of fight or flight.

Winter creeps in. Snow swirls in November. Ice makes patterns on the windows at night. I start cutting out squares for a baby quilt and wonder when it will happen. We're in no hurry, but I want to give him this. He's given me so much.

But we can wait. I'm safe. He's there.
All is right in our small corner of the world.

CHAPTER FIFTY-NINE

WESTIN

It's January when Sovereign and I finally make the sale that melds our two farms together. Now, Carter Ranch and Sovereign Mountain sit side by side, separated only by a thin fence line. In the spring, we'll put a gate in it so we can ride our horses back and forth.

Maybe someday soon, our children will do the same.

"How's Keira?" I ask one day while we're in the city getting the papers finalized.

"Pregnant," he says.

"I knew that," I say. "She's been pregnant since summer."

He pulls the door open to the general store and takes his hat off. I follow him inside, grateful for a bit of warmth.

"She sleeps most of the time," he says. "Can't blame her. Looks exhausting."

I nod, like I know what the fuck I'm talking about. We get our things, and I pick up a bag of lemon candies and a bolt of flannel for Diane. Sovereign heads up the mountain, and I take the road that loops around to Carter Ranch.

Snow falls softly over a frozen landscape. The air smells clean, like new beginnings.

I rewrote my story. I'm still the gunslinger. I'm still my father's son. I still come home at the end of the day with those fucking candies in my pocket.

But she chose me, and that makes all the difference. Every day, she chooses me. It's in the collar on her neck, the ring on her finger, her name on our contract and marriage license.

It's in the way she falls asleep in my arms, melted into me, trusting me with every breath in her lungs.

She was broken, but she gave me her trust. I'll never take that for granted.

Back at the house, she's in the little corner of our bedroom where I built her two bookshelves. She's in a dressing gown, her bright hair falling almost to her waist. Her back is to me as she stacks her books up. A guide to the flowers of northern Montana. A sketchbook with all her pictures.

When I kiss her head, she jumps and turns around.

"Don't scare me, Westin," she says.

I kiss her. "Are you hungry?"

She shakes her head. "I'm tired. I made soup and biscuits. Yours are in the microwave."

"You go lie down," I say. "I'll lock everything up."

She goes to bed without protest. After I've eaten and the dogs and horses are settled in for the night, I lay down beside her. She's fast asleep, snoring softly with nothing but the top of her golden head visible.

One second, I'm out cold. The next, I wake with a start to the patter of her bare feet running across the floor. The bathroom door slams, shaking the house. Something falls off the sink and crashes onto the hard tiles. Then, I hear her vomiting loudly on the other side of the wall.

My stomach flips.

No, it can't be.

I'm up in a second, pulling on my sweatpants. I tap lightly on the door. When she doesn't answer, I walk in to find her on her knees by the toilet. She looks up and wipes her mouth with the back of her hand. Her eyes are perfectly round.

I just look at her, my heart going too fast to speak.

She smiles weakly. "I was trying to knit these...little socks to surprise you, but I think the surprise is ruined."

It sinks in slowly. Then, all at once. I lift her in my arms and carry her reverently back to the bed. She's shy, holding herself as I tuck her in. Her eyes follow me, hesitant, as I brush her hair back and kiss her forehead.

"Are you alright?" she whispers.

I nod.

"I thought you wanted a baby," she says, "so I stopped taking the pill. I hope that wasn't the wrong thing to do. You seemed really certain."

I clear my throat. "Darling, I think this is the happiest I've ever been."

Neither of us know what to say. She starts laughing and falls into my chest as her laughter turns into tears. I hold her and stroke her hair.

Just like that, the entire world has changed. We're no longer hunkered down for the winter. Now, we're just waiting on spring.

"I'm so tired," she says after a while. "Do you mind if I just nap this morning?"

"Anything you need," I say, helping her lay down. "I'll get you some water. No food?"

She shakes her head. "No food. I just want to sleep."

I get her some cold water, and she's already sound asleep when I return. Her beautiful face is relaxed. I stroke back her hair and press a kiss to her temple.

In the living room, I open the chest by the window where she stores our keepsakes. Inside are the quilts her Nana made, a few old recipes, my father's pistol, and her copy of *Canterbury Tales*.

I pick it up, turning it over in my hands, and open the first page. At the end of a long row of names, written in faded cursive is her name, and beside it is mine.

Diane Lemon Carter m. Westin River Quinn, July 17th.

There's no trace of those brief months she was married to a Garrison. Our children and grandchildren will only know that we met and fell in love on Carter Farms and lived happily ever after. To them, our past will be as bright as the future Diane and I will build together.

I touch her name, sitting next to mine where it belongs.

My girl. Diane Carter is my girl.

CHAPTER SIXTY

WESTIN

THREE YEARS LATER

The air is cool. The grass is a deep, rich green.

Spring is here.

I'm leaning on the paddock behind the barn. Gracey had a foal a year ago, a stallion with a blaze down its nose. They stand at the crest of the hill, tails switching, mist rising around their feet as they forage. At my feet, Billie sits with her chin rested on my boot.

Everything is so still. The fields are rich with tall grass already. We'll have a good haying season.

Last spring, unexpectedly, Sovereign gave me another strip of land, bringing the property line even closer to his ranch house. I think that was his plan all along—to meld the farms as closely as he can. That way, we can have our separate homes, but nothing changes all that much.

A door slams behind me. I turn, squinting against the sun. Matthew Hewitt's truck is parked next to mine. The door opens, and he steps out, putting his hat on. He's a quiet, bearded man with silver hair. Last spring, he showed up at the house and asked if I minded if he proposed to my mother. I said I was happy to give my blessing and a few acres of land as well. During the summer, with Jensen's help, we built a house over the hill for them to live.

Everything is good now. The world is peaceful.

I start down the hill, Billie running ahead to jump on Matthew. He digs around in his pocket and comes up with a crushed biscuit. She takes her prize and flops down on the porch.

"Here to pick up the little one," Matthew says, shaking my hand.

"Is she spending the day with you?" I ask.

He nods. "Eve called early this morning and talked to Diane," he says. "Wants me to take them into town for the fair. You all are welcome to tag along."

I shake my head. "I've got a full day of work, but thanks."

We step into the cool front hallway. I take my hat off and hang it up, dusting off my hands. From deep inside the house comes a soft patter. It comes closer, full pelt, and then my daughter veers around the corner and throws herself against my leg. My heart warms as I bend down and pick her up, hoisting her on my shoulders.

I never thought anybody could get me as wrapped around their little finger as Diane did. Then along came Allison Lilly Quinn. Curly blonde hair like my wife. I hope to God she doesn't have an ounce of me in her, but time will tell.

She digs her damp, sticky hands into my hair as I carry her to the kitchen. Diane is at the counter, packing a picnic basket. She's just as pretty as the day I met her, maybe more—golden hair braided down her back, skirt tucked around her belt, long legs and feet bare.

"Matthew's here for Allison," I say.

She looks up, offering her mouth for a quick kiss. I set our daughter on the floor, and she scampers around me to jump into Matthew's arms. He laughs, patting her on the back.

It means a lot to me that he's the person my mother chose to be a grandfather to my little girl. He's a good man; I've never heard a harsh word from his lips. He has got endless patience with Allison, and anything my mother wants, she gets.

My daughter will grow up never knowing my father. That's the way I want it.

"Eve made her a dress for the fair," Matthew says. "Pink, lots of frilly stuff around the edge."

"That sounds about right," I say.

"Just make sure she wears her sunscreen," says Diane. "And her hat, or her hair will bleach white."

We pack my stepfather and my little girl into the truck along with the picnic basket. Then, I stand with my arm around my wife's waist as she waves goodbye. The crunch of the truck's tires fade away until we're left in silence. I bend to kiss her temple, breathing in her sweet, familiar scent.

"What's your plan for the day?" she asks.

I slide my hand lower to grab her ass. "Thought I might fuck my wife."

She steps back, gathering her skirt in one hand. Her head tilts. A little blonde curl grazes her cheek.

"Maybe if you can catch me," she says.

She hitches up her dress and takes off, running towards the barn. Diane is quick, running through the fields with our daughter every day, but my legs are long enough that I know I can catch up to her. I still let her think she'll win, just for the fun of it.

She dashes into the cool of the barn, and I follow, not breaking a sweat, just in time to see her scramble up the hayloft and disappear. I catch the top of the ladder and swing up. She's at the far end, a little glitter in her eyes as she backs against the wall.

I take a step closer. She bites her lip.

She tries to dart around me, but my arm shoots out and snags her waist, throwing her down into the soft straw. My body falls over hers, and she gives up, palms open. She didn't have much fight in her anyway.

I kiss her neck, then down where the neckline of her dress gives me a glimpse of her breasts.

"I love you, darling," I murmur.

She sighs, turning her head to the side so I can kiss her neck. "I love you too."

I nip her shoulder. "Love me enough to make another baby with me?"

She goes serious, her fingertips coming up to touch my cheek. She runs them through my beard, letting them rest on my mouth. We've talked about having another baby a few times before, but before now, it was just talk. Now, it feels real.

"Maybe," she whispers.

I kiss the top of her nose. She's got early summer freckles already.

"What do you want?" I ask. "Another girl?"

She shakes her head. Then, she shrugs. "Anything."

"I'd like a little boy," I say.

She purses her mouth. "What, so he can grow up and be as rough and rowdy as you?"

"Hey now, I haven't been rowdy in quite a while, darling," I say. "I'm behaving."

She slips her arms around my neck and pulls me in for a deep kiss. I'm lost in her taste and her warm body beneath mine. The longer she kisses me, the harder I'm getting in my pants. Mindlessly, I push her skirt up to find she's naked underneath.

Fuck me.

She moans as I slide my fingers over her pussy, wet, warm, and as soft as velvet. Her lips part, and my tongue swipes against hers. I shift to brace my knee so I can undo my belt and pull my zipper down. Her body lurches as I position myself and push inside. Her mouth breaks from mine, and a soft moan escapes it.

"Oh, you feel so good," she breathes.

I thrust in a short stroke. "So do you, darling."

We fuck in the straw, panting and sweaty. I roll over onto my back, and she straddles me, sinking down on my cock. I can't bite back the moan the sensation elicits. Her hands tangle in the front of my shirt, her eyes shut. Her hips work hard, taking her pleasure as it comes. When I come, we both collapse against each other.

She lifts her hand, tracing the beams up above.

"I'll have another baby," she murmurs. "Just one more, I think."

"And whatever it is, that's fine by me," I say.

We lay on our backs for a while. Then, I help her down, and we go inside to clean up. The day passes like any other as I head out to repair fences, then into town for supplies. I run into Jensen at the feed store, so we have a coffee and a cigarette on the curb outside. He's on his way up to Sovereign Mountain to do some work. Later in the month, Keira is having Diane and I up for a few nights while I help reroute the river.

The summer tumbles by in a haze of warm nights. Some of them we sleep; others, we stay up and play. When we need privacy, I take her out to the barn or the field so she can be as loud as she wants.

The haying season is good. We bring in a better yield than I anticipated.

Fall creeps in on silent feet. One second, the world is hazy with heat, and the next, I wake up in my cold room with my wife curled up against me for warmth and ice on the windows. Sleepily, I run my knee down her thigh and check her ankle for the little gold anklet. It's there, warm against her skin.

I duck under the covers, rolling her onto her back. She smells so good, it makes my brain hum pleasantly. She's in her little blue slip, the one she knows I like best. I pull it to the side and open her thighs. The scent of her pussy hits my nose a second before my tongue does, her taste spreading through my senses.

She moans, and I slip the tip of my tongue inside to feel her muscles clench around it. Then, I lift my mouth to her clit and lick, back and forth, one palm on her lower belly so I can feel the muscles in her hips tighten, two fingers in her cunt. Her spine rises, a ripple moving through her body. A soft moan comes from somewhere above as she comes, pumping around my fingers.

I love that—the rush, the release, the fluttering of her helpless body in my hands.

Drunk, I move up and roll her onto her stomach. Her lashes flutter, her eyes fixed on me, barely conscious.

Bodies entwined, I fuck my wife, my eyes fixed on the gold chain around her neck as I come, emptying myself into her pussy.

She's still sleeping after I shower and get dressed. I draw the blankets aside, my dick twitching at the sight of her wet inner thighs. She's such a good girl, so fiery but so sweet at the same time.

That image of her floats around my mind as I work through chores. The chilly morning is bright, the sky blue overhead and the trees gold.

Somehow, I got everything I wanted.

CHAPTER SIXTY-ONE

DIANE

SUMMER

I'm just inside the front door, hand on my hip as I survey the lawn. There are men out by the barn, standing around, hats on their heads, talking in a circle. Everybody has come to place bids for hay and grain.

Gerard Sovereign.

Jensen Childress.

And my husband, Westin River Quinn.

Behind me, in the kitchen, I can hear Keira talking to Allison and her son, Cash. They're both around the same age, and they spend all their time getting into trouble. The ceiling fan on the porch whirls. Cows low from the cool shade of the grove over the hill.

A truck comes up the drive, slowing as it pulls in next to the barn. The door opens, and Deacon Ryder jumps out, boots hitting the gravel hard. That means everyone is here, and we can start serving dinner. I push the door open and call out for my husband.

Westin comes, standing on the lowest step.

“You need me to bring in the barbeque, darling?” he asks.

I nod. He takes off his hat, setting it on my head. Smiling, I follow him down the hall and out the back. Cash and Allison dart around us, running as fast as they can for the creek. Keira dashes past, close on their heels.

“I better go help,” I say.

He catches my elbow, kissing me quickly. “You get the kids. I’ll do the rest.”

I nod. He gives me a short smile, the kind that creases around his eyes. I pluck his hat off and fit it back on his head. He gives me a light spank as I leave. My heart is so full, I don’t mind having to run down the hill and catch the children before they jump in the creek.

Keira takes them upstairs to wash, and I help Westin set the table and lay the food out. Then there are boots clattering down my hall as everyone fills up the dining room, all talking, laughing, joshing each other. The mood is light.

Everything is the same, but so different from the day I met Westin. This time, my house is full of people I chose, people I want to sit at my table.

Westin claps his hands. “Hats off, sit,” he calls.

Everybody settles down. Westin pulls out my chair beside his at the head of the table. Feeling like a princess, I sit and let him push it in. To my left is Keira, and on her other side is Sovereign. The children sit on Westin’s right, behaving for once.

Everyone fills their plates, and the talking starts back up again. It’s a dull roar, but this time, it’s good. We clean our plates and talk business. I stay quiet because I’m feeling especially sleepy today. My spine aches; I can’t wait to crawl into bed and beg Westin for a back rub.

He glances over at me, eyes going soft. His hand slides over my thigh, up to my lower stomach.

I’m three months along. We haven’t told anyone yet, but we plan to when I start showing. For now, we’re enjoying having a secret just for the two of us.

This pregnancy is easier than the first. I'm not sick anymore, and my appetite is strong. Westin thinks it's a boy; I'm inclined to agree.

That night after everyone is gone, I go to check on Allison. She's a lump under the sheets, snoring. The moon glows through the open window. My heart swells, and my palm slips over the tiny curve of my lower belly. A rough hand curls around my waist, and Westin's chin rests on my head.

"Hey, you ready for bed?"

"Yeah," I whisper. "I've been ready all day."

I turn, letting him usher me down the hall and into our room. The door clicks shut, and I sink to the edge of the mattress. He kneels down, unstrapping my sandals. His hands move gently over my sore ankles and calves, massaging them. Our eyes lock, and I'm lost in his gaze, remembering why I chose him.

He's so strong. At the end of every day, I feel my burdens slide right off my shoulders when he touches me.

"You happy?" he asks, voice low.

I nod, unable to keep from smiling. He leans in, and I bend to kiss him. His beard is scratchy, his chest rising and falling. He tastes like Westin, like the man I'll love until the day I die. Reluctantly, I pull back. He reaches behind me to unfasten the necklace he gave me for my birthday this year: a little golden locket. He sets it in my jewelry dish on the bedside table with my rings.

Nobody forgets my birthday anymore. Westin makes sure of that.

"Let's get you into bed, darling," he says, voice low.

He helps me lay back, and then he kisses me again, once on the forehead, once on the mouth, and once on my lower belly. He tucks me in and brushes back my hair.

"You get some rest," he says. "I'm going to lock up the barn, and then I'll be back."

Curled up, I listen to the night birds cry. An owl screeches. The horses nicker from the stalls. From the bed, through the window, I can see Westin come around the back of the house with Billie at his heels. He checks the chicken coop. Then, he sinks down on the back steps and takes out a cigarette as Billie settles her head on his knee.

He's at peace, just sitting under the stars that stretch over his ranch like a net of pure silver, hat on his head and dog at his feet.

I watch him for a long time until he finishes his cigarette and gets up. The back door slams, and I hear him coming up the stairs. It's only when his presence fills the room that I finally close my eyes.

His lips brush my temple. "Goodnight, darling."

THE END

OTHER BOOKS BY RAYA MORRIS EDWARDS

The Sovereign Mountain Series

Sovereign
Redbird - novella
Westin
Darling Bride - novella

The Welsh Kings Trilogy

Paradise Descent
Prince of Ink & Scars

The King of Ice & Steel Trilogy

Captured Light - Lucien & Olivia
Devil I Need: The Sequel to Captured Light
Ice & Steel: The Conclusion to Captured Light & Devil I Need
Lucien & Olivia: A Christmas Short

Captured Standalones

Captured Desire - Iris & Duran
Captured Light - Lucien & Olivia
Captured Solace - Viktor & Sienna
Captured Ecstasy - Peregrine & Rosalia

Acknowledgments

First and foremost, as always, thank you to my husband. You, like Westin, walked in with a plan and pulled me up when I couldn't do that for myself. Thank you for your patience, your generosity, and unfailing support.

A special thank you to Corinne, who worked closely with me on this book from the very earliest drafts to the final edition. Thank you for letting me send endless messages trying to work through each stage of this book. Thank you for your support, your kindness, and irreplaceable knowledge of romance novels, especially in my genre.

Thank you to Lexie, my developmental and line editor, for putting up with my endless DMs and for reading the book before it's technically done to assure me everything is going to be okay.

Thank you to Alexa, my copy and proof editor, for your encouragement and hard work on this colossal manuscript.

Thank you to my beta readers, especially Emilie, who was able to step in and read both *Westin* and *Darling Bride* in record time! Your support means so much!

Thank you to Michelle for your wonderful cover photography and thank you to Sandra for bringing my vision for this series to life and designing this stunning cover.

Thank you to my street team and my ARCs readers, many of whom have been reading my books for a long time!

A special thank you to you, who supported and read my books! I couldn't have gotten through writing Westin without your kind words and encouragement.

Made in United States
Orlando, FL
27 September 2024

52026635R00240